The Love at Stake anthology brings you six captivating paranormal tales featuring vampires and their sacrifices, made in
the name of love. Blood lust and romance are all consuming
for these vamps and their lovers. Six stories of seduction in
the shadows that lead to a happily ever after for all.

Love At Stake Anthology
Copyright © 2019 Charlie Richards, Lynn Michaels, A.J. Llewellyn, Catherine Lievens, Jo Tannah
ISBN: 978-1-4874-2451-0
Cover art by Angela Waters

Published by eXtasy Books Inc or
Devine Destinies, an imprint of eXtasy Books Inc

Look for us online at:
www.eXtasybooks.com or www.devinedestinies.com

LOVE AT STAKE ANTHOLOGY

BY

CHARLIE RICHARDS, LYNN MICHAELS, A.J. LLEWELLYN, CATHERINE LIEVENS, JO TANNAH

An Altered State of Mind
A Loving Nip Short Story

By

Charlie Richards

Just a little Love Bite: When a vampire's beloved attempts to kill another's soul mate, his loyalty is tested.

Darian Striplan accompanies others in his vampire coven to a secret lab in New York with the intention of shutting it down. They planned to capture the scientists, discover their backers, and free the paranormals trapped there. While inside the facility, Darian scents his beloved—his soul mate—in a human dressed as a guard. Oddly enough, the man also appears to be trying to free the paranormals. Talking to the man, learning his name is Claude Missandel, Darian quickly realizes that there's something wrong. Claude is confused, believing he is rescuing prisoners of war. Darian uses his vampiric mental manipulation abilities to search his human's mind and recognizes the touch of magick. After the rescue is complete, Darian takes Claude home with him, hoping their coven's resident demon, Balthazar, can assist Claude. When the attempt goes horribly awry, and Claude nearly kills his coven master's beloved, Master Adalric banishes Claude. Darian has a hard choice to make—his coven or his beloved?

DEDICATION

*In family life, love is the oil that eases friction, the cement that
binds closer together, and the music that brings harmony.*
~Friedrich Nietzsche

CHAPTER ONE

Darian Striplan crept down the hall on silent feet, watching his brother Daystrum's back. As their coven's second-in-command, Daystrum led their trio of vampires while Gerald, one of the coven's enforcers, brought up the rear. Their task was to clear the wing of guards and confirm how many paranormals were being held in B-wing so they could be transported out of there.

The facility's A-wing was being cleared by a group led by their coven master, Adalric Bachmeier.

The distinct sound of a muffled scuffle reached Darian's sensitive ears. Touching Daystrum's shoulder, he urged his brother to stop. As the lead tracker for his coven, Darian's sense of hearing and smell exceeded even the master's.

"There's someone to the left," Darian murmured, indicating the direction at the T-junction they were ten feet away from. "There was a scuffle. I heard the thud of a booted foot on the floor, then the slide of cloth."

"That could be a fight or someone getting it on," Gerald commented just as softly, his thick lips twisting into an amused smile.

The left side of Daystrum's mouth curved into a wry smile. "Let's go see."

After pausing at the end of the corridor, Daystrum held up a hand. He flipped up his pointer finger, then added his middle finger, and finally his ring finger. As soon as the third digit popped up, Daystrum sprinted around the corner.

Having utilized the one-two-three technique for centuries,

Darian instantly followed. Relying on his peripheral vision, he saw that Gerald was on his heels. Darian spared a glance to his right, confirming his suspicion that the corridor in that direction was vacant.

Darian refocused on what lay ahead of him, taking in the situation at a glance. A black-haired guard lay on the ground, and a blond man dressed similarly in camo pants and a black t-shirt crouched next to him. The conscious man appeared to be rummaging through the other man's pockets.

The blond's head snapped up, and his green eyes widened upon spotting them. He shifted to one knee and began to draw the pistol strapped to his right thigh. His intention was clear—shoot them.

Putting on a burst of speed, Darian surged past his brother. While he could probably dodge a bullet—and even though only one right through his heart or his head would take him down—he didn't want to chance it. Growing his claws, Darian allowed his eyes to haze in preparation for a lethal strike. His vampiric ability to see a body in what was similar to infrared so that he could track the flow of blood in a person would make it easy.

Darian was within six feet of the stranger when an intoxicating scent flooded his nostrils. His blood instantly heated in his veins, and his mouth watered. Even his gut clenched, and his groin warmed.

Holy fucking shit! One of these guys could possibly be my beloved!

With that knowledge rocking his system, Darian hesitated. Daystrum caught up with him, lifting his claws. "Wait!" The shouted word was out of Darian's mouth before he could think better of his actions.

Daystrum didn't pause, but at least he didn't go for a killing blow either. His brother retracted his claws and grabbed the human's wrist. Using his momentum, he rounded the man, forcing him to drop the weapon—probably by squeezing a pressure point. Daystrum pushed the blond's arm up behind his back — pinning it between their bodies — while wrapping the guy in a headlock.

Peering over the human's shoulder, Daystrum scowled at Darian. "Explain yourself fast," he hissed.

"I-I —" Darian began.

At the same time, the blond muttered, "Oh, thank fuck! I didn't know base was sending reinforcements." His voice sounded a little raspy, probably from the pressure Daystrum had on his throat, but his words were clear — even if they were confusing. "I haven't been able to reach them for two days."

Huh?

What the hell is the human talking about?

"Base?" Darian questioned, revealing his confusion.

Darian met his brother's gaze, whose lifted brows revealed that he was equally perplexed. Even Gerald, who was rising from where he had been checking the downed human's pulse and was shaking his head, had one brow ratcheted higher than the other quizzically. Swallowing hard, Darian prayed to the fates that the intriguing scent came from the blond.

"Yeah." The human tried to peer over his shoulder, but the prick of Daystrum's claws on his throat must have stayed the action. "I saw your knives, so I know you're not with these guys. You're here to rescue the POWs, too, right?" He grimaced. "Sorry for tryin' to shoot ya, but I didn't know."

"You, shut up," Daystrum ordered, giving the human a narrow-eyed look even as he eased the claws of his left hand away from the man's neck. Next, he met Darian's gaze. "You, tell me why."

"I smelled something . . . ball-tingling," Darian replied before clearing his throat and glancing at the downed human. To his relief, now that he was standing next to them both, he could easily parse their different scents. Darian held his brother's gaze. "I-I *need* to taste him."

Daystrum groaned even as Gerald snorted. "Make it quick,

bro." His brother released the human, pushing him toward Darian in the process.

Darian grabbed the human's upper arm with his left hand as he cradled his neck with his right. He liked the feel of the muscles under his palm as well as the way the human's nostrils flared. Dipping his head, Darian ignored the shocked gasp that escaped the man when his human finally realized what Darian intended to do.

Sealing his mouth over the human's, Darian slipped his tongue between the surprised man's slightly parted lips. He ignored the stranger's surprised grunt as he explored his mouth. The man's masculine flavor burst across his tongue, flaring his taste buds to life.

To Darian's pleasure, the human got over his shock swiftly and began kissing him back. He eased his body closer as fire coursed through his veins. His blood flowed south, and his dick thickened.

Unable to help himself, Darian used their tongue-play to slide the blond's slick appendage along his fang. He felt the human start in his arms just as a heady, iron-rich flavor tantalized his taste buds, and even his cock twitched. Groaning with pleasure at the exquisite taste, Darian tightened his hold as he pressed closer to the man. At the same time, he lowered his left hand and wound it around his beloved's waist, urging him flush against him.

Just as Darian felt the exquisite sensation of his human's erection pressing against his upper thigh, he felt a hand land on his shoulder. He broke the kiss, a growl escaping him as he turned to peer at whoever interrupted him. Meeting Daystrum's gaze, seeing his brother's smirk and shake of the head, Darian remembered where they were and more importantly, their mission.

Right. So not the time.

Clearing his throat, Darian eased his grip on his strong human even as he grinned unabashedly at him. He admired his broad, fit form, square jaw, and buzzed hair, even going so far as to slide his right hand up to pet the back of it. The soft strands teased his fingertips invitingly. His beloved's green eyes were widely dilated, and his lips were a bit puffy from the kiss.

Gorgeous.

"Got a little carried away, didn't I?" Darian mused, his voice husky with arousal. "Can't say as I mind, though."

The human blinked several times, obviously attempting to gather some composure. His cheeks darkened as he glanced to Darian's left and right. He cleared his throat while pressing against Darian's chest.

Darian eased his hold, releasing the man, even though it was the last thing he actually wanted to do.

"Wha—" He paused and cleared his throat again. "Who are you guys? You *are* here to rescue the prisoners of war, right?" His brows furrowing, he continued, "So, uh, I guess your friends are okay with you, uh"—he waved absently between them—"you and guys."

"Yeah," Daystrum confirmed. "I'm Daystrum. That's Gerald." He smirked while keeping watch down the hall to the left. Gerald was doing the same to the right. "The guy you were making out with is my brother, Darian. What's your name?"

"Claude Missandel," he replied, still sounding more than a little confused.

"Great. Now that we're acquainted, we need to get back to work," Daystrum stated. "What were you looking for on the body?"

Right. The mission.

"A key card, so I can open this door," Claude told them. His expression still held a wealth of uncertainty as he looked between them.

"Yes, we're here to free the people held here," Darian assured his beloved, hoping to get his cooperation so he could figure out where the human's ideas came from. "And shut down this facility, too."

"Good. Good," Claude mumbled. "These guys deserve a chance to go home and heal."

As Daystrum made quick work of locating the key card Claude mentioned, Gerald stepped close to Darian. "Congratulations," he whispered, grinning at him. "He may be a little crazy, but he's your other half."

Darian muttered his thanks, wondering at his beloved's state of mind.

I'm gonna have to take a second to peer into his mind. Maybe he hit his head or something.

CHAPTER TWO

His body thrumming with a mixture of arousal and confusion, Claude Missandel tried to rationalize the last ten minutes of his life. The men had been holding knives, right? The red in their eyes he'd thought he'd seen must have been a trick of the light.

But how did they move so fast? And how the hell could a kiss be so overwhelming?

Claude also couldn't figure out how such a facility could have been constructed in the jungles of Cambodia. Also, who would ship POWs there for experimentation? And who was doing the experimenting?

His information was so full of gaps, but Claude had worked with less. Normally his job consisted of working as a sniper for an incursion. Strictly speaking, he was supposed to be on reconnaissance, but because he hadn't been able to raise anyone on coms for two days, he'd decided to enter the structure and see if he couldn't rescue the POWs himself.

It'd been going damn well, too, until he'd been interrupted by the odd party he now traveled with. What was even stranger was the fact that the two guys didn't even bat an eyelash when the third man had laid one on Claude. It was almost as if they'd expected it.

And what do the comments about scenting something intriguing and congratulations and beloveds mean?

"Calling in five for B-wing," Daystrum ordered, his focus on his phone. Then his attention shifted to Claude. "Two shifters, two vampires, and a confused human beloved." His lips curved into a half-smile. "That last one will be sticking with Darian." After another pause, Daystrum said into his phone, "He seems to be confused. After we move the paranormals to the west exit, we're going to pick his brain a little bit."

Claude glanced around the group, trying to decipher what he was hearing. They had found only four drugged prisoners. Why were they reporting five? And how did Daystrum know one of them was confused?

Once that question slid through his mind, Claude realized the answer.

I'm the fifth man. So what the fuck do they think I'm confused about?

Time would tell.

Over the next ten minutes, Daystrum led the way back through the wing. While Darian released the metal straps holding the prisoners to the tables—that seemed overkill to Claude—Daystrum and Gerald accessed the computer in each room and downloaded information to a flash drive. The trio worked swiftly together, proving they'd been a team for some time. They hurried from room to room, each picking up an unconscious prisoner and taking them with them. Even with a man draped over their shoulders, they still moved impressively fast.

And why does that cause a twinge of the green monster in my gut. That's so stupid. One is the guy's brother and the other . . . well . . . maybe that's why I'm jealous. Although, Gerald didn't seem in the least bothered by Darian kissing me, so they're obviously not together.

"Claude?"

Darian's deep voice drew Claude out of his thoughts. Meeting the bigger man's gaze, he saw that Darian was staring at him with concern in his eyes. The guy even had a hand on Claude's shoulder, and now that he was aware of it, the gentle weight caused the hairs on his nape to stand on end.

"Yeah?" Claude stared up the three-inch height difference,

which was new. Normally when he hit a bar for a pick-up, he ended up with a twink. His well-muscled frame and obvious military bearing drew them like moths to a flame. Realizing he was sinking into his head again, Claude focused on Darian and noticed he peered at him with concern. "Did I miss something?"

Daystrum snorted, peering over his shoulder at him where he was standing at the computer. "He only called your name three times. Did you hit your head or get injured by someone before we found you?"

"Daystrum," Darian snarled, the man's name, drawn-out, was a sound of pure warning.

Scoffing, Daystrum returned his attention to his computer while he answered. "I need to know if he's a liability to us, Darian." He growled softly before adding quietly, "And to you, brother."

"I—" Claude paused. He was a kickass sniper and a badass martial artist. Still, these men were the good guys, right? "We're on the same team, so why would I hurt any of you?"

"Exactly," Darian immediately replied, giving his shoulder a squeeze. "I'd called your name to see if you were willing to carry this guy, since he's fairly small, but if you've hit your head—" Darian snapped his mouth shut, using the sentence as an implication.

Was Claude safe to carry an unconscious man?

Am I?

Claude mentally did a quick physical assessment. His body felt fine—strong and pain-free. Even though he was confused about his assignment and where these men fit into it, they were getting these guys away from there, so he would go along with it.

For now, anyway.

"Yeah, I got him," Claude assured, sliding his arms under the prone male. Assessing the brown-haired man's features, he guessed he couldn't have been more than twenty-two.

"Damn, he's young."

"Let's go," Daystrum ordered, shoving the flash drive Gerald handed him into his pants pocket. Then he hefted the man he carried off his shoulder so he could cradle him in his arms. "We won't have much time once we reach the exit."

Lifting the soldier into his arms, Claude followed behind the others. The fact that the man was a little small for a soldier pressed into his mind. Maybe some recruiter had been desperate to make his quota.

Claude traipsed behind the others, finding his gaze sliding to Darian's ass every few seconds. His boner, which had never completely softened after that hot kiss, began to thicken again. He lifted his gaze to the bigger soldier's broad back, but that wasn't much help either.

This guy is ripped everywhere. Day-am!

Just then, Darian peered over his shoulder and caught him looking. He grinned as heat filled his eyes. The man even hummed and gave Claude a once-over that appeared almost lecherous.

Claude felt his prick twitch just from that look alone.

Geez. Never had that happen before.

Darian focused forward again, and another thought struck Claude.

Bet he's not a bottom.

His stomach tightened as his asshole clenched. He'd only caught on very rare occasions, but even his groin tingled at the idea of feeling Darian pound into him. He would wager the man was hung.

"Okay. Let's lay them out on the floor here," Daystrum ordered, placing the large, dark-haired man he was carrying on the floor about twenty feet from the emergency exit. "Garner has disconnected the alarms, so we won't have to worry about the noise." Daystrum glanced at his watch, then turned to Darian. "We have seven minutes. Get to it."

Darian rested the man he carried on the floor. After Claude

had done the same, he straightened. Finding Darian easing into his space again, he took a step backward.

As much as Claude would enjoy another make-out session with Darian, he didn't think his dick could handle it, and he was *not* an exhibitionist. "Whoa, wait." He lifted his hand to ward him off. "Here really isn't the time, stud."

Chuckling, the sound husky, Darian waggled his brows. "I agree in that regard," he all but purred. Still, he lifted his hands and cradled Claude's skull, his thumbs teasing along his jawline. "But this is different." Darian's expression turned pained. "You're a little confused, Claude. I need to check your mind for injuries."

"What?" Claude stilled, trembling under the broad male's gentle touch. Lifting his hands, he gripped Darian's black polo shirt, needing the contact to ground himself. "What do you mean?"

"Just relax, Claude," Darian crooned roughly. "I would never hurt you."

Then, much to Claude's shock, the deep brown irises of Darian's eyes bled to red. His jaw sagged open, but it was the light pressure on his mind that pulled the gasp from his lungs. It was the strangest sensation . . . as if someone somehow brushed his brain ever-so-lightly.

You're okay, Claude.

Claude heard Darian's voice, but the man's lips hadn't moved. "D-Darian?" he squeaked, a cold sweat breaking out on his skin. "What?"

Keep breathing, Claude. Slow, deep, and steady.

For some reason, Claude's body instantly obeyed.

That's the way.

"H-How are you d-doing this?"

Claude was a soldier—a down-to-earth fighter for his country. He didn't—pain stabbed through his forehead, yanking a cry from his throat. His eyes slid closed, and his body shook. Black spots danced across his vision, and in the next instant, his eyes rolled to the back of his head as his brain shut down and his body collapsed.

CHAPTER THREE

"Magick? Are you certain?" Darian stood in Master Adalric's office, having explained how he'd met Claude and what he'd discovered by searching his mind. "I'm not certain what type of magick, but yes. Someone definitely tampered with Claude's mind. He thinks he's in Mongolia rescuing prisoners of war." Rubbing the back of his neck, Darian scowled at the floor. "When I tried to delve deeper, to see if I could undo the damage or even figure out his real memories, the pain was so great that he passed out."

The agony Darian had inflicted on his beloved tore at his soul. He desperately wanted to apologize, but he couldn't do that until the man woke. Knowing he needed to report to his coven master, Darian had left Claude in his bed, and he shifted from foot to foot, wanting to get back there.

"Well, since we don't cast spells, we need someone who can," Adalric mused slowly, narrowing his eyes. Then he brightened. "Go back to your beloved, Darian. I'll see if Balthazar is on this plane, and if not, call for him. When Claude wakes, do your best to explain things to him." Adalric winced as he shook his head. "I can't imagine that this will be a good way to learn about paranormals, but the mate-pull is intense. I'm sure he'll come to his senses before too long."

Darian could only hope so. He'd watched as friend after friend in their coven had found their beloved. All of them had needed to overcome a speed-bump or two, but they'd all done it. And each time, Darian had hoped he would be next.

And now I am.

Rising, Darian murmured, "Thank you, Master."

Adalric nodded, already lifting his phone to his ear.

Taking advantage of the dismissal, Darian strode swiftly from the room. He hurried to the central staircase and made his way down it, taking the steps two at a time. Upon reaching the bottom, he headed to the kitchen.

"Hey, Darian," Patrick greeted, glancing up from whatever he was mixing in the bowl. "Didn't expect to see you here." Continuing to stir the contents, Patrick cast a cheeky grin his way. "The rumor mill is working fast. You found your beloved on that raid?"

Darian nodded. "I did. He's" —after a second of hesitation, he decided on—"not feeling well. Do you have anything savory that would be easy on the stomach?"

"Does he have any allergies?" Patrick asked as he turned off the mixer and set it down. Then he began moonwalking toward a large refrigerator that Darian knew from experience contained oodles and oodles of prepared meals and snacks. "Favorite foods? Things he hates?"

Shaking his head, Darian admitted, "We haven't actually had much of a chance to talk about that kind of stuff, yet." He lifted his hands as he shrugged abashedly. "Not a clue."

"All right." Patrick did a spin, then stuck out his foot and undulated his hips. At the same time, he pulled open the refrigerator while mumbling, "Let's see what we got."

Humming a song Darian didn't recognize, Patrick pulled out a covered bowl with each hand. He set them on the counter, then grabbed a large blue and white serving dish. It was divided into five different compartments around the outer ring with a round section in the middle.

As Darian watched, Patrick filled a couple of the slots with what was in the bowls. He put them away and pulled out two plates, doing the same with the items on it. Finally, he pulled out another plate and bowl. After Patrick had put those away, he brought the full plate to the bar, setting it before Darian. Then he grabbed two rolls of fabric-napkin-wrapped utensils and placed those next to the plate.

"That's red *Jello* with banana and strawberry chunks in it," Patrick began, pointing to a red mass. "Here is potato salad. These are California rolls with a tub of soy sauce next to 'em."

Darian realized he must have blinked at some point, because there was indeed a small plastic container of brown liquid next to the five rice-covered rolls sitting in that section.

Patrick must have scented his confusion for he laughed before telling him, "I have these soy-filled containers tucked in with that dish of spring rolls in the fridge for convenience."

"Ah," Darian hummed. "Nice."

Nodding, Patrick continued his explanation of the food. "These are turkey and cheese wraps with lettuce and tomato. Then prosciutto and cheese roll-ups, and finally some raw veggies with a cup of ranch."

"Damn, thanks, man." Darian grinned at the coven chef. "I owe you one."

"Naw," Patrick replied glibly, executing a slide-step so he was back in front of where he'd been mixing. "It's my job, Darian." He winked at him. "Helps that I enjoy it."

A low growl sounded behind Darian, causing him to peer over his shoulder. Upon seeing Patrick's beloved, Allen, stalking into the room, he fought back a snicker.

Allen glared at Darian, but his features softened when he slid his focus to Patrick. "You wanna tell me why you're winking at someone other than me, baby?" he questioned, annoyance in his tone. As Allen rounded the end of the counter, he added, "And what do you enjoy, hmm?"

Instead of responding, Patrick licked his lips and offered his lover a saucy come-hither look.

As soon as Allen was close enough, the human wrapped his arms around Patrick from behind. He growled low in his throat and began nibbling up his neck. "You're not going to get any work done until I get my answers," he vowed.

Rolling his eyes, Darian grabbed his food and napkin rolls. He quickly left the kitchen, having no desire to be a voyeur to the chef and his beloved's shenanigans. After all, with a glance down at the massive amount of food in his hands, he reminded himself that he had his own beloved to care for.

Darian would forever deny the bounce in his step as he made his way back upstairs to the wing housing those in the inner circle. He was the head tracker. He did not bounce — ever.

Except maybe today.

Smirking at his own thoughts, Darian shoved the rolls of utensils under his arm, giving him a free hand to open the door. He slipped into his room, closing the door behind himself. After toeing off his house shoes, Darian crossed his front room and turned left into the bedroom of his suite of rooms.

To Darian's pleasure, Claude lay right where he'd left him. Except, now however, the human's eyes were open. Darian moved slowly toward him, pasting a warm smile on his face. He noted the way Claude's brows were furrowed, and his scent of confusion filled the room.

"Hey, Claude," Darian murmured, revealing that he knew the man's name and hoping that jogged his beloved's memory. Even as he placed the platter on his nightstand, he continued to glance Claude's way. "How are you feeling?"

Claude swallowed hard enough to cause his Adam's apple to bob. As he slowly levered himself into a sitting position, he muttered in a rough voice, "Like I got hit by a *Mack* truck. Darian, right? What the hell happened?"

Seeing Claude struggling, Darian eased an arm under his upper back and helped him. Pleasure filled him that his human remembered him. He placed an extra pillow behind his beloved's back, then parked his ass on the side of the bed so he was facing him. Unable to resist touching, Darian took

Claude's hand between his own.

"Yeah, I'm Darian. You're in my home because you passed out when I tried to remove the block someone put on your mind." Seeing Claude's throat working and how he narrowed his eyes, Darian reached over and grabbed the glass of water he'd left on the nightstand for him before leaving the room earlier. "Here. Take a sip."

Claude obeyed, using his free hand to drink deeply. Lowering the glass, he rested it on his knee. After licking his lips, he asked, "Block on my mind? What does that mean? What are you talking about?"

Darian sighed, wondering the best way to explain. Hearing Claude's stomach grumble, he released him and leaned over. He grabbed the platter and placed it on Claude's lap.

"Eat," Darian urged, picking up the roll of napkins next and handing one to Claude. "Everything is always better on a full stomach."

Even though he was obviously confused, Claude did as he was told. He placed the water glass on the nightstand, unrolled the napkin so he could place it on his lap, and chose the spoon. Then he took a bite of *Jello*.

Smiling at his choice, Darian spread his own napkin before popping the top off the soy sauce. He peered at Claude through his lashes as he snagged a California roll, then dipped it in the dark liquid. Using his napkin to catch drips, Darian popped it into his mouth.

Darian watched his beloved eat steadily for several minutes. It seemed he enjoyed all the items on the platter, for he tried some of each. His favorite was definitely the cheese-wrapped prosciutto, since he ate all of it. The wait gave Darian time to decide where to start, and that was with the basics, seeing as the man was in a scientific facility that experimented on shifters and vampires.

Taking another California roll, Darian asked, "Have you

ever heard the term paranormal, shifter, or vampire?" Then he took a bite and waited.

CHAPTER FOUR

Claude opened his mouth, intending to scoff. *Who believes in shit like – except. Wait.* He *did* recognize those terms.
But where have I heard them before?
"I-I have."
Claude struggled to sort through memories that were oddly murky. Had he hit his head? If so, when? Images flashed through his mind — him dressed similar to the guards he'd just taken out sitting in a conference room. There was a man and woman dressed in suits, as well as a half dozen others wearing lab coats. Information was being presented on a screen.
They were sharing information about . . . different kinds of paranormals.
But when would this have taken place?
A sharp pang spiked through his temple, yanking a hiss from Claude. Pressing his forefingers to the side of his head, he rubbed. Taking a couple of slow deep breaths, he felt the pain ease.
"You okay?"
Upon hearing Darian's deep concerned voice, Claude opened eyes he didn't remember closing. He hated appearing weak, so he forced a smile as he shrugged. "Yeah. Just a bit of a headache." Peering side-eyed at the big, handsome man, Claude grabbed a turkey wrap. "So, uh, tell me about these paranormals, will ya?" Before popping it into his mouth, he indicated the food. "Thanks for your help and for this."
"The building you were in wasn't actually a prisoner of

war camp," Darian told him slowly. "It was a building utilized by scientists. They were holding different paranormals.
The men we pulled out were vampires and shifters."

"But, my information—"

Darian lifted his empty hand, stalling Claude's denial. "I
told you there was a block on your mind. Someone implanted
the idea that it was a POW facility into your brain. That's why
it hurts your head when you struggle with certain memories."
His serious expression remained even as he picked up his fork
and slid it through the *Jello*. Darian's deep brown eyes held
commiseration as he told him, "I'm a vampire, Claude. So I
have a few abilities in mental manipulation, but what was
done to you is far beyond my skills. Fortunately, we have a
demon living at the edges of the coven. His name is Balthazar,
and he's very well versed in spell-casting."

As if he needed food in his mouth to shut up his rambling,
Darian shoved the forkful into it. Then his lips curved into a
half-smile, and he hummed. He obviously enjoyed the *Jello*,
too.

Listening to the big, handsome man's explanation, Darian
couldn't stop the way his jaw sagged open. His brows
ratcheted higher and higher. He felt his heart rate spike as he
swept his gaze over Darian's face and torso.

Darian set down his fork and grabbed a turkey wrap. He
held Claude's gaze, his expression appearing calm. With his
serene brown eyes and handsome features, he looked . . . normal.

"V-Vampire?" Claude finally managed to stammer. Tension thrummed through him. "Y-You're a . . . a vampire?"

Darian nodded once. "I am." Reaching out with his free
hand, he rested it on Claude's blanket-covered thigh. "You're
completely safe here. No one will hurt you."

Claude's thigh clenched under Darian's palm, but it wasn't
from revulsion at being touched by a paranormal creature.

Instead, tingles of desire flowed up his leg and spread to his groin. His gut clenched as blood flooded his prick, and his dick began to plump and thicken.

"H-Holy shit," Claude whispered, shock filling him. "What?" He wasn't certain what he needed to ask.

"It's okay," Darian rumbled huskily. "What you feel is natural. You're my beloved. My soul mate." He rubbed his hand up and down Claude's thigh, squeezing and massaging. "I feel the same for you, Claude."

With his mind reeling and his senses on edge, Claude struggled to assimilate everything he'd just been told. His head pounded, and he gasped for breath. Black spots danced across his vision.

"Easy, Claude," Darian crooned. His hands slid over Claude's hair, then down his neck to his shoulders. "You're okay. Take a deep breath for me."

Claude tried, but he found his lungs didn't seem to want to work. He cast about for a means of escape. Realizing Darian must have moved the platter at some point, Claude shoved the blankets aside and tried to flee.

Darian's arms came around him, drawing him against his chest. "Breathe in my scent, Claude." He slid one hand up to cradle his jaw and urged him to press his face against his neck. "It'll help calm you. Breathe, handsome."

As soon as Darian's earthy, masculine scent touched his senses, Claude finally managed to get his lungs to work. He sucked in a deep breath, and to his surprise, his pulse began to slow. Tucking his nose against Darian's flesh, Claude groaned softly as his pulse slowed even more.

"That's the way, Claude." Darian rubbed his left hand up and down his back soothingly. "You're safe."

Claude gripped Darian's upper arms, using the hold to ground himself. "Why the hell did that work?"

Darian chuckled softly. This time he used the hold he still

had on Claude's neck to urge him to lift his chin. When Claude met Darian's gaze, he saw hunger in the man's dark brown eyes.

"Because you are my beloved, Claude." Darian pressed his lips to the corner of Claude's mouth before adding, "I am yours, and you are mine. Soul mates."

"I-I'd never believed in such a thing," Claude admitted, cocking his head. "Except, if vampires are real . . ." He allowed his voice to trail off as he peered at Darian in silent question.

"Definitely real." Darian grinned broadly, revealing a sharp set of fangs. "Although the myths got most everything wrong," he added with a wink. "I happen to love garlic, and the sun doesn't bother me in the least."

"Damn, those look sharp." Claude lifted a hand, intending to reach out and touch. Except, right then, the sound of knocking on the outer door filled the room.

Sighing, Darian released him as he eased off the bed. "That'll be my coven master and hopefully Balthazar."

"The demon." Claude couldn't help the slight hitch as he spoke the words.

Darian paused in the doorway and looked back at him. "You're safe here." Then he disappeared.

As Claude waited for his return, he realized Darian was telling him that a lot. *For good reason I suppose.* Not wanting to meet guests while in bed, Claude slid to the side of the mattress.

At least I'm still fully clothed.

Claude spotted his boots under a chair to the left of the bed, but he had no idea where his socks had ended up. Pushing to his feet, he thought about raiding Darian's drawers to find a clean pair.

Claude didn't get the chance. Darian reappeared, and he wasn't alone. The first man seemed normal other than the dominant presence he exuded. The second guy — creature —

being . . . that could only be the demon—Balthazar.

The demon was, in a word, massive—six-foot-six of solid muscle. He sported swarthy black skin and hypnotic black eyes. It was the huge black, bat-like wings that caused his mouth to sag open.

"Oh, fuck me," he muttered. Even though he stared like a slack-jawed yokel, he couldn't seem to get his mouth to close.

Balthazar rumbled a low, amused laugh. "No thanks. My *amina* wouldn't care for that."

Claude glanced in confusion at Darian, watching the big vampire return to his side.

"An *amina* is a demon's beloved," Darian explained, slinging his arm around Claude's shoulders. He smiled down at him, then waved at the smaller male. "This is Master Adalric Bachmeier, leader of our coven. Master, this is my beloved, Claude Missandel."

"N-Nice to meet you," Claude murmured.

"Same to you, Claude," Master Adalric replied, just a hint of a smile curving his thin lips. "We'll see if we can't get you sorted." Then he turned his attention to Balthazar and lifted one brow.

"Let's go out to the front room," Balthazar stated. "Where we can all get comfortable."

Claude nodded. That sounded good to him. As he followed the new arrivals, he couldn't resist pressing into Darian's hold a little. There was definitely something to all the soul mate, beloved crap, because Claude certainly felt more at ease with Darian at his side.

And his smell. The feel of his hands on me. His — damn it. Focus!

For some reason, probably because Claude had known about paranormals for some time, even if he didn't remember the how or the why of when he'd learned about them, Claude found himself accepting his new reality pretty easily.

Of course, that meant he needed to get his brain back on track.

Claude cautiously took a seat on the small sofa where Balthazar indicated. To his relief, Darian settled next to him. "What will this entail?" Claude asked cautiously as he watched Balthazar pull the coffee table closer, then sit on it so he was directly in front of him.

"Just look into my eyes and relax," Balthazar told him, resting his forearms on his thighs and leaning close. "You shouldn't feel a thing."

Famous last words.

Still, Claude did as he was told. He stared in wonder as Balthazar's black eyes appeared to swirl hypnotically.

Claude didn't remember anything after that.

CHAPTER FIVE

Darian watched as Claude's eyes glazed over. His beloved's body swayed a little. He rested his hand on the back of Claude's neck in an attempt to steady him.

Claude jolted. His eyes widened. Then he leaped to his feet. With a panicked look, Claude swept his gaze around the room.

"Easy, Claude," Darian murmured, slowly rising to his feet. He lifted his hands in a placating manner as he took a step toward his clearly spooked beloved. "You're okay. You're safe here."

"Gotta save 'em," Claude muttered. Then he pivoted and bolted for the door.

Glaring at Balthazar, Darian snarled, "What the fuck did you do?" even as he started after Claude.

"Nothing," Balthazar denied, also rising. "It's—"

"We'll discuss it later," Adalric cut in. "Let's find Claude first."

Nodding, Darian sprinted out the open door. He followed his beloved's scent and rushed down the hallway to the right. Reaching the main stairway, Darian hustled down them three at a time, all the while sweeping his gaze over the area in search of his beloved.

Damn. He can sure move fast.

Darian heard Adalric and Balthazar behind him as he turned to the right and headed deeper into the house. Rushing through the massive formal dining room, he shot through the rear swinging door and into a small, much more informal dining space.

Skidding to a stop, Darian whispered, "Oh fuck."

Taking in the scene, Darian felt his heart skip a beat. Claude stood in the middle of the kitchen. He held a chef's knife in his right hand, and his left arm was wound around the waist of Seth Goodwin—Master Adalric's beloved. Claude pressed the knife to Seth's throat as he stared at Allen.

"If you don't tell me what I want to know right now," Claude was demanding, "your friend gets it. Where is the compound?"

A feral snarl echoed through the room from behind Darian, and he knew that Adalric had arrived. While concern for Seth filled him, it was the spike of fear for his own beloved that got him moving. Injuring the beloved of a vampire carried a serious penalty, and killing one was a death sentence.

"Claude." Darian called his beloved's name in a soft, firm voice. "Put the knife down, Claude," he urged. To his relief, Claude turned his attention to him, but the feeling was short-lived. His beloved's gaze appeared vacant, and no recognition lingered there. Still, Darian had to try, for both men's sakes. Easing forward a step, Darian stated, "Remember what I told you? There is no compound. There are no POWs. It's all in your head. Look around you. This is a kitchen in a mansion."

Claude blinked once, twice . . . and for just a second, Darian thought he saw a spark of recognition. Then he shook his head, backing up a step and taking Seth with him. "No. No, you're just trying to confuse me. You're—"

Patrick leaped through the pantry doorway, which was only a couple of feet to Claude's left. Even as Claude began to swing the blade toward the small vampire in an attempt to defend himself, the chef brought the frying pan he held down on Claude's head. The sharp thud rang through the kitchen, and Claude began to drop.

Lunging forward, Darian attempted to reach his falling

beloved. Fortunately, Patrick caught him. With a pained smile, the chef eased the unconscious Claude into Darian's arms.

"Sorry about hitting your beloved," Patrick offered, a concerned expression on his face. He curled into Allen's embrace, since his human had quickly rounded the counter to reach him. "What's wrong with him?"

"A demon messed with his mind." It was Balthazar who answered. "If I had to guess, I'd say it was Lindemere."

Darian winced as he glanced from where Balthazar leaned against the kitchen counter to where Adalric held Seth. His master growled softly as he glared at Claude. Seth rubbed his back and chest, murmuring platitudes and assuring him that he was fine.

It was probably only Seth's soothing that kept Claude's head attached.

"Can you fix it?" Darian asked, focusing on Balthazar. He knew that Lindemere was a demon under the Horseman of Death, too. He was the one who'd brought them the information on the scientists' facility in the first place.

The thousand-year-old demon let out a long sigh as he shook his head. "No. I'm sorry. I don't even know if Lindemere could correct what he did."

While slowly rubbing his left hand up and down Claude's back, Darian kept his beloved pressed against his body with his right. "So, what are you saying? That there's no hope for my beloved to lead a normal life?" Just the idea caused a spike of anxiety to fill him.

Balthazar lifted both hands in an *I don't know* gesture. "You saw what happened when I tried to repair his mind. If you want to tie him to a bed, I could try again." A grimace twisted his features as he shook his head. "But it could permanently damage his mind. Otherwise, my suggestion would be to keep him away from magick."

27

"How—" Darian began, but Master Adalric cut him off.

"If his mind cannot be mended, he cannot stay here."

Sucking in a sharp breath, Darian gaped at his master. He took in the hard expression on his leader's face. Darian's mind whirled at the implications.

"You would . . . you would have me deny my beloved?"

"I'm sorry, Darian," Adalric stated, the cold glint in his eyes easing just a little. "I have to think of *all* our beloveds." His focus shifted to Claude, who was beginning to stir in Darian's arms. "It's obvious that when Claude is under the influence of whatever Lindemere did, he considers humans the threat. Not paranormals."

"It's actually an ingenious altered state of mind," Balthazar commented, sounding impressed. "He turned a human guard against the scientists, which gives the guard access to the inside. It could create havoc from within."

A thought hit Darian, and he swallowed hard. "Lindemere never expected Claude to live, did he?"

Balthazar chuckled—*fucking chuckled!* "I'm sure he expected him to be gunned down at some point." He jerked his chin in Claude's direction. "Your beloved is quite skilled . . . military speaking."

Master Adalric growled. "Exactly why he can't stay. Two minutes out of your sight, and he had a knife to Seth's throat!" he roared.

Claude stiffened, having obviously returned to consciousness.

Darian kept his right arm's grip tight on Claude, uncertain what frame of mind he would be in. Sliding his left hand up his back to his neck, he cradled the silky flesh he longed to sink his fangs into. He used his thumb under Claude's chin to urge his beloved to peer up at him.

Once their gazes clashed, Darian smiled warmly. "Hi, handsome." He couldn't quite keep the sadness out of his tone, even though he was flooded with relief, too. Darian saw the recognition in Claude's eyes. "How're you feeling?"

With his brows furrowed, Claude peered back at him. He then swept his gaze around the room. When he returned his focus back to Darian, there was a definite hint of fear there.

"Darian? What happened?"

Chapter Six

Claude settled on the sofa in Darian's room while rubbing his palms over his face. Staring at the floor, he tried to put together the last five minutes. Unfortunately, everything was a blank.

And an aching head.

Sliding his hand to the back of his skull, Claude felt around the goose egg there.

"Here's an icepack," Darian stated quietly, drawing his attention.

Claude lifted his focus and took the offered item—a hand towel wrapped around something. Palming the item, he realized it was a half-dozen ice cubes. He moved it to the back of his head.

Feeling the coolness, even through the cloth and his hair, Claude let out a relieved sigh. He spotted the pensive gleam in the vampire's eyes and grimaced. "I can't remember what happened after I sat down across from that demon." Seeing the wince on Darian's face, Claude felt his own heart rate spike. "I fucked up, didn't I?"

Surely that was why his head hurt, and he didn't remember going to the kitchen.

Hell, I don't even know how I found the kitchen.

"It wasn't your fault," Darian told him. He opened his mouth, probably to say more, but the knock on the door made him pause. Offering a growl, he grumbled, "Now what?"

Claude watched as Darian headed to his door. Uneasiness thrummed through him with each beat of his heart. He didn't know what the fuck had happened, but he hated the discomfort he saw in the bigger man's expression. Somehow, he knew he was the cause of it.

"Daystrum," Darian greeted, his voice deep and rough. "Hey."

"Brother," Daystrum responded, entering the suite.

Claude straightened, recognizing the man. He'd been part of the rescue team. Since Darian was a vampire, it made sense that Daystrum was, too. How easily the trio carried the unconscious men also suddenly made sense.

They have increased strength and speed, so be damn careful. If they see you, you won't be able to make the shot.

Frowning, Claude tried to remember who'd said such a thing . . . and why.

"I just talked to Master Adalric. What are you gonna do?"

Daystrum's comment drew Claude out of his thoughts. He focused on the pair, glancing between them. While both men were big and broad, standing six-foot-three, Claude found Darian's wider shoulders and rugged good looks made him much more stunning. Recalling the feel of Darian's brawny arms around Claude, heat began to swim through his veins.

"He's my beloved, Daystrum. You know I can't walk away from him."

"Then you'll leave the coven?"

"Wait. What?" Lowering the icepack, Claude rose to his feet. His vision swam for an instant, so he rested his hand on the arm of the sofa. While still blinking, trying to clear his gaze, Claude felt an arm slide around his waist, supporting him. Instinctively, he knew it was Darian. "Why would you need to leave your home?" Meeting the bigger man's gaze, Claude saw the warmth, the need and lust, simmering in their depths. "Because of me. I fucked up that bad?"

Daystrum sighed deeply as he flopped onto the reclining chair to the right. "This isn't something you have control over, but it *is* something dangerous," he stated flatly. His dark eyes glittered with annoyance. "The demon Lindemere played in your head because you were helping the bad guys. Now, you have these . . . episodes."

When Daystrum paused, stumbling over his words, Darian picked up the explanation. "You've heard how some soldiers develop PTSD, right? Do you know much about it?"

Swallowing hard, Claude rubbed at his chest. "Are you talking about the flashbacks where they think they're back on the battlefield?" He glanced between them, racking his brain for any information he'd picked up along the way. It wasn't something he'd really looked into. "Or maybe the panic attacks or the night terrors?"

Darian sat down next to Claude, taking the icepack from him. "The first, actually. When Balthazar probed your mind, you reverted right back to thinking you had to find the facility holding prisoners of war," he told him quietly as he lifted the dish towel full of ice cubes. He placed it against Claude's head while stating, "You raced out of here and made your way to the kitchen where you ran into a couple of humans who were beloveds to vampires in the coven. You, uh—" Darian paused, heaving a big sigh.

"You accosted them, Claude," Daystrum told him bluntly. "It seems that, somehow, Lindemere gave you the ability to differentiate between humans and paranormals, so you left them alone, but you targeted the humans."

"Shit." Claude fought his urge to lean into Darian's chest. He did give in and rest his hand on the big man's thigh. Just that simple touch calmed something inside him, allowing his pulse to slow. "Is just magick the trigger?"

"We don't know," Darian replied, obviously being honest. He rested his free hand over Claude's where it was on his leg, threading their fingers together. "That's why there's an issue."

"And it can't be fixed," Claude guessed.

Daystrum shook his head. "Afraid not."

Claude sighed deeply. Even as he squeezed Darian's fingers, holding tighter, he muttered, "Then I should go. I'm a danger to the people here. I—"

"And we will," Darian cut in. "We'll find somewhere safe."

His eyes widening, Claude shook his head. "You can't walk away from your coven just for me! That's crazy!" No matter how much he wanted to experience being a beloved like Darian had offered, Claude couldn't allow the vampire to throw his life away for him. They'd just met, after all. "If you guys could tell me who my contact in the military is at this point, I'll check-in, and maybe I can utilize their medical services to fight this. I—"

"No fucking way," Darian snarled, his grip on Claude's hand tightening. "You are my beloved. My soul mate. You will not leave me, and I sure as hell am not allowing you to try to deal with this on your own when it was a paranormal that did it to you."

"I . . . but—" While Claude's pulse spiked and his body warmed at Darian's vehemence, he worried the vampire would come to despise him for turning his ordered life upside down. "Why would you give up everything for me?"

"Do you mean other than the fact that my brother will die if you walk away from him?" Daystrum commented coldly, giving him a narrow-eyed scowl.

"Daystrum!" Darian snapped, glaring at his brother.

Claude gaped as he glanced between them. He saw the way Darian sneered at Daystrum and how Daystrum shrugged one shoulder in a *so what* gesture. Realizing he hadn't been given all the information—hell, Claude figured he'd been given hardly *any* information—he squeezed Darian's hand. When that didn't get the vampire's immediate response, he lifted their twined fingers to his mouth and nipped Darian's knuckle.

Darian's sneer fell away as he snapped his attention back to Claude. He glanced from Claude's face to their clasped hands, and back to his face. His cheeks took on a pinkish hue as his nostrils flared.

"Tell me," Claude demanded. "Die?"

While Darian's cheeks lost their color, he muttered, "It's a closely guarded secret of our kind. If a beloved walks away from a vampire, or a vampire is kept away from his beloved by someone for any length of time, we'll die." Claude's confusion must have shown clearly on his face, for Darian explained, "Even if we never bonded, the blood of other donors would sour, and we would eventually no longer be able to drink it. We would weaken and die." The corners of Darian's lips kicked up a bit as he stated in a dry tone, "Fate likes to get her way, and she punishes those who thwart her."

"Wow!" Claude swallowed hard, a little wigged out by the idea of some mystical invisible goddess having so much control over people. Pushing that thought aside, he offered Darian a cheeky grin. "So, how does bonding work?"

Daystrum chuckled. "While you explain that, I'm gonna make a call." Rising to his feet, he grinned at them. "You guys have fun." Then his mirth faded, his expression filling with remorse. "While I will miss you brother, I understand why you have to leave, and I have an idea of where you can go."

Darian rose to his feet, tugging lightly on Claude's hand. As Claude rose, Darian asked, "What are you thinking, bro?"

"I'm gonna give Spieron a call," Daystrum stated as he headed toward the door. While his smile appeared sad, he glanced between them. "Not much magick on a cattle ranch, right? Plus, the gargoyles should easily be able to keep an eye on Claude."

Without another word, Daystrum left the suite, leaving them alone.

When Darian focused on Claude, his smile appeared a little

tight. His next words explained why. "I never wanted you to find out about that issue. I wanted bonding with me to be your choice." Tossing the dampened icepack to the coffee table, he muttered, "I don't want you to feel like you have to stay with me out of obligation."

Claude lifted his free hand and cupped Darian's strong jaw. The move drew the vampire's attention back to his face.

"You'd turn your life upside down to help me. I would be grateful to offer you the same consideration." Claude knew it wasn't a declaration of love or anything, but they'd just met. "You're willing to help me, and I won't deny my attraction to you. I have a feeling I'll be honored to spend a lifetime with you." Scoffing, Claude couldn't help but add, "Especially since you're getting the raw end of the deal and putting up with my crazy."

CHAPTER SEVEN

Even though Darian wanted to thrash Daystrum for sharing the fact that his life was now on a timer unless he bonded with Claude, he marveled at how easily his beloved took everything in stride — even his handicap.

Leading his soon-to-be lover to the bedroom, Darian couldn't help but comment on it. "You seem to be accepting everything very easily, Claude." Walking backward through his suite allowed him to read his human's expression, not wanting to rely only on his scent. "Most humans don't."

Claude's lips curved into a wry smile. "To be honest, nothing you've really told me has come as a surprise." His smile faded as his eyebrows drew together. "It's like . . . I already knew it but just didn't remember."

"That makes sense," Darian quickly assured. Reaching the bedroom, he paused at the foot of the bed and skimmed his fingers over Claude's closely shorn blond hair. "I'm sorry for what happened to you, my beloved."

To Darian's surprise, Claude shook his head. "I'm not." Lifting his hand, he placed his palm on Darian's stomach, then skimmed upward. "I don't know if I would have met you if I hadn't run afoul of that demon . . . and it's my guess that I wouldn't have been as open to the advances of a paranormal" — he met Darian's gaze, his green eyes full of warmth and hunger — "your advances, Darian." Claude's voice lowered, taking on a husky note. "And I sure like where this is going."

Darian couldn't stop the hungry growl that burst from him.

Seeing the way Claude grinned back, then feeling his beloved tweak his thumb over his nipple, he realized his human didn't mind at all. A low moan escaped Darian as tingles burst across his skin, and his nipples tightened, causing his breath to catch.

"Oh, handsome," Darian ground out around a moan. "You keep doing that, and we won't be talking about bonding."

"Really?" Claude released Darian's hand so he could use both to grip Darian's hem. As he lifted it and slid his fingers along the grooves of his abdominals, he asked, "So what will we be talking about?"

"We won't be *talking* at all," Darian stated gruffly, resting his hands over Claude's where they touched him. He squeezed gently in warning, drawing his beloved's focus to his face. Curving his lips into a feral grin, Darian warned, "I'll be *showing* you, instead."

Claude's nostrils flared as he sucked in a swift breath. His green eyes darkened, and the scent of his lust perfumed the air. He flicked out his tongue, swiping it over his bottom lip even as he returned Darian's hungry smile.

"Good." Claude pushed his hands upward, so Darian let them go, and his mate began lifting his shirt. "You've had my dick hard as nails almost every minute since I met you." His eyes glimmered with a hint of amusement. "Even when I was confused or being given bad news. Weird."

"Not weird," Darian countered, resting his hands on Claude's shoulders so he could start doing a little touching of his own. "Just as it should be."

Then Darian grew his claws and carefully curved them under the neckline of Claude's t-shirt. Drawing down, he easily sliced the material. In seconds, the remnants of Claude's shirt fluttered to the floor in strips around his bare feet.

Mmmm . . . even his feet are perfectly proportioned.

Hearing Claude's chuckle yanked Darian's focus away from his sexy man's feet. His beloved's green eyes twinkled as he stated, "If you intend to suck my toes, we might have a problem."

Darian barked a laugh, enjoying Claude's teasing. After bending at the waist and allowing his beloved to yank his shirt over his head, he again met his gaze. Darian shook his head.

"Maybe if we were playing in the tub, but no. Not right now." Darian winked, giving his man a cheeky grin while watching him drop his shirt to the floor. "Just admiring you and deciding if I should give your jeans the same treatment."

Shaking his head, Claude stepped backward. "I'll handle them," he told him, then proceeded to do so.

To Darian's absolute pleasure, he saw that Claude went commando. His long, swollen length jutted from between the flaps of his jeans, then disappeared from view as Claude bent to shove the fabric down his legs. That was okay, because with one step to the left, Darian had the opportunity to ogle his beloved's very fine, very firm ass.

Eager to enjoy touching and exploring every inch of his muscular human, Darian made quick work of his own jeans. By the time he straightened, Claude had crossed to the right-side nightstand. He was bent over, the flexing globes on gorgeous display, and he rummaged through the drawer.

"Looking for something?" Darian asked roughly as he crossed to stand behind his beloved.

"Condoms and lube."

Darian would have guessed that, but hearing confirmation caused his heart rate to spike. He palmed Claude's cheeks, squeezing rhythmically as he bent over his beloved's back. With their size differences—Darian standing three inches taller with a broader frame—the position was perfect. Rocking forward, Darian pressed his dick between his human's cheeks, rubbing along his warm trench.

"No condoms needed between us," Darian purred into his

human's ear before licking a stripe up the soft flesh behind it. Liking the way a tremble worked through his beloved, he did it again, then as he nuzzled the damp flesh, Darian added, "Paranormals can't get or give human diseases, and I need to spill in you to complete our bond."

When Claude replied, his voice was low and rough with his arousal. "And the lube?"

The simple acceptance caused Darian's heart to soar. It also made his fangs ache. Or that could have been the scent of Claude's blood flowing through the swollen vein so close to his mouth.

Exquisite.

Opening his mouth, Darian prepared to wrap his lips around the point where Claude's neck met his shoulder. He wanted to bite, to drink, to give his beloved the sweetest of ecstasy. Then he remembered Claude's question.

Right. Lube.

"That's in the second drawer along with my toys," Darian told him before giving in and sucking on the flesh before him. His cock throbbed, and pre-cum leaked from him, leaving a trail along Claude's cleft.

Claude shuddered in Darian's hold. His hips bucked, pushing back against him. He groaned roughly even as, with a shaking hand, he closed the drawer and opened the next.

Another moan ripped from Claude's throat, probably at the sight of not only the lube, but Darian's collection of butt plugs, anal beads, dildos, nipple clamps, and other things.

"Yeah, I like my toys." Darian hoped to use plenty of them on Claude . . . but another time.

Done waiting, Darian straightened. He grabbed Claude's hips and easily hefted the large man onto the bed. Then he grabbed the lube—the warming kind—and slammed the drawer shut.

Darian turned back to the bed. Climbing on, he found that Claude had rolled to his back. He had his hands behind his head, and his legs were slightly splayed. The cheeky grin on his face, along with the hard shaft curving over his abdominals, made his mouth water — for different reasons. Even though Darian longed to kiss his beloved's smirk off his face, he decided to go for option two.

Gripping Claude's left thigh, Darian pushed it to the side, forcing his man to spread his legs wider. He then rested his weight on that hand as he positioned himself between his forever love's legs. Peering at Claude through his lashes — unable to resist seeing his beloved's response — Darian opened his mouth and swallowed his man's erection to the root.

Seeing Claude's eyes widen and his jaw sag open, Darian smiled around the tasty, hefty piece of meat in his mouth. That did the trick. As he sucked up on Claude's prick, then sank back down, he watched with satisfaction as his lover's chest heaved and his abdominals clenched.

The pre-cum flowing across Darian's tongue tasted better than the finest wine. It exploded across his taste buds, sending zings of pleasure through his own body. His cock throbbed and jerked, hanging heavy between his legs, wanting to get in on the action.

Soon. And now I'm talking to my dick.

Darian pushed the inane thought away and refocused on pleasuring his lover. He sucked hard with each draw up, then swiped his tongue over his leaking glans. On the way down, he pushed at his frenulum, then traced over the thick vein running along the length.

His mouth watered for a taste of the blood coursing within, and he could no longer resist. On the next upstroke, he twisted his head a little so he could lightly nick the swollen vein with one fang. The sweetest nectar exploded across his tongue, drawing a harsh groan from his throat.

That also threw Claude over the edge. In the next instant, his beloved grabbed his head and thrust up. Burying his erection in the back of Darian's throat, Claude shouted Darian's name as he came.

Darian happily took it as Claude pumped burst after burst of hot seed down his throat. Using his vampiric strength, he managed to pull up just enough so the next few shots hit his tongue. Darian moaned blissfully at the exquisite taste of his beloved.

CHAPTER EIGHT

Claude blinked rapidly, trying to clear the dark spots from his eyes. It was tough, especially since the blissful pings of endorphins were causing his senses to float. His body felt rung out in the best way possible.

Holy fucking hell, my vampire has the best mouth on him.

Then Claude felt the mild stretch of a finger in his chute, and he realized they were far from over. Peeling his eyelids open, he stared down his body. He met Darian's gaze, noticing how he sported a *cat that ate the cream* smile on his lips.

Guess he did, too.

Claude grinned as he managed to gather enough coordination to spread his legs wider. "Another," he urged, surprised at the hoarseness of his voice. "Please."

God, I'm begging.

Except Claude wanted what Darian was offering so damn badly. He'd never had a regular lover—never thought he would be in a position to have one. Plus, Claude had never met someone who tempted him to leave behind his nomadic lifestyle.

Darian, however . . . Darian pushed all his buttons and then some. He was kind and strong, not to mention thoughtful and attentive. Less than a day in his presence and Claude wanted the man like he'd never wanted another.

"You with me, Claude?"

Hearing Darian's rough question, Claude snapped his attention to the man's face, having realized he'd been lost in his head for a moment. The burning desire lighting his vampire's dark eyes, eyes that were beginning to take on a distinctly reddish hue, caused a fresh rush of arousal to burn through his veins. His breath caught in his throat as he stared into Darian's gaze.

"I'm with you," Claude managed to gasp out. Feeling Darian's fingers easing out, then back into his ass, pegging his prostate, he groaned with the pleasure of it all. "So fucking with you."

"Good," Darian snarled. The irises of the vampire's eyes bled to a deep red, beating out the brown. His focus slid to Claude's neck, and he licked his lips. "Do you have a preference on how I take you?"

As Darian spoke, he eased his fingers out of Claude's channel. He gripped his own dick, drawing attention to the thick piece of meat jutting from a thin thatch of dark curls. Wrapping his fingers around his length, Darian greased himself up.

The sight made Claude's mouth water. His empty hole clenched with need. "My knees," he chose, his gut tightening with anticipation. "I want you to pound me into the mattress with that beauty."

Darian took Claude at his word. Without another word, he rocked back onto his knees, then gripped Claude's hips. Exhibiting super-human strength, Darian easily flipped Claude, then lifted him, making it easy for him to get his knees under him.

Spreading his knees wider, Claude went down on his elbows and arched. Never in his life had he presented his ass to someone, but his desperation had him doing it right then. His cock twitched and throbbed so hard it tapped against his abdominals.

"Now, my vampire," Claude urged, peering over his shoulder at his lover. "I'm yours."

"Hell yeah, you are." The feral smile that creased Darian's features sent a wash of pride through Claude. His man's need was clear to see on his features. "Mine!"

Claude felt the touch of Darian's flared crown against his hole. It was the only warning he got before the vampire thrust. Fighting his first instinct—to clench—Claude focused on the comforter between his forearms and pushed out.

His body welcomed Darian's thick erection as it sank deep into him. He groaned at the stretch, having never felt anything like the heat of his vampire's bare cock sliding along his inner walls. Even the slight pinch of pain soon faded, as with impressive accuracy, Darian slid his dick's head across his prostate.

"Darian!" Claude moaned, shuddering at the sensations firing through his rectum.

"That's right, my beloved," Darian responded, his voice guttural and rough. "Cry my name. Tell me how much you love my taking."

As soon as Darian's balls teased along Claude's crease, the vampire reversed direction. The new sensations pulled a cry of delight from Claude's throat as his nerve endings flared to life. Goose bumps spread across his groin. His balls rolled, and zings of pleasure shot down his thighs.

Moaning Darian's name, Claude rocked into each of Darian's thrusts. His lover set up a punishing rhythm, slamming into his channel over and over. He felt his groin warm, and tingles began at the base of his spine.

To Claude's shock, he realized he was already dangerously close to coming a second time. Wanting his vampire with him, he did his best to milk Darian's dick. He squeezed each time he pulled out and pushed back against him with each thrust.

"Yesssss," Darian hissed, his warm breath ghosting over the sensitive hairs at the back of Claude's neck. "My cock was made for your ass. Milk me, beloved. Show me how much you need my seed."

Claude barely had enough brain cells to continue, but he

managed it . . . until he felt Darian's hand on his dick. His vampire began stroking in time with his movements, and that was the end. All Claude could do was shudder in his lover's hold as his balls drew up and his orgasm swelled through him.

Shouting hoarsely, Claude poured his seed into Darian's coaxing, talented hand . . . and all over the comforter. He cried his lover's name, shaking with the intensity. Black spots swam across his vision as wave after wave of endorphins overwhelmed him.

Through Claude's haze of ecstasy, he heard Darian's roar. He felt him embed his erection deep inside him as the rush of hot seed warmed him from the inside out. A wave of satisfaction hit him that he'd pleased his lover.

Claude sighed deeply. Then he felt Darian's mouth on his neck. Remembering his vampire's needs, he tilted his head, offering more room. That must have been the right move, for Darian's deep moan of pleasure echoed through the room.

Then the vampire bit.

For an instant, Claude tensed at the spike of pain from Darian sinking his fangs into his flesh. A heartbeat later, the most euphoric sensation swept through him. He let out a gasp as his mind swam and his nipples beaded. The zings traveled straight to his cock, and another orgasm blindsided him.

Floating on clouds of bliss, Claude groaned roughly. He reveled in the sensation of Darian's pulls at his neck, and it transferred straight to his cock. His dick kept coming, pulsing and throbbing in time with Darian's sucks.

Claude's senses spun, and his body overloaded. His eyes rolled to the back of his head, and he knew no more.

CHAPTER NINE

Even though the coven threw a going away party, it was a subdued affair. Word of why Darian was leaving had been quick to go around the estate. If it happened outside of a secure meeting of some kind, it was fair game for gossip.

Darian kept Claude close to his side. Daystrum and his beloved, Korbin, stuck nearby, too. Darian appreciated his brother's solidarity and faith in him, especially since his own beloved was human.

On more than one occasion, when someone came up to wish him well, Darian could scent a hint of guilt rolling off his beloved. Most of the donors didn't make an appearance, but that wasn't surprising. After all, it was impolite to prance a string of ex-lovers in front of a newly bonded beloved.

Under the usual circumstances, a vampire holed up with his beloved for a number of days. That way, when he or she ran into a donor, their relationship was on solid footing. Plus, it gave the vampire time to explain why a harem of donors was so important to most covens — secrecy and convenience.

"I *am* sorry to see you go, Darian," Master Adalric commented, his expression a mix of regret, compassion, and resolve.

Darian nodded. "And I understand why Claude can't stay." He squeezed his hand where it rested on his beloved's hip while casting a quick smile on his man before returning his focus to the master. "So does he."

Master Adalric's beloved, Seth, offered his hand to Claude. "No hard feelings, man. I get it."

Claude's brows shot up, but after a few seconds, he reached out and took Seth's hand. "Thank you." After a heartbeat, he added, "Most wouldn't."

Seth released Claude's hand even as he stated with a grim smile, "In another life, I was a firefighter. I was on more than a few calls where the danger was caused by a PTSD flashback." Seth shrugged. "This was no different. Too bad it's magick induced. I hear that shit can be unpredictable in the hands of a novice."

While Claude was nodding his agreement—or maybe just acceptance of Seth's words—Balthazar announced his arrival by saying, "Lindemere isn't a novice. He's lived over a thousand years." His black lips kicked up at the corners. "That also means his idea of justice is a little different than a human's."

Darian understood, and he didn't hold it against the demon. There was no point. Instead, he introduced Claude to Balthazar's *amina*, Peter. Knowing his beloved would be curious as to why a demon and human were considered part of the coven, Darian explained how Peter had been their ward for almost two decades—eventually becoming a donor—before meeting the demon. Peter was family.

Another big vampire arrived, and Darian introduced him as Toni. At his side was another demon, Abyzou, although this one was pale and slender with gray eyes and white, batlike wings. Their arrival also caused Balthazar and Peter to wish them well and move on.

Once that pair were out of earshot, Darian whispered a very condensed version of why there was still a hint of tension between Toni and Balthazar. When the big demon had met and wooed Peter, Peter had been Toni's favorite donor. Fortunately, Toni had been seduced by Abyzou—a demon under the Horseman of Pestilence—a couple of months later, and most of the vampire's ire against demons had dissipated.

Balthazar and some of the other vampires had even given

Abyzou advice on how to win Toni.

Once the party broke up, Darian took Claude back to his suite and spent the night making slow, sweet love to his human. He knew words were cheap, so instead, he physically did his best to express how Claude was everything to him. Darian wanted his beloved to know that walking away from his coven, his position, and his brother was nothing compared to the joy and peace he derived from having Claude at his side.

Darian hoped he'd convinced his handsome human, but even if he hadn't, he intended to spend the rest of his life convincing him.

There was nothing that could happen that would cause Darian to walk away from Claude.

The next morning, Daystrum and Korbin, as well as Gerald, helped load Darian's things into his SUV. He'd learned that Claude kept a storage unit and a small studio apartment in Buffalo, Wyoming. That was where his human was originally from, but it had been almost three years since he'd been back there.

When Darian had asked Claude if he wanted to swing up there and get his stuff, his man had agreed. That extended their road trip by almost a week, but Darian didn't mind. It gave them plenty of time to cuddle in hotel room beds, enjoy whirlpool tubs in high-end suites, and many long conversations while driving.

By the time they arrived at the cattle ranch owned by Nicholas Lindson, Darian felt as if he'd known Claude forever — and he knew there was so much more to figure out about the man.

"So this ranch is owned by Nicholas, who's mated with a gargoyle, huh?" Claude queried as he swept his gaze over the fenced rolling hills. Once Darian confirmed that information,

Claude questioned, "Tell me again why your vampire buddy is living here?"

Darian flashed a grin Claude's way. He'd given his man a lot of information, so he wasn't surprised that some of it hadn't stuck.

"Spieron Virche was an enforcer in my coven. Uh, my old coven," he amended absently. "He was sent here by Master Adalric to clear the mind of Nicholas's father when he discovered information harmful to a gargoyle elder's mate." Darian explained the bare bones to Claude, since he didn't know all the gritty details himself. "While there, Spieron discovered that the man Nicholas knew as his father wasn't *really* his father, so he helped him be reunited with his Uncle Albert, who *was* really his father, and in the process, discovered that Albert was his beloved. So he moved here."

After a few heartbeats, Claude muttered, "Ooooookay."

Darian barked a laugh as he thought over his words. "Yeah, that was a little convoluted, wasn't it?"

Claude shrugged, smirking at him. "I get the gist. He found his beloved and rearranged his life to make it work."

"Exactly." Darian grinned.

Reaching over, Claude squeezed Darian's thigh. "Kinda like what you're doing."

Since the house had appeared in the distance and Darian saw that a few people stood waiting on the front porch, he slowed his approach. That gave him time to squeeze Claude's hand and tell him, "A life with you by my side is worth any sacrifice."

Claude nodded, although his expression still appeared a little troubled. "I'm just wondering how you don't think I'm a danger to all these ranch hands."

Darian gave his beloved a reassuring smile. "Because Elder Bodb has gargoyles here that protect him. When Daystrum explained the situation to the elder, he was more than happy to extend their services to monitoring you, too." Realizing how that could sound, Darian added, "No offense. It's just until we learn if you have any non-magickal triggers."

Even though Claude winced, he still nodded and squeezed Darian's hand back. "I get it. I really do." His lips curved into a wan smile. "I'll have to thank them."

Darian nodded as he parked to the left of the house. He pointed to the four people on the porch. "The younger, dark-haired man is Nicholas. The older male with long, slate-gray hair who's holding him is his gargoyle mate, Bodb. Remember, when you're amongst humans, don't use his title. The ranch hands don't know that some of these guys are paranormals." While Claude nodded, Darian pointed out the older, burly guy, whose beard was peppered with gray. "That's Albert, and the shorter man next to him is Spieron." After another round of nods from Claude, Darian shut off the SUV and asked, "Ready?"

"As I'll ever be."

Figuring that was as good as it was going to get, Darian pulled the keys from the ignition, opened his door, and slipped out. Spieron—who like the rest had all been waiting on the porch for them to park and exit—immediately bounced down the couple of steps. Sporting a wide grin that showed off his fangs, he grabbed Darian and gave him a bone-crushing hug.

"Welcome, Darian," Spieron offered, grinning from ear to ear. "It's so good to see you."

"You, too, Spieron." Darian took in the smaller vampire's lightly tanned features and how his green eyes gleamed with happiness. Since he remembered Spieron as always being somewhat somber, he couldn't help but add, "Ranch and bonded life agrees with you."

Spieron chuckled, nodding. "Hell yeah, it does." Releasing him, he took a step backward. "Looks like bonded life agrees with you, too." Spieron's focus slid to Claude, who had paused a few feet away, having been stopped by the others who were introducing themselves. "How's your man doing?"

"As good as can be expected," Darian replied, lowering his voice. "Has everyone been briefed?"

Nodding again, Spieron told him, "Those who don't know about paranormals know that he's ex-military and think he suffers from standard PTSD and can have flashbacks." The fellow vampire offered Darian a tight smile. "Your beloved will be safe."

"Claude is worried about others, not himself."

Spieron clapped Darian on his shoulder. "Sounds like a good man. Now come and introduce me so we can get you both settled."

Darian did just that.

CHAPTER TEN

Claude found he liked ranch life. The work was hard, manual, and kept him busy. Sadly, after three weeks, he still couldn't throw a rope to save his life. He had relearned how to ride a horse and had become a deft hand at fixing fences. The long days riding fence lines with only his vampire at his side began to ease his mind.

The noon-day blowjobs helped with that, too.

On more than one occasion, one of the ranch hands had come up and thanked him for his military service.

Claude found the easiest response was, "It was my honor."

Then, more often than not, the hand would tell him, "If you ever need anything, just holler."

The family atmosphere filled something inside Claude that he hadn't realized he'd been missing. The rest of the time, all his needs, wants, and desires were met by Darian. The vampire was the most attentive, thoughtful, and amazing boyfriend—and lover—a man could ask for.

"Hey, you going hunting with us this weekend?"

Claude rose from the boot box where he'd been pulling on his boots. Turning, he found the ranch's foreman, Stanley Redfeather standing nearby. The man was a handsome fellow of Native American descent, although Claude had no clue what tribe and probably wouldn't ever ask.

"Hunting?" Claude grabbed his cowboy hat and plopped it on his head as he commented, "It's spring. What's in season?"

Stanley flashed white teeth in his high-cheek-boned face.

"Wild hogs. They're considered a nuisance animal in Texas, so they're always in season."

"Hogs." Claude nodded. "Okay. Uh . . . when? Why?"

"They're tearing up the fences on the southern side of the property that abuts to the national forest," Stanley told him as he led the way onto the back porch. "We're gonna snag a couple of them, drive most of them off, and have ourselves a massive barbeque."

Claude nodded again. "Sounds like fun. Just let me know what time you plan on doing that."

"Will do." Stanley slid a bandana over his head, tying it in the back. He didn't wear a cowboy hat over the long, black, twin braids he kept his hair in. "See ya at dinner."

Claude nodded and lifted a hand in a wave, then started toward the barn. He intended to saddle a horse and get another lesson on roping from Keith. The ranch hand had the patience of Job and never minded trying to help Claude learn how to throw a lariat.

Hog hunting. Huh. Never done that before.

The first time Claude had practiced with a rifle after arriving at the ranch, he'd feared the noise or scent would throw him into a flashback. Fortunately, it hadn't. At that point, his prowess as a sniper had become known, and he'd even had a few hands ask for help to improve their accuracy.

Claude loved feeling needed.

Entering the barn, Claude strode past the ranch's farrier. He nodded at the big man, who was in the process of trimming a gelding's hoof. The big man jerked his chin in acknowledgment but continued with his work.

Just as well, Claude thought. *Can't remember what Spieron said the guy's name is anyway.*

After making his way to the tack room, Claude grabbed a halter, lead rope, and a box of grooming supplies. He had just left the large room and was on his way to halter Ivan—a kind-hearted ranch gelding—when a loud ringing noise filled the barn. That was followed by a sharp pain in his temple, as if someone had decided to stab him with an icepick.

Gasping, Claude dropped the grooming supplies and gripped the top of the nearest stall wall. He swayed as a second burst of pain shot through him . . . then a third. His gaze swam, and his body shuddered.

Claude wasn't certain how long he stood there. Finally, the ringing in his ears faded, and the pain in his head subsided. He blinked open his eyes and peered around slowly.

Confusion flooded him.

Where am I?

Recalling his mission, Claude knew he needed to get his bearings damn fast. He dropped the halter and lead rope he carried on top of a nearby box of spilled grooming supplies, snagging a hoof pick in the process. Then he crept slowly along the walkway, ignoring the friendly horses that stuck their heads over the half-doors, obviously looking for attention.

Claude came to a corner and peered around it. He spotted a big man hunched beside a horse. The guy held the gelding's hoof between his thighs and was thoroughly focused on his work.

Striding confidently, Claude walked right past him. The guy didn't even look up. Outside the barn, he took a step to the right, which kept him in the shadow of the building.

He saw a house straight ahead across a good hundred-foot, gravel-covered clearing. The place exuded a welcoming western-country living. There were corrals and paddocks and pastures as far as the eye could see.

From Claude's information, the facility was supposed to be in Cambodia.

So where the hell am I?

Just as Claude thought he would have to try his luck at subduing the big farrier in order to extract information, another man rounded the corner of the barn. While he was taller than

Claude by several inches and broader in the shoulders, he was older, too, judging by the gray in his bushy beard. Claude knew he could take him.

Claude lunged forward and grabbed the brawny man's flannel-covered bicep. Yanking the guy toward him, he wrapped his other arm around his throat and pressed the pointy end of the hoof pick to his throat. It wasn't a sharp instrument by any means, but Claude was willing to bet the bigger man wouldn't realize that.

"Claude?"

Hearing his name issued by the stranger, his deep voice sounding questioning and concerned, Claude tensed. Did he know this man? He didn't think so.

"How do you know my name?" Claude demanded, keeping his voice soft and harsh. He didn't want the farrier to hear him. "Where am I? Who told you I was coming?"

The older fellow turned his head just enough to glance at his face. His deep brown eyes went from holding confusion to understanding. He even smiled just a little.

"We knew you would be coming, Claude," the man stated softly. "Darian told us to expect you."

"Darian?" Claude repeated softly. That name sounded familiar, so why couldn't he place it? "H-How did he know?"

"Your superiors," the man explained. "Darian is their inside man. We're with the resistance, and we're helping him. If you loosen your grip, I'll take you to him."

Claude nodded slowly. That sounded plausible. "Okay. But no funny business." He eased his hold, and the man relaxed a little. "I wouldn't want to have to gut you," he threatened, although he wasn't certain his current weapon would manage the job.

Still, Claude shifted the hoof pick's edge to the older guy's surprisingly trim waist.

Must be due to ranch life.

"No funny business," the older man assured. "He's in the

ranch house in a meeting with a few others." He pointed toward the back door. "That way, please."

Claude figured he didn't have too much of a choice but to obey. While praying that the guy wasn't lying to him, he started them both toward the house. After climbing up the porch, the older man opened the unlocked door and led the way inside.

They passed through a foyer with a boot box, a couple of boot racks, and many coat and hat hooks. After that, they went through a large dining room and turned down a hallway. The man stopped at a closed door and knocked loudly three times.

A few seconds later, the door opened, and Claude found his breath taken away by the handsome man standing there. His deep brown eyes swept over them before his brows furrowed. He cast a questioning look between them.

"This is Claude. You were expecting him." The man lowered his voice as if keeping secrets from whoever else was inside the room. "POWs."

Darian's lips parted, and he peered at him in a new light. He nodded. Then, without a word, Darian lunged at Claude.

Faster than Claude could track the impressive man, he was disarmed and pulled against his chest. To Claude's surprise, instead of hurting him, Darian dipped his head and captured his lips. He thrust his tongue between Claude's lips and delved it into his mouth.

For an instant, Claude froze. The idea of struggling occurred to him. Then the man's taste and strength seeped into his senses. He groaned as he gripped Darian's upper arms and began kissing him back, sliding his tongue along the other man's and giving as good as he got.

His brain seemed to fuzz out as pleasure swamped Claude. His blood heated, and need thrummed through him. His dick quickly began to throb so hard he feared he would come in his jeans.

When breathing became paramount, Claude turned his head and gasped. He panted harshly as he peered up at his vampire's face, spotting the worry within the depth of his eyes. Then Claude realized they had an audience.

Claude swept his gaze over the assembled group. Spieron had his arms around Albert, who was rubbing a hand over the vampire's chest and whispering assurances in his ear. Bodb had his arm slung over Nicholas's shoulder, and both men were glancing between Claude and the other pair.

That was when it hit Claude.

"How did I get in here?" Claude grimaced, letting out a growl. "Damn it. Did I hurt someone?"

"Not a chance. You were just a little confused." Albert offered him a smile that looked almost fatherly. "A little sweet talkin' to get ya in here and a thorough tongue-fucking by your vampire, and now you're right as rain again."

Claude nodded even as his cheeks heated, telling him that he blushed. "Thank you for your understanding."

"We would like to know what triggered it, however," Spieron stated. "What's the last thing you remember?"

Thinking quickly, Claude explained how he'd been about to snag his mount when a sharp ringing filled the barn followed by a pain in his head. Then . . . nothing until he was making out with Darian in the house.

"The high-pitched clang of a striking hammer, maybe?" Nicholas hazarded. "The noise of a hammer on a horseshoe nail can make anyone's ears ring."

"We might just have to do some tests," Bodb commented, nodding. "It would be good to find out."

Claude nodded. "Sure. Yeah." Although he hated being lost inside his head, he understood the importance of controlled tests. "I need to know what to avoid."

"But later," Darian snarled. "Right now, *I* need to strip you down and check you over." He growled softly as he rubbed his hands up and down Claude's back and sides. "I need to be sure you're well."

With his body still keyed up from his make-out session, Claude shuddered as he pressed into Darian's touch. "Y-Yeah. Okay."

The others either chuckled or smiled indulgently. Relief filled Claude that none of them seemed to mind his momentary lapse. From what had happened, he realized they'd already come up with a plan to counter it.

When Darian grabbed Claude and hefted him onto his shoulder, he decided he would have to thank them later. For a few seconds, all Claude heard was the pounding of Darian's boot steps on the stairs as he carried Claude up to their bedroom. Then the door slammed shut, and Claude bounced as his back hit the mattress.

Staring up at Darian, he felt as if his heart skipped a beat. The hunger in his vampire's eyes took his breath away. With his claws out, Darian leaped on top of Claude, but he didn't feel an ounce of fear — only anticipation.

Claude opened his arms and welcomed his vampire, more than happy to help calm his fears — even if that meant losing another change of clothes.

ABOUT CHARLIE RICHARDS

Charlie started writing fantasy when she was eight, and after stumbling onto her first erotic romance at age nineteen, she realized her true calling. She now focuses on writing gay erotic romance, normally of the paranormal variety, with heroes of all kinds. With the help and support of her husband, Charlie finally fulfilled one of her life-long goals . . . move to acreage with her horses. You can often find her curled up with her laptop and a cup of tea or glass of wine, creating her next adventure. Charlie enjoys exploring the mountains of her new Oregon home on horseback, 4-wheeler, or motorcycle.

She can be reached at ch.richards2010@yahoo.com
Or visit her at www.charlie-richards.com

CONTRACTED BY BLOOD

BY

LYNN MICHAELS

Vampires, gypsies, and blood-sacrifices.

These are the things you get with a blood-contract. But vampires need to feed. They rule with bloody hands. Conrad was destined for the same, until his new blood-partner helps him change. The prince in blood, Conrad, no longer plays by their rules.

DEDICATION

This one is for Nicki for putting up this challenge, and Jo for always pushing me hard.

CHAPTER ONE: THE CELEBRATION

Celebrating my one hundredth anniversary of becoming a vampire was not as I had imagined. I watched the festivities below from the second-floor mezzanine. A riot of color and noise cavorted beneath the gaslights. Streamers, confetti, and balloons contrasted sharply against the cold stone floor. People danced, jumped around, or merely bobbed their heads to the raucous music. Many of the guests wore corsets and flowing skirts. Some had on fancy top hats and lace gloves that covered their arms from fingers to elbows. Frankly, it bored me.

My sire, Felix, had opened the ceremony as the night began with a few heartfelt words. As king, he had that right. I'd listened to him elaborate on what a wonderful prince I'd been. He'd spoken in past tense as if I was no longer those great things. Maybe it was only a way to transition from past to present. I knew he was going to give me a regency to rule within his kingdom. Things were changing, but it seemed odd.

I was put off by everything around me, particularly the behavior of Tiziano. He was King Felix's blood-partner. I understood he had a place here, but he pranced around like the life of the party. His hair, so blond it was more of a white in color, hung past his shoulders and parted on the side accentuating his pixie-face. He'd lined his eyes with coal as black as his vest. He'd lost his jacket, so his puffy white sleeves showed, and unlike most other blood-partners, his shirt had a high collar that hid his neck, rather than showing off his marks. Perhaps he thought hiding that long, pale throat would be more alluring to Felix. I didn't know, but Tiziano had obviously helped organize this asinine party. And his choices differed greatly from tradition.

What did Felix see in Tiziano? He was pompous, flamboyant, and Felix pampered and spoiled him. Felix had never ever been one to spoil those he loved, assuming he loved me and the others he sired. He wasn't my biological father, but he turned me into the vampire he wanted by blood and by raising me from a boy and into my manhood.

Maybe I shouldn't judge. One hundred years as a vampire, and I still didn't have a blood-partner. I couldn't bring myself to take one. I'd witnessed too many bad pairings that ended as most things in a vampire's life do — with blood.

The crowds below parted, and the music stopped. A large platform on wheels was rolled to the center of the ballroom. My brother-of-blood, Devyn, stood beside it. "In honor of my brother, Conrad, I present my gift. To properly open the festivities!"

I knew what Devyn would be gifting me, even before I saw his blood-partner in his red hood and cape step up on the platform. His head bent forward, and even from my place on the mezzanine, I could see him tremble.

The ceremony was at once the highest of honors and one of the few legal ways to get rid of a blood-partner. Gifted.

As a blood-sacrifice.

"Conrad! Come down. Partake." Devyn beckoned me with outstretched arms. "Come on!"

I huffed. I didn't want any of this, but despite it being *my* party, I had no choice. With a little wave to the crowd below, I headed to the stairs. Reinforced cement risers set within an ornate, carved railing that deceivingly appeared delicate like lace, spiraled down to the floor below.

As I made my way toward the platform, the party-goers parted before me, clapping and offering congratulations as I passed by. I stopped in front of the platform and looked up to the poor soul who was about to lose his life. I could see his face. Pale blue eyes were framed with wrinkles. He was past his prime. *Shame on Devyn.*

"Thank you," I told the sacrifice. I didn't even know his name, but I'd bet he was glad of this, even though he was sad and scared. He nodded, and a wry expression crossed his face. Damn that Devyn. I didn't want this.

Devyn was young, eager. He still had much to learn. He'd never been a threat, but neither had he been a friend. He'd been brought over some twenty-five years ago. Not much in the scope of a royal vampire's life.

He stepped up on the platform beside his partner. He whispered in his ear and received a nod in return. He pushed the hood off his partner's head, exposing his long, golden hair, streaked with the first signs of gray, and kissed his temple. That wry smile morphed into a sad frown as Devyn's partner realized that this was truly happening. His fingers shook, and he tucked them under his robe.

I didn't miss the evil glint in Devyn's eye as he grabbed the ceremonial knife and chalice. One of the elite guards stepped up beside him and placed his hand on the sacrifice's forehead, tilting his head back. The sacrifice was shorter than Devyn and the soldier. The positioning was perfect. Devyn slid the knife over his throat in one smooth move. No hesitation. Then he caught the lifeblood in the vessel.

The crowd cheered.

Fucking cheered.

I hated them all. At that moment, Devyn worst of all. He stretched out the cup to me, even as the guards moved to catch the rest of the blood from the sacrifice in a large pitcher. Behind Devyn, they leaned the sacrifice forward. They wanted every drop.

Reaching up, I took the monstrosity. It was gold, encrusted

with fine jewels. The least I could do was honor the poor soul's sacrifice. It had been made for me, after all. I drank, deeply. The blood was rich, metallic.

I didn't understand why Devyn would do such a thing. Blood-partners were meant to be cherished to their final days. Not disposed of so callously. Although, the ceremony was supposed to be an honor. Voluntary. I knew better than that. Royalty always had a way around laws and customs. We used them to our advantage. I knew this event was no different.

"Thank you, brother." I nodded and handed him the mostly empty cup.

He licked the edge and smiled, showing his long fangs. Before I had the chance to make a fool of myself by attacking him, he winked and motioned for the guards to share the rest of the blood. They poured from the pitcher directly into the mouths of waiting partiers, human and vampire alike.

All that was left for me to do was watch the festivities and wait. Afterward, Felix would bestow his gift. A piece of his territory for me to govern. My own regency. Surely, that would be worth enduring this nonsense. Felix's lands had expanded too far and wide. It was necessary, and I'd been groomed for it.

The music started up again. I pushed through the crowd, making my way to the edge. I didn't care to be pressed in the center of all these bodies, hot and cold, moving together. Others enjoyed that sort of thing, but I never had.

Eventually, my next gift arrived. Tiziano had arranged performers to entertain us. Jugglers, firebreathers, and exotic dancers made their way through the guests as the music changed to something more cutting-edge. They were greeted by applause and wild cheering.

A young man walked in, his steps high and precise, from the far-right doors that led to a staging area behind the ballroom. He carried a large hoop over his head and dressed in some kind of tight material that clung to every muscle, showing them off as he moved, flexing and contorting. He kicked his leg up over his head, toes pointed.

He twirled, his long black hair wild around him, mimicking the strange cape. Dark eyes flashed. Painted lips smiled. He was beautiful. He was also the first creature to arouse me in many years.

It took a lot to get my attention. I preferred to feed at the clinics, rather than take a blood-partner. I bored too easily, and disposal was not something I thought I could bring myself to do.

But this one . . . he moved like an angel.

My eyes locked onto him, and the rest of the ballroom disappeared. He lowered the hoop and stepped through it. He flung it around. The silver hoop was as tall as he was and sparkled beneath the overhead lights. It spun around his waist, over his head, around his legs, arms, and shoulders. He bent over, touching the floor behind him, and pulled the hoop over his body. He lifted one leg, spinning his toy around it. The movement emphasized his hip bones erotically. Then he dropped the hoop on the ground and performed rhythmic gymnastics around it. I'd hardly even noticed the rest of his troop and the guests moving out of the way to give him room.

A slight young girl moved in, dressed similarly and turning many heads with her dark hair and lithe body. She handed the hoop-dancer two batons with red ribbons streaming behind them.

He danced, prancing around the circle our patrons had made. He jumped in the air. He tumbled. He flirted with the crowd. All with these red ribbons trailing behind him, complimenting his dark, untamed hair.

He stopped in front of me. The music stopped.

He smiled brightly. "Happy birthday, Your Royal Highness." His voice was breathy from his exertions and so fucking sexy. I reached out to grab him, but he tumbled away in a series of backflips. Never had I seen anyone like him, so exotic and sensual. I wanted to see him in my bed with all that dark hair spread across my crimson sheets.

Most of the humans in our territory were fair-haired with light skin as fits with their heritage in this colder climate. My hair was also blond, and before I'd been turned, my skin had been creamy. It had become the palest of white, more translucent by the year. This performer who caught my eye was my opposite with raven hair and skin the color of a fawn. He must spend his days dancing in the sun. I was thoroughly intrigued and wanted a taste. I began to hatch a plan. If Devyn could manipulate rules of feeding—contracts, agreements, and sacrifice—then so could I.

Tiziano touched my elbow, snagging my attention. What a dangerous thing to do. It showed how his status had risen in our king's house. Another manipulation of laws and customs.

"The king is coming to bestow your gift now." Tiziano's eyes flashed with mischief. The gift from our regent was traditionally given at the very end of the party, but it wasn't over by far.

CHAPTER TWO: FELIX ARRIVES

Felix stormed into the ballroom with a complete entourage of bodyguards and sycophants. The Elite Guard marched behind him and his hangers-on. Behind them, The Savage-Guard brought up the rear. They were rarely warranted for such a situation, a rare breed of mutants who evolved into a class that was neither human or vampire but a weird combination of both. They were super strong, could walk in the sun, and were exceedingly loyal. They were also as stupid as fuck, and easily side-tracked from their jobs. They were incapable of making complex decisions, not to mention exceedingly ugly with misshapen heads, and instead of elegant fangs, their mouths sported thick, short tusks, good for nothing but looking fearsome.

This fanfare was unprecedented. A tinge of worry shot through my gut.

Tiziano patted my arm. If he meant it to soothe me, it didn't. Perhaps he meant to get my hackles up because that's exactly what it did. I glared at him, and he merely pushed his thick, white locks out of his face with a smirk.

"Tizi!" Felix strode forward then embraced his blood-partner before acknowledging me. That was a very bad sign. His blood-life could be seen flowing through his veins beneath his almost clear skin. He wore thick layers of clothing to guard against any chill and hide the markings of age from our human guests, but his hands were bare, and as he stretched to hug his lover, his shirtsleeves pulled up, exposing more skin.

"My Sire," I interrupted.

"Yes. Prince Conrad." He grabbed me by the shoulders as he had in my vampire-youth. "Today, we honor you. Tizi set this up, and we're honor-bound to thank him." He narrowed his eyes, daring me to disrespect his partner.

"But of course. What a marvelous fete it's been. Tiziano, I thank you." My words were rote, emotionless, but the motions made were more important than true feelings—lesson number one of being a prince.

Felix chuckled. He knew all this put me off, and rightfully so. "Nevertheless . . . I have a gift for you. Happy hundred, Conrad." He leaned in and kissed the side of my head. Then he stared over at Tiziano, who smiled shyly—*as if the man has a demure bone in his body!*

With a snap of his fingers, Felix directed his commander of The Elite Guard to step forward. He handed Felix a pristine white envelope. Felix practically flung it at me. He stared at Tiziano, completely avoiding eye contact with me.

I put aside my offense and jealousy and opened the envelope. Soon enough, I'd be out of there and on my own estate. I'd been waiting a long damn time for this.

I pulled out the paper that I expected to be a proclamation of my regency.

It wasn't.

It was the deed to a house on the coast. A vacation property.

Was this a joke? I looked over at Felix. He had Tiziano wrapped up in his arms, ignoring me. Tiziano's kohl-lined eyes flashed, mocking me. This had all been orchestrated by Felix's blood-partner. The realization overwhelmed me. He was a threat.

How could Felix let a blood-partner rise so high? He should have turned him, if that's what he'd wanted, but he hadn't. A human would never out-rank a vampire, especially me.

"What is this? Felix?"

He glanced my way. "Your gift. I know you've admired that home."

"This is . . . not." I cleared my throat, trying to buy time to squash my emotions and speak clearly. "I thank you, but this isn't what I expected."

Tiziano smirked. "You shouldn't let your expectations rule your life, my prince."

Felix chuckled. "Indeed."

After a hundred fucking years of being in my sire's shadow, being groomed to rule, this cheap whore captures Felix's heart — and his ear — in a heartbeat.

"Sire . . . Felix . . ."

"Now, now, Conrad. Appreciate this gift. Take it. Enjoy!" His eyes turned threatening, red rimming the irises.

I knew better, but I'd had enough. "I was expecting regency. The highlands —"

Felix straightened. "I was expecting a grateful prince. Obviously, you're not ready."

A hush fell around us. Everyone tuned in to what was happening.

"Challenge!" My fury reached boiling point and a loud hiss escaped through my teeth.

It was the only way. Felix's guards wouldn't let me touch him. But a challenge? That had to be answered one-on-one. If he wouldn't give me my regency, I'd take everything.

Felix merely laughed. First a chuckle, then he burst out into a full-blown belly laugh as if he'd seen the most hysterical thing ever. *Right. Me.*

I didn't have a chance to do anything about it. Felix shifted and threw his arm around my shoulder, squeezing gently. "Conrad . . . we're not doing this. It only proves my point. If you're so easily angered, you're not ready to rule. You must be patient."

"I've been patient. For a hundred years," I said through

clenched teeth, my tongue scraping against a fang.

"Tut-tut, Conrad. We'll speak about this in my office later. For now . . . your party is almost over. Go find someone to play with." He shoved me forward into the gathered crowd. They turned away, unwilling to look me in the eye, and started chatting with each other as if they'd been doing that all along. I hated all of them.

Except one.

CHAPTER THREE: MEETING MERI

As I scanned the crowd, I caught the gaze of the lissome performer. The acrobat was standing on the corner of the platform that had been used for the blood-sacrifice. It seemed he only wanted to see above the crowds. He held my attention, looking surprised then glanced around. The body of the sacrifice was still lying prone. The performer quickly stepped off the platform, then turned to leave. He headed toward the rear door, but I was faster.

I rushed through the crowd, shoving some out of my way. They didn't part for me as they had before. I was tarnished, but at that moment, only catching him mattered. Before he could open the door, I grabbed his arm. "Stop. Please." If I wasn't going to receive my regency, at least I could drown my sorrow in this beautiful, young man.

He faced me, eyes like the midnight sky. He gasped in surprise. The tiny sound imprinted on my heart—what little of it I had left. He smelled like cake and sweat and something made of strength, like iron. Delicious. He tilted his chin up. "What do you want with me?"

"Everything . . ."

He started to pull away, mumbling under his breath.

"Let's start by getting to know each other. Okay? You can leave at any time, but you don't know me, yet. Give me a chance." He had all the power at this point in the relationship, before things started, as we were only two potential partners with no contract, no proposal. He could legally walk away from me without any recourse. But I couldn't let that happen.

Not after seeing those deep eyes staring at me, and those pink lips pulled together in surprise.

"Okay."

That one softly spoken word made my heart soar. Maybe I could better understand why Felix looked at Tiziano *that* way. Although, this sweet performer was nothing like that double-crossing sycophant. *Maybe. I still don't know him, after all.*

"Come on. Let's go somewhere quieter where we can talk."

He bit at his bottom lip as if thinking about it for a moment, then he nodded. "Okay . . ."

I led him out the door we had been standing in front of, then through the staging area where many of his clan were preparing their acts, dressed in colorful costumes and makeup. Some waved to him, some stared, but none approached or called out.

On the far side of the room, we pushed through another set of doors that led into the kitchen area. The huge open area had stone floors and walls and a massive fire pit with iron racks. I didn't concern myself with this part of the house. It'd been included for our human servants, guests, and of course, blood-partners. I knew my way around, though. I'd traveled these seldom used passages for a hundred years. There wasn't one inch of the castle I didn't know.

I led him behind the main house to a small set of stairs that climbed up to the higher floors. It was a simple staircase, nothing like the elaborate monstrosity in the front hall where the revelry could still be heard. My personal domain was on the third floor. We said nothing as we climbed. My boots tapped on the tread, but his bare feet didn't make a sound.

My suite had several rooms attached, the main one being a sitting area. I led him to the smaller of the two sofas and sat as close to him as I could. His black hair was a wild mess around his head. He shoved it out of his face. "I don't even know what I'm doing here with you."

"Talking. It's not that hard."

"I know what you want. I-I . . . I'm nobody." He twisted his hair, pulling it away from his face, but it fell right back the second he released it.

"You're adorable. What's your name?"

"Merivel, but, uh, no one calls me that. I go by Meri. Please."

"Merivel? I like that."

"Please, I'm only Meri." He glanced away from me.

I tipped his chin up with a finger. "Meri. Thank you. Please call me Conrad."

He trembled. "I cannot. You're the prince of this kingdom."

I noticed then he had a slight accent different than my own. "Where are you from?"

"Everywhere. Nowhere. We're gypsies. We've traveled, performing for others, for generations. Who knows where we began? We don't."

"Fascinating. The lands you must have seen . . ."

"Oh, I have been everywhere." He started fiddling with his hair again.

I didn't know if it was a nervous habit, or that he wanted it out of his face. "Let me. Please." I gently turned him then knelt on the couch behind him. I ran my fingers through those luxurious black locks, then proceeded to braid the silky strands over the top of his head. When I finished, he had a long braid down his back, ending between his shoulder blades. I ripped a piece of my shirt tail off to tie it.

His shoulders were irresistible, slim but muscular like everything else about him. I trailed my hands along them and down his arms.

He turned with a jerk. "Thank you."

With his hair away from his face, I could better admire his beauty. "Gorgeous."

"I'm not." His eyes flashed with something desperate.

"I, uh, must tell you, Meri. I've never taken a blood-partner. You do know what that is?"

"Yes. I understand the laws of your land. We're required to know them when we enter." He leaned back and stretched his long, firm leg forward, posing like a sexy nymph. "But you're royalty. I know that it's . . . what? Different. Right? You can get around the laws. If you want."

"Maybe, but I won't. That's not who I am."

"And who are you, exactly, Prince Conrad?"

Hearing my name on his lips did utterly fantastic things to my insides, stomach flipping, chest fluttering, cock rising things.

"Well?"

"Who am I? Maybe after a hundred years, I don't even know."

Meri frowned. Perhaps he was looking for a sexy, playful answer, but I didn't have that in me.

"Well, then what do you want?" he asked, more serious this time. He probably expected me to fuck him and drink from him without a contract, then discard him like trash. I wasn't going to do that.

What am I doing, though? "I want many things. I want you. I want my regency. Looks like I can't have either of those."

"Regency? I heard that when you were arguing with the king. What does that mean?"

"It means I would have my own small kingdom within this one." I swirled my finger around for emphasis.

"Why?"

"Why what? Why is it inside this one?"

"No." He pushed on my thigh with his toes. "Why do you want it?"

There was the catch—the crux of everything that had happened. It was why I was always on guard, and why I'd never taken a partner. When I finally answered, it wasn't more than

76

a whisper. I'd never admitted such a thing out loud. "I want out from under his rule."

"King Felix?"

I nodded, unable to say more.

"But . . . a, what did you call it? Regency? That's still under him. Ruling *under* him. He's still in charge, right?"

I didn't answer. I stared into his deep, dark eyes. He understood more than I'd ever thought he would in only a few short sentences.

"Conrad, why don't you leave? Wouldn't that be easier?"

"No. He wouldn't let me go. A hundred years of grooming . . ."

"He doesn't seem to want you to take a bigger part. He would have given it to you years ago. Wouldn't he? And he still denies you? I don't know. I think I'd leave. Unless . . ."

"Unless what?"

"Unless you really want to rule. The only way to get your own kingdom." He tilted his head back and forth. "But I kind of thought you meant you wanted to be away from him. The ruling thing was only secondary. Am I right?"

"Yes."

He held his hand up. As if it were that simple. Maybe it was. I didn't know. I hadn't had time to think it through. The only thing I was sure of was that there was a lot more underneath the pretty exterior of my acrobat.

"I want to offer you a contract." The words blurted out without thought, but I didn't need any more time to think about it. It had been churning in my mind since I'd first seen him.

"Before we've even kissed?" He winked at me.

I didn't need to kiss him to know we would have sparks between us. Meri was like lightning. He set my soul on fire— if I had a soul to set on fire. I wanted to spend another hundred years finding out—with him.

"Meri, what are your terms?"

"I've never had a contract. How would I know? What can we put in there? What would I be bound to?"

"You're considering it?" Even though I hadn't said please, the begging was in my voice all the same. "We can have so much more."

"Are you letting your . . . uh, *sexual desires* rule your thoughts?"

"This goes beyond sexual." I grabbed his arm below the elbow then pulled him to me. I had to touch him. He willingly came and sat in my lap. "Do you need a kiss to decide?"

"Maybe—"

I didn't let him continue. I pushed my mouth against his and slid my tongue between my fangs and his pretty lips. He moaned into my mouth, making me wish I could drink his sounds like blood.

He wiggled his ass over my hard cock. "Conrad . . . tell me about this contract . . ." His eyes were half closed, and he licked at his lips as if he had something delicious lingering there.

I chuckled. "I can make it whatever you want. We can put a trial clause in it."

"What's that?" He reached up and shoved his fingers in my hair. It wasn't nearly as long as his. I chose to keep it above my ears and collar, but it was thick. I loved his hands tugging and pulling as he carded his fingers through the strands.

"Uh . . . it's . . . difficult to think with you doing that, Meri."

He removed his hands, but I wanted them back. I huffed. We needed to finish the business part so that I could take him to bed.

"It's a clause that says we both have a certain amount of time to try this thing out. Like three days or a month. Or whatever. Either of us can end the contract for any reason without notice during that time. Once the trial period is over, the contract is permanent."

"That sounds like an out for you to throw me away when you're finished."

"It's not. I don't want that."

"How could you know? You said you've never taken a partner."

I kissed the side of his neck. "I know."

"Conrad . . ."

"We can put that only *you* have the option to terminate the contract during the trial. Not me. I'm stuck with you."

"Until you're not." He stood up.

"What?"

"I saw the, uh, the body. I know what was done. That's how . . . how you get rid of a contracted partner. It doesn't matter what's in the contract. The law of sacrifice overrules a contract."

"You're very smart."

He crossed his arms over his chest and glared at me. I couldn't resist his fiery attitude.

"Meri. I'm not trying to trick you. That's the way it is. I can't change it, but I don't like it. I don't like a lot of the laws, but I'm bound by them. Will you let that stop you? Stop us?"

"I don't want it to, but I barely know you. Prince Conrad. Vampire. Ruler."

"I'm vampire first. That's something you should know. That means at my core, I'm a killer. We all are, even with those fancy laws."

Meri smiled then. His face lit up. Why had that made him so happy? I raised an eyebrow, and he laughed. "Gee . . . Conrad, that's the most honest thing you've said all night."

"I haven't said anything dishonest." I pursed my lips together. *Have I?*

"Ah . . . no, but in the middle of convincing me to be your blood-partner, you admitted what you really are, and I can trust you—only so far. You still want me to give up my life for you."

"Tell me what you don't want to give up?"

"Freedom. I want to be able to come and go as I please. I don't want to answer to anyone. Don't want to answer to you." He pointed at me. "Any more than you want to answer to Felix. Understand?"

I did. "So take the contract. You can break it whenever you want. We can make the trial period a whole year. Or two. We can travel. We don't have to stay here."

"Can we travel with my family? They're expecting to meet up in a few days at the Eastern border. We're leaving your kingdom. We only came here for your celebration."

I nodded. Troops like his rarely came to Felix's territory. There were strict laws that were difficult to navigate. "Why'd you come?"

"Tiziano. He arranged it."

"Of course." I sneered.

"You don't like him?"

"No."

"Neither do I. So, about that contract?"

He was going to do it. I knew he would. "I didn't answer you. About traveling with your family."

He smirked. "I don't think I care."

We spent the next hour hashing out a contract. It included the things he wanted, but also some parts that could not be changed. They were law. He signed. In blood. So did I.

I set the drying contract on my desk then laced our fingers together. "Come."

Getting him naked was my only priority. I helped him peel the leotard thing he was wearing off his shoulders and torso. The material hung around his waist while I explored his chest. His muscles weren't huge. His chest was very flat, but the definition in them was unmistakable. I flipped my thumbs over his nipples and enjoyed watching them perk up. "So sexy."

Meri blushed. "You need to be undressed, too. Come on, Conrad."

I'd dispensed with tie and jacket for the evening, but I had worn a vest with formal trousers. Meri made quick work of the buttons and slipped the vest off. He ran his deft fingers over my shoulders and down my sleeved arms. He took his time, unfastening my cuffs. I'd worn the gold cufflinks that had Felix's signet pressed into them. Meri carefully placed them on my bureau.

Meri unfastened the top button at my throat. He smoothed the material across my chest as he made his way down. "You feel so hard . . ."

When he finished, my shirt slid off my shoulders and onto the floor. I pulled him close, our skin touching, chest to chest. He was only a little shorter than me. A perfect height. I ground my hips into him, so he could feel how hard I was for him, and he tilted his head up to me in response. I kissed him gently, wanting to go slow, but the kiss quickly turned desperate. Our tongues dueled, and our hands grabbed at each other. I reached down to touch his dick. The material covering him was soft and padded beneath my fingers like I was grabbing a pillow rather than a cock. It made him giggle.

"I have a dancer's belt on."

I eyed him carefully.

"It's for protection. Hang on." He pulled the material over his hips, exposing what looked like a thick, padded jock strap. He bent and pulled the leotard off his legs, hopping a bit as he got his feet out. Then he stood up straight, hands on his hips. "See?" He snapped the elastic around his waist before rolling it down to expose his hard cock beneath the thick covering.

"Damn. Amazing." He wasn't small at all. On the contrary, his cock was long and lean as was the rest of him. He'd trimmed his hair around it and his balls very tightly. His legs seemed smooth, though he had such dark hair —

Meri lifted one leg high over his head. "I shave," he confirmed. "It looks better in the costume." As he lowered his leg, he ran his hands up his thigh from knee to torso, then up his sides, tickling over his ribs.

"That's some show."

He smiled. "Hm . . . you like?"

"I do . . ."

He hummed softly as I cupped his ass and gave it a little squeeze. I lowered my head and ran the edge of my nose along his collar bone, teasing myself as much as him. I wanted to draw this out. Imprint every second on my memory. Lower, I flicked my tongue over one pert nipple. A flush of color bloomed across his chest and throat. Meri made a soft groaning noise as I bent over, pressing my face into his stomach. So soft and pliable.

I turned him around and guided him to sit on the edge of my bed. He ran his hands over the soft comforter and lifted his chin to gaze up at me. I stepped between his legs, and he reached for my waist. "Can I?" he asked.

"Of course."

In a moment, he had my trousers unbuttoned, and shoved down my hips. Beneath them I wore a snug undergarment, but nothing like the contraption he'd had on. He shoved it all lower, exposing my hard cock, then pushed the material to the floor. He reached for me and opened his mouth, so I let him play. He sucked my cock down then pulled off it and licked at the tip.

"Damn, Meri," I growled when he did it again. "I want inside you." I pushed his shoulders back and crawled over him, our bodies touching everywhere. His smooth legs wrapped around mine, and our cocks danced together as I undulated above him.

There was no doubt that Meri loved what we were doing. He made all the right sounds, and rubbed his hands over my skin, clutching at me here and there .

Meri sighed. "My aunt said this trip would be important. But I never expected this"

"Aunt?"

"She tells the future." Meri frowned. "Vaguely. Still . . . look at me now."

"Is this what you wanted? Is this why you came here?" Doubts crept in, leaving me more vulnerable than I wanted to be.

"No. Conrad, no. This is . . . completely unexpected." He rolled his hips, pushing up into my groin. "But not unwelcome."

I pressed against his lips and snaked my tongue along his. Wet, velvety, and not nearly enough. I poured my desire into that kiss, scraping my tongue against my fangs, dangerously. I pulled back and gazed into his eyes. "I have something to help. In my drawer." I pointed to the small cabinet beside the bed, but I didn't want to get up. I didn't want to part from him, not for even one second.

"I'm not impatient, normally . . . but come on, get it."

His words spurred me on with another growl escaping my throat. He moved farther up the bed as I retrieved the goop that would slick everything up and make it pleasurable for both of us, especially him. I didn't want to hurt him any more than I had to.

Meri spread his legs, planting his feet on the mattress, knees wide open, so I could see everything he had waiting for me. His balls were pulling up tight, exposing that sweet puckered hole.

"Have you done this before?" I asked him.

"No, uh . . . not this, like this. I've . . . dabbled." He blushed.

"I want to suck your cock like you did mine, Meri, but I can't." I flashed my fangs at him. I could sense his heartbeat kick up when I did that. "I'm not going to hurt you."

He nodded and gestured for me to come closer, so I lowered over him again. He whispered in my ear on an exhale of hot breath, "I want *everything* you have to give me. I can handle a little pain."

If I wanted him to trust me, I needed to trust him. I took him at his word, but I still intended to make it enjoyable. I sat up between his legs and looked my fill, then I grabbed the pot and opened it. I scooped out some of the lube and smeared it over his taint and down to his hole, making him wiggle.

He gasped. "Cold . . ."

I chuckled. "It'll warm up fast enough." I pushed the stuff inside him. It was slick and made my finger glide. Meri moaned softly, his eyes rolling. He was enjoying it. Something warm and bubbly radiated through me. I swallowed it down and moved faster, adding fingers, and when he started to squirm, I crooked those fingers and hit his spot.

Meri practically flew off the bed — eyes wide. "What was that?"

"Pleasurable, no?" It had been a long time since I'd taken a lover, but I hadn't forgotten how to pleasure a man.

"No? Yes! Do it again!" He eased down to the mattress, and I repeated my trick. This time, he stayed put, but the sound he made was far beyond simply moaning. He fluttered his eyes, and I wanted nothing more than to give that to him again and again.

Torn between continuing to fill my new partner with ecstasy and wanting to take some for myself, I slowly lifted over him, aligning myself with his hole.

"Conrad!" he called out as I pushed inside his slick heat.

He closed his eyes, and they crinkled at the corners.

"Relax. Easy."

He settled down a bit, and as he did, Meri grunted with a delicate frown on his face.

"Meri . . . sweet Meri. It'll get better soon. Push against me some."

We held still when I finally bottomed out. My pubic area was flush against his balls and lower thighs — everything squashed together. I loved how it felt, how it looked.

When I started moving, pumping in and out with small strokes, his eyes opened, and his mouth opened, too, forming an *oh*.

"You like, Meri?"

"Y-yes. By-the-moon! Why haven't I done this sooner?"

"You were obviously saving it for me." I grunted and pumped harder, fucking him and canting my hips to ensure I hit his spot.

The noises he made were layered with high-pitched ecstasy. Exactly what I wanted to hear. He ran his hands over my thighs and gripped the muscles tightly, urging me on. I rolled my hips, fucking into him fluidly. The need built from around my groin, spreading outward, up my spine, and out to my legs. I couldn't fight it. Instead, I leaned forward and latched onto his throat, sinking my fangs in deeply. His blood-life poured effortlessly, tasting of iron and promise. I came hard, overwhelmed by the sensation of feeling him tight around my cock and pouring into my mouth. Even after my orgasm, I found it hard to stop drinking from him. So delicious and comforting.

A banging on my outer door forced me from my prize. I licked at the wound to help seal it, and when I stood to admire the view, Meri had come all over his stomach and chest. I'd barely noticed in the heat of the moment, but I happily rubbed my stomach where the cum had been shared with me. "I'll be right back. Don't get dressed."

He nodded with half-lidded eyes and a serene smile. That satisfied expression made it so hard to leave, but the pounding came again. I grabbed my trousers from the floor then pulled them on, hopping to the door.

It flew open as I approached. "Hey! Wait a minute." Outrage consumed me as one of The Elite Guard stepped in, backed by two huge monstrosities from The Savage-Guard.

CHAPTER FOUR: CONRAD CAPTURED

"We have a contract. I assure you. No need for this intrusion."

It would be just like Tiziano to send troops in, thinking I was breaking the law with my new partner. *Bastard*! But he had nothing to stand on. I hadn't cheated.

The elite guard glanced around the room. "That's good." He stepped closer, then smiled, flashing a bit of fang in the process. "That's not why we're here, but you're going to need it." He snapped his fingers. "Take this one, too."

One of the savages stepped forward to seize me and grabbed my arm. "What is this?" I snarled at the guard and nipped at the Savage who strode past me into my private quarters. Protecting Meri was more important to me than my own predicament.

They dragged us both from my suite and down the hallway leading to the main house. Meri gave up struggling when the guard told the savage to pick him up. He threw Meri over his shoulder. Everything inside me cried out to defend my blood-partner. I needed to be sure he was safe more than I needed to live.

I had no idea what this mess was about, but I knew that I'd fucked up. Meri would not be allowed to break the contract until this was cleared up, and how long would that take? I had no way of knowing. If it went on too long, Meri would miss meeting up with his family, or worse, be stuck in the contract permanently. I wanted that, but I didn't think he truly did. He'd trusted me that he could break it.

CHAPTER FIVE: THE INTRIGUE

I was a prince. I'd lived over a hundred years as pampered royalty, and more. I'd been born on this estate and lived my first life here. I was groomed from the womb. I knew I was fated to be turned from an early age. Being arrested had never been a possibility. I'd never once considered such a thing. My shock at the situation didn't stop the Savage Guards from tossing me into a cell.

I'd been brought below to the basement levels where thick, stone walls had held up the manor for thousands of years. This part of the structure was older than what even a vampire brain could understand.

The air was cold and damp, but the cell had been made comfortable for me as if Felix couldn't bear to have me uncomfortable, even if he did allow my incarceration. Someone had added thick carpets that were soft under my bare feet. A double bed, made up with all the splendors of royal bedding, took up the majority of the space, and an extra blanket waited at the foot of the bed. I could see by the gaslights hanging on the walls through the silver bars outside my prison. Every bit of luxurious indulgence here angered me beyond belief. I kicked the leg of the bed.

The elite guard tsked, grabbing my attention.

"What is this all about?"

He shrugged and walked away. It wasn't his place to answer my questions. The first of those being where the hell had they taken Meri? The second was what the hell was I going to do about this?

I was obviously being set up for something, though I had no idea what or who was behind it. I suspected Tiziano, but what did he have to gain here? He already had Felix's attention. He was treated far better than any other blood-partner Felix had ever had. What more could he want?

Felix was probably still pissed about my backlash at the party. I should never have tried to challenge him. He'd blown it off like I was a child. *Does he still think of me that way? Incapable? Immature?* I thought I'd shown him how serious I was. I'd taken on more and more responsibility over the years and had always proved capable.

At least there were no windows in my cage. Two sides were stone from the foundation. The third was a solid wall of plaster, though I suspected something much stronger beneath it. Stone or steel—I had no clue. The fourth wall wasn't a wall, but iron bars laced with silver. I could almost feel the sting anytime I paced too close. I'd felt it reverberate through me when I'd passed into the cell. This was a jail built to hold vampires.

Pacing across the front of the bed, hours seemed to pass before I heard footfalls. Finally, someone was coming and . . . I could smell my Meri—vanilla and metal rolled together. I was relieved to see him.

The guard unlocked the cell then pulled the barred door open, letting the savage that carried Meri come forward and drop him to the ground. I rushed over, pulling him into my arms.

"You have about an hour with your partner. I'll be back." He nodded and left. He wasn't nice, neither was he overly cruel. His indifference shuddered through my heart, scarier than if he'd been malicious.

"Meri . . . I'm so sorry. Are you all right?"

He nodded, looking down to his legs. He'd been dressed in a cotton tunic, leaving his legs and feet bare. I grabbed his face, tilting it so I could see his dark eyes. They stared at me with all the depth of the night. "I'm okay," he whispered, but I could see the tear tracks streaked down his cheeks. I kissed them, softly.

"I'm sorry."

"What did you do?"

"I have no idea." I hugged him, letting his warmth bring me some small comfort. "I'm scared."

Meri huffed. "Scared? You're the prince. Surely, this will be cleared up. Is it about . . ." He motioned between us.

"No. I don't think so."

He exhaled loudly, relieved. "Okay. So?" He held a hand up.

I took it and kissed his palm. "You won't be allowed to break our contract until this is settled, one way or another. I'm sorry. I hadn't intended this."

He leaned into my shoulder. "I know. It's fine. I don't mind, really. I was thinking . . . I . . ."

"What?"

"Maybe I don't want to break the contract, anyway. I don't know. It's silly." He snuggled against my chest. "Seems it doesn't *ever* matter what I want."

"It matters to me. Even if I can't do anything about it . . . it still matters. *You* matter." That piece of information was etched in my heart, completely unexpected and true.

"Thank you." He sighed. "They brought me so you can feed. You need your strength." He tilted his head, exposing that long, elegant neck.

Irresistible. I sank my fangs in over the bruise where I'd already marked him. I loved that my mark stood so boldly against his bronze skin. I relished the nourishment he gave me. I wanted more than that but couldn't even think of making love to him in this harsh place. Felix might have had it decorated, but I could still see exactly what it was. A prison.

I finished drinking and let myself be content to hold him for the moment. Too quickly, the guard returned.

"Don't fight them, Meri. I don't want you hurt."

He nodded, standing then walking away. He waved and followed the savage.

"Hey!" I called out to The Elite. He turned to me. He had blondish-brown hair that poked out beneath his cap. "Where is he being held? You *are* treating him well?"

"Of course." He sighed as he hung his ring of keys at his waist. His hands were covered with thick gloves that protected him from the silver of the bars, but the gloves also hid his skin, so I could only guess at his true age. His face was still fairly solid. "Felix said to treat him well. Don't worry. I've no need for punishing the innocent."

After that, Meri was brought to me in intervals, some longer than others. I fed, but never anything to overtax him. He told me he was eating well, and they were keeping him in a room a few floors up. He thought it was nicer than anything he'd ever stayed in before, but it was lonely. He was used to having a large family around him all the time. The only one he could talk with was me. The guilt crushed my heart. I never wanted him to be so sad and tried hard to make the moments we were together better for him.

Finally, the guards came and brought me before the king. He sat behind his massive desk in his office. I'd been there a million times before, but never in chains. They'd cuffed my wrists behind my back. I could feel the silver itching against my skin as I stood there. Felix lifted his eyes to me, peering over the desk. "This is very disappointing, Conrad."

"For you or me?"

He scowled. "Don't. You're playing a harsh game, and you don't know the rules."

"Teach me." He'd taught me so much over the years, but

not this. Where was his head on this? I had no clue. "I don't understand."

"No, you don't. That's the problem." He stood, placed his hands on the edge of the desk, then leaned forward, looming over it. "You think you can rule? You don't have what it takes. You aren't subtle. Everything you think or feel is written all over your face. You've never been able to hide anything from me."

"That's a bad thing?"

"Conrad! Ugh! It is. This pains me, but you're so naive even after a hundred fucking years!"

"Felix, please!" I wasn't beyond begging.

"To rule you must be shrewd. Calculated. Never let anyone know what you really think or feel. You have to put aside your emotions and make decisions—hard decisions—based on fact."

"Are we talking about me or you?"

Felix sat back in his chair. "It doesn't make a difference." For the first time ever, he looked sad. I could see how miserable he was, but even in that moment, it was as he said. *Calculated.* He wanted me to see it.

"I'm in trouble here, but I still don't understand."

"Devyn is going to rule. I'm giving him the regency."

Everything snapped into place. Clarity at its most ruthless. The laws Felix was bound by for inheritance would not allow anyone else but me to have the regency. I'd thought it was a given, but I had been so wrong. This wasn't about Tiziano at all. It was all Devyn. "You're listening to what that sniveling brat has to say?"

"Now you show some backbone. Of course." He threw his hand in the air, full of disgust.

"Don't do this. There must be another way."

There wasn't. I knew it. Just like Devyn's blood-sacrifice. Spilling blood was the only out.

"You're being charged with a terrible crime, Conrad. The reason you're here is that it has come to my attention that you've recently taken a blood-partner. We must finalize how to dispose of your assets."

"No." I pulled against my bonds. I had thought the silver cuffs were overkill. I was wrong about that, too. They were the only thing keeping me from tearing his throat out. "You will not harm him. No!"

Felix stood and walked around the corner of the desk. He leisurely dragged his finger over the stacks of paper and books lined along the edges then glanced up to the wall behind me. I knew without looking that a portrait of him with his Sire hung on that wall. It was old. Maybe as old as the estate. I didn't know. The picture of a young Felix was stunning. He'd been so beautiful with his golden hair and bright smile. He wore clothes that were no longer available to us — denim pants and a thin, cotton pullover. His shoes were made of canvas and rubber.

He stood in front of me. "You can thank Tizi for this, Conrad. He's taught me, ugh . . . well, a lot. About love."

I opened my mouth to ask him more, but he put his finger over my lips.

"No. Listen. He taught me. I love him. He's asked that you have a choice about your new partner. I would just assume sacrifice the gutter trash. He's nothing. Not worthy of you at all. And how legal is this temporary contract you have, anyway?"

"Let him go."

"Tizi has asked this of me." He shrugged. "Take him out of my sight."

That was it. Accused. Charged. Judged. Sentenced.

None of it needed to be said. The charges were bogus. He didn't want me to rule, and the only way to make that happen was to get rid of me. For Devyn to take my place, I had to die.

For the first time, I hoped Tiziano did have sway over Felix. I wanted Meri to live. I wanted to die knowing he would go on. That he would dance and perform. That he would fly.

CHAPTER SIX: SORTING LIES

When I returned to my new abode in the basement, Meri sat waiting for me on the bed. His legs were crossed in front of him, his shiny hair cascaded over his shoulders free of the braid, and he bit at his bottom lip with worry.

The guard stopped me to remove the shackles, then shoved me through the door, slamming it behind me. He didn't say another word. I didn't want him to, either. My eyes were locked on Meri the entire time. I wanted to kiss the anxiety from his beautiful, exotic face.

I rushed to him, pulling him tight against me. "Meri . . ." I buried my face in his shoulder.

"What? What happened? What's going on, Conrad?"

"He's decided that Devyn should rule in my place . . ." I barely gasped the words out. They were laced with heavy meaning and weighed down with Devyn's malicious intent.

"What? I don't understand." He pushed at my head to get me to move off him.

Complying, I looked at him . . . carefully, tenderly. "There's only one way. I have to be—" I swallowed hard. I didn't want to say it.

Meri glared at me. "Dead? They're going to kill you?"

"Yes. I didn't do anything wrong. They—Felix. He wants me out of the way. Gone. This is the only way to do it."

"To manufacture a non-existent crime? Fuck! I was right about vampires."

I shook my head. "No. Not completely. It's not me. I wouldn't—"

"That's probably why they want you gone, Conrad. I'm surprised you don't see that." His voice rose with his anger. Then he looked at me, pursed his lips together, and cupped his hand over the side of my face, rubbing against my bare cheek. It hadn't needed to be shaved in a hundred years. "It's also why I love you."

"You love me?"

"Shut up."

I kissed him. I couldn't help myself. I wanted to be so close that we'd never part. We had so little time left. "They promised to set you free, though. Felix agreed to it. You'll be able to go back to your family and forget this whole thing ever happened."

He burst out laughing, but it was a rough, ugly sound. "You think? I doubt that." He pulled me to him, rubbing his hand down my arms. "I don't believe that for a second. As soon as you're gone, they'll sacrifice me and dance in our blood."

"No—"

"Yes. Don't be naive about this. I'm sure he *said* he'd let me go. Probably to keep you calm. Docile. Going willingly to your grave."

I had to doubt Felix's intentions. He'd also said it was Tiziano's request. He could go against it. What real power did Tiziano have? Had he really taught Felix to love? I doubted it. Meri was right. "I'm so stupid."

"Oh, you're not. Conrad, baby. You have a big heart. It's not your fault that you shouldn't have been a vampire prince. You're too gentle for that."

"What should I have been?" As if I had ever had a choice. My fate was dictated before I was ever conceived in my poor mother's womb. I'm sure she thought she had done right by me when she had contracted with Felix, but maybe not.

I didn't know if I'd change a damn thing, though. If I did,

I'd probably never have had Meri in my arms and in my bed.

"I don't know. You could be a gypsy? Like me?"

"I would. I really would." I hugged him. The embrace was for his words and his heart, and for his bravery. "You should have walked away from me, Meri."

"You asked me to stay. Asked for the contract."

"I didn't think it would mean your life."

He pushed away from me and off the bed. He grabbed hold of the bars, trying to look down the hall. "We need to go. We have to get out of here. I can help. I am a gypsy . . . and an acrobat."

"How will that help?"

Meri sized up the bars, then contorted himself, sliding between them to escape the cell. He put his fingers over his lips to shush me as he snuck down the hall.

My heart pounded in my chest, sending blood to my extremities. I could feel it moving through me. I could barely breathe. If they caught him . . .

He slid around the corner where I couldn't see him. I could hear him speaking. Could hear the guard . . .

Holy Blood-Anointed! He was going to get himself killed.

A moment later he came back. I could smell his blood. "What did you do?"

He held up his wrist. Fang marks pierced his skin. I wanted to bust through the cells and kill the fucking bastard. How dare he bite *my* partner?

"Calm down, Conrad." He held up the keys in his other hand.

"How did you?"

"Gypsy. Remember?"

I could still smell blood. It had me growling. "He sampled *our* blood. I'll kill him."

"No. I offered it. Come on. I did what I had to. Let's get out of here. Be quiet."

Meri was right. This entire situation was wrong, but it couldn't be helped. None of it could. If we didn't escape, we'd be killed. I could handle my own death. I'd lived too long, but not Meri's. Not my beautiful Meri. He had so much life left in him.

I stepped out of the cell. Meri pulled at my arm. I tried to follow him away from the guards, but I couldn't. "Wait."

"No. Conrad, no."

I marched down the hall, my bare feet slapping against the stone. I charged around the corner and leaped. The guard wasn't expecting it. He hadn't even noticed me coming. I grabbed his head and twisted, snapping his neck. The only way to kill a vampire—remove his head, snap the chords connecting his brain to the blood. It worked. He slumped to the floor.

Two savage guards were standing there, only a few feet away, watching the whole thing go down. They were slow. Fierce and strong, but their brains operated at a dawdling pace. They were incapable of making quick decisions. I searched the guard and found his trainer, a short black stick he held in his hand. It was charged with vampire blood and used to control the savages, to teach them. I held it up. They both cowered. "You're both off duty. Go to your quarters. Do not speak to anyone."

One of them hesitated. I pointed the trainer at him. I had to be firm, or I was dead. I stroked the sleek, black box with my thumb. It shot out a volt of light that struck the savage in the chest. They weren't smart enough to know I wasn't in charge. They couldn't tell the difference between prisoners and guards. They only did what they were told. After the quick jolt, they both fled. I didn't know if they'd get help or simply return to their quarters as instructed, and I wasn't going to wait around to find out.

I stripped the dead guard, taking his shirt and boots. They

fit well enough. He didn't have anything useful for Meri, but we'd make it work.

CHAPTER SEVEN: THE ESCAPE

I led Meri through the tunnels and lesser known hallways of the estate. I'd played there as a child, hid as a sullen teen, and even had a few sexual trysts as an adult before I'd been turned.

We made it to a seldom-used exit. The door opened to the surrounding forest. We ran through them, holding hands, not looking back. When the forest floor became thick with undergrowth, I carried Meri to save his bare feet and legs. We desperately needed to find more suitable clothing for him and somewhere to hide during the day. The sun was threatening me in the distance.

We broke through the woods on a hillside and looked down at the roof peaks, barely visible in the early morning.

"Conrad." Meri slid from my shoulders onto the soft grass. "Morning is coming fast. What are we going to do?"

"You're going to go down there." I pointed at the village. "People will help you."

"Without you?" He lifted one dark eyebrow. "I don't think so."

"Meri . . . be reasonable. They won't continue to search for you."

"No. There's no argument here." He stamped his foot. "Together. Us. That's what you said." He gestured between us. "Now what do we do? What will happen if the sun rises?"

"It will kill me. I can't tolerate it at all." There'd been a time in my vampire youth when that might not have been the case, but I'd grown too old.

"You need somewhere safe to hide." He bit into his lower lip as he scanned the valley below. "How fast can you move?"

I almost laughed. "I'm vampire. We're stronger. Faster. Some say smarter, but I'm doubting that about now."

Meri snorted. It was adorable. I couldn't help pull him to me, but he pushed away. "Conrad. Stop. We don't have time for this. Look there." He pointed to a barn farther down the hillside, but still a few good miles outside of the town. "Get there. Fast. I'll follow. I'm going to explore and find some clothes. But you get in that barn. Now."

I loved the way he ordered me around. He was right. I hated him going without me, though. "Meri. Just come with me. We'll go together—"

"Enough. Conrad. I'm capable of taking care of myself. Gypsies are very resourceful. The sun is coming up. We are out of time. Now go!"

There was no other choice. "Fine." Despite how easily I'd given in to Felix, I didn't actually have a death wish. Before I left, I turned to him, grabbed his wrist in one hand and his hair in the other. "Do not let anyone else touch you. Don't ever let another drink from you. And bring yourself to meet me soon. Understand?"

"Yes . . ." he choked out.

I kissed his pink lips, but then self-preservation kicked in. I ran as fast as I could go. It probably looked as if I'd disappeared to Meri's mortal eyes.

Inside the barn, I found a corner in the back that would be shaded from the sun. To be safe, I stacked a few hay bales in front of my hiding spot and dug myself under the loose hay. There I waited. Away from the sun but not my worried thoughts. Thinking about Meri in the village on his own, wearing nothing more than that thin shift. I hated it.

The sun came up outside and didn't scorch me. I had no idea how long it had been, but Meri didn't come. I tried to stay awake, but the higher the sun rose, the more my eyelids drooped, calling me to sleep. Eventually, I gave in.

CHAPTER EIGHT: RENDEZVOUS

When I woke, a warm body was pressed against my side. He smelled like grass and cigar smoke, but underneath that was the familiar warm vanilla and musky sweat that was only Meri. I pulled him tight against my chest. I ran my nose through his hair. Then I held him at arms' length while I inspected his naked body, making sure he was unhurt.

"Mmm . . . Conrad . . . you are awake!"

I thrust my hips into him so he could feel my cock. He turned then wiggled his way to the floor, wasting no time unbuttoning my trousers and yanking them lower.

"You may not be able to suck cock, but I can." He flicked his tongue over the head of my cock, then sucked me.

"By the blood . . . Meri . . ." I'd never felt so good. He was everything. This was everything. I shoved my hands in his thick, dark hair. "I want to fuck your mouth, Meri . . ."

He pulled off me with a loud pop.

The pressure in my dick demanded more attention. "Meri . . ." I begged him.

"Yes. Whatever you need." His breathy voice had my heart fluttering.

When he sucked my cock again, I pulled at his hair and rolled my hips. He was ready for me. I fucked into his beautiful mouth, watching him take all of me. His wet heat wrapped around me was bliss. I sped up the pace, thrusting harder. Meri was perfect with his hollowed cheeks and half-lidded eyes. My hands entwined in his midnight hair. The tingling rushed up my cock, everything sparkled behind my eyes, and

I came hard inside his mouth, down his throat. He drank it all.

Afterward, Meri pulled off with a chuckle. He held up his hand, showing me his cum. I held him by the wrist, pulling him to me, then licked his palm and fingers, tasting his salty, tangy essence. He laughed again as I cleaned him up. Then we snuggled down in the straw. The sun hadn't completely set, so we had time simply to be together.

"Conrad. I have a plan. If you want . . ."

"What's that?" I was simply glad he'd made it back to me safely.

"I found a steam-cart of sorts. We'd, uh . . . have to steal it."

"Did you find clothes?"

"Yes. They're hanging up. I had to try and wash them. They kind of stunk, but they'll work."

"Good. And this steam-cart?"

"We need it." He snuggled into my chest. "Or horses—"

"No. I'm not fond of horses, and they've no love for vampires, either. Too smart, I think."

"I'd heard that but didn't know if it was true. My family has several carts pulled by horses. We also have oxen and sheep. Is that going to be a problem? I mean if we meet up with them. And stay with them. I know where they'll be, but we have to hurry."

"That's why we need the steam-cart?"

He straddled my waist and loomed over me, staring down at me. "That and to keep you out of the sun during the day."

I reached up and pulled a strand of hair from his face. "You want to? With me? What will your family say?"

"They're family. They'll take us in. They'll help us. If we can get there."

"Well, if they're as clever as you say, that seems our best bet."

He smiled. If hijacking this machine that he'd found made

him happy, I'd do it a million times over.

We dressed, and when the sun finally dipped below the horizon, we set out. Meri had found pants, boots and a shirt that fit. The clothes were stained and ripped, and the boots hardly had a sole left, but they'd work.

Meri led me to a run-down business that seemed to be abandoned. The husk of the steam engine loomed over a cluttered lawn, strewn with debris. "This is it? Are you sure it's going to even work?"

"Yes, I checked that out. And look." He pointed to a side building. I strode over to see an old coal bin and several sturdy boxes. "We'll need that."

"Indeed." I shoveled coal into the boxes then loaded them into the front housing where it would be easily accessible to shovel into the furnace. The big iron engine was set on top of tracks that ran on six wheels that stretched the length of the machine.

It wasn't hard to understand the general idea of how it worked. You dumped coal into the big fireboxes, and the energy produced from burning turned the gears between the engine and the tracks, they rolled the six wheels, and then the whole thing moved along the tracks. It was big and heavy enough to roll over almost anything. How exactly the inner mechanics worked was beyond me, but apparently not beyond Meri.

He had the machine running smoothly in no time at all. He started the fire and filled a huge tank with water. On the back side of the contraption was a compartment to ride in. Meri stepped in and climbed to the top where he could see where we were going. Obviously, my gypsy-partner would steer the rig. He'd found a pair of goggles and pulled them over his eyes, then he started the machine up, and we simply drove it away.

Before we left, Meri pinched some day-old bread from

outside the local bakery and a few other things from around town. Olives, sausages, bruised fruit. I felt bad that I hadn't even thought about finding food for him. I should have. If he didn't keep up his strength, I wouldn't be able to keep up mine. Despite being so old, I still had a lot to learn.

Once we were on our way, I rubbed his shoulder. "I'm sorry about all of this, Meri."

"It's fine. Right now, we have what we need. We may have to find more coal before we get there, but that's okay."

"I mean it, though. You wouldn't be in this position if I hadn't been so selfish. You should be with your family."

"I'm an adult, Conrad. I made my own decisions. You didn't coerce me. I wanted to. Besides . . ." He turned that bright smile on me. It was almost enough to light up the night sky. "We're only a few days behind them. They'll wait for me."

I hoped he was right.

The steam-cart lurched through the streets of the city, then Meri turned it to the main road, heading out of town. The road ahead was barren but lit by the gaslights on posts every thirty meters, casting a golden glow over the cobblestone.

"It's very quiet," Meri whispered. The only sound was from our engine, huffing and puffing and letting off steam every so often.

Instinctively, I leaned forward, trying to listen for anything else ahead of us. I heard the shouting a moment too late. "There! Stop them!" Vampires poured from the side streets, racing alongside us, calling out to stop us.

"Go faster, Meri," I urged him, though I knew he'd never make it go fast enough.

One of our pursuers caught up and jumped at us. He pulled himself up by the railing on the edge of our compartment. The moment I had his head in my sights, I kicked him, sending him flying.

"Conrad!" Another, dressed in The Elite Guard's uniform, had leaped onto the front of the engine. He lurched side to side, balancing himself as he moved toward us. I wasn't sure what his intentions were until he jumped down onto the side platform that ran along the motor-works. *Sabotage.* I couldn't have that. I crawled over and shoved him away, but he held onto a lever and pulled himself closer. I punched him in the face.

He turned and spat blood, then grinned at me. "Shouldn't have done that. My orders say I can kill you, Prince."

"Vile creature."

The second he let go of the lever, I kicked him in the chest. This time he flew backward, landing on the road below.

Meri screamed.

Another had climbed onboard. I rushed to help him, but another soldier had his claws around my leg, tugging at my trousers, trying to haul himself up or yank me down. I caught a handful of long, golden hair, and slammed his head into the edge of the platform. He wailed as his legs were caught up in the engine's track. I let go of him as he was slid away with a sickening crunch.

I glanced over at Meri through the small window he used to see where we were going. He was trying to fight off a vampire. I could not tolerate another's hands on Meri. He was *mine*.

I maneuvered to the cabin. The guard had Meri in his arms. My low growl filled the cabin, and the guard turned to face me with surprise in his eyes. He was as good as dead, and he knew it.

"Mine." I almost didn't recognize my own voice. It sounded animalistic like a deadly predator.

The guard lifted his hands in the air, and Meri ducked down, but the vampire wasn't finished. He narrowed his eyes. I read his movements. He flinched before he lunged, but that second was enough. I punched out as he dove forward. A loud crack rent the air as we connected. The guard's chin caught the worst of it, snapping his head. Before he hit the floor, I had my claws at his throat, digging through his skin. Few things could tear a vampire apart, Blood squirted out from his wound. I tossed his body over the rail and into another would-be attacker, knocking them both from our engine.

Other shouts could be heard behind us, but Meri had kept us on course. "Are they done?" he asked, as we pushed out of the town and into the dark.

"I don't know. Let's get off the main road. This thing will plow over rough terrain. Right?"

"It will." Meri turned the big wheel, and the machine yawed to the left. We plowed over the open land, picking up some speed.

There was no sign of the attackers. I couldn't hear them or see them. "I think they gave up."

A chug and a whir came from the engine. "Needs more coal. I'm going so fast, it can't keep up."

"I'm on it." I leaped to the platform and pulled out the box of coal, thankful it hadn't been disturbed during the fight.

Once I'd shoveled plenty of coal inside, I returned to the compartment. "Are you hurt?"

"No." He pointed to the eastern sky. "They stopped chasing because the sun is coming up. There's blankets." He pointed to a compartment I hadn't noticed. "That opens. Pull them out. We can't stop now. Cover up and stay low."

I listened to my Meri, but only after I kissed him. "Thank you."

"Shut up and do it." He pushed at my chest to get me going.

After the second night of travel, Meri was no longer

smiling. The food was gone, and we had very little coal left. Plus, the water had burned off faster than Meri had anticipated. We'd need all three of those things very soon, and there wasn't a town in sight. "I can run faster than this thing. I can go ahead and find something. Food for you at least."

He shook his head. "Not yet. I-I don't want to be alone yet. Okay?"

"Of course." I stepped closer to him, offering what little comfort I had. If they attacked again while Meri was alone, I'd never forgive myself.

"I'm afraid that maybe they won't wait for us, Conrad. It's been days. We should have seen some sign. Something . . ."

"They're moving, too, right?"

"Yes, but they'd be slower. The caravan, well, it travels sluggishly at best."

"Worse than this thing?" It was slow and getting slower. It started chugging oddly as if it knew I was criticizing it.

"Ugh. It needs more fuel."

I moved over the railing to shovel in the last of the coal. "That's it, Meri." The beast stopped lurching and pulled ahead smoothly. "How far do you think it is to where your family will be camped?"

He'd said they planned to stop on the border of our territory and the Vandals' for a few days. They were to wait there for him and any other family members who might have found trysts of their own. Afterward, the family would proceed into the next country.

I knew it was more difficult to come inside the borders of our country than to leave. The Vandals hardly cared who came and went. They were a poor and weak empire that made money from travelers passing through but had little products of their own to offer.

Meri didn't answer. I could see him frowning in the darkness.

"Tell me about your family, Meri."

"Ha. They're going to love you and that blond hair. I can't wait to see little toe-heads running around camp. That's if you want kids."

"Meri, oh . . . sweet boy. Vampires can't have children. That's why we contract women. Then their offspring are . . . turned. It's a complex ceremony."

"Oh. I thought . . . well, I'd heard something like that, but I thought Felix was your biological father. No?"

"No. Perhaps we have a distant relation. He's nearly a thousand years old, but if you want children, I'd stand in as father to any dark-haired beauties you might gift us with."

Meri shrugged. "I wanted blond boys." He shook his head. "No worries. It is what it is. Still, I'll have you."

He would. He'd have me until he no longer wanted me, or he died. I didn't even want to think of what I'd do after that. "I love you, Meri. I'll follow you anywhere."

That made him smile. It warmed my heart.

After a time, the machine started jerking again. Meri didn't bother even commenting on it. "Do you think Felix will send anyone to look for you?"

"Maybe not. He hadn't wanted to kill me. Not really."

"He—"

"Sh . . . I know." I patted his arm. "He was most certainly going to kill us both. That doesn't mean he didn't love me or care for me in his own twisted way."

"What about Devyn?"

I shrugged. I stared out at the night sky and the tree line in the distance. I'd misjudged Devyn completely. How would I know what he was thinking or what he was capable of?

Felix had been right. I wasn't fit to rule. If I had been, I would have seen this shit coming and put a stop to it before Devyn had ever had a chance to whisper in Felix's ear. "I don't know for sure, but I think we'll be safe. Particularly once we move into the Vandals' land. They won't bother searching for me there. If I come back, I'm dead. But . . ." I lifted a hand. "Meri! Look. What's that?"

Ahead in the distance, I saw light flickering through the trees.

"Listen!" Meri said.

Sure enough, music floated on the breeze, teasing us with its joyous sound. "Is that them?"

He nodded, practically jumping up and down. The machine made a final lurch and hissed as the last of its steam was released. "Well. Good timing that." He patted the big wheel he'd been using to steer the contraption with. "Come on."

I carried him on my back as we made our way to the gypsy camp. Not because we needed to, but because I wanted to. I wanted to keep him close. I had no idea what would happen upon meeting Meri's family. I squeezed his leg that was wrapped around my waist, seeking comfort in any way I could get it.

Meri's family gathered around us as we entered the camp. He dropped to the ground then stepped forward. "Mama!"

A rotund woman hugged and squeezed him before pushing holding him at arm's length. "You smell . . . ugh!" She waved her hand in front of her nose.

"I know." Meri turned to me and took my hand. "This is Conrad. I, uh . . . contracted with him."

They weren't entirely happy about taking me in, but Meri was family. After some grumbling, and Meri telling our story, they welcomed us. They had waited for him, and he was right, they would help.

I had to avoid the animals for the most part, but Meri's steam-cart was like a tiny version of the engine we'd been traveling in. It was painted red and gold. All the gypsy carts were as colorful as the people. I instantly loved them.

Meri's folks helped us clean up, then Meri dressed in his

own clothes that were a different style than I was used to, but fashion suited him well. He had loose trousers, held up with a red, silk sash with a vest that matched it. He left it open, and I could see his firm chest. He also had a red and black head scarf that was folded over and shoved over his head to keep his hair out of his eyes. He was bold and beautiful.

His family banded together to find similar clothes that fit me as well. "Here. It's mine." Meri handed me a scarf like his for my head. "It'll cover your beautiful hair, but that'll be good if they come looking for you."

I didn't think I'd ever truly blend in with his family, but I took the material and let him help me fix it on my head.

Then the celebration began. The men shared alcohol, and the women brought food. Musicians played and many danced, including Meri.

A lovely, thin woman with a colorful dress sat beside me. Her skirts were cut short on the sides, exposing much of her bare legs. "I knew something was in that boy's future."

"You must be his aunt?"

"Lavi."

I shook her hand. "I'm Conrad—"

"I know who you are. Even before Merivel started spouting his story. I'm not surprised he landed the crown prince. I *am* surprised you couldn't hold onto it."

"I guess, it wasn't meant to be. I think I'll be far happier with Meri than I would be there. I-I . . ." I took a deep breath and tried again. "I'm not the same. I was trained to be merciless. But I'm not."

Lavi patted my leg. "No, you're not at all."

It was a vampire's nature to rule. To take charge. Or so I'd been told. I was a complete failure. I liked Meri to be in charge. He'd proven he knew what he was doing, and I tended to be utterly useless. Meri didn't seem to mind, so I silently vowed to follow his lead.

Chapter Nine: Grand Finale

L ater that same night, I fed from Meri. We loved each other. Then we joined his family for refreshments and dancing. He was a skilled performer and each time he'd danced and sang with his family, it made me love him more.

The gypsies planned to set off for the border at dawn, so they packed up early and crawled into their wagons to sleep. After a few hours, I was the only one left awake. I walked around the campsite, wondering how my life was changing so quickly.

I'd not moved this fast, made spur of the moment decisions, or leaped without looking since I'd been turned. Vampires were cool, calculated. We thought things through at our own pace. Perhaps that had also been a mistake. Devyn seemed to move quicker — behind the scenes like a flea-bitten rat.

No sooner had I thought his name, then I heard his voice. "Surround!"

I heard the stomping of feet as his guards moved through the brush, and once I realized they were there, I could smell the iron taint of their blood.

I had to do something. "Devyn. Face me, you coward!" This needed to end.

He appeared from between the trees, glaring at me. "You're a fool, Conrad. It's over."

"Challenge, Devyn. You're in charge now? So I challenge you." I pointed at him. This time it would stick. His soldiers may have been obeying his orders, Felix's orders, but they knew the law as well as I did. A challenge like this had to be answered. Felix had been wrong to deny me that, but Devyn wasn't powerful enough to do the same. I hoped.

A challenge meant a one-on-one fight to the death or surrender, but surrender normally meant death for the loser, anyway. He'd be sacrificed. The challenge meant live or die. I'd die to keep Meri safe. But I wanted to win. "If I lose, your goal will be met, Devyn, and you can leave these people alone. They aren't ours."

"Tiziano said something of the same when he told me *exactly* where to find you." He grunted and took off his jacket. Beneath, he wore a vest and shirt with puffy sleeves — vampire finery not meant for fighting. "I promise nothing but your death, my *prince*."

Devyn would slaughter them all, and I couldn't let that happen. I didn't wait for Devyn to finish unbuttoning his fancy vest. I sprang at him, shoving him in the chest. He hadn't expected it and fell, landing on his ass. I couldn't give him a chance to regain his footing. I jumped on him then punched him in the face.

He bucked his hips to knock me off and scratched his sharp nails down my bare arm. Still, I punched him again. I made to grab his throat and rip it out, but my fingers slipped in blood that dripped down my arm. He threw me then, and we wrestled in the dirt. Devyn pulled the scarf from my head, tossing it aside, and cursed under his breath. "Mother fucker."

I caught his knee in my gut. It knocked the wind out of me. He pushed his advantage and slammed his elbow into my jaw. The pain radiated through my head.

Pushing to hands and knees, I growled at him as I charged again. I knocked him on the ground, grabbed a fistful of his long, blond locks, and used it to tilt his head to get at his throat. It was about to be over.

Then Meri screamed.

I glanced up to see one of the savage guards dragging him out of his wagon. In that moment of panic, Devyn punched up with a palm-strike to my chin with the butt of his hand. It knocked my head back. Devyn slashed out, digging into my throat.

I grabbed his wrist and twisted. He cried out when his radius bone snapped.

I tightened my thighs to grip his legs and keep him from moving. Balling my fist, I slammed the side of it into his temple. His eyes fluttered, and I grabbed his throat again, nails digging into his flesh.

"Please, brother . . . Conrad . . ." he hissed.

"Despite how evil you are, I don't want you dead, Dev. We've been brothers in blood. But you don't deserve to live after your betrayal."

"Ugh! It's not personal . . . please—"

"My life is very personal. Surrender or die." I shook his throat, proving I could rip it out in a heartbeat.

"S-surrender." He slumped down to the ground.

"I'll make a deal with you, Devyn." I meant what I'd said. I only wanted to be away from them.

Meri stepped up beside me. "You can go home now, Conrad." He put his hand on my shoulder.

"No." I stared up at him. Nothing had changed in my heart. "I'm not going."

Devyn stood up when I released him and slapped at his pants to dust them off. "What is it you want, Conrad?"

"I want you to go home to Felix. Tell him whatever you want. Take the regency. I don't care. Just leave us alone. Don't come after me."

"You'll never be able to return, Conrad." Devyn cocked his head to the side as if he couldn't understand what he'd said.

"I don't want to."

He huffed, but he had no choice. The eyes of his soldiers

were on us. "I swear it. By the blood. But if I ever see you again, the deal will be undone." He reached his hand out to the nearest soldier. "Give me your silver blade."

"Agreed." I stretched my hand out to him.

Devyn sliced both our palms with the silver-tainted dagger. It stung. But so did Devyn's treachery. Both would scar me. He gripped my bloody palm with his own. "I swear it."

"It's done. Now take your soldiers and leave."

He motioned with his hand, and his troop followed him into the surrounding forest. That's when I noticed the rest of the gypsies. They'd all been woken, and they joined me in the center of the camp.

Lavi stepped forward. "We should thank you for protecting us, putting your life on the line, but you brought the trouble here. I respect your decision to take care of the problem. We still welcome you. If this is done, let's move out."

Meri picked up the headscarf I'd worn and shook off the dirt. He handed it to me. "Thank you."

"No need. Lavi was right. This was my fault."

"But you could have gone with them. You stayed? Why?"

"I love you, Meri. I could never have contracted better." With him in my arms, everything would be fine. "Let's go." I kissed his lips, then turned him toward his little wagon. We had to get moving. It was time to start our new journey.

About Lynn Michaels

Lynn Michaels lives and writes in Tampa, Florida where the sun is hot, and the Sangria is cold. When she's not writing she's kayaking, hanging with her husband, or reading by the pool. Lynn writes Male/Male romance because she believes everyone deserves a happy ending and the dynamics of male characters can be intriguing, vulnerable, and exciting. She has both contemporary and paranormal titles and has been writing since 2014. Her stories don't follow any set guidelines or ideas, but come from her heart and contain love in many forms.

Julian

By

A.J. Llewellyn

Lieutenant Mick Fielding moves to the quirky California country town of Julian, to take up a position in the San Diego Sheriff's county substation. With the biggest problems being vandalism and theft crimes, he's stunned when he lands a homicide investigation. The case takes some nasty twists and turns involving drugs, love, and betrayal. Meanwhile, Mick has met an amazing man, local baker Julian Jarrett. Yes, Julian, who lives in Julian. Why does this man haunt his days and nights? And why do locals whisper that he's a vampire?

Julian Jarrett has close ties to the law enforcement community in Julian. Not the least because his cousin is the captain of the Julian Sheriff's Department. His passion is baking. Hot men have been off his menu for er, decades. But something about Mick is appealing. And frightening. Could he be falling in love? More to the point, should he let his freak flag fly for the hunky lieutenant?

CHAPTER ONE

The morning started with spoiled milk, no coffee, moldy bread, and a peculiar stench from the camel dairy across the road. Mick Fielding gazed out of the window. Old Julian Highway was still in the grip of a rare, frigid fall. Twenty-seven degrees. Up from twenty-three the day before. *Balmy!* The locals—most of them apple farmers—were freaking out that the unusual cold snap would kill their late seasonal crops and drive away the area's most important source of income—tourists.

They came in droves each year to pick apples, buy apple pies, apple cider, apple butter or jelly, and even purchase their own apple trees. They also got to indulge their inner child with hayrides, pumpkin carving, and scarecrow building.

Mick fiddled with the thermostat, but it wouldn't budge. Yet another thing in the house that was on the blink.

Why did I think this was a good idea? He let out a breath, condensation evaporating as he peered out of the front window, his gaze sweeping up and down the quiet, snow-sprinkled street. It looked like icing sugar. *Oh, don't think about food. It'll just make you hungrier, fool.*

He checked the broken thermostat again. Nope. Broken. *Maybe it's a fuse again. I'll fix it after a cup of coffee. Coffee? What coffee? I forgot to buy some, but I swore I had some in the freezer.* Mick sighed, suspecting that all of this was a bad sign that the day would only get worse. He checked the fridge again in case some decent food had magically appeared in it. It hadn't. There was still a single lemon and two takeout packets of

120

ketchup.

Then his cell phone rang. A text from his boss. The San Diego Sheriff's sub-station watch commander. *Attention all units. Tonight's a full moon. Expect the unexpected. Be careful out there.*

Mick knew it wasn't a joke. But so far, every day in the town of Julian had been filled with crazy, startling activity. He wondered again why he thought moving to a California country town would ease his severe case of *generalized anxiety*. He turned on his gas oven, right up to four-hundred degrees and left the door open. The poor man's way of warming up his home.

It wasn't that Mick was poor. His mountain cabin was. In poor condition, that is. Each day brought yet another calamity. He wondered how long it would be before it completely fell apart. It was obvious now that it had been this way before he moved in, and the landlord had cleverly disguised its defects with appealing online photos. Sweet touches like crisp white, heat-resistant Roman window shades, hurricane-lamp wall lights, and rustic, hardwood flooring had fed into his desire for a woodsy lifestyle. He'd only been here three weeks, and Mick worried about his sanity the longer he stayed here.

He moved to one of the two rickety chairs by the kitchen table. He'd loved them at first. There had been four then. Now he had two left and hoped neither of them collapsed underneath him. He almost laughed except that this was his first day off, and so far, it was a miserable one.

Why can't I sleep in? He contemplated his breakfast options, or lack thereof, surprised that after a straight nine-day shift, he was even up and at 'em at six o'clock in the morning. Habits died hard with him, however, and he eyed the three unpacked boxes lined up in the kitchen. His back creaked at the mere thought of more work.

He thought about driving down the road to the local diner, but his last visit there had apparently been broadcast on some invisible wireless network. One by one, locals had trooped to his corner table to air their grievances about law enforcement and some weirdo called Julian.

They were all full of unspecified complaints about him.

It had taken Mick a minute or two to realize Julian was an actual person. Which was weird, given that they were living in Julian.

I just had to get the yen to simplify and move and fall off the grid.

He sighed again. He was hungry because he'd skipped dinner, which hadn't been difficult considering he'd been chasing a fugitive fire-starter all over the mountain. He took a sniff of the shirt he'd been wearing the day before and had slept in out of sheer exhaustion. It still stunk of fire. As did the rest of him. The mere thought of taking a shower was both delicious and painful. *Why couldn't I wake up to hot coffee and a slice of toast?*

Mick hesitated to leave the oven on while he dragged himself to the shower. He was not only afraid the oven would malfunction, and the place would burn down, but the Julian Sheriff's department had a firebug in town. Still, he had to spruce himself up. He'd worked so many hours at the station that he'd grabbed fitful hours of sleep in the cot in one of the back rooms. It should have felt great being home in his own bed. But it wasn't. The lonely ache in his heart gave way to morbid thoughts. If the house did burn, then he'd be with Laurence so much faster.

That's a terrible thing to think. I'll take a shower and maybe find something to eat at another local place to improve my mood. He glanced again at the boxes awaiting his attention. No food in there. They could wait.

A quick, hot shower felt wonderful, and for a moment, he allowed himself to relax. Eyes closed, he let the needle-like spray fall from his head down his tired shoulders. His eyelids flew opened when he heard a noise from the showerhead. *Oh man, was it falling off?*

No. He heaved a sigh of relief and dipped into the array of mini travel shampoo bottles his sister had sent him. He kept them on the window ledge of his shower stall where they shared space with a tiny house spider he allowed to camp there, and a half-empty bottle of Jack Daniels for *ahem*, medicinal purposes.

Eva flew everywhere as an international media consultant and worried about Mick paying for items that she could provide for free. Ever since his early days as a corporal with the Los Angeles sheriff's department, she'd viewed Mick as a struggling student and herself as the Robin Hood of first-class plane travel. He unsnapped the cap of the bottle in his hand, and the faint smell of cherries wafted into the hot, damp air, making him think about pancakes. He'd bought a discounted box at the grocery store, but that was missing from his kitchen cabinets. Maybe he'd put it someplace else and forgot about it.

How could I have no food?

He sighed, contemplating jerking off. It was his favorite thing to do while he was soaping up. Unless he was getting his cock sucked, and that wasn't going to happen any time soon. It had been months since he'd had any action.

Mick thought about last night's fire-starter and how the guy had eluded him and his partner, Gonda. The arsonist had been active for four months and set blazes in odd places using rudimentary incendiary devices. The department had kept important details out of the media, but it struck Mick, not for the first time, how easy it was to set a deadly inferno.

Agitation gnawed at his soul, and he turned off the taps. It was horrible to know that his suspect, dubbed Fly Boy in Julian, was still out there. Somewhere. Stepping out of the tub, he reached for a towel. Like his clothes, it smelled like fire, and he wondered why. Thankfully he had a few clean towels in the linen closet. He dried off, wondering if he should have jerked off after all. It would have taken the edge off things.

I need coffee and breakfast. I can head on over to that swell place on Fourth Street. What's it called? The new one. Everybody talks about it. Got a nice big, screened-in heated porch. Yeah. And great coffee, too. And I could do with some of their avocado toast. I shouldn't eat pancakes, even though I want them. I should get me a slice of their Dutch apple pie to go. I wonder if that hot-looking waiter still works there. Man, he was hotter than a slice of warm cherry pie. Now why did I have to go and think about that? That's made me really hungry. And that waiter? I couldn't catch his eye. Wouldn't give me the time of day. Then again, that place was slammed. And he was juggling a bunch of tables.

He tugged a comb through his thick, brown curly hair and sprayed his pits with B.O. killer. He put on jeans and a black, zippered sweatshirt, shoving his feet into clean and dry socks and work boots. Mick had a lot to do today, and a fresh set of clothes improved his outlook on life. He returned to the warmth of the kitchen and the faint smell of teriyaki sauce. He hadn't cleaned the oven since he'd reheated a dish given to him by his partner's wife a couple of weeks ago.

Mick thought fondly of Walter Gondo, known to everyone as Gondo. He had baby triplets. The boys looked just like him. Bald. His wife, Jenn, was his best asset and Gondo always said so, too.

Gotta get out of here, but first things first. He had big plans for the lemon in his fridge. He'd boil water and squeezed the fruit into it. *A good, healthy start to the day.* He opened the fridge but jumped back when his front door flew open.

Holy cow! Did I forget to lock it?

He reached for his duty weapon but stopped, stunned, when his neighbor—the bossy and boring—Mrs. Louise Shirley dashed inside, shotgun in her grip. She had the grace to look embarrassed.

"Sorry, Mick. I remember from the last tenant that the door doesn't lock."

Her lips kept moving, but he'd stopped listening. *It doesn't lock? How did I not know this? Oh man, I'm moving out today.*

"And so I think he's got my daughter."

Mick blinked. "He who?"

"She posted on her *Snapchat* and *Instagram* last night that she was going to see him. Nobody's seen her since."

"Who are we talking about?" Mick was trying to follow her meandering nonsense.

"That man!" Her eyes glowed like a damned forest fire. "I think he's got my Gemini."

Mick knew Gemini. She was a nightmare. Nobody would want to take her on willingly. Not even a kidnapper. *Note to self. Keep on this one's good side.* "Which man?"

"The weirdo I've been telling you about for weeks. That Julian-guy. Julian Sangway or something. I brought my gun, just in case."

"You won't need that." He moved over to her, trying to extricate her ancient Parker shotgun from her steely grip.

"This is worth twelve grand!" she hollered. "It said so on *Google*."

She tells me the same thing every time I see her.

Louise waved the gun around. "Can you vouch for its safety? I mean, your door doesn't lock."

"Well, I'm law enforcement and—"

She gripped her weapon to her chest. "Whad-d-ya gonna do about him, Lieutenant? He's a menace to society."

Mick squinted at her. *You should talk.* "We don't know that."

"You mightn't, but I do. I know lots of things. Ever since the army did those illegal experiments on me—"

Oh, no. Not this again.

He snatched the weapon out of her hands. "You know it's illegal to walk around with a weapon." He checked the gun for bullets and glanced at her. "Even if it's unloaded." He stowed it in the hall closet. The door had a lock on it he'd installed himself because he kept a couple of weapons in it. "I'll vouch for its safety."

So far she had filed a few vague gripes about Julian with him, and more definitive reports with the Sheriff's department, but nothing that could result in an arrest.

"She's a headcase," Gonda always said when Mrs. Louise Shirley became the topic of conversation. From what Mick understood, she'd been in the army during the first gulf war and had driven a tank close to the frontlines. A gunshot wound to the head—her own doing during a routine cleaning—had resulted in a skewed personality and galloping paranoia. She had become a survivalist with a Winnebago packed to the gills with emergency rations in her driveway. According to his department's captain, it had been waiting there for two decades, and she'd forgotten to leave room for her and her dogs should a crisis arise.

"I'll vouch for its safety," he said again.

"You cookin' teriyaki chicken?" She sniffed suspiciously. She pronounced it like Terry-yucky.

"No." He walked over and switched off the oven and closed it.

She gave a haughty shake of the head. "Gemini said he hired her to help him bake his pies. He—"

"He bakes pies?"

"Yeah. He owns that new place down on Fourth Street."

Man. Am I salivating? He bakes pies! "He bakes out of his house?"

She blushed a little and shuffled her feet across the floor. It was the first moment he took in her weird ensemble. Camouflage overalls, a purple, floral sweater underneath, a pink pussy hat on her head, and huge Doc Martins on her feet. Built like a Mack truck, she didn't need a weapon of any kind. She could bulldoze a man with a single step.

"Well . . ." She pointed the toe of one boot across the wood grain, her head hanging low. "He's baking pies for the kids' contest." Glancing up at Mick, she mumbled, "For free."

Mick opened his mouth, but she pointed a finger at him. "He's still got my Gemini."

Pie. He bakes pie. "I think you're right." Mick gave her his most serious expression as he slipped on his holster and duty weapon. He liked his trusty Sig Sauer snug on his right hip. Pity he couldn't think of a reason to use it on Louise. All their neighbors hated her. She peered through people's windows and made wild accusations about them for no apparent reason. "Let's go check on this guy, Louise."

As he passed by her and opened the door, she chortled, "That's the spirit." She gave him a hard slap on the back that sent him head first down the three steps leading to the snow-covered ground outside. He gripped the handrail, but it came away from the stairs.

"Arrgh!" he screamed. He tried to get his balance but somehow tripped and flipped over landing flat on his back. For a moment he was in so much pain he was certain he'd broken it.

"Are you okay?" a gravelly voice asked.

Mick opened one eye, then the other. Staring upward, he became aware of Louise's wide-eyed gaze, and then, something wonderful. An Adonis standing beside her, looking down on him.

Maybe I died and went to heaven. Who is this gorgeous man? Did Laurence become even better looking in the afterlife?

"Are you okay?" the man asked again. He had raven black hair, piercing blue eyes, and gave Mick such a dazzling smile that it made it hard to squeak.

"I'm not sure," Mick muttered. "Am I dreaming?"

The man's eyes twinkled. "I don't know. Are you?" He reached down and with a firm grip, hoisted Mick to his feet.

"Hey," Mick protested. His law enforcement background had taught him that one never moved a person who'd had such a severe fall in case of breaks or other injuries.

"Wuss," Louise said in a stage whisper.

"Hey," Mick said again. What was the Adonis doing to him? Mick was in agony as the man steadied him with one hand and ran the other down Mick's spine. Tendrils of warmth moved through his body. *What the . . .*

All the pain fled his body. Even a persistent twinge in his right shoulder from rotator cuff surgery was gone. He wasn't sure if he'd imagined it, but the Adonis' hand seemed to linger there. "What did you do?" Mick asked when he could breathe again.

"I did nothing. Just making sure you could walk. Why don't you come to my house? I just finished baking, and I have an extra pie. Bayou Goo Pie. You like pie, Lieutenant Fielding?"

Louise gave a harsh laugh. "If he doesn't, I do." She lifted her hand and seemed to be about to give Mick another whack. She frowned and mumbled, "Wuss," again.

"Is this your gun, Lieutenant?" The Adonis bent and picked up Mick's duty weapon.

Mick took it and shoved it into his holster. The Adonis had magic in his hands. Nothing else could explain the sudden sense of complete well-being Mick experienced.

This is better than sex. Geez, Louise. I'm that hard up that a guy helping me to my feet feels like a miracle cure. As the Adonis led Mick away from his front yard, Mick was surprised how good he still felt. Pain somewhere in his body had become so customary that he'd forgotten what it was like to be free of it. *The robbery*, he reminded himself. Two years ago, he and Laurence had responded to a convenience store robbery in Hollywood. They had gone as backup for another unit already on the scene. They'd been told there was one armed suspect, only to discover there were two.

All four responding officers had been shot. Laurence and another officer died. It had not only been painful to get over the loss of the man he loved, but his shoulder required extensive repair work. But his fallen comrades' sacrifice was his daily fuel. He'd learned to live with pain because it was a reminder that he was alive.

And free.

For the first time, he became aware that the Adonis had his arm around him, helping him along the highway. Mick was cold but had never felt such delightful body heat. Laurence's face swam into his mind. *Don't. Stop it.*

"Here we are." The Adonis stopped outside a well-ap-pointed cabin. Mick stared at it. He'd never been to this place, but he now realized his landlord had used the exterior in the online picture gallery to lure an unsuspecting Mick and other, unsuspecting renters into jumping at the chance to live in it.

The Adonis even had a sturdy wall out front with a gate that opened and closed like it should. "Come on in," he said, letting go of Mick. As he turned to push the gate open, Louise clutched at Mick's sleeve.

"They say he's a vampire," she whispered.

Oh, for corn's sake. Mick ignored her and stepped through the gate. He caught the flash of anger that flashed across the Adonis' features.

He recovered quickly and extended a hand to Mick, which he took. "We haven't been formally introduced. I'm Julian Jar-rett."

Mick blinked when a frisson of heat, heck, a flame of carnal desire seared through him. He started to sweat, and then Julian let him go.

"Well, you know who I am, I guess. And you have tea and Bayou Goo Pie." Mick grinned like a simpleton. He suddenly got hard. Very hard.

CHAPTER TWO

"Of course I know who you are," Julian said, the alluring smile returning. "I saw you on the news last night chasing that fire lover through the mountains. You have courage, Lieutenant."

"Please call me Mick. And I didn't catch him. It's infuriating." Mick hadn't had any idea how much this notion depressed him. He never usually spilled his thoughts to members of the general public.

"You will." Julian winked at him.

"Where's my daughter?" Louise trilled.

The annoyed expression returned to Julian's face. Mick didn't blame the guy for being pissed. She'd called him a vampire, and she wouldn't let up about Gemini. Louise was as obnoxious as they came. She followed them to the front door then forced her way past them.

"Where's my Gemini?" she shouted, darting from room to room.

Mick should have cared more, but he knew Gemini could take care of herself, and besides, he was here on official business. Serious pie business. The house not only looked wonderful inside but smelled amazing.

"Is that pecan?" he asked, his senses going into an orgasmic overdrive. He wished his cock didn't have a mind of its own and shoved his sweater down farther to hide the front of his pants.

"Yes. That's the base of my Bayou Goo Pie. Please, take a seat." Julian swept a gracious hand over toward the kitchen table with its pristine farmhouse table and chairs. The baking smells were intoxicating.

Mick took in the numerous barrels of different types of apples lining two walls. That wasn't a surprise since the town of Julian was known for its apples. Locals had been protesting for a year, however, that the almost one-hundred-year-old tradition known as the Julian Apple Days Festival had been scrapped. In its place, the local council had created numerous small holidays, including the kids' fishing derby held at Lake Cuyamaca. *Ah, that's the contest Louise was talking about.*

Mick sat, stunned by the magnificence of the well-appointed kitchen with shelves crammed with interesting looking bottles of dried herbs, flowers, and colorful liquids. Framed, artistic photos of pies dotted the walls. His gaze fixed on the frothy culinary creation to which Julian was adding a final handful of shaved chocolate swirls. It was like something out of *The Great British Baking Show*.

"You bake a lot of apple pies?" Mick asked.

"Tons." Julian's warm voice filled Mick's soul. "My bakery provides pies during the harvest festivals and holiday contests, and I plan on entering the pie baking contest this year." He waved at the barrels. "We've run out of room at the bakery for these."

"Where's your bakery?"

Julian slid him an amused glance. "You've been there a time or two. I own JJ's down on Fourth Street."

"I was thinking about that place while I was taking a shower this morning. I was going to head over there for breakfast. That's you?"

Julian chuckled. "That's me."

Louise huffed back into the kitchen, her face red from her exertions. "She's not here."

She seemed surprised. Maybe she'd expected to find Gemini trussed up in a closet in latex and chains. Her gaze fell on the heavenly looking pie, and her mouth fell open as Julian sliced up generous portions of it.

She swallowed. Visibly.

For the first time ever, Mick sensed a kindred spirit here. Louise looked like she was drooling. "What's that?" Her voice came out in a kitten-like purr.

"It's nirvana." Mick couldn't believe the plates Julian slid in front of them. Mick's belly rumbled like an old truck, but he'd become so immobilized by sheer awe that Julian had to physically put a fork into his hand. Mick took a deep breath, flicking a glance at Louise. "I'm going in," he said.

His fork slid like butter into the thick but defined layers. He took a huge bite. *Oh. God.* He'd never tasted anything like it. He let the creamy fillings roll around his tongue. The pecan pastry at the bottom was crisp and rich. "Is that cream cheese at the bottom?" he finally asked.

"It's a pecan cheesecake, yes." Julian was watching him, seeming pleased by Mick's response.

"And above that, chocolate custard?"

"Yes." Julian's face shone.

Mick closed his eyes, savoring the full impact of the flavors. He hated swallowing. He wanted that delicious goo on his tongue all day long. "And it's got chocolate chunks. Man, that chocolate is like velvet." He opened his eyes and stared at the pie. The custard was laced with generous pieces of milk chocolate, and all of it topped with a thick layer of whipped cream, a faint dusting of powdered sugar, and chocolate shavings

"You like the chocolate?" Julian asked.

"Yes. It's unbelievable."

"It's made out of camel milk."

Mick stared at him. "Seriously?"

"Yes. I buy the milk from the dairy across the road and make it myself."

Mick shook his head. "Wow." He didn't think he'd ever

eaten anything that had been given such loving treatment.

"I know you're a coffee drinker—"

Mick looked at him, surprised. "How do you know that?"

Julian laughed. "My wait staff told me how they had to keep customers away from you. We'd all heard about how you got ambushed at that diner on the highway here while you were trying to enjoy breakfast and a cup of coffee. We wanted you to have at least one place in town where you could feel comfortable."

Mick was touched. "That's so nice. Thank you."

Julian grinned. "I heard people had lots of complaints about me that day at the diner."

Mick's face went beet red. He couldn't deny it, but he also had no desire to discuss it.

"Anyway, I know you like coffee, but this mint and honey tea I made perfectly complements the pie. Tomorrow, I'm baking an Elvis pie. Coffee goes great with that."

"Elvis, as in Presley?" Louise asked, lifting her face from her plate. It was the first thing she'd said since she'd stopped squawking about Gemini.

"Yes. It's almost like his favorite sandwich, but gooier and much, much creamier. It has a peanut butter and banana filling, a lot of cream, and of course, a bacon and peanut crust."

Mick grinned. "Yes. Of course." The idea tickled him. He had no idea such a thing existed. *A bacon and peanut crust. I'm gonna get fat hanging around this guy. Fat and happy.* He shook the thought from his mind.

Julian moved over to them with a silver teapot and a pair of porcelain teacups. He had the most captivating gait Mick had ever seen on a man. He was like a panther. Stealthy and luxurious. He poured out the fragrant contents into the cups. Mick squirmed in his seat the moment the sweet scent of honey rose in steamy swirls. He wanted to bury his face in it.

"That's raw wildflower honey from my family's ranch in

Louisiana." Julian beamed at them. "We just harvested. I got back a few days ago."

"You're from Louisiana?" Mick couldn't detect a Southern accent.

"Yes, sir. My family's from Bossier Parish, in the north-western part of the state."

"I know it well." Mick sipped his tea then swept his fork across the whipped cream on his pie. Julian was right. The tea brought out all the nuances of the sweet fillings. And to think a diner burger was the height of gourmet cooking.

"You've spent time there?" Julian asked, an odd look crossing his dazzling features.

"Yeah. I went to Northwestern University." Mick's cell phone rang. It was Gonda. A text with three numbers. 9-1-1.

"You have to go?" Julian asked.

"Where's Gemini?" Louise asked again.

Mick bent his head, quickly demolishing his pie. He didn't care what the emergency was. He was going to finish every last bite.

Julian sighed. "She came here yesterday. I gave her twenty dollars to buy some butter for me at the market. I usually buy at the dairy farm across the road. She never came back. I would have reported my car stolen because I let her drive it."

"Why didn't you?" Mick asked, scraping his fork tines along the bottom of the plate.

"Because she brought it back early this morning and left it in the driveway. It's out of gas, dirty, and a bit dinged up, but it's back."

"How dinged up is it?" Mick thought he might finally have enough evidence to get a warrant out on Gemini Shirley. The girl was a menace to Julian's residents. She'd allegedly shop-lifted an expensive vintage ring at a consignment store, but the footage had been too grainy to prove it. Wherever she went, things went missing. She was also totally crackers. Just like her mom.

Julian sighed. "There's a dent in the right rear panel. I can't prove she did it, but I'm certain it wasn't there before."

That was the story of Gemini's life. She got away with stuff. Again and again.

Julian gave Louise a hard look. "Please tell her I need for her to return my keys."

Louise went red again. "I'm sure she has an excellent excuse." Her gaze went everywhere but to Julian.

Mick rose to leave.

"Hold on a moment." Julian held up a hand. "Take the pie with you, Mick. I'll put a cover on it."

"You don't need to do that, but thanks. That was crazy good."

"Are you going to eat it if I give it to you?"

"Of course I will." Mick texted Gonda back with three question marks and waited for a response. He'd learned the hard way that Gonda's 9-1-1 calls were often not emergencies but designed to get an immediate response, even if one wasn't required.

"Then I'll give it to you. Just wash out the pan when you're done and bring it back to me." Julian slanted a hooded look in Louise's direction. "As soon as you return the six pie plates you have at home, I'll give you a pie, too." He pushed the covered plate into Mick's hands. "You're welcome here anytime. Would you like some tea in a to-go cup?"

Mick's eyes glazed over. "Hell, yes. And thank you. That was the best meal I've ever had in this town."

"That wasn't a meal, but I'm planning on cooking one tonight. Stop by if you feel like it." Julian's gaze seemed to penetrate right through Mick, making him feel good in places that had been dormant way too long. "I'm making a traditional northern Louisiana meal. Natchitoches meat pies, fried chicken, purple hull peas, collard greens, hot water cornbread, and for dessert, strawberries in port wine over homemade honey ice cream."

He's seducing me with food. I haven't had those wonderful meat pies in years. "That sounds amazing. Who else is coming?"

Julian's gaze was hotter than a forest fire. "Only you."

Man, I think I'm sweating. He likes me. He really likes me!

Mick's day was getting better by the second. He ran a finger across his top lip, surprised to discover he really was sweating. *It's the tea. That's all. And I bet his central heating works. Damn. Unlike mine.* He tried to shift his gaze from Julian's. Did he have the courage to come back here for dinner? Alone? Julian was sexy as hell. Fascinating, charming. *Dangerous* was the word that next came to mind.

"What about me? Am I invited?" Louise asked.

"Certainly not." Julian's indignant tone made Mick laugh. "I want the butter I sent your daughter out to get, or my twenty dollars. And the pie plates and my keys. If you get me all those things, then I'll consider it." He pressed a travel cup into Mick's free hand. "Enjoy."

Mick intended to, and he hoped nobody would come into his house and steal the pie from his unlocked cabin.

Outside, he peered over at the driveway. It was empty, so he shot a glance at Julian, who watched from the doorway. "Didn't you say she returned the car?"

Julian shook his head. "That girl. Honestly. She did bring it back. She must have come and taken it again, and I didn't realize it." He frowned, staring at the vacant space. "The engine on that thing's loud. I should have heard it."

"What's the make and model? And the license plate?" Mick went to hand Louise his cake plate and mug, but Julian gave a distracted wave.

"You can't miss it. Powder blue sixty-seven Mustang." He gave Mick a lopsided smile. "License plate is HOTPIES."

Of course it is. Mick nodded. "Got it." He turned to Louise. "Let's get you your gun back and in the future, leave it at home please."

"Oh, you're no fun," she grumbled, but her eyes danced with merriment. "You should have seen your face when I walked into your house!"

Mick said nothing. Gonda hadn't called him back, which meant his problem wasn't so urgent. Mick made it home quickly though he wished he hadn't raced out of Julian's. The man's house was comfortable and warm. And everything seemed to work. But then again, Louise had been there. Talk about a cock block.

What am I thinking? I'm a cop. I can't go all bayou goo on the guy. Though sex'd be nice. Man, he has the most erotic voice. Gravelly and deep. I wouldn't mind a roll in the hay with that voice in my ear. I want to eat his pie and make love to his voice. And not necessarily in that order.

"I'm much more than that."

"What the—" Mick gave a start and whirled around, but Julian wasn't there. Mick glanced at Louise, who was already trudging up his stairs. Mick shivered. *Oh, great. Now I'm hearing things.* Louise threw open his door and hurled herself inside. She parked herself at his locked hall closet and tried the door.

"The lock on this one works," she griped.

"Sure it does." Mick deposited Julian's gifts on his kitchen countertop. The alluring scent of teriyaki had vanished. And he was still hungry. He'd get rid of Louise and help himself to another slice of pie then figure out his plan for the day.

"He has such a lovely voice, doesn't he?" Louise leaned against the doorframe, looking moon-faced. "So romantic and dreamy."

"I like that low rumble. He doesn't talk. He growls. Like a tiger."

Louise straightened herself and stared at him. "He doesn't growl. His voice is like honey." Her gaze moved past him to the covered pie. "Are you going to eat that all by yourself?"

"Yes," Mick lied. He actually intended to visit Gonda and Jenn and treat them to a couple of slices. They were so good to him. It was about time *he* took them something tasty to eat.

"You really think he growls?" Louise asked. Before he could respond, she said, "He makes me feel so calm. When I'm with him, I feel . . . I don't know . . . girlish somehow. Then I'm away from him, and I become a total bitch again."

Mick laughed. She looked so surprised by her own admission. He unlocked the closet and handed her the shotgun, checking once more to see if it was unloaded.

"I'm gonna find my daughter." She glowered. "Stealing the vampire's car."

"He's not —" Before he could finish his sentence, she'd regained her usual seething disposition and stomped out of the door. "Don't shoot her!"

The second she was gone, Mick called Gonda a second time, leaving a voice message. He loathed texting and had no idea why so many people preferred it to making a call, which was so much quicker and easier. "Hey, you. I got a nine-one-one call. Everything okay? I have an incredible pie here and thought I'd maybe bring it over. Hit me back." He had the crazy impulse to call Julian and thank him for the impromptu breakfast but got a hold of his senses. Next, he called his landlord, Billy Hudson.

"Hi, this is Billy. I'm not here right now. Leave a message after the beep. Beeep!"

Mick yelled into the phone. "Billy, I know it's you. Knock it off."

"What gave me away?"

Mick rolled his eyes. "The heavy breathing." He sighed again. "Look, this place is falling apart. Either you send a handyman to fix everything today, or I'm moving out."

"It's not that bad."

"Not that bad? It's worse than bad. The front door doesn't

lock."

"I thought I'd fixed that."

"You mean you knew there was a problem?"

"A while back. But I fixed it. I swear. Maybe someone broke in and wrecked the lock again."

That wasn't a pleasant thought. Mick shook his head. "So, the front door lock. The front handrail. The thermostat—"

"Again?"

"Yes, again. I know we take turns replacing the fuses, but the whole unit needs to be replaced."

"I don't have time today."

"You'd better make time. There are other things, too. Broken towel rods. The kitchen window's hard to open. Or close. And I think there's some kind of rodent in the bedroom wall. It's driving me insane."

"Anything else?" Billy's tone turned snarky.

"I'll write out a list. And it all needs to be done today. I've called you three times now."

"But your list keeps growing."

"Today," Mick insisted and ended their call. For a moment, he wondered if Billy would show. The guy was a local who'd run off to join the circus in Australia as a trapeze artist and after a bad fall, had moved back to Julian with a very young Thai wife and two small, cute children. He'd told Mick his dream had been to become a *capitalist, home-owning, land-renovating baron.* What he really was, however, was a slumlord.

I should tell Julian he's been using photos of the exterior of his house to rent this property. Mick snapped the cap of the travel mug and drank some of the tea. Still warm, and delicious. He cut himself a thick hunk of pie and ate it fast. *Hmmm. Delicious.* He popped the rest in the fridge and drained the tea, leaving the mug in the sink to rinse before returning it to Julian. There was no point in putting it in the dishwasher. There was nothing else to wash. *Damn. I should have told Billy that's on the fritz, too.*

139

He took a couple of minutes to jot a note to Billy with all the broken parts and pieces to the house. His hand shook from the chill in the house. Mick then got the bright idea to take another shower to warm up before setting out to shop for groceries. If he had to, he'd change his own front door lock and get a new set of keys. He mentally listed all the things he'd need to buy at the Julian Market. He got a thrill out of the notion that he could drive to Main Street, hit the market and cross the street to visit the hardware store. No driving around for miles like he had back in L.A.

Mick stripped off and ran the shower faucet until he achieved a decent heat. He stepped under the spray, adjusting the nozzle until he got a soft rainfall effect and closed his eyes. He moved his hand down to his cock and got the strange and sudden sensation of a mouth on him. It jolted him at first, but he enjoyed the effect. *God, that feels great.*

He moved his hand down his treasure trail, letting his fingers stroke upward from the base of his cock to the springy head. Before he knew it, he was hard, his cock bouncing against his curled fist. He moaned. His orgasms were intense whether he was fucking, being fucked or sucked. He enjoyed the sensations the human body could produce, and he had no place to be.

I can take my time. He stroked up his hefty shaft, wishing he'd done this earlier.

Suddenly, through swirls of steam, he glimpsed a dark-haired man kneeling before him in the shower. Mick brushed the hair and water from his eyes.

Hot damn! I never had a wet dream like this before. It was Julian grinning up at him. He moved Mick's hand away, and Mick stared at his palm in surprise. The pleasurable sensations had him rocking on his feet. *What the hell is happening to me?* He let out a strangled cry as his cock appeared to be devoured by Julian. His mouth worked up and down his length, lips tightening on him.

Mick fucked Julian's mouth, almost laughing at the realistic feeling of getting one hell of a fucking blow job. He jumped when Julian moved his hands around Mick's hips, pulling him closer. When his nose collided with Mick's treasure trail, Mick's inhibitions fled him.

"That's it. Suck it."

Julian pulled him closer still, and Mick gripped the shower stall's walls when Julian dug his fingernails into Mick's ass cheeks.

"Oh, fuck!" Mick came in a blinding roar, gripping Julian's head to him. *Don't stop now. Please don't stop.* He kept coming. Julian swallowed everything he gave him, and when he finally pulled back, Mick's cockhead was resting on Julian's bottom lip.

He looked up at Mick, sheer lust in his eyes. "I told you I was so much more than pie." Then he vanished. Mick almost screamed. *It was a dream. One hell of a fantastic sex dream.* He turned off the taps and got out of the shower. He ran his towel over his body. When he reached his butt, it stung a little. He turned around to look in the mirror, stunned to see scratch marks where Julian had held his butt cheeks. He gulped. *It can't be.*

A knock at the front door hastened his drying and dressing, and he ran to the living room in time to see Billy and his young wife and toddlers taking up space.

"Hi," he said. The entire family's faces turned as one, and their grave eyes rested on him. The word dried in his throat.

"Hey," Billy said. "Quite a list you have here." He held up the page, a look of reproach in his gaze.

"Yeah. Well. Um. Don't worry about the front door. I'll fix the lock myself."

Billy's expression brightened. "Okay, cool."

"And I'll just get out of your way in the meantime."

"Do that," Billy muttered as he prepared to work on the thermostat.

Mick rushed out the front door, and his cell phone rang. The wind chill reached him, and he realized he'd left his coat inside but felt weird returning for it. *That's so weird. It's my house!* He had an old hooded, fleece-lined flak jacket in his trunk. It would have to do. He checked his cell phone. A call from Gonda. He took it as he unlocked his off-duty black pick-up truck.

"Hey," Gonda said. "I was going to invite you over for breakfast, but I got a funny phone call from somebody up on the ridge where we were last night. Got a report of gunfire and a woman says there's an abandoned car up there."

Instinct pricked at Mick. "What kind of car?"

"She says it's an old *Mustang*. She smells fire, but there's no evidence of it. Says there's water underneath the carriage, but no visible burning. The lady says something is off and she won't go near it."

"I don't blame her."

"I'm heading up there now. Wanna meet me?"

"Where, on Farmer Road?" Mick asked.

"Yep. At the parking area near the Volcan Mountain Trail."

"Exactly where we were last night. I'm on my way. I think the *Mustang* belongs to one of my neighbors. Call me and let me know if you see a license plate."

"Will do."

They ended their call and Mick jumped in his truck, fired up the engine and headed north up the highway. He loved the wild outdoors, and Julian had plenty of it. He felt more clear-headed than he had in weeks. *I should jack off more often.* He tried not to think about the weird illusion that Julian had been in the shower with him. It had been so erotic yet real. It put a smile on his face that he thought might last for days. If bad news wasn't awaiting him on Volcan Mountain.

He glanced at the passing scenery — mostly sprawling apple farms whose family generations had worked hard to preserve their properties. They'd faced many challenges over the decades, not the least of which had come from the gold rush.

For a brief thirty-year period in 1870, San Diego county had been gripped by gold fever, like other parts of California. In fact, San Diego's very first gold nugget, a tiny one, had been found in Julian. But apples had been the town's real gold.

His truck gave a lurch as he climbed higher. The crisp, cold weather was perfect for hiking the often-difficult trail. It had little shade from the relentless sun, no restrooms, and a plethora of pesky gnats, hungry mountain lions, and rattlesnakes lurking close to the trail. There were two trails, the second being Five Oaks, but within minutes, he'd approached the parking area, surprised to see Gonda only just pulling up behind him in his wife's sporty family wagon.

Mick realized Gonda lived a few miles farther away from him. More toward civilization. He too lived in Julian, but Gonda preferred being close to the business end of things.

Up ahead, a vehicle was parked, but it wasn't a *Mustang*. It was a *Dodge Avenger*. Mick hadn't seen one in a few years, but a lot of people kept older vehicles in Julian. This one was at least ten years old. There was no license plate on the back or the front. Everything about the appearance of the vehicle was wrong, beginning with the fact it was parked under a straggly tree in a haphazard way, a huge pool of water beneath it.

"Ominous," Gonda texted him.

It was an anomaly for sure. Mick parked, got out, and Gonda exited his vehicle, too. He was wearing his trademark skinny jeans paired with a heavy navy knitted sweater, and a scrunched beanie that matched it.

Bet Jenn knitted both. "Strong smell of fire," Mick said. "Somebody set fire to that vehicle then doused it with water."

"And moved it here. I don't think the fire happened here."

"Agreed." The air crackled with menace. Mick could feel it, and a cold, clammy feeling gnawed at him.

"How fucking weird." Gonda pushed the beanie farther back on his head.

"So we potentially have two crime scenes."

They scanned the ground for footprints, and there were tons. Many were unclear, but some might be useful. "I'm gonna call for the tech guys to come and get plaster copies of the footprints," Mick said.

Gonda gave him a long look. "You think it's that serious?"

Mick nodded. He didn't know for sure but had a bad feeling about this one. "I think there's a body in there."

"A lot of scuffling going on," Gonda said, pointing to various sets of prints. "One set of tire tracks heading down the mountain."

"Two sets coming up here." Mick studied the tire tracks.

"So whoever was up here had a getaway car," Gonda responded.

They donned gloves from the glove compartment of Mick's truck. Careful to avoid the evidence around the vehicle, they approached it. The last thing Mick wanted to do was mar a fire investigation. He knew that fire chiefs dreaded cops sticking their noses into their cases when they weren't arson investigators, but he and Gonda had to make sure nobody was trapped inside. The burnt smell was more acrid the closer they got.

Gonda checked the front of the vehicle. "No license plate here. No evidence of fire."

Mick checked the doors of the car. Locked.

One glance inside the windows told a story of a frenzied attack. The rearview mirror was broken and dangled over the dashboard. The glove compartment hung open, the contents tossed on the floor. The passenger side door panel had been ripped open.

"Looks like they were searching for something. Wonder if they found it?" Mick noted scattered junk food wrappings, a half-eaten burger on the front passenger seat, spilled drinks on the center console, takeout cups dripping onto the driver's seat and all over a blue tooth portal.

"Blood," they said in unison once their examination reached the backseat. Mick used his pocket flashlight to focus on the blood splatter. It was obvious that the trunk had been pushed toward the backseat. The latches barely held.

"I think somebody's in the trunk," Mick said, his senses on red alert.

He grabbed his cell phone as Gonda snapped photos and made contact with his station captain. "Sir," he said when Byrne Conrad took his call. He reported their findings.

"If you think there's somebody in the trunk, open it," Captain Conrad said. "I'll stay on the line with you. If we do have a victim, I'll contact San Diego for their crime scene crew."

San Diego was almost a two-hour drive from here. "Can't we get someone local?" Mick asked.

"Let's see what we have first," Conrad said. "What's the license plate number?"

"No plates."

"Christ," the captain said.

Mick knew that whatever he found, he and Gonda would have to stay on the scene and protect it, regardless of whether or not there was a body inside the car.

"Please don't screw up the evidence," Conrad commanded.

"I'll record, you open," Gonda said to Mick.

Thanks a lot. Mick hated having to open the trunk, but somebody had to do it. The stench of fire almost made him gag.

"What's going on?" the captain asked.

"Figuring out how to open the trunk without

compromising the scene more than it already has been. Whoever doused the fire went a long way toward ruining the evidence."

"You got a crowbar?" the captain asked.

"Yeah."

"Use it."

Mick retrieved it from the bed of his truck and pried the *Avenger's* lock open. Gonda filmed the whole thing as the trunk lid creaked upward, the smell of fire and blood was engulfing. Mick had expected it, but he was still shocked by what he saw. A body. What he hadn't expected was a gigantic, unburned log laying atop it.

"Freaky," Gonda murmured.

"What's going on?" the captain bawled in Mick's ear.

"A log," Mick said. "A heavy one."

Once Gonda finished snapping photos, they lifted the log off what looked like a man, judging by his bare feet. They set the log on the ground, and Mick studied the feet, which were remarkably untouched. They had been bound with wire, and the victim was curled in the fetal position, his head jammed right up against the rear of the back seat. Mick took a second to absorb the cruelty capable of human beings. The man was wrapped in black garbage bags, and what looked like a shower curtain and possibly a bedspread.

"I know what they were looking for," Mick said. "He's wrapped in household items—"

"There's a body?" the chief asked.

"Yes, sir. And I think he was killed someplace else. Beaten. Extensively, probably in a home. Looks like they wrapped him in everything they could lay their hands on. There's a bathtub with a lot of blood evidence somewhere. And he's been bound with a ton of camping rope and electrical wires."

"Stereo cables. That's why they tore his car apart," Gonda said. "Somebody knew this car very well. Back in the day, they used to install stereos this way, with wires sometimes stashed in door panels."

"Right. And there's another thing," Mick said, leaning forward. "Sir, we need an ambulance. This poor guy is still alive."

CHAPTER THREE

A s they started working on getting the bindings off the
man in the trunk, for the sake of police reports to be filed
later, Mick announced, "Time is nine a.m. Pacific Daylight
Time. Body was left here sometime between four o'clock and
now. Gives us a five-hour window. Gonda and I were up here
until four, and the vehicle wasn't here then." He glanced at
Gonda. "When did you get the call alerting you to this?"

"Two minutes before I called you. A little after eight-thirty.
It was an anonymous number. I almost didn't answer it. I'm
getting so many damned spam calls lately."

They both stopped talking. Puddles of water settled in the
trunk, and the complication system of wires wrapped around
their victim seemed endless. Gonda produced scissors from a
first aid kit in his own car to snip away at the mound of plastic
bags wrapped around their prone victim. After several black
garbage bags, they came across a plastic military seabag.

"Fuck," Mick ground out. "This is army-issued. Wonder if
he's a vet, or whether one of the perpetrators is." He let Gonda
take photos before they proceeded.

The captain bawled in his ear. "What have you found?"
Mick told him.

"Any chance you can remove it without cutting it?"

"No, sir. I've never seen so many layers of plastic before."

"Carry on."

Mick and Gonda worked feverishly to release the ligatures
from around the victim's neck. One of the wires went down
to his hands. They cut the bindings, but the man's hands

remained bound tightly behind him.

"There's another set of wires going from his hands to his feet," Gonda said, desperately trying to release the knots. "Jeez. They went to town on this guy."

Hogtied.

"I think they were trying to stage the scene, but something went wrong," Mick said as he worked to loosen the wire wrapped around the man's neck.

"That struck me, too." Gonda reached between Mick's fingers and snipped the wires. "Damn, that's tight."

Mick had no idea how their victim was still breathing with his head obviously suffering severe blunt force trauma, not to mention fire. The man's breathing was shallow, agonized. Mick knew he had endured total torture.

Half the victim's face showed some signs of fire, the other half, which was pressed into the floor of the trunk, was still intact. His skin was mottled and blistered. He didn't look good, but he was still recognizable as a human being.

He has a strong will to live, this one. Mick's sense of right and wrong went into overdrive. *The guy didn't deserve this.* He put his gloved hands to the man's mouth, trying to open it farther and help him breathe. The first thing he saw was soot. Lots of it.

"Shit!"

"What?" the captain asked in his ear.

"He's got something stuffed in his mouth. Looks like a damned sock." Mick couldn't believe it. He gripped a piece of the fabric and tugged. The man gagged and moaned, his body contorting. The sock didn't stop coming. It had been shoved down his throat. It was some kind of striped tube sock — the kind guys wore playing soccer.

"I'll bag it." Gonda raced over to his car.

Mick noticed the victim had stopped breathing. He felt for a pulse. It was very faint. *Oh, no.* He leaned over the victim's face and began rescue breathing, one breath every five seconds, keeping his fingers on the carotid artery. By law, he wasn't supposed to give mouth-to-mouth resuscitation due to risk of infection. There was no time to run to the car to fetch the CPR kit or even yell at Gonda to bring it to him. *Where the hell is that ambulance? And why oh why did we come up here in our personal vehicles? Because it's our day off and we weren't expecting this.*

"We need an ID on this guy," Gonda said.

"No time to check his clothing. These wrappings are all stuck to him," Mick said quickly in between breaths.

"Roger that," Gonda said. "I'll check for a wallet in the car. I'm gonna bust open the driver's door." Gonda moved over to the driver's side of the vehicle and using the crowbar, popped open the door.

Mick counted the seconds, and breathed, again, and again.

"No wallet. No sign of any keys," Gonda called out. "I'll get the VIN and call it into DMV." He crouched down, muttering a string of numbers into his cell phone.

Mick kept working, but then the painful breathing stopped, and he couldn't feel a pulse anymore. He immediately began chest compressions, thirty compressions to two rescue breaths. He felt for a pulse again, but still nothing. "No! Stay with me!" He sped up resuscitation efforts, but the man's sightless eyes told him everything. A tear crept from the corner of the victim's ruined eye and down his burned cheek.

"Hurry! Help me," Mick shouted to Gonda, but when he looked over at him, he noticed an old sedan pulling into the parking area. Gonda rushed over, waving the occupants away. One of them tried taking pictures with his cell phone. Gonda blocked his line of vision.

Mick put his lips over the victim's and continued mouth-to-mouth. He had been trained years ago in traditional cardiopulmonary resuscitation, and it was a natural, life-saving process for him. Even if law enforcement agencies advised against it. He tried not to think about the twisted, burned and bloodied flesh beneath his and blew air into the man's mouth.

Gonda forced the people in the car to back down the hill, yelling at them. "This is an active crime scene, and you need to leave. Now!"

Mick continued applying CPR. As Gonda raced over to him, Mick resumed mouth-to-mouth, letting Gonda take over pumping his hands against their victim's chest. The frail, bound body made noises, but it sounded like bones cracking. Not breathing.

"He's gone," Gonda said after a few minutes.

Mick gave up and slumped against the trunk. *Why?* Why did this happen to this poor guy? What had he done that was so terrible that he'd been destroyed this way? Mick tried to compose himself but couldn't. *I wanted to save him.* Laurence's face loomed in his mind. He said, like he always had to Mick, "You can't save them all."

Sirens blared coming up the hill.

"Give the sock to me, Mick." Gonda was tugging gently at it, and a devastated Mick who hadn't realized he still held it, had to release it and put it inside Gonda's paper evidence bag. He checked his watch. It had taken the ambulance nine minutes to arrive, the local fire crew right behind it.

As soon as the emergency services crews pulled in beside the *Avenger*, Mick was forced to let them take over.

"How is he even still breathing?" one of the paramedics muttered as they loaded the victim onto a gurney.

"He's breathing?" Mick asked, his spirits lifting.

"Barely." He flicked a glance at Mick. "You gave him mouth-to-mouth and applied CPR?"

"Yes."

"What's the story with this guy? I've never seen trauma like this on a patient." Another paramedic stuck a needle in the victim's chest, then a catheter. Mick knew it was to decompress collapsed lungs. A hissing sound followed soon after, the air escaping from the lung.

He felt a twinge of guilt. *I hope I'm not the one who caused that with my CPR. Or Gonda.*

"We found him in the trunk, a log on top of him—" Mick stopped, realizing the victim's assailants had known he was alive when they poured water on the trunk fire. *I bet he put up a damned good fight and they put the log on him in case he got the crazy idea to save himself.*

He turned to Gonda. "They put out the fire because they were afraid of getting caught. Wonder where they started it?"

"Can't have been far away for water to pool like this." Gonda looked at him. "You think this case has anything to do with the firebug we chased around up here last night?"

"Good question. But I have no idea." Mick felt helpless. So many questions and right now, there were few answers.

Gonda nudged him. "You've got blood all over your face. You may want to let the emergency room staff give you a blood test."

"I'm fine." Mick swiped at his mouth with his jacket sleeve.

"We've still got a heartbeat. Faint. But it's there," the paramedic told them. "Probably due to your life-saving efforts."

Mick couldn't believe it. For a moment, they stood, watching the paramedics loading their victim into the ambulance. He already had an oxygen mask on, but they needed to get a needle into his arm.

"Can't find the veins. This is unbelievable," one of the paramedics muttered.

"All the stuff they wrapped him in helped preserve the body," Gonda said, glancing at Mick. "Maybe there's still a ton of trace evidence."

Mick nodded. "We gotta get that Vehicle Identification Number."

"Yeah. I'll call 'em again. Hey, I see the captain coming up the hill now. I'll let you handle him." He rolled his eyes at Mick. "Yippee-ki-yay."

Mick wondered what he'd done with his own cell phone and realized he'd left it in the car's trunk. The fire crew processing it weren't happy about letting him collect his phone, but he *was* a first responder to the scene, after all, and he needed his phone.

"Hello?" he said into the receiver, but the captain had ended their call. "Maybe we should drive around and look for the first crime scene," he said to nobody in particular, but the fireman standing beside him said, "No. We'll handle that."

"Okay."

"I'm going to be the lead investigator on this case. I need you to tell me exactly what you saw in here."

Mick dropped his gaze to the ground around the *Avenger*. Gonda had taken photos, but any attempts to make molds would be futile now. He went through the story again, thankful Gonda had recorded the moment he'd popped the trunk.

"My partner took photos and shot footage. The victim was in here, curled in the fetal position, an unburned log on top of him."

"What did you make of that?"

"It could mean nothing." Mick spread his hands. "My partner and I suspect they were trying to stage the scene. Or they could have put the log on the victim knowing he was still alive. He had soot in his mouth. I'm sure the hospital will check his carbon monoxide levels. It staggers me that he's been in there fighting for his life. His assailants probably thought he'd suffocate to death."

The fireman just looked at him. "And what brought you up here in the first place?"

"My partner received a call from a woman. He can tell you more. She said there was a vehicle up here and that it seemed suspicious."

"Any idea who she was?"

Mick shook his head. "No name. We can get his cell phone

records, but that may take a while, so it doesn't help us right now. We shoulda started trying on that already," Mick fretted.

"Don't be too hard on yourself. This was a crazy situation. You saved that man's life. You and your partner thought on your feet. What were your impressions of the scene, the immediate ones, that is?"

"I felt the body was dumped in broad daylight, which was nervy. But then again, this trail is pretty remote, and this wasn't the original crime scene. From the endless wraps used on the victim, I'd say this happened in someone's residence. A crime of passion, maybe. It got way out of hand."

The fireman nodded. "And why do you think they doused the flames?"

Mick had been asking himself the same question since he'd opened the trunk. "You want my honest opinion?"

"I wouldn't be asking otherwise."

Mick stared straight ahead. "This was an act of torture. They wanted this guy to suffer. They stuffed a tube sock down his throat. Beat him. Burned him. I think somebody put out the fire because he wanted him to suffer as long as possible."

"I hadn't considered that," the fireman said. "There's a lot of evidence in here that seems to have nothing to do with the case at all. To your point, it seems staged. They had zip ties in the front seat but didn't use them to bind his hands."

"I didn't see those. We just looked in the windows, and I felt there was a body inside the trunk."

"What made you think so?"

"The backseat hinges had come loose from the trunk side of the vehicle. It seemed to me that there could be a body in it. As you can see, the victim is tall, and it was probably difficult to cram him into the trunk, which was why his attackers jammed him inside it."

"And this is the log you found on top of him?" The fireman

indicated the log Mick and Gonda had put aside.

"Yep." Mick hesitated. "Can I ask you a question?"

"Sure. Whether I'll answer, is another matter."

"Do you think this has anything to do with the firebug from last night?"

"Beats the heck outta me. I'll keep you posted. That guy's a slippery character, and in my experience, he enjoys fire too much to put one out. He likes to see things *burn, baby, burn.*"

"I appreciate your perspective," Mick said as the paramedics shut the door on his victim and prepared to race down the hill.

"Gimme your card, and I'll call you when I have more substantial information." He paused. "I'm guessing this has nothing to do with the firebug because none of his usual tools are evident."

"Right. We looked," Mick said.

Only a handful of people in law enforcement knew that the firebug used the same starter kit each time. A lit cigarette, three matches tied with string to a piece of newspaper, and a rubber band over the entire incendiary device. Easy, cheap, and devilishly successful.

The ambulance's sirens drowned out their conversation as it backed down the hill.

When the noise subsided, the fireman said, "I'm guessing that whoever did this wanted it to look like the work of the firebug and initially intended to burn the vehicle with the victim inside."

"I thought about that myself," Mick said.

The fireman gave him a wan smile. "I know you did." He peeled off his gloves, pulled his own business card from his pocket, then donned fresh gloves again.

Mick read it. *Taylor Conrad, Chief Arson Investigator.*

"You related to Captain Byrne Conrad?" *Where is the captain anyway? Gonda said he was on his way up here.*

"He's my brother. Anyway, thanks for the help. I need to

ask you to stand back, please."

Mick obeyed, and Gonda joined him.

"Any news from the DMV?" Mick asked.

Gonda frowned. "Still waiting for a callback."

Thanks to California's rigid stalking laws, cops had a hard time getting immediate help from the DMV. Their credentials had to be verified, and nothing happened as fast as it did on TV.

Mick had hardly noticed that the captain had arrived. He was anxious to get an ID on the driver and begin his own investigation.

Gonda's cell phone rang. He cradled the phone against his ear as he jotted quickly into his small notebook. "Thanks," he said, ending the call. "Car's registered to a guy called Arturo Ruiz. They're sending a photo." His phone buzzed, and he checked it.

"Looks like him," Mick said when Gonda showed them the image. The man in the photo had been handsome, had a charming, crooked grin, shaved head, and an intense look in his dark brown eyes.

Christ on a cracker. This is the waiter from JJ's. The one who wouldn't look at me. Man, he looks different with his shaved head. Julian will know something about him. Wonder if he still works at the bakery?

Captain Conrad walked over to them, away from a group of uniformed officers.

Gonda showed him Arturo Ruiz's photo. "You know him, chief?"

Conrad's face paled. "That's our vic?" He seemed stunned. He paused. "Yeah. I know him, and he's the last guy I'd expect to see burned alive in the back of his car."

"Who is he?" Gonda asked.

Conrad ran a hand through his hair. "Arturo's a former corporal in our sheriff's department. He quit four years ago to join the army. I was a sergeant back then. He did two years in Iraq. He came home two years ago. He had a tough time of it I heard. Bad PTSD." He paused as a Julian squad car came up the mountain. "I've asked patrol officers to check the other trail entrance and points up the highway for evidence of fire."

"Good," Mick said, wondering how the captain's arson investigator brother would like police interference. On the other hand, this was a small town. Taylor Conrad would need all the help he could get.

"What grills my cheese is that this kid is only twenty-six," the captain said. "He survived an actual war to come home to . . . this."

Mick said nothing for a moment and did an internet search on the guy. He had spotty cell phone reception one moment, nothing the next.

Gonda's phone worked, but he shrugged after a couple of minutes. "He doesn't even seem to have an *Instagram* account."

"I'm not surprised. He was always a quiet guy. Real family type. Coached his half-brother's little league team. He had a dog. No idea if he still does." Conrad's eyes reddened. "He's had trouble finding work. I thought he was okay because I haven't heard from him." He stared into the middle distance. "I should have checked in with him more. Damn."

Mick and Gonda exchanged glances as Conrad went on.

"Last time I spoke to him, he told me he was staying with his mom. On and off. He had a wife, and she left him when he went to Iraq. They had a daughter. I think he had high hopes of winning her back, but she left town without a trace. I put one of our guys on her trail." He flushed guiltily. "I never did find out if they located her."

"But you were in contact with him when he first came home?" Mick asked.

The captain nodded. "His mom was the one who called me. Oh, over a year ago. Said he was super depressed. That's not uncommon with returning vets, as you know. I wanted to help. We met for coffee, but he's not a real chatty type. Tried to say he was okay. That he'd connected with a couple of his old friends, but he wasn't himself. I could see that."

Conrad stared at the *Avenger*, watching as the fire crew continued processing it. He didn't show any recognition of his brother being there. "He promised me he'd talk to a therapist. I put him in touch with a good social worker at the VA's office in San Diego." He looked devastated. "I don't want to be the one to tell his mom." He swiveled a gaze to Mick. "Marisol won't be able to handle it if he doesn't make it. Can you do it?"

"Yes, sir," Mick said. "We'll head there right now, and we'll start with interviewing family members." He paused. "I'm certain I saw him at JJ's bakery, working as a waiter."

Conrad gave him an odd look. "Check that out."

"We will."

"He didn't deserve this," Conrad ground out.

"I know." Mick looked over at Gonda as he jotted the address the captain gave them for Marisol Ruiz. Mick shivered a little at the irony of the street name. She lived on Firefighter Steven Rucker Memorial Highway.

"She has a nice little grey and white house. Even has a white picket fence. She's a wonderful, hard-working woman." Conrad seemed to be fighting his emotions. "I'll text you her phone number."

"Roger that." Gonda ran a hand across his forehead, looking exhausted. So far, their longed-for day off had taken a sinister turn with no detour in sight. Arturo's last known address was close to Gonda's neighborhood. "Let's drive to my place. I'll drop the truck off, and we'll go in your car."

"Sounds good."

"Stay in touch," the captain said. "And get rid of your gloves. Bag 'em. They're covered in blood." His cell phone rang, and he took the call, holding a finger up to Mick and Gonda.

Oh, no. Before the captain could give them the news. Mick wasn't surprised but felt crushed by Conrad's words.

"Arturo just went into cardiac arrest. They have him on a respirator, but he's flatlined. I don't think he's gonna come back this time." Conrad's eyes reddened once more. His cell phone rang again, and he took the call. He kept saying, "Uh-huh," then turned to Mick and Gonda. "They just called it. Arturo's gone." His eyes filled with tears.

Mick was fascinated. He'd never seen Captain Conrad act even remotely affected by *anything*. For Mick, this desolate experience was a reminder that he, too, knew a couple of guys who'd endured PTSD. He hadn't checked on them in a while. He vowed to contact them before the end of the day.

"Captain, this isn't your fault."

Conrad nodded. "No. I know. I wanted him to come back to his family of sheriffs, but he knew his head wasn't on right. I thought if I left him alone, if I gave him time to heal, and if he got help, he'd walk into the station one day with his killer smile and crazy duck jokes." He gave a faint smile. "He had a plethora of them." He waited a beat. "This is bad, guys. We don't get murders here. Our biggest crimes are theft and burglary. Find out who the hell who did this." He jabbed a finger into the air. "I'll get you all the help you need. Arturo was one of our own."

CHAPTER FOUR

After dropping off Gonda's truck, Mick and Gonda drove in silence until they were out of earshot of the emergency crews.

"You ever seen the captain get so worked up before?" Gonda asked.

"Nope. Never."

"I don't recall anyone at the station ever talking about Arturo Ruiz, and I've been here for a couple of years." Gonda scratched his chin. "This case is getting weirder by the second. Didn't you say he worked at the bakery? Why would anyone murder this guy?"

"And who's the mystery woman who called you?"

"No idea, but I'll call our IT guys and ask them to look into my cell phone records." Gonda picked up his phone and called the tech unit out of San Diego. As he told them what he needed and stressed the urgent nature of his query, Mick thought about what they had so far.

He wanted to call Julian, but he felt a visit was a better option. He wanted to see his reaction when he told him the news.

"I wish we had security cameras," Mick said. A part of him had liked the fact that Julian was really a big, country town. Another part railed at the lack of useful, vital investigators' tools such as cameras. The only place that had one was the local bank. He'd bring up the topic at the next council meeting.

"You know, I was just thinking about that, and it *sucks*,"

Gonda said finally.

"Agreed." Mick craned forward as they neared his driveway. A pale blue *Mustang*, license number HOTPIES was parked in it, and his front door was wide open.

"That's Julian Jarrett's car," Mick said.

"The pie guy?"

"Yeah. What the hell is it doing in *my* driveway?" Mick waited only until Gonda pulled up behind the *Mustang* and Mick jumped out.

"Wait for me," Gonda shouted, but Mick was already sprinting up the stairs to his house. No handrail. It still lay on the ground right where he left it. He took his *Sig Sauer* out of his holster and ran inside.

"Hello?"

Nothing. In the kitchen, his unpacked boxes were gone. He tried to remember if they'd been there when he'd left this morning. He checked the thermostat. Still broken. He opened the fridge. The pie plate stood empty, the cover missing.

Gonda raced in, weapon in hand. Mick glanced at Gonda whose preferred weapon of choice was a *Glock*. "On the count of three," his partner said.

Mick nodded, and they moved as one, fanning out to the bedroom and bathroom. It was there that Mick detected the smell of smoke. His towels, all of them lay puddled in a heap in his tub. A streak of what looked like blood led to the drain.

"Somebody turned my house into part of the crime scene," Mick said. "And where the fuck is my landlord?"

"You wanna call it in, or you want me to do it?" Gonda asked.

"You do it. I need to call Julian and tell him we found his car, but we need to get it to the crime lab." Before he could call, however, Mick's cell phone rang. He didn't recognize the number, but he sure recognized the voice.

"Julian?"

"Yeah. Listen. I just heard. Is it true?"

"About your car? Yeah. Somebody left it in my driveway."

"I don't care about the car." Julian's tone was cold and angry. "I'm talking about Arturo. I just heard he was murdered."

"Where did you hear that?"

"His mother just called me. Some woman called her. Said, quote, he'd been taken care of. What the hell? Who does that?"

Some kind of monster. "Did she recognize the voice?"

"Marisol says she's never spoken to this woman in her life. She called the hospital, but they won't tell her anything. She needs to get there. Arturo's car's been missing since yesterday, and she's been frantic."

"Did she call the police?"

"No. She had her reasons, and I will explain." Julian's breath grew ragged. "If it's true that he's dead, she won't be able to handle this, Mick. He's her whole world. So. Is it?"

"Yes," Mick said. Silence fell between them.

"I'm at the bakery, and I've got no car. I *Ubered* here." He paused. "And what the hell is my car doing in your driveway?"

"No idea. I was—my partner and I were on our way to see Mrs. Ruiz, and I saw your car here. My front door was wide open."

"I want to be there when you talk to her. Can you pick me up so that we can arrive together?"

"You're that close to her?"

"She's one of my best bakers. She talked me into hiring Arturo. Best decision I ever made. The kid started as a waiter, but I recently discovered he makes the best hot water crust of anyone I ever met." Another pause. "Damn. This is so wrong. So wrong and unfair."

"I couldn't agree more." Mick knew where the bakery was,

of course, but Gonda had called in a report on Mick's house. They'd have to wait for officers to arrive. "Listen, somebody's been in here. We're waiting for a squad car now. And I'm sorry to tell you that your car's going to be towed."

"I'll take an *Uber* to Marisol's."

"Please don't. Wait for us. It'll be a couple of minutes, that's all. And please don't call her. The news should come from us."

"We don't have to wait," Gonda said. "Captain's pulling up right now. Dispatch must have called him."

The captain's black Escalade rolled to a stop outside Mick's house. Mick and Gonda walked down the stairs to greet him.

"We'll be on our way in a few minutes," Mick told Julian and ended their call. He grabbed his toothbrush and paste from his bathroom cabinet. Mick didn't care if he was smudging useful prints. But still, he couldn't use the bathroom sink because it was part of the crime scene. His mouth tasted of blood and fire. He raced into the kitchen and cleaned his teeth in the sink. *Ah, much better.* He removed his blood and smoke-infused jacket and shirt then washed his face and hands. There seemed to be no hot water, and it set his teeth on edge.

"Good idea. We can't go like this to visit Mrs. Ruiz." Gonda took his turn at the sink as Mick patted himself dry with paper towels.

"Congratulations," Gonda gasped. "You have no hot water."

Mick shook his head and raced to his bedroom, where he pulled out a clean sweater from the closet and a hooded jacket. He returned to the kitchen.

"What the hell's going on?" Conrad asked as he hovered at the front door. He looked at Mick as though he was to blame. "And what's Julian's car doing here?"

"You know him?"

Conrad gave him a weird look. "Of course I know him. He

bakes friggin' great pies." He sounded almost hysterical. "And he's my cousin."

"I didn't know that." Mick saw no family resemblance at all.

Conrad shook his head. "Somebody keeps stealing his car and returning it. We quit dusting it for prints because it's always wiped clean." He peered at the car's exterior muttering, "Wonder if we'll find anything this time." He straightened, giving Mick and Gonda meaningful, penetrating gazes. "I'll secure the crime scene."

Oh, yeah. I see the family resemblance now. Mick almost shivered.

Conrad gave them a dismissive wave. "And you're gonna wear that stinky shirt, are you?" His baleful stare at Gonda seemed to make Mick's partner cringe.

"Well, I could borrow something from Mick, but I don't think it'd fit. I buy from Big and Tall, ya'know."

"He's hardly a midget," Conrad snapped.

"I've got a couple of big sweaters." Mick ran back to his bedroom and grabbed the biggest sweater he could find. When he returned, Gonda changed with a miserable look on his face.

Mick filled the awkward silence by asking the captain to make sure a female officer could meet them when they visited Mrs. Ruiz.

"Yeah," the captain said. "You're meeting at her house?"

Mick's cell phone rang. It was Julian. Mick welcomed the small moment of delight hearing that man's seductive voice again, even if his words were strained.

"Marisol's here at the bakery. Don't worry. I haven't asked her any questions. She just turned up saying she was afraid to be at the house alone."

Mick felt a pang of anguish for the woman. This was common among the surviving family members of violent homicide.

"Thanks for letting me know. We're on our way." Mick ended the call and gave the captain the update.

"Very good."

"We'll need a female officer to accompany us," Mick said.

"Yes. Of course." He paused. "I'm thinking Corporal Washington. She's very calm and very bright." He seemed to be waiting for Mick's approval.

"Great choice. We handled a couple of burglaries together."

"Yes, I know. She admires you. Said you were great to work with." His mouth lifted in a Lurch-style smile. "I think she has a crush on you."

Oh, no.

"I'll have her meet you there. Carry on."

"Yes, sir," Mick and Gonda said in unison. Sometimes Mick felt like a kid being dismissed by the headmaster after detention. They went outside and climbed into Gonda's vehicle.

"He's such a tool." Gonda frowned and started the engine, peeling away from the house.

"It's my fault. I should have brought out a sweater for you to begin with." Mick fought the urge to clutch the roof and the dashboard as Gonda wove recklessly down the highway.

"Brother, I'm not faulting you. We don't need to speak sometimes. You probably sensed I'd stop at my place and grab a clean sweater. He's such a tool," he repeated.

Gonda was right. They had good communication between them. Mick felt bad for Gonda. For some reason, the captain liked to ride him. A lot.

"You might have to move," Gonda blurted. "Freaky shit happens in that house."

"Tell me about it." Mick felt depressed as he called his landlord. This time he got the guy's real answering machine. He left a message. "Billy, what did you do to my house? Call me immediately." He added a *please* though it wounded him to be polite. He wondered if and when Billy would get back to him.

As they approached the downtown end of Julian, Mick observed all the things he'd come to cherish about it. The trees were beautiful. Big, leafy, and bright green, they defied the cold weather. And whatever mayhem human beings brought to the place. The cider mill on Main Street seemed to always smell of baking apples. He inhaled as they whizzed past. Delicious.

There was a new apple vineyard two doors down. He hadn't tried their wines and wasn't sure he'd enjoy apple-flavored vino. He smiled at the sight of the sawmill where people bought their own wood to make furniture. There was a rocking horse for sale out front. He also loved the eclectic cluster of restaurants and cozy breakfast bars.

JJ's was in a quirky triangular-shaped building next to a hardware store on one side, and a steakhouse kitty-corner to it.

Julian was waiting outside for them, still wearing the clothes he'd had on earlier, with a white chef's apron atop it. Mick's spirits lifted at a little. *Man, that guy is sexy.* His stomach rumbled. In spite of everything, he was hungry, and somebody had eaten all the pie Julian had given him.

"That's him." Mick pointed.

"I know," Gonda said. "He's one of Jenn's dearest friends. She's been wanting to set the two of you up since you moved here."

"She has?" The idea tickled Mick. He was beginning to like Jenn more and more.

"Sure thing. Julian saw you at the bakery one day and asked her about you. As a matter of fact, she'd almost convinced him to ask you out, but he's kinda shy."

He wasn't shy in my shower this morning. Heh, heh.

Mick sighed. He reminded himself that it was a sex dream. And in sex dreams nobody was shy.

Gonda pulled up beside Julian, lowered his window, and said, "Hey, J.J."

J.J.? Mick hated the name. He thought Julian was so sexy and classy.

"Gonda! Good to see you. You too, Mick, but I'm sorry that it's under these circumstances. Why don't you leave your car out front here? Marisol's inside, waiting for you. I just gave her a cognac." He held up a hand. Neither Gonda nor Mick spoke. Mick didn't want Arturo's mom drunk. On the other hand, she'd just had a terrible shock. They parked and stepped out of the vehicle.

Julian shook both their hands, his grip lingering on Mick's. Mick felt a flash of warmth infusing him in dangerous places. He glanced over at Gonda, who was busy rolling his eyes. Neither Julian or Mick let go, and Mick had an absurd desire to run down the street with Julian and find someplace dark and private to—

"Lieutenant? Lieutenant Fielding? I'm here!" a female voice called. "Yoo-hoo!"

Mick turned and smiled at Corporal Annette Washington. He let go of Julian's hand with great reluctance and introduced them to each other.

They all went inside. Mick was surprised to see the *closed* sign on the door, the place empty.

Julian closed and locked the door behind them. "I felt under the circumstances that it shouldn't be business as usual."

"That was thoughtful. Where is she?" Gonda asked.

"This way." Julian led them beyond the counter with its gleaming shelves loaded with delectable looking pies, into the kitchen area. It was huge and as compelling as Julian's home kitchen.

"Can I get any of you a coffee? I just made some, fresh."

"That'd be great, thanks," Mick said.

"I'd love some, thanks," Annette said, making a beeline for Marisol Ruiz.

"Me, too." Gonda nodded.

Apart from the fact Mick was desperate for coffee, he knew that getting the victim's mother to open up about her son's life would be easier the more conversational it seemed.

Marisol Ruiz sat at a large wooden farmhouse table, similar to the one in Julian's house. She was an attractive, middle-aged woman with long, chestnut tresses. She wore a plum-colored sweater and ink-black pants.

Annette moved into a seat beside her and took her hand. That simple gesture seemed to unravel Marisol. Her agonized expression and unstoppable flow of tears tore at Mick's conscience. Annette did a wonderful job of introducing herself and letting Marisol know she was there for her, willing to listen and to talk, to take care of her.

"I'm here for the town of Julian, and everyone shares your pain."

Mick gave her a moment then spoke. "Good morning, Mrs. Ruiz. I'm Lieutenant Mick Fielding, this is my partner, Lieutenant Walter Gonda. We are very sorry for your loss. We—"

"They won't let me see my boy," Marisol burst out, tears shaking her whole body. Mick and Gonda sat opposite her and waited for her to calm a little. It would be like this for her, this seasickness of the soul, Mick knew, for a long, long time. A therapist once told Mick that grief was love. Love that a person wanted to give but couldn't. She'd said that grief was love that had no place to go. He knew all about it because he still grieved Laurence so much.

"I know this is hard for you, but we do need to ask you some questions." Mick leaned closer to her. "I know this is a bad time, but we need to catch whoever did this. We need your help."

She bit her lip. "But I don't know anything." Her face flushed and she glanced away. He knew she was lying. Whatever secret she thought she needed to protect was a moot point now her son was gone.

Mick kept his tone gentle. "You told Julian that Arturo disappeared last night. When did you last see him?"

"Last night. At my house. He moved into a guest house behind my friend's place a few weeks ago, but he had trouble sleeping." Her voice wobbled. "He has bad dreams." She blinked and burst into tears again.

Annette gripped her hand and patted it with her free one.

"Does he come to your place when he can't sleep?" Mick persisted.

"Yes."

"And what time did you last see him?"

"About six o'clock. He brought his dog, Thor, with him. Thor's getting old and he's started having seizures. Arturo falls apart each time it happens, even though we have medicine for him. Arturo doesn't handle pressure very well, so he brings Thor to me. I have more space than Arturo has at the guest house." She paused. "He can't handle being alone at night. He says the shadows scare him."

"So he came over?" Gonda asked. "Then what happened?"

She glanced away at again, looking over at the sink area as though the pile of plates loaded on the bench was suddenly fascinating.

"He was agitated. He brought stuff and put it in his room. I always keep it ready for him. Arturo knows my home is his home. It would kill him if he couldn't sleep in his old bedroom."

Kill. She seemed to be aware that she'd used the word. Her hand trembled as she put it to her lips. "Oh, my God. He's never going to sleep there again." Tears ran down her cheeks.

"And what happened after he came over?"

"He was worried, like I said. Nervous."

"About what?"

"I don't know."

Once again, Mick knew she was lying.

"Please trust me. Whatever happened, all I want to do is catch whoever did this."

She was a stubborn woman. Her eyes took on a hard cast, and she downed the contents of the glass in front of her. She swatted at her tears with a massive wad of tissues. "Why won't they let me see my son?"

Gonda looked at Mick. He believed in honesty, and he had no time to waste.

"I'll be honest, it's bad what they did to him," Mick said. "Besides, the, ah—" He didn't want to say coroner—it would be too harsh at that moment. "The, ah, doctors will need to look at him."

"You mean they need to examine his body. Will they do an autopsy? What did they do to him, lieutenant?"

Julian arrived with coffees for Annette, Mick, and Gonda. He put cream and sugar on the table then poured a little more cognac into Marisol's glass from a cut-glass decanter. A finger's length.

"Tell me," Marisol said. "Nobody's told me a thing. I called the police. I called the hospital. *They* wouldn't even admit he was there."

"He was beaten," Mick said. "They did some very bad things." He knew no medical expert would allow her to see Arturo in his current condition. And no doubt, whichever funeral home she worked with would insist on a sealed casket.

"*Pinche pindejos*," she shouted.

Mick knew it meant fucking assholes. And she was right.

"Who are the assholes? Can you tell me?" Mick asked.

She closed her eyes, squeezing out a few more tears. "I do not know," she said again, then her voice came out a panicked whisper. "I'm afraid."

"Nobody is going to hurt you. I can promise you that," Julian said, moving to her other side and covering her hand with his. "There have been too many secrets."

She hung her head and wept. "Too many," she agreed, putting her head on Julian's shoulder. He slipped his arm around her and shot Mick a helpless look.

A few minutes later, she said, "He let people borrow his car."

"When?" Gonda asked. "Last night?"

"All the time. Whatever happened last night had nothing to do with Arturo. They did it."

"Who?" Mick asked. What was she doing? Why was she lying? "Mrs. Ruiz, you said he came over about six-thirty. How long did he stay?"

"Not long. He was upset because he couldn't find his friends. He kept calling them. And then he left."

"Who are his friends?" Gonda asked.

She sat, sullen, and on the verge of tears again.

"Please, Marisol, you have to tell them," Julian coaxed. "Tell them what you told me. They can't hurt him anymore, and nobody can hurt Thor. You're both coming to stay with me. Tell them. Please."

"People threatened to hurt Thor?" Mick asked.

"My boy . . . he loves that dog. And Thor tries to protect him. Always." Fresh tears sparked her eyes. "Something happened a few months ago, and Arturo wouldn't tell me, but somebody attacked him, and Thor bit the attacker. The attacker hit Thor in the head and ever since then he's been having seizures." She sobbed again. "My son blames himself." She sobbed into Julian's shoulder. "Oh, my God. My baby's dead!"

It took her a moment, but she blurted the words as though she needed to purge her soul. "He's been so lost and in so

171

much pain. He started taking drugs. I don't know when he got into them. I only know his personality changed a few months ago. He was involved with these two friends of his."

"What kind of drugs?" Mick asked.

"Methamphetamines."

Oh, boy. Friends and drugs did not mix well.

"His friends have been selling them, and they started to sell some to him. They gave him free samples. That's what Arturo told me. I've researched that drug, and there's no such thing as free samples. It hooks you. And it hooks you hard. They say it's the most addictive, lethal drug out there. He told me when I caught him one day that he can't afford prescription meds and the meth helps him. What's happening to our country? Our young people are in crisis, and nobody's doing anything about it."

That was a whole other valid discussion point, but right now, Mick had one focus. A brutal murder.

Mrs. Ruiz was on fire now. "I know those drugs are bad. His friends . . . they laughed when I asked them to stop. They were the ones who told me Arturo was selling the drugs, too."

"Who are these friends?" Gonda asked.

"The ringleader is the one that scares me. People say he's the one that brought meth here," Mrs. Ruiz said. "Ever since he came back . . ." She stared at the tabletop. "They say he used to be in a gang, but I don't know . . . he deals in drugs and intimidates people. My boy used to hang out with him until he went to Iraq. I thought when he came home, his friends would be gone, but they were right here."

"What's the ringleader's name?" Mick asked.

"Billy."

Mick had a bad feeling about this. "Billy who?"

"Billy Hudson." Her words came out in a petrified rasp.

Oh, my God. Mick ran a hand over his face. Some puzzle pieces were falling into place. Others were floating around, leering at him in his mind.

Mrs. Ruiz looked at the expression on Mick's face. "So you know him. Am I right? He's bad news."

"Yeah." Mick's day was getting worse and worse.

"Who's the other guy?" Gonda asked.

"He's bad, too, because he does whatever Billy tells him." Marisol took a deep breath, her hand shaking again as she pressed the tissues to her face. "Tom Francisco. He used to be a good kid, but his teeth are bad now, and he's skinny, skinny."

Mick and Gonda had come across Tom Francisco a couple of times. He was a habitual thief, his favorite things to steal were women's purses and anything he saw left lying around in a vehicle. He seemed a bit squirrely but not a violent kind of guy. If he was a meth-head, however, Mick knew only too well the way it fucked with people's minds.

"Mrs. Ruiz, this may have nothing to do with anything, but I heard that Arturo used to be married. I heard his wife left him and took the kids with her. Was he ever able to find her?"

She looked at Mick, a bitter expression in her gaze. "Oh, he found her. He's gotten over her now, but she caused him a lot of problems. She gave up those babies. Adopted them out of state for money. Signed away her parental rights. Forged his signature, too. He couldn't fight it because he wasn't here." She grabbed for the cognac glass, but it was empty, and when she glanced at Julian, he shook his head.

After a moment, she went on. "That . . . he could never get over. He loved those children. But she never moved away. She was here. How do they call it? Hiding in plain sight." She slapped at the tears streaking down her face. "It was his dream to take her to court and get those babies back." She glanced at Julian. "This wonderful man gave my boy a job here, and he's tried to help him. He said as long as Arturo came to work every day, he'd pay for a lawyer. But his friends ruined everything for him."

"You said the ex-wife is here? Who is she?" Mick asked.

"I'm sure you know her, but he stays away from her, and she stays away from him. It's that girl. That big troublemaker around town. The one they call Gemini."

CHAPTER FIVE

It took Mick a couple of minutes to absorb the shock of knowing that his landlord may have been involved in Arturo's murder. Not to mention Gemini's potential part in it.

No matter what he asked her, Marisol claimed not to know what the fight between Billy and Arturo was over. She kept saying he left the house around seven-thirty, but that somebody picked him up.

She gave Mick her son's cell phone number. It was jarring when he tried calling, and he heard Arturo's voice. "Leave me a message," he said. But his voicemail was full.

"Any idea where his cell phone is?" he asked her.

"No. He kept it on him. It wasn't a fancy phone. It's one of those pay-as-you-go phones."

Law enforcement called them burner phones. *Ugh.* That seemed so inappropriate, and creepy, under the circumstances. He knew calls and cell phone tower pings on these throwaway items were harder to trace than subscription phones. He asked her for the address to Arturo's guest house, and she gave it to him.

"You said he left around seven—"

"Yes. He left the house but didn't drive his car. He left it in the driveway and said he'd be right back." Her face twisted in torment. "I wish I knew who picked him up. I wish I'd looked out the window. He didn't come back, and I was worried about him. He always calls if he's going to be late, and since Thor was injured, he hardly leaves his side. He didn't call once, and he didn't return any of my texts, which isn't like him. I looked out of the window around midnight, and his car was gone."

He believed that part of her story. Whoever had taken Arturo had beaten and tortured him, came back and collected his vehicle to burn him alive in it.

Mick called Captain Conrad and gave him his updates. Conrad put out APBs on Billy Hudson, Tom Francisco, and Gemini Shirley, sending out all available squad units for the hunt. Much as Mick wanted to search through Arturo's guest house himself, he and Gonda had plenty to do. Captain Conrad assured Mick he'd assign another team to it.

The captain did tell him there were no fingerprints found on Arturo's *Avenger*. "There are none on Julian's vehicle, either. Somebody went to a lot of trouble to disguise their crimes. We're waiting for DNA results on the blood in your bathtub." His voice became muffled, and Mick realized he was issuing commands in the background.

He came back to Mick. "Send Annette back to the office since Julian's taking care of Mrs. Ruiz. I'd like you to take Mrs. Ruiz and Julian to her home. Check it out. Make sure everything's okay. Check Arturo's room. Let's see if there's anything of evidentiary value. Then you can take them and the dog to Julian's. They'll be very safe there."

"Roger that," Mick said.

Corporal Washington didn't take it too well when she learned the captain wanted her to return to the station.

"They need your help," Mick said. "They need all hands on deck."

"Bet they put me on phones," she muttered darkly and stomped off to her duty vehicle.

Mick couldn't say anything. They weren't a huge station, and they needed everybody to help hunt for three dangerous people. He and Gonda drove Marisol and Julian to her house.

Thor, the dog, turned out to be a lovable German Shepherd

who nuzzled Mick and Gonda in turn. He'd been sleeping on the sofa and returned to his spot, one eye on the activity around him.

They visited with him for a minute then donned gloves to go through Arturo's room.

Before they could that, Julian helped Marisol get some clothes and work things, as well as essentials for Thor.

Outside, reporters had gathered, and Mick groaned when people started pressing the front doorbell. Marisol became unglued, and Julian kept hugging her. Thor started pacing and barking, making things worse.

"Calm down, baby." Marisol got to her knees and held the dog hard.

"We need to get you out of here," Gonda told her. He'd parked in the driveway but called a squad unit to come to the laneway behind the house. "Don't use sirens or lights," he warned.

When they arrived, Gonda waited in the house with Marisol and Thor. Mick went out with the suitcase and carry bags Marisol had thrown together. They stuffed the trunk of the black and white.

Julian kept glancing at him. On their way back to Marisol's, he stopped Mick. Keeping his voice low, he said, "I'll look after them. I promise. Please come over later if you can."

"I will."

Julian waited a beat. "If I learn anything more from Marisol, I'll let you know. I don't think she had a clue what Arturo and Billy fought about, but I think I do. I just don't know for sure and hate to lead you astray."

"Why didn't you say something before?" Mick was incredulous.

"Like I told you, I don't know if I'm right and I don't want to do anything to stir that rattlesnake Billy Hudson."

"Was it over drugs or money?"

"No. I believe it was over his wife, but I could be totally wrong."

"Kanya?" He had Mick's attention now. He'd met her a couple of times, but she always seemed subservient and nervous around Billy. She barely spoke to Mick. "What about her?"

"It's complicated, but they really were just friends." He hesitated. "I think she found a kindred spirit in Arturo. But she may have played up the connection a little to make Billy jealous."

Oh, boy. Mick thought fast. "Okay. After we check the bedroom, Gonda and I will go look for her."

"Okay." Julian seemed less than thrilled about the idea. "You watch yourself with that lunatic."

"I will." Mick had the absurd desire to hug the guy but had no idea why. He forced the idea from his mind and helped Julian get Marisol and Thor into the squad car.

He returned to the house. Now that he and Gonda were alone, they could check things uninterrupted.

The media was still outside in full force. A news crew from L.A. had joined the San Diego crowd, apparently unaware their quarry had vanished. Mick ignored them, took a deep breath, and stepped into Arturo's bedroom. He wasn't surprised to see that it was neat to the point of being sterile. One pair of shoes stood neatly by the closet. Every surface gleamed. He could almost see Arturo standing at attention beside him.

"I've gone over it, didn't find much," Gonda said. "Nothing here. He's definitely military. You could bounce a quarter off that bed."

Mick took it all in. Very few personal items took up space on the desk Arturo must have occupied as a teen. There was no computer on it or any sign of some kind of portable tablet. The top shelf was occupied by three pristine military craft that looked like he'd made from craft kits. Beneath those, he had half a row of books, mostly military and business-related. *The Mammoth Book of Special Forces Training* almost broke Mick's heart. He knew Arturo had put up a good fight to save his life. He blew out a breath and did a double-take when he saw one title that read, *The 4-Hour Work Week. Escape 9-5, Live Anywhere, and Join the New Rich.*

He pulled the book off the shelf and opened to a page at random.

Practice the art of non-finishing. Hmm. He planned to do just that. He closed the book and put it back on the shelf. Did anyone actually believe the author? He felt a stab of sympathy for Arturo who probably wouldn't have chosen to live in Julian if he'd figured out the secrets of the rich. He *had* figured a way around working 9-5, though. Drug dealing however, wasn't a livelihood he'd recommend to anybody. He knew from his work in the field that it had an almost one-hundred percent death rate.

There wasn't much else, just like Gonda said. A closet with his army uniforms, some pants, a couple of shirts, and a bedroom dresser that was empty. Something made him dive under the bed and look. It was often a good place to find discarded cell phones.

This time it wasn't.

He and Gonda spent the next several hours driving around Julian and nearby towns of Banner and Pine Hills, chasing up reported sightings. There was even one from the old, abandoned Eagle Mine. Well-meaning residents had followed the story of Arturo's murder and wanted to help capture his killers. Or maybe they were interested in the ten-thousand-dollar reward the mayor had just offered.

Mick wanted to revisit the crime scene, but it had been cordoned off, and he most likely wouldn't find anything useful there anyway. He called the captain, who was busy holding a press conference. He checked in with Corporal Washington, who, true to her prediction, was at the station fielding phone calls.

She was most informative, even if she felt like Cinderella before the ball. "Well," she said. "So far, Billy and his family are missing. Gemini and her mother Louise Shirley have vanished. They left the campervan at home, but Louise's Ford truck is pretty ramshackle. They won't make it out of the state even if they head to Mexico."

Mick hoped they were just hunkering down someplace local. If they actually made it to Mexico, relations were so bad between the two countries they'd never get an extradition order to bring the two women back.

Five minutes later, Annette called Mick back. "A store clerk saw Tom Francisco trying to get his hair dyed at a dog groomer's off Main Street. He texted nine-one-one when Tom showed up with a box of Clairol and an old shotgun."

Mick almost laughed. He suspected Tom had used Louise Shirley's weapon. That thing sure was making the rounds.

"Yeah," Annette went on. "Like cheap hair color's gonna be a good disguise." She paused. "They just arrested him. I'll keep you posted."

A few minutes later, she called back, sounding out of breath. "Mick, if you thought you might come in and question him, you're out of luck. He lawyered up as soon as they brought him here. Sheesh. I didn't think he had any brains at all. Guess he's not as stupid as he looks."

It was frustrating for everybody, but it was how things often went in real law enforcement. Lengthy, tearful confessions only happened on TV. At least one of the monsters was off the street.

Mick and Gonda were starving and hit one of the few stores left open. Everybody had closed up. Even the gas station was empty.

"This is eerie," Gonda said as he got out of his car and stretched his legs. "I feel like we're in that scene out of *High Noon*, where everyone's gone into hiding because they know shit's gonna go down."

Inside the store, the owner seemed nervous but determined. She told Mick and Gonda she wasn't sure whether she wanted Gemini and Louise to be found by the police or if she wanted to shoot them herself. "I've been taking lessons at the range. I'm keen to practice on a live target."

"You really want to do that?" Mick asked, a little shocked.

"Hell, ya. I want them suckers caught. Or dead. Preferably dead. Then I'll sing, *Happy Days are Here Again*."

Mick nodded. "Just give us a call if you see them. We'd prefer them alive, not dead."

"I wouldn't," she said in a pert tone. Clearly, she had a grudge. She wouldn't hear of Mick and Gonda purchasing the bottles of water they brought to her counter.

"No, no. This is on me, boys. Go get 'em." She even gave them a couple of pre-packed cheese sandwiches and a pair of slightly bruised apples to go.

Back in Gonda's vehicle, they debated their next move when the captain called.

"I'm gonna eat," Gonda said, unwrapping his sandwich.

Mick put the captain on his cell phone's loudspeaker.

"Hey, Mick. We found Billy Hudson. He had no idea we were looking for him. Guess he's not keeping up on current events. Believe it or not, he'd just gone back to your house with a new front door lock. He's pissed that we arrested him. Says you owe him thirty-four dollars for the lock."

Mick snorted. "I hope he doesn't hold his breath. Where are his wife and kids?"

"No idea. He doesn't know either. By the way, he says he's the one who left the blood and towels in your tub. He cut his hand with the knife he used to slice up the pie you had in the fridge. He says he and Kanya had a fight and she took off with the littlies. We're bringing him in right now. He'll cave like one of his own brick walls.

"I just got some interesting news from the hospital." Conrad rattled some papers and said, "The hospital emergency room staff tells me that Arturo Ruiz's blood work results are coming up weird. He had some strange infection they can't identify. Apparently, it resembles some kind of animal, possibly a bat, or a flying fox. I'm not sure about the latter. I've never seen one of those around here." He paused. "He may have been bitten at some point. But he's ex-military.

What if the army was doing secret experiments on these guys? I know it sounds farfetched, but it's possible. I'll look into it. Anyway, stay in touch with me." He ended their call.

Gonda glanced at Mick, circling his index finger around his ear if to say, *he's crazy.*

Bats. Foxes. Blood. Mick recalled Louise Shirley's words about Julian. *People say he's a vampire.*

Gonda started the engine. "So we've only got Gemini and Louise to look for. Maybe we should take a pass by their house."

"Good idea." Mick buckled up and grabbed his water bottle as Gonda moved out into the street. He screamed. A truck was coming right at them from the other side of the road. It hit two parked cars then zigzagged toward them. Mick's life flashed before his eyes.

"We're gonna hit!" Gonda shouted.

Neither man could escape the rutting truck. Mick glimpsed the driver's face. Louise Shirley. Her mouth was open, her eyes closed. She hit the driver's side of the car, spun out of control, then her truck rolled three times and stopped upside down in the middle of the road.

People came running. Gonda stirred.

"You okay?" Mick asked.

"Yeah. My cheese sandwich has seen better days, though."

Mick unbuckled his seat belt and ran to the truck. He and the shopkeeper pulled an unconscious Louise and a spitting Gemini out of the vehicle. Somebody must have called 9-1-1 because an ambulance came hurtling down the street.

Louise lay on the ground. "My heart," she murmured, grabbing at her chest.

"You, stupid old bitch!" Gemini shouted. "None of this would be happening if you'd just let that car burn. You had to get creative and put out the fire." She kicked at her mother's foot. Louise moaned again.

Mick grabbed Gemini's hands behind her back. She spat at him as he cuffed her.

"Please let me shoot her!" the shopkeeper begged.

Mick asked her to check on Gonda, but his partner was already out of his car. He was limping, but he was alive. Mick held onto Gemini as the ambulance put Louise on a gurney.

"She's had a heart attack," one of the paramedics said.

"She was having it as she was driving," Mick said.

They loaded her up. Mick watched, astounded that Louise Shirley had put out the fire in Arturo's trunk. When a squad car arrived to collect Gemini, Mick and Gonda went through her truck. Several bundles of crude fire starters sat in the glove compartment. There was a map of Julian with various points marked in red felt-tip pen.

"She's our firebug," Gonda said, as shocked as Mick. The shopkeeper gave them a ride back to the station and casually asked about the ten-thousand-dollar reward.

"Ask the captain," Mick said.

"Don't worry. I will."

Gemini didn't wait for questions. She said she had nothing to do with Arturo's murder. "I suggested after Billy and Tom tortured him that my mother could set fire to him. That's all I did."

And that was a lot. She was looking at murder charges along with the others.

"Mom did it then changed her mind. She wanted him to suffer more. If we left him in the trunk, his death would take a bit longer."

It was a chilling confession. Mick felt dirty after their conversation. She offered no real reason for her ex-husband's death except that, "He spoke to Kanya Hudson when he shouldn't have. He had no right."

Knowing all of the participants in Arturo's senseless murder had been caught and would do serious time, left Mick feeling relieved but drained. He wanted a shower, a hot meal, and he wanted Julian.

Jenn Walter picked up Mick and Gonda, dropping Mick outside Julian's house.

She took off, and Mick hesitated. *What am I doing? Am I nuts?*

But Julian was waiting at the front door for him. "I miss you," he said. "I miss you, and I don't even know you."

"I could say the same about you." Mick thought he might stop breathing. There was a man standing off to the side.

It was Laurence.

CHAPTER SIX

What the hell is happening to me?
Julian came to him. "Laurence and I both know you miss him, but it's my turn now."

"He's really here? How?" Mick had always longed for one more day. One more hour. One more kiss. But here was Laurence looking happy and wonderful, smiling at him.

"Who do you think gave me the idea for jumping in the shower with you this morning?"

Tears came to Mick's eyes. "That was real?"

"Didn't it feel real?"

Mick couldn't respond. He was acutely aware of Arturo's mom sleeping in the guest room. This was a very private, emotional moment, but he guessed she'd had a few herself lately.

"Laurence will always be with you. He never wanted to leave you, but he had no choice. He hated seeing you suffer for so long. I noticed him walking behind you the very first day you moved here."

Julian took him into his arms and kissed his head. "This is not what he wants. He wants for you to be happy. To love again. If you let me, I can love you enough for both of us. I can help you see him, talk to him, whenever you want."

"How? How is it possible?"

Julian pulled away from Mick, his face a mask of pain. "He's always with you. Just think of him as being in another room." Without another word, he took Mick inside. Past the wonderful-smelling kitchen, past sweet Thor who lay on the living room sofa, a crackling fire going in the fireplace.

In Julian's bedroom, time seemed to stop. Julian led him to the bed and lay across it, watching Mick strip off his jeans and boxer briefs. His smile was one of predatory pride when he saw Mick's cock.

"Oh . . . Mick. Please let me touch it." He sat up, his fingers running up and down the shaft. He placed a kiss on the tip. Mick wanted to touch Julian, too, but Julian was in control. He let Mick kiss him, then stood, grinding himself against Mick's body. The sensation of Julian's hard and massive cock left Mick dizzy with desire. He lowered his hand to stroke the rigid shaft, but Julian moved away from Mick's touch, moving his hand from Mick's balls then up to his belly then down to his ass.

He touched Mick's cock. *Leaking.* He stripped off then, and Mick moved his hand to Julian's beautiful body, but Julian grabbed Mick around his hips and got to his knees, his fingers going to his ass the same places where he'd dug his nails into Mick's ass cheeks in the shower. It seemed so long ago now.

Unbelievably, Mick started coming, and Julian wasn't even touching him. He moaned as Julian went right to his cock, licked his come, then made him hard again. He suddenly stood, pushing Mick to the bed roughly. He mounted him and kissed him then turned him face down, pulling Mick to his knees. He went down on Mick's ass. He licked and sucked Mick, his hands gripping Mick's heels. Mick's feet came off the bed, and Julian flipped him onto his back.

Mick lifted his knees toward his chest. "I can't wait any longer. Just fuck me. Please."

Julian moved two fingers into him, stroking him. Their eyes met in a moment that seemed to Mick as though Julian had struck a match that lit a fire in him. Julian removed his fingers and stuck his cock into Mick, panting as he moved in and out of him.

Mick held onto him, his hulking, hot lover. It felt as though they'd done this forever, even though it was all so new.

Julian held him tightly, pulling Mick closer, closer and then they came, red and gold fireworks blinding Mick. Julian didn't let up. He began again, urging Mick to another orgasm. He didn't think he could come a third time. His head pounded.

"It hurts," he whispered in Julian's ear. And then he came. He screamed Julian's name, as the pain spread from his head to his neck and he was still coming so hard and that it felt like nothing else on Earth. Seconds later, his whole body relaxed.

"Rest now," Julian growled in his ear.

Mick woke up alone, threw on his clothes, then looked for Julian. He was in the kitchen, kneading dough.

"You're a vampire," Mick said. "I sound crazy even to myself. But I accept it, and I don't know why."

"Because we're falling in love and when you know, you know."

That was as good an explanation as any.

"You'll learn I'll never hurt you. Our love will just grow deeper. I can bite you and turn you. Or not. The choice is yours."

Mick took a gamble. "Is Kanya Hudson a vampire?"

Julian looked surprised. "Yes, she is. She was trying to help Arturo. She'd trusted him with her secret. He needed a friend, and she knew if he turned, it would cure his addiction. She had to bite him three times."

"You'd have to do that with me?"

Julian looked him right in the eye. "Yes, but for you, it will be much more pleasurable. Arturo still needed one more bite, but Billy thought it was an affair." Julian took his frustration out on the dough.

"Where is she now?"

"In hiding. We need to keep her safe from Billy. And his gangbanger friends. He never had a clue about her real origins. She's a good girl. Just married the wrong guy. Tomorrow, you can take her to the captain. He'll understand when you explain."

"Explain that she's a vampire?"

"Of course. He's one, too." He tilted his head at Mick. "There are whole communities of us. Byrne Conrad came out here first, then Taylor. My brother Dan is a butcher. He lives close by in Santa Ysabel."

"So you're the baker. What about a candlestick maker?" Mick kidded.

"We have one of those, too. Taylor's wife, Francesca, makes incense, candles, and oils."

Mick gawped at him. "How can um, you be awake and walking around in daylight?"

Julian moved over to him and took him into his arms. "I'm a baker. I have to be able to function like most people. Francesca has a harder time. She needs to be awake at night to make her potions. People just think she's an insomniac." He kissed Mick then walked back to his dough.

"I love you, and I don't know how," Mick said as Julian put his dough into a bowl, covered it in plastic then put it in a drawer. He wondered why, but Julian told him without him having to ask.

"It's a proving drawer. The bread needs about an hour to rise. Now, you were saying?"

"You can read my mind?" A voice in his head said, *yes.* "Ah, um, I believe in love at first sight. I just never thought it would happen to me. I thought it only happened to kids."

Julian smiled. "I was a kid once, you know."

"When? How long ago?"

"Mick, you never ask a vampire his age."

"That old, huh? Well, I always did like older men." He

moved over to Julian. "I hope I don't wake up and find this was a dream."

"Not a dream. But we'll go back to bed soon, and I'll wake you with kisses, hot bread, and coffee. We'll spend time with Marisol and Thor. We'll help them heal." He held Mick's face in his hands. "Finally, you are real." He swallowed Mick's mouth with his.

When Mick caught his breath, he said against Julian's lips, "So we've got an hour? I'm thinking I'd like to try out your shower trick again."

"Your wish," Julian said, giving Mick another lingering kiss, "Is my command."

ABOUT A.J. LLEWELLYN

A.J. Llewellyn is the author of over 250 M/M romance novels. She was born in Australia, and lives in Los Angeles. An early obsession with Robinson Crusoe led to a lifelong love affair with islands, particularly Hawaii and Easter Island.

Being marooned once on Wedding Cake Island in Australia cured her of a passion for fishing, but led to a plotline for a novel. A.J.'s friends live in fear because even the smallest details of their lives usually wind up in her stories. A.J. has a desire to paint, draw, juggle, work for the FBI, walk a tightrope with an elephant, be a chess champion, a steeplejack, master chef, and a world-class surfer. She can't do any of these things so she writes about them instead.

A.J. started life as a journalist and boxing columnist, and still enjoys interrogating, er, interviewing people to find out what makes them tick.

How to find/friend me:

email: ajllewellyn@gmail.com
website: www.ajllewellyn.com
www.facebook.com/aj.llewellyn
www.twitter.com/ajllewellyn
Newsletter sign-up: ajllewellynnewsletter@gmail.com—each month I give away a free ebook!
I'm an app! Download my FREE A.J. Llewellyn App for Android here: http://tinyurl.com/lkbc4wm

THE KNOCKERS

BY

JO TANNAH

Can a vampire be mastered?

On Thosolla, a world where humans live in peaceful co-existence with the prevalent race, the Reter family have ruled and exacted justice for over a millennium. When a beloved prince is found dead along with his newly wedded husband, both humans and Thosollans point accusing fingers at The Knockers.

Ezmet Reter is enjoying a quiet time with his human lover, Francis, on a private island on Earth when word reaches him of a rebellion on Thosolla. The reason? Supposedly, The Knockers have exacted punishment on his beloved cousin, Ezra, who he thought was on his honeymoon with his husband of two weeks.

Legend has it The Knockers are a trio of vengeful creatures who neither forgive nor spare anyone who dares break the sacred agreement between Thosollans and humans. They are feared for their uncanny ability to hunt down the guilty, and no one knows of their origins or the true extent of their powers.

The whole situation perplexes Ezmet, for the last recorded incident when The Knockers wrought their vengeance was five hundred years in the past. Worried, he journeys back to Thosolla to hunt down the killers. When Francis' life is endangered back on Earth, Ezmet's anger unwittingly unleashes the wrath of The Knockers.

The seconds ticked by. Trickles of sweat ran down Ezra's temple. It made his skin itch, but he dared not move a muscle. One moment of distraction and he could lose Christian. His gaze flicked to the wall clock. As though in slow motion, the long hand moved from ten to eleven, then settled next to the shorthand already beneath twelve. More seconds ticked by, and the hand moved again.

Outside, an owl began to hoot, but Ezra didn't dare look out. That moment of distraction was all it took, and the hand moved closer to twelve. Ezra felt his heart thunder in his chest. He tightened his hold on Christian's hand as the sound of wings in flight broke through the dark, silent night.

"Ezra." Christian's raspy voice lured Ezra from his silent vigil.

With trepidation, he looked into the eyes of his beloved.

"You must go. Leave me. Save yourself."

"I'm not leaving you alone," Ezra said. A tear fell on his cheek, followed by another and another.

"You must go, my love. Go to your family. They will know what to do."

"I'm not leaving you alone," Ezra repeated, shaking his head with vehemence.

"They're coming. *The Knockers* are coming."

"They will never take you away from me."

"There is no stopping them. Nothing can stop them."

Three knocks on the door stopped whatever words Ezra was going to say. He inched closer to Christian when the door opened, and three hooded figures stepped inside. Ezra could swear they never took a step. The shadows hid their faces from him, but he didn't need the light of the three moons to know what lay beneath the thick fabric. Ezra crouched low over Christian, sobbing out his fear and anguish into his neck. Any moment now and *The Knockers* would exact their vengeance.

"Please, we are innocent." Ezra's plea fell on deaf ears.

The sound of silence dropped over him. Not even the

animals outside made a sound. Like a tsunami, a whispered word swept through the hut.

Revenge.

Seconds ticked by. The long hand passed the short one. The three hooded figures moved as one, turning their backs on the princes' lifeless bodies. *Payment accepted. Vengeance enacted.*

CHAPTER ONE

"Harder," urged Francis, gripping Ezmet's naked hard-muscled butt, arching his hips up even higher, groaning loudly when Ezmet did as he asked. Ezmet drove his cock deeper with every thrust, slowing down when Francis' grip on his hard shaft tightened, increasing his speed when it relaxed.

Ezmet did as requested. Always, when making love to Francis, he was driven to make Francis feel good. He needed to see to it that whatever sensations he was giving from the heated friction their bodies created together would bring Francis to a slow crescendo. He knew it was the only way to get that moan, and when that happened, he would lean down and bite. He loved to watch Francis grip the sheets before he reached orgasm.

Beneath them, the bed squeaked, every sound forced out in rapid, staccato, uneven rhythms—the perfect accompaniment to their passion. It was music to his ears and drove him to thrust even deeper into the welcoming heat.

From over his shoulder, Francis looked up at him beneath his lids, his long, auburn hair falling over his eyes as he turned his head on the pillow.

Ezmet grinned, baring his teeth. "How much more can you take?"

A smile spread across Francis' features, but when Ezmet moved his hips for an extra hard sharp thrust, Francis narrowed his eyes and let out a hiss. When he opened his eyes once more, there was a clear challenge in their green depths.

"I could do with more," Francis countered. Adding emphasis, he pulled himself from Ezmet's downward thrust. He then twisted and lifted his legs before flipping over. With Francis lying on his back, Ezmet found easier access to the hard cock that lay on Francis' flat belly.

Francis shifted his hips once more, sliding his legs up and wider apart. With his legs almost over his head as he angled into the right position, his change in position made it easier for Ezmet to reenter him. From the way he was positioned, Ezmet knew Francis would be able to see where they joined.

Ezmet let go of the throbbing hot cock. He took up his own and pointed it directly into Francis' hole. He paused for a moment and looked at the loosened muscles. These were spread wider than normal. They had to, so as to compensate for Ezmet's girth. He grinned as he held onto Francis' sweaty hip with one hand. He took his time running one palm down the length of Francis' chest. With the other, he took hold of the cock that lay there. It leaked copious amounts of precum that mingled with their combined sweat. Leaning forward until their lips were a hair's breadth apart, Ezmet breathed in that fresh, sweet, spicy scent he had developed a craving for.

It was a highly addicting scent, and he could never allow anyone else to be alone with Francis. It would be too dangerous, and Ezmet would never tolerate it.

Not for the first time, he wondered how he had ever been granted the gift of his lover. They had met for the first time just over six months before on Ezmet's home planet of Thosolla. Even after all this time, not once had Ezmet heard of anyone who would foolishly cross hundreds of light-years, alone, to an alien planet as a backpacker of all things, and without any identification.

Francis had been detained by the roving night police when he was seen walking along an empty road. At first, the police hadn't known what to do with him. As a human, Francis was not an oddity — humans lived among the Thosollans, after all. No, it had been the fact that his presence had an odd effect on those who arrested him.

Down to the last one of them, those who came in contact with Francis found themselves catering to everything he asked of them. One even made an effort to bake him bread, even though Francis hadn't requested it. When asked why, the only reason the Thosollan had given was that Francis might like it, and it was imperative that Francis be given whatever he wanted. That was when the captain claimed that he thought something was not right. The situation escalated when Francis asked to meet the king, and the captain didn't think twice to take it upon himself to contact a friend, who had a friend in higher places, who had another friend who knew of someone working for the royal family. That man had used his influence to contact Ezmet's personal assistant, who broke royal protocol and took it upon himself to take the request directly to Ezmet.

At first, it had angered Ezmet that Thomas would stoop so low as to ask Ezmet to look into a curiosity that seemed to be brewing in the lower quarters of the capital. In those days, Ezmet had been easily angered, but when Thomas continued with his tale, Ezmet's anger had morphed into amusement and then curiosity. Before he knew it, he was instructing Thomas to connect him with the captain. Six days after Francis had first been picked up, Ezmet found himself looking up at the building that was the capital security headquarters. He didn't know why, but he had no other choice.

Somehow, something drove him to see for himself. He had to know. Who was the human tourist who held such influence over the night police — vampire men who were in their position because of their capabilities? The moment he crossed the threshold of the headquarters and their gazes met across the marbled floor, Ezmet knew he was screwed.

Figuratively.

A gasp brought Ezmet back to the present. He looked down and saw the way Francis had his eyes rolled back. Felt the way his hips met his every thrust. There was no fear in him — no hesitation in accepting his power.

Literally.

Francis was a gift. His gift. A gift only bestowed to very few vampires.

Ezmet continued his thrusts as he leaned forward until their lips met. He smiled to himself, pressing closer when Francis latched onto his lips with a hunger that called to Ezmet's soul. Yes, he had a soul, and for the first time in his long life, he felt complete, replete, satisfied. *Loved.* Such was the intensity of his desire, his feelings for his lover. The thought struck like a whip against his fragile self-control. Something inside him stirred. His cock, already thicker than humanly possible, began to throb. Recognizing the sign, he jerked back from their kiss and balanced his weight over his knees. He was ready. More than ready to lose himself in his lover.

"Don't you dare," came the growl, and Ezmet opened his eyes. His hips stilled — he was unable to resist the command.

"Tell me what you want." Ezmet's whisper drifted across the small space of their bedroom. The sound echoed smoothly, beguilingly, wanting to know what it was that was expected of it.

Ezmet pulled out of Francis, who took his own cock into his hand. Doing a back crawl, Francis moved up the bed until his back was flush against the headboard. Ezmet missed him already, but Francis crooked a finger, and Ezmet had no choice. No, he did have a choice, but he didn't want to resist, so he crawled up between the long, lean legs. He knew what it was his lover wanted, but he still needed to hear the words.

"What do you want me to do?" Ezmet stopped where he was, bent over that gorgeousness of a hard cock, the thick vein pulsing under his gaze.

"Bite me," Francis said, and he moved his hand to expose the vein some more. With his other hand, he pointed a long-nailed, slim finger at the vein that called out to Ezmet. "Right. Here."

There was nothing he could do, and there was nothing he wanted more than to please his lover. His fangs dropped — needle-thin, harder and sharper than any weapons ever invented. With a hiss and a growl, Ezmet bent and bit. Gently. Oh, so gently.

The flavor of his lover's blood tasted more intoxicating than the best brews the royal family of Thosolla indulged in. It flooded Ezmet's mouth, coating the soft tissues there before flowing down his throat. Above him, Francis urged him to suck on him some more, and Ezmet did what he always did when it came to Francis and his requests. He sucked and sucked, feeling the blood enter his system and pacify the monster inside him.

Ezmet was a Thosollan vampire. Even among his kind, he was considered the deadliest. As for the lover who moaned above him, the human who fearlessly gripped his hair and pulled on it until the pain on his scalp throbbed, Francis ruled over him. He was his life.

Francis was his *Mastre*.

CHAPTER TWO

Swaying his hips in time with the classical music playing in the background, Francis tucked his hair behind his ear, only to grimace when the strong scent of garlic hit his nose. He'd have to make sure to wash his hair twice when he took a shower later. Although he loved to cook, one of the pitfalls was he always managed to smell like the ingredients afterward. A smile tugged on his lips. It was a good thing his lover loved his cooking. Otherwise, he'd have to stop, and he never wanted to stop.

When the garlic was minced the way he wanted, he used the sharp edge of the knife to slide the bits onto his palm. He scraped the garlic bits into a flat metal dish where the other ingredients were neatly arranged. Before turning to pick up one of the three potatoes soaking in water, he smiled at the plate full of ingredients, liking the way the vegetables were arranged in a rainbow of colors.

Turning once more to the potatoes, Francis began the meticulous process of first cutting them into thin discs, stacking them, and then slicing them into thin strips. Finally, he diced them. He placed the potatoes back into the water where they had been soaking before and was just about to pick up an earthenware bowl so he could begin cracking the eggs into it when a muffled sound made him stop. He looked over his shoulder in the direction of the bedroom. The sound was followed by that of a door closing from inside. A curve of a smile formed on his lips before he turned back to what he was doing.

Francis began cracking eggs into the bowl in front of him, his movements relaxed and unhurried. He hummed to the music, adding salt and spices into the eggs before whipping them until they were light and frothy. By the time he heard the sound of the bedroom door open fifteen minutes later, he was pouring the egg mixture over the sizzling cheesy vegetables in the pan.

Hard, muscled arms wrapped around his waist, followed by a tender kiss on his nape. Francis leaned into the touch, but he didn't pause from his task.

"Did you sleep well?" Francis asked, stepping back from the stove and turning within the embrace to face his lover.

Instead of an answer, warm, soft lips covered his, and Francis sighed into the kiss. Their tongues met and dueled lovingly with each other, the kiss deepening, their desire rising. It was always like this with Ezmet, and he could never resist him. When they finally parted, it was to lean their foreheads together and breathe in each other's scents.

Francis loved these moments. Ezmet was always tender with him. He really should be afraid of this man, but for some reason, he never had been. Even that first time they'd met, on Thosolla, when he'd finally gotten the chance to take the journey there, he'd never felt even the least bit nervous around his Ezmet. And Ezmet really was his, just as he was Ezmet's.

The first time they'd embraced, he had not felt the slightest twinge of doubt that he belonged to the Thosollan vampire. The sizzle of cooking food distracted him from his thoughts, and he dropped a soft kiss on Ezmet's cheek.

"Go, take a seat. Oh, and there's coffee in the carafe." He didn't wait for Ezmet to reply and turned back once more to his cooking. "This is almost ready."

"Thank you." Ezmet ran his hand tenderly down Francis' thigh when his plate was placed in front of him a few minutes later. He sat at the breakfast table, nursing his coffee, dressed in a long flowing robe of cream linen. The V where the two panels met showed the pale skin of his bare chest, and it was all Francis could do not to reach down and touch the soft skin there.

"I hope you like it," Francis said instead as he smiled down at Ezmet, dropping a kiss on the top of his head before moving away to sit opposite him.

"Ah, sweets, you've not disappointed me yet." Ezmet's voice was like a whisper of a caress. His eyes reflected what Francis knew as the vampire's love for him.

Francis wanted to preen under the indulgent look Ezmet gave him. He watched Ezmet take up a bite, the whites of his teeth a stark contrast to the ripe pinkness of his lips, and it was all Francis could do not to squirm until he heard that his efforts had not been for nothing.

"Oh, this is wonderful," Ezmet said, forking another bite into his mouth. "The mixture of cheeses is just the perfect blend." Ezmet looked up and threw him a kiss. "Perfect as always, my love. Thank you."

Francis swore his heart nearly burst with happiness. There was nothing he wanted more than to please his lover. "There's more, if you want." He didn't mind sounding eager. Not at all.

"Maybe after I'm done with this?"

"Of course. I made enough so you can have your usual second or third serving. Not that I assumed you would want more, but I'd hoped you would."

"No need to hope, sweets. I have a huge appetite."

Francis smiled as he looked down on his plate, his heart thundering in his chest. He forked some of the omelet into his mouth and ate in silence. He didn't need to look up to confirm Ezmet was watching him, probably listening to his heart pound and his blood rush through his veins. Knowing what he did, it should have made him anxious. Instead, he felt his excitement rise, and his lust threatened his logic. Ever since they'd first met, he had felt those ice-blue eyes watching his every move. He should have been creeped out, but with Ezmet, it felt like he was soaking in a warm bath that never cooled. He took up his glass of water and raised his eyes, only to meet Ezmet's loving gaze.

Francis sighed internally as he took a sip of the cool water. Ezmet Reter, king of Thosolla. The most powerful vampire in the known galaxies was his.

Ezmet had stood before him across the marbled floors of the police headquarters all those months ago, looking the very image of a vampire king.

Francis had thought he would never get to see him. His imagination had failed in comparison to the real thing. Behind Ezmet, blurring in the shadows of the night, he could clearly make out three hooded figures. They were slender and incredibly tall. For a moment, Francis had stood mesmerized, only that time it wasn't because of Ezmet's magnificence. It had been because memories had taken a hold over him. He'd seen those three figures before, but that had been back on Earth, when he had been but a little boy accompanying his mother to see the archeological site her team had unearthed from the layers of dirt and rubble that had hidden them for over five hundred years. When his eyes had flicked back to Ezmet, the three figures faded into the dark and became forgotten memories. His eyes filled with the presence of the beautiful, powerful creature.

Ezmet stood half a foot taller than Francis' six feet, his pale skin glowed under the lights, and his eyes were a translucent icy-blue color. His features were sharp and angled, as though they had been sculpted by an artist who had been seeking perfection and succeeded. It was a faultless combination that betrayed his bloodline. Part human, part Thosollan, and part something else. It was that unknown element that made him different among all the rest of his kind. His flowing silvery-white hair hung down over his shoulders and framed his face like some exotic headdress. It emphasized the electric blueness of his eyes. As for his voice, Francis thought his heart would explode from the beauty.

"So, you are the human who has managed to cause havoc amongst my night police." Ezmet had looked him up and down, playing with a pair of white gloves he held in his hands. A faint smile had curled his thin, pale pink lips.

So beautiful.

Hearing the words that came out of his mouth — that had been the moment when Francis had realized what it was that had called him to Thosolla.

Soft. Musical. Deadly.

Ezmet had taken a step forward, only to stop immediately. Francis remembered how it had taken all his strength to control the unbidden desire to tear off Ezmet's clothes and run his hands over his naked skin. He'd stood there, his eyes wide and hungry, all thoughts coming to a halt when, in a blink of an eye, he'd found himself face to face with the vampire king.

Ezmet's fangs had dropped. The two silvery, needle-like apparatuses that should have frightened Francis instead only managed to make the blood rush to his cock and his imagination to go into overdrive. He'd stared at the sharp teeth, his breathing rapid, his heart thundering in his chest, and all he could think of was how it would feel to have them pierce his skin. In hindsight, what he did next — he didn't know who had been more startled, him or Ezmet. There they were, several policemen and royal guards watching their every gesture, and Francis had made that risky move. He had done the very thing he had wondered about, and he acted on it without thought. His tenuous control over his instinct had snapped.

He'd leaned forward until he was so close he could see the

minuscule pores on that smooth, alien skin and cupped Ezmet's face. Then, he'd licked the fangs. Even now, thinking about what he'd done, he could feel his cock harden beneath the pajamas he wore.

"I hope you're thinking about me, sweets. I can smell your arousal." Ezmet licked his lips.

Francis knew it was not to taste the food he'd been eating — rather, it spoke of a much darker, needier drive. He looked up and met Ezmet's gaze. "I was thinking about the first day we met, actually." He didn't know how he kept his voice steady, as his heart was about to explode from wanting.

Ezmet's eyes widened, his mouth open, the fork he'd been about to take a bite from hovering mere inches from his mouth.

Francis took up a bite and chewed on it thoughtfully. "I was thinking about how it felt when I licked your fangs that first time. How they pierced my tongue. It really should have been disgusting, I *am* human, after all, and the thought of blood makes me faint. But you, my dear lover, you made me want to climb you in front of all those police of yours and fuck myself on you."

Ezmet had lowered his fork and now gazed at him with a need that Francis knew would end with his ass in the air and getting fucked to oblivion. But he had to have his fun first. He opened his mouth to continue his tale, to tease the creature, when he found himself whipped out of his chair. One second, the room blurred — the next, his pajamas were ripped off his hips. Ezmet looked down on him, the tips of his fangs barely visible between his lips. It was a clear betrayal of his desire.

Francis laughed in delight when Ezmet cupped his cock in his hand and went down on him. His breath hitched in his throat, and he groaned out loud when the tip of his cock touched the back of Ezmet's throat. He thrust his hips upward so he could get further up there. It felt hot and cold, and the points of those sharp teeth added to the intensity of the sensations. He wanted to keep thrusting into Ezmet's throat. He wanted those fangs to pierce his skin, and he wanted —

"Oh, your majesty, I am so . . . excuse me . . . oh, my lord! Pardon me. Pardon me. Oh, my lord!"

Still trapped in a haze of desire, Francis peeled his eyes open to see who'd spoken. At the same time, Ezmet growled deep in his throat, and before Francis could stop him, Ezmet launched in a blur of a naked, pale body toward the man who'd so rudely intruded upon their privacy.

With one hand, Ezmet held the man up by his throat, held his back against the wall, feet dangling two feet in the air, and face going purple. Ezmet's growl deepened, and Francis found his vision blurring. He closed his eyes to clear them, feeling the anger swell around him. It was like electricity crackling the air with its energy. Francis opened his eyes once more and saw there were more than three people in the room. The shrouded trio was back.

From out of the shadows they appeared, hands outstretched, as though they meant to join with Ezmet's hand. Francis had no doubt what was going to happen next. The old man was going to be killed. He knew he had to stop them. Somehow.

CHAPTER THREE

"Ez? Let him go, my love."

Ezmet let out another growl, his anger an all-encompassing emotion. He looked at the man who had dared step into the same room where his *Mastre* was. He opened his mouth to unleash his verdict when, once more, he heard that voice. It was the one voice that had the power to silence him.

"Ez? Please, my love. Let the man go."

No matter how much he wanted to squeeze the life out of the intruder, he was left with no choice but to do as he was requested. He loosened his hold and held back his anger. But unlike other times, when his actions had been prematurely halted, he didn't resent the interruption. He started to slowly turn around, eager to please his *Mastre*.

Ezmet flashed his fangs and hissed a final warning, but he finally released the old man. He belatedly recognized him as his emissary to Earth. Ezmet's gaze held the ambassador's for a long moment before taking a step back and slowly lowering him, making sure he was in his line of sight so as not to witness Francis' nudity.

"How dare you intrude upon our privacy, Katala?" His voice had lowered to almost a whisper. To all those who knew him, it was a clear sign that he was barely holding on to his anger.

Katala had sunk to his knees, one hand massaging his throat, the other on the floor. He gasped for air as his color slowly returned to normal.

"Ez?"

Ezmet flinched at the feel of a cool hand on the small of his back. Without taking his gaze off Katala, he raised a hand and pointed a finger to the open door.

"Wait for me outside."

"Yes . . . yes, your majesty," Katala gasped out. He didn't even rise. Instead, he crawled on his hands and knees. When he was through the door, he closed it behind him.

Ezmet watched every move with narrowed eyes, gritting his teeth, fighting every muscle to keep himself from leaping through the barrier and killing the old man and whoever else had opened the door to this suite.

Slender arms wrapped around his chest and a tender kiss was placed in the middle of his back.

He closed his eyes and leaned back into the touch as the arms moved higher until they reached his chest. "I apologize for the intrusion, sweets. It won't happen again."

"I'm sure it won't," Francis said into his back, his voice sounding muffled. Another kiss from him, and his arms loosened.

Ezmet dropped his head and turned to face his lover. "I promise you that will never happen again. Forgive me?" He bent his knees so he could gaze into those gorgeous green eyes.

"Oh, Ez, there's nothing to forgive. I'm sure that man, whoever he is —"

"That was Ambassador Katala. He's my representative here on Earth," Ezmet said, sighing in relief that Francis didn't seem angered.

"Okay . . . that Ambassador Katala has learned his lesson. He would never do such a foolish thing as to interrupt us having sex again."

"We weren't having sex!"

"Uhm, yes we were, honey. Now, why don't you go out there and see what drove him to such a foolhardy act as to interrupt your royal majesty's sex life."

Ezmet pouted. "You're being sarcastic."

"Yes, of course, I am. Ez, you were about to kill him in front of me, and he's so old. Are you not feeling in the least bit guilty that you were about to off someone who is old enough to be your great grandfather?"

"He's actually my nephew, sweets," Ezmet said. "He's a full human."

The only display of surprise from Francis was his eyes widening a fraction before he rolled them and stepped away from Ezmet. Immediately, Ezmet felt the loss.

"I can't believe you just said that," Francis said. He crawled back into their bed.

At the show of his naked ass, Ezmet felt his cock stir once more and his mouth watered.

"Ah, ah, ah!" Francis wagged a finger at him. "No! Go. Get out there and find out what that man . . . your nephew who looks like your grandfather . . .came in here risking his life for. I'm pretty sure it was important. Now go!"

Ezmet smiled. His Francis was obviously a little irritated.

"I'll go find out now. Wait here for me?"

Francis' brows rose, and his chin lowered to his chest. "And where do you think I'd be going?"

"Nowhere without me, I hope?"

"You're such a wuss," Francis said, but his smile brightened up the room.

"When it comes to you, I am. I won't take too long," Ezmet said and turned around to open the door.

"Sweetie? Please put something on. I don't want anyone seeing all that skin. Even if that man *is* your nephew."

Ezmet didn't reply, but he threw a reassuring smile at Francis and took up his robe from the floor. He couldn't remember when he'd taken it off. As he did so, he opened the door and closed it softly behind him. His smile vanished when he saw Katala sitting on one of the three sofas in the middle of the living room. He flicked a glance at the Thosollan royal guards standing stiffly against the walls. There were seven in all. Ezmet's left eye narrowed.

"Nephew? What brings you here?"

"I'm sorry, your majesty. Uncle. I came as soon as I heard the news, and it didn't enter my mind that you would have a companion."

"His name is Francis, and he is not my companion. He's my . . . fiancé."

Katala's eyes went wide as saucers. He threw a look between Ezmet and the closed bedroom door several times.

"Uncle? Does he know he's your fiancé?" He gulped.

Ezmet smiled to himself when Katala dropped the use of his title. "Not yet, but he will. I was going to ask him after I . . . let's just say I was going to ask him before you rudely disturbed us."

"Once more, I'm sorry." Katala grimaced and swallowed again.

"So?"

"What?" Katala was scratching at his cheek, still looking at the bedroom door and not paying attention to Ezmet.

"Why are you here?"

Katala jerked and straightened in his seat. His hand fell from his face. "I bring you bad news. Our cousin, Ezra, and his husband Christian were found dead, murdered in the basilica."

"When?" The news was both worrying and devastating. Ezra and Christian had only just gotten married. Ezmet strode to one of the chairs and sat on it.

"Last night. But there's more," Katala said in a hurry when Ezmet opened his mouth to ask more question. "All signs point to *The Knockers* doing it."

"*The Knockers*?" This time, it was Ezmet's brows that rose

210

high on his forehead. "Why are they saying it's they who murdered a royal prince? What great crime did Ezra or Christian commit? That Ezra married his lover of twenty years?"

"The investigators said the act was one of revenge. At least, that's what they told me. I haven't got all the details."

Ezmet regarded his nephew for a long moment, studied his face to observe for signs of lying. He didn't see anything. "Katala, the last time *The Knockers* exacted their justice was over five hundred years ago. During my father's time."

"That is what I also thought of, Uncle, but the investigators said that all the signs and conditions were met exactly as *The Knockers* would. But revenge? I didn't know that the trio would stoop so low as to exact revenge. For whom?"

As Ezmet leaned back, his lips thinned and he shook his head. "They don't. They exact justice to keep the sacred covenant in place, not to spit on it or to instill fear in our peoples."

"Which brings me to the third part of my bad news. There's an uprising in Thosolla as we speak. The people say that what *The Knockers* did was not according to our sacred laws, that Ezra and Christian were innocent souls. *The Knockers* must be brought before the people and be judged."

Ezmet scoffed. "They think to judge the judges?"

Katala shrugged. "The people are afraid. The fact that the last time anyone had heard or seen *The Knockers* was five hundred or so years ago has made many question their existence. Some are even questioning their right to exist. They think that it should be a thing to question and doubt, as no one has as yet determined their origins."

"Are you questioning them as well, nephew?"

"No, Uncle. I was taught well by the royal tutors and have found their presence to be the one factor that keeps the peace on Thosolla. However, the people have not, and many are thinking of the trio as mere fiction. Urban legend."

"What do you want me to do?"

"Uncle — your majesty — you need to go back with me. Back to Thosolla. You need to show yourself to our people and appease their fears. Things are escalating to dangerous levels there. Only your presence will quell their panic."

"You think they are strong enough, that they have the numbers to succeed?" Ezmet leaned back and considered Katala.

"There's only three hundred of us versus the millions of humans there. Not to mention the Thosollans themselves, both the half-breeds and the pures."

"We are all Thosollans, Katala. How many times have I said that?"

"I am merely verbalizing what many have come to think, Uncle. I am human, but I am also Thosollan. Of course, I know who and what I am."

"What do you think of Francis?"

Katala threw another glance toward the closed door before turning back to Ezmet. "I would advise that you leave him here, but only for the short while!"

Ezmet threw him a glare.

Katala rapidly added, "He may be in danger on Thosolla. Ease your people first, then bring him into our fold. He will need to be assimilated into our family, as well, so it is best to let them get used to your having a companion before bringing him planet-side."

Ezmet considered his nephew's words and found no fault in them. "I'll have to talk to Francis, but I'm afraid he won't like it."

"What won't I like? What's going on?"

Ezmet quickly turned around in his chair. Francis stood in the bedroom's open doorway. Like him, Francis had put on a robe. He didn't know how many he would have killed if Francis had walked out naked. He glanced at the guards, who had turned their heads in Francis' direction. From the looks on

212

their faces, they were affected by his presence just like the night police had been. Ezmet sighed. He really needed to marry his Francis, and soon, or lose all sanity and kill anyone who looked at him.

CHAPTER FOUR

Francis considered the two men before him. His eyes flicked toward the guards standing by the walls and he narrowed his gaze at them. He had told Ezmet he didn't want any bodyguards around on their vacation. No one should be able to reach them where they were holed up. Mount Toubkal was not only a private and highly secure property of the Reters, but it was also the highest peak on the damaged Earth. There were no communities, no cities, within a twelve-hundred-mile radius. Only water.

"Leave us," he whispered.

There was no hesitation. The guards bowed their heads as one and silently filed out of the room. They didn't even ask for either Ezmet's or Katala's leave. Francis walked over to sit by Ezmet's feet, not missing the way Katala's eyes had widened in apparent surprise. Francis smiled to himself when Ezmet dropped a hand over his head as he leaned against his lover's leg. He looked up at Katala and saw the way the Thosollan was looking at him. The shock was apparent, but the shadow of fear in his eyes made Francis smile wider. He obviously didn't know what to make of Francis, and Francis didn't want it any other way. He didn't like explaining anything to anyone. He didn't need to explain to Ezmet, and he was the one who counted the most in his life.

"What is it that I would not like, Ez?" He didn't look away from Katala. Ezmet's hand stilled for a moment on his head before he continued his petting.

"I may have to go back to Thosolla, sweet. Would you

214

mind staying here?"

"Why would I not like it if you leave, Ez?"

"You'd be alone here, and I would worry."

Francis turned to look up at Ezmet. The hand on his head dropped to his nape. "I wouldn't mind. And why should you worry? You've left me alone before when you attended your cousin's wedding."

Ezmet shrugged. "I worry if you're not around. You'd be alone."

"Something's happened on Thosolla, hasn't it?" Francis rubbed on Ezmet's leg.

"Yes." Ezmet made a grim nod. "My cousin and his husband have been killed, and there's some rioting in the streets. Ezra and Christian's wedding was the one I attended. They were quite popular."

"Then you should go."

"But what about you? Are you going to be safe?"

"I'm quite certain I'll be alright."

"If you're sure?"

"Very." Francis grinned reassuringly at Ezmet before he looked at Katala. "Ambassador Katala, have you eaten?"

"No, I haven't." Katala looked at him nervously then at Ezmet and then back at Francis.

"Oh, good! I'll just heat up some of the breakfast I made earlier." Francis pushed himself off the floor, using Ezmet's knee as leverage. "Ez here interrupted our breakfast, and I'm a little hungry. Give me a few minutes."

Francis dropped a kiss on Ezmet's head and walked toward the kitchen. He looked at the food he'd made earlier and decided it was good enough to reheat. He remembered the guards he'd asked to leave as he walked over to the three-door refrigerator. He tapped the touchscreen on the door and checked its contents. Ten minutes later, he poked his head out of the kitchen door and saw that Ezmet and Katala were still deep in conversation.

"Ez?" At the sound of his voice, both Thosollans looked up. "Food's ready. Oh, and Katala? Please ask the guards to come and join us." He didn't wait to see if they would do as he asked. He arranged the food on four platters and placed them on the counter where everyone could make their choices. For Ezmet and himself, he took up two dishes and plated them. When he turned around, one plate in each hand, he saw the doorway crowded. Katala looked hesitant, while the guards behind him were sniffing appreciatively at the air. Francis grinned.

"Come! Let's eat. Where's Ezmet?"

Katala walked over to the counter and took up a plate. "He went back to your bedroom."

"All right. Go ahead and begin without us, I'll just go and get him. I don't want to have to reheat the food all over again." Francis placed the plates on the table and left the men to the fare. When he opened the bedroom door, he walked into an empty room. Frowning, he looked at the closed bathroom door.

"Ez? Are you in there?" Francis knocked on the door. When he didn't hear anything, he turned the knob and opened the door to an empty bathroom. He exhaled noisily, wondering where Ezmet had gone to. A movement on the balcony to his right caught his attention, and he let out a relieved sigh. He slid open the glass door and stepped out. Sitting in one of the three deck chairs was Ezmet, and he seemed to be lost in thought.

"Hey, what are you doing out here? Breakfast is ready. Again."

Ezmet didn't move, so Francis moved closer. This time, Ezmet turned his head. That was when Francis saw the tears. He hurried over and curled up on Ezmet's lap.

"Oh, sweetie, what's wrong? Is it your cousins?" He took

Ezmet's face between his hands and gazed into his eyes. The tears flowed faster. "Talk to me?"

Ezmet didn't speak. Instead, he wrapped his arms around Francis and buried his face into his neck. Francis hummed softly, knowing his lover needed to let out his grief. He hadn't known or met Ezra or Christian, but it was obvious to him that Ezmet had loved his cousins. When the tears finally dried, Ezmet still didn't speak. But from the way he was breathing, it was clear that he'd somehow fallen asleep.

Francis lay in Ezmet's arms, watching the shifting cloud-bank undulate beneath them. The sun was hidden behind a thicker layer of clouds above them, so he didn't feel the heat. He closed his eyes and settled more comfortably, making sure he didn't move so much as to wake Ezmet. He could still remember, as a young boy, how the clouds were feared. Thanks to the technology the Thosollans had loaned them, the atmosphere was now cleaner and breathable without having to wear a gas filter.

Sitting safe in the comfort of his lover's arms, Francis allowed his thoughts to wander, thinking of how his life had changed ever since he'd met Ezmet six months before. Before that time, he'd had no obvious idea what his purpose in life had been, only that he needed to find Ezmet. Now he had a clearer picture, but there was something else he was missing. He released a sigh. Ezmet's trip back to Thosolla worried him. Time was his enemy, but with Ezmet beside him, he would have the chance to beat it. He would be okay for a while, but not for much longer. They needed to bond.

When Francis next opened his eyes, he found himself lying in bed with the comforter draped over him. He glanced at the window and saw that outside the sun had lowered. A glance at the digital clock on the wall opposite the bed showed that it was not even noon. It was an improvement. He could still remember the days that lasted only a few hours, and still, those days had been dark.

No, Earth had not seen daytime for hundreds of years. That they were getting more and more sunlight these past few years was a gift, and it was all thanks to the Thosollans and their aid.

He stretched until he felt his muscles strain before he got out of bed. After a quick splash of water on his face, he wiped the dampness off with a towel and went out to the bedroom. Looking about, he didn't see anyone around, but his stomach growled and he shook his head. He'd missed breakfast twice that morning—should he take a third chance at it? The suite was empty when he walked out of the bedroom, but he didn't mind. He knew that Ezmet was somewhere, just not there.

His hand stilled midair, reaching out to open the fridge, frozen at his realization. The more he thought about it, the more it became clearer that yes, he could feel Ezmet and had done so for some time. In fact, the more he thought about it, he knew that somehow, that had been the reason why he had traveled to Thosolla in the first place. The pull he had felt had been the driving need to be near Ezmet. Although Francis couldn't quite understand it, he found that he didn't mind it. It didn't scare him, either. All he knew for certain was that being with Ezmet completed him. The question was, did Ezmet feel the same about him? He pulled on the doors and opened the fridge.

Francis looked at the plate of food inside. It was wrapped in plastic, ready to be taken out and heated up. On it was a note. Taking it up, he opened it and smiled at what Ezmet had written.

I'm sorry I left without saying goodbye, but I won't be gone long. I promise I'll be back as soon as I settle the problem back home. Three days max if I have anything to say about it. If I can't, I'll send some-one to bring you up. Wait for my word. I love you. Ez

Francis smiled and pressed a kiss onto the paper. "I love

you, too."

His eyes filled, for he'd never imagined Ezmet would be the first to say the words. Well, not say, but he had written them. He would make sure the note never got lost so he could remind Ezmet, should he forget. Not that Ezmet was the type to forget. He vowed that as soon as he and Ezmet were together once more, he'd make sure he would say the words and kiss him to oblivion.

Whistling a tune under his breath, Francis watched his reflection on the glass as his food heated up. His reflection looked content. He felt content.

CHAPTER FIVE

Ezmet worried over his lip. He had been staring at the report Katala had handed over to him as soon as he'd entered the royal palace. He'd wasted no time in traveling to Thosolla and had arrived within hours of leaving a sleeping Francis. No matter how many times he read it, he still couldn't understand how *The Knockers* could have gotten involved in the death of Ezra and Christian. In fact, he knew there was no way they could be involved. Across from him sat his Uncle Maxim and Aunt Xephine. Among the royal family, they were the ones he was closest to, and seeing them broken angered him. They didn't deserve their grief. Ezra had been beloved by all Thosollans, so whoever had murdered him and his husband had more than just him or the royal family to answer to. Thosollan and humans would drain their blood.

"You need to do something, Ezmet," Uncle Maxim said. His hands trembled as they gripped the arms of the chair he sat on. "Whoever has done this to my son and son-in-law needs to be found. Immediately."

"Ezmet knows what he's doing, Maxim. That's why he's the king and not you." Xephine turned a grave face to Ezmet. "Nephew, I grieve for my son, and it's breaking my heart. I know it's painful for you as well. He and you were very close."

"We were, Aunt. Ezra was like a brother to me."

"I know." Aunt Xephine sighed. She looked down at the handkerchief crumpled in her hand. "However, Ezra's murder is only a symptom of a bigger problem. *The Knockers'* suspected involvement is something you should look into at once. Once you find out where they are, you'll find his murderer."

"I know, Aunt." Ezmet met his aunt's gaze and saw the pain in her eyes. His aunt was most assuredly one of the most astute of all the royals. He could only imagine the hurt and confusion she felt over not knowing who or what had killed her son and son-in-law.

"One more thing, Ezmet, before your uncle and I take our leave. It has come to my understanding that you have taken up with a young human. Is he your companion, a simple lover, or is he someone who should be looked into by the family? I can find out, but I am too depressed, and I would rather hear it from you before anyone else."

Ezmet looked away, annoyed that his aunt would bring Francis up now. He knew he shouldn't have hoped that she wouldn't know—that had been foolish of him. Xephine would eventually know everything. She had connections that he could only dream about.

"I didn't want to tell anyone, not until after I'd found Ezra's killer, but since you asked, Francis is my fiancé."

Xephine gave a brief nod. "All right. Let me know when you're ready to reveal his presence in your life. Now, one last question before we go."

"And what question is that?"

"Is Francis your *Mastre*?"

"Xephine! Of all the questions to ask your king," Maxim huffed and turned a red face to Ezmet. "I apologize, Ezmet."

"Oh, don't be foolish, Maxim." Xephine stood and smoothed her hands over her skirt. "As if Ezmet can hide anything from me. Now, is he or isn't he?"

Ezra took a deep breath. "He is."

"Oh, my . . ." Xephine paled and swayed, and for a moment, Ezmet thought she would fall, but she grabbed on the arm of her chair and dropped back into the chair, taking deep breaths.

"Are you sure, nephew?" Maxim stood behind Xephine and rubbed her shoulders. "Are you very sure?"

"I am, Uncle. I am." Now that he had actually said the words out loud, he felt more stable in himself. Fulfilled.

"Have you told him?" Xephine asked. She touched Maxim's hand on her right shoulder as though to steady herself. Her hand trembled visibly.

Ezmet frowned. Xephine never trembled. He shook his head and ran a hand through his hair.

"Not yet, but I did leave him a note telling him I loved him and that I was going to bring him here in three days' time." He smiled at his aunt and uncle, but flinched back when they glared at him.

"You left him a note? What's wrong with you, boy?"

"Maxim! Don't you dare raise your voice at your king!" Xephine rose to her feet and placed both her hands on the table. "What were you thinking? Oh, Ezmet, if I could slap the back of your head like I did when you were a child, I'd do it. But I'm a lady, and I respect you, no matter that you are . . . never mind. All right, hand over the details to where you left him. I'm sending my people to get him and place him under tight security."

"He doesn't need security, Aunt," Ezmet said. His voice dwindled to a whisper when her eyes narrowed. "He won't like it."

A feminine brow rose.

Ezmet sank into his chair. "He's at my mountain home down on Earth. Mount Toubkal."

"You left him on . . ." Xephine closed her eyes and took a deep breath. Her nostrils looked pinched when she finally opened her eyes. If glares could kill Thosollan vampires, he'd be dead. "I'll let you know as soon as he's on Thosolla. He doesn't stay there. No *Mastre* deserves to stay on that dead planet."

"It's not dead, it's recovering, actually."

"Tell me that in a century and I'll think about it. Now, I go." Xephine turned around and walked toward the door. "Maxim, come. We have a *Mastre* to rescue. The gods save us from immature vampires who think they are king without their *Mastres*."

The door closed after Xephine and Maxim.

Ezmet closed his eyes and leaned back into his chair. He had not had a moment of rest since arriving back on Thosolla, and he desperately missed Francis. Whenever he was around his lover, he felt calm and in control. Even when he'd lost his temper with Katala, he'd still been in control. For hundreds of years, he'd wondered when he would finally lose his hold on his sanity. With Francis beside him, he wouldn't have that worry.

CHAPTER SIX

Francis sat on the very chair he'd last been in with Ezmet. Before him, the sun began to drop behind the clouds, its last rays of warmth touching his skin. It didn't take long before everywhere turned black. There was none of the afterglow of Thosolla's sun. The moon that he knew was out there somewhere remained where it was—hidden behind thick clouds of volcanic ash. Once, over a thousand years ago, Earth had been a thriving planet.

The simultaneous eruptions of the volcanoes around the world had hastened Earth's atmospheric death. Ash released into the atmosphere already compromised by ozone holes and pollution pushed the planet's temporary cooling. The larger particles had wreaked havoc over the surface, causing cataclysmic damage. The smaller particles formed the dark clouds in the troposphere. The curious shades of colors had fascinated the population at first, causing them to ignore the signs. It hadn't taken long for the land and seas to turn into poison and the rain to acid. For a planet that was already on the edge of global warming, the cataclysmic events had only hastened the inevitable planetary catastrophe.

Earth died three years later when the land cooled, the seas rose, and the earthquakes began. If it hadn't been for the arrival of the Thosollans, humans would have become extinct. Citing a long-forgotten link between humans and Thosollans, they had come, and they had helped. They even opened their planet, so those who chose to risk space travel could seek asylum. Many had volunteered, but more refused to leave Earth.

Those who chose to leave were only now starting to come back.

Francis and his parents had been among those who had come back to Earth, over twenty years ago. Two years later, his mother had died. He and his mother had been part of an archeological team on the outskirts of the dam that held the waters back from the Thosollan fort. The land had been a gift given to the royal family of Thosolla, as partial payment for the aid given. That was where he was now — this vacation home which Ezmet hadn't visited until six months ago when he had first brought Francis there.

After the earthquake that had buried Francis' mother alive, it had taken his father's team another weak to find him. They'd thought him dead when they finally found his broken body, but he'd opened his eyes and breathed. He didn't know what had happened, for he could barely remember anything. What he did remember were the voices that never let up encouraging him to breathe and have faith.

The voices that sounded like thunder and the gentlest of his mother's kiss on his cheek. Somehow, Francis knew the voices belonged to the same trio he kept seeing lurking around now whenever Ezmet's emotions were heightened. Curiously, he didn't feel frightened whenever they appeared. Instead, he always felt at home and at peace. Not like right now, though. His head ached, and he could feel his energy level sinking.

A smile curled on his lips. At least he'd had his time with Ezmet. He couldn't wait to be with Ezmet again. He'd only been gone two days. Francis closed his eyes, feeling drowsy all of a sudden. He'd barely eaten the food he'd prepared for himself, and now he didn't even have the will to load the dishes into the sanitizer. Maybe if he slept a little, he would wake up feeling better. Just then, a thump from inside the suite made him look over his shoulder.

His brows furrowed. There were no animals here, and he was sure he'd placed everything in the sink. Another thump followed by a curse made him sit up in his chair. His heart thundered in his chest as he looked around him, trying to assess whether he could get out safely and not be found. But then the doors to the bedroom opened and robed figures rushed in. Francis froze at the sight. He'd never seen these people before, but they were too tall and slender to be fully human. Thosollans. He met the gaze of one of the figures. The blue eyes revealed nothing. Even when he raised his weapon and pointed it at Francis, it revealed nothing. Francis reached out.

"No. Please."

A soft popping sound came from the weapon held up to him, and it was immediately followed by a sharp pain on his forearm. Francis looked at the odd-looking thing that had penetrated his skin. The world tilted, his vision blurred, and then he blacked out.

The next time he opened his eyes, Francis found himself lying on a bed, a soft blanket tucked over his chest. He also felt like he'd been washed and cleaned, and that realization made him feel uneasy and dirty. He frowned down at himself, lifting the edge of the blanket, hoping he was still wearing the clothes he'd been in. He wasn't, and the feeling of violation made bile rise in his throat. Closing his eyes, he mentally checked the rest of his body and thankfully didn't feel any of the soreness he usually had after a round of sex. However, his right forearm felt really tender, and he raised it to see what was causing the pain. Memories of something being shot into his arm rose, and he rubbed on the spot. He'd been drugged, of that he was certain. Probably so he could be kidnapped.

Looking about, he found he was in a basic looking room, much like a hospital. He wasn't sure if he was in one, though.

The last time he'd been hospitalized had been when he was rescued. Before attempting to sit up, he checked himself over once more. Discovering he wasn't feeling dizzy, he pushed aside the blanket and swung his legs over the side of the bed. There were no slippers, and the floor looked cold. Grimacing, he pointed a toe and touched the surface. Flinching at the icy temperature, he knew he couldn't risk getting sick. He needed to stay strong so he could escape.

Francis didn't know where he was, so his plans were going nowhere until he did. The minutes passed until Francis lost track of time. When he thought he had been sitting there for at least fifteen minutes, the door opposite him slid open to reveal a woman in a nurse's uniform. He frowned at her broad smile and flinched back when she took his wrist in her hand.

"How are you feeling?" Her accent didn't reveal where she came from, but Francis didn't hear any judgment in it.

"A little sore. Otherwise, I'm good. Where am I?"

"I'll give you something for the pain. It's your right arm, isn't it?" Francis nodded, and the nurse let go of his arm. She turned to look at a masked man standing at the door. "Please have them bring in the medical tray?"

The man gave a brief nod. He disappeared but came back almost immediately, this time pushing a metal tray before him. In the course of the next few minutes, the nurse had given him another injection and had rubbed an ointment over the sore spot. Her movements were sure and methodical, but she didn't say anything to him other than checking whether she'd hurt him or not. Francis didn't think she was there to hurt him, especially when she kept patting his arm. When she left with the masked man and the door closed behind them, Francis' confusion only increased. He checked the door, flinching at the coldness of the floor and found that it was locked. Sighing, he went back to bed and lay still, staring at the ceiling. After a few minutes, the overhead lights went dark. When nothing happened, Francis closed his eyes and sighed again. *Might as well get some sleep.*

The next time Francis opened his eyes, he didn't bother thinking about what time it was. He'd read about this somewhere, where a subject was denied any concept of time. It was a common type of torture, he guessed, so thinking about it would only confuse him more. He began to count, and when he reached one hundred eighty, the lights came on.

Another one-eighty, and the door unlocked. Once more, the nurse came in to check him out. Once more, the masked man stood at the door. He didn't bother to interact, just allowed her to do her job. Six hundred had the nurse give him another pat. One-eighty more and she and the masked man left. One-twenty and the lights went off. Francis smirked. *Rinse. Repeat.* He knew this was going to be a boring wait.

By the time Francis had gone through the whole act four more times, he knew he was getting impatient. Still, he allowed everything to happen. He had to know what they were trying to get out of him. To pass the time, he thought about Ezmet and wondered if he knew what had happened.

A thump outside the door made him tense up. He waited for something to happen, but when nothing did, he relaxed once more in his bed. At least whatever it was they were giving him was keeping him from getting hungry. However, it was worrying that he didn't feel the need to relieve himself.

Francis lay down and thought of Ezmet. He wanted to cry. His heart rate began to increase as his eyes drifted closed and he felt tears building behind his eyes. He missed Ezmet, wanting him to be there for him. With Ezmet's image in his mind, he began to pray that he would be taken out of this hole. He didn't know how long he was going to last. Without knowing what day or time it was, he didn't know how much time he had left. The only wish he wanted was that he would still be alive to see Ezmet once more. And then he could die happy.

CHAPTER SEVEN

Ezmet looked out the window. Outside the palace, the sky had darkened and looked almost black. Min, Eze, and Xem, the three moons of Thosolla, were high in the sky, their radiance cast onto Thosolla, lending a gentle purple light all around. The shimmering night-blooming flowers nodded in the wind, their scent perfuming the air. A flap of wings, followed by the shrill cries of the lunar bats, drew Ezmet's gaze, but he couldn't see them. He'd been back on Thosolla for three days, and he was no closer to finding out who had killed his cousins. He was missing Francis keenly. All he could see were the green eyes of his lover, the way their corners crinkled when he found something amusing, the skin on his neck going taut when he threw his head back in laughter.

Physically, Francis was more than beautiful, at least to Ezmet's eyes, but what really drew him to Francis was the calm manner with which he approached everything. Ezmet knew there was something wrong, but he didn't want to ask Francis. He knew he could always investigate without Francis knowing, but Ezmet felt it would be a betrayal. The more he thought about his lover, the more he wanted him here. On Thosolla. Now.

A knock on the door pulled him from his thoughts. Ezmet frowned when Katala stepped inside before he could permit entry. Katala closed the door behind him and gave a brief nod before speaking.

"Your Majesty, there's someone outside wanting to see you. He says it's urgent."

Ezmet slumped in his chair, sorely tempted to leave all kingdom matters on Katala's shoulders. He just wanted to find the killers and get back into Francis' arms.

"What's so urgent, Katala? What's more urgent than finding Ezra's killers?"

"It's Dr. Michael Nikolaj. The archeologist. From Earth."

"Show him in."

Katala gave a brief nod and opened the door. He peered outside and waved someone in. Ezmet stood up when a middle-aged man stepped into the room. He hadn't realized that the man was on Thosolla. Katala made the introductions and stepped out after Ezmet thanked him.

"Dr. Nikolaj. What can I do for you?" Ezmet waved toward the chair in front of his desk. He observed the man make a hesitant bow before sitting down.

"Ah, I'm so sorry to disturb you, your majesty," Nikolaj said. He ran a nervous hand over a thigh, then his hair before he settled into his chair.

"That's all right. If I had known you were on Thosolla, I would have invited you over. Francis has spoken of you."

"He has?" Nikolaj looked startled for a moment. The surprise turned to confusion, and his brows lowered. "Ah, your majesty . . . Francis spoke of me?"

Ezmet frowned at the man's confusion. "Of course he did." He gave a small smile. "Now, what can I do for you?"

"Ah, I . . . ah . . . look, your majesty —"

"Call me Ezmet, Nikolaj."

Nikolaj blinked several times, speechless. Ezmet gritted his teeth. Patience had never been one of his virtues.

"Ezmet? Uhm, I have sent you several messages over these past months and never got a reply. I thought I'd risk your anger by coming here myself."

Ezmet frowned. "Messages? What about?"

Nikolaj brightened up. He sat up straighter and smiled

broadly. "I found them, Ezmet. I found them."

Ezmet stilled. His heart thundered inside his chest, and for a moment, he felt himself splinter. "Where?"

"It was right there, in front of me, and I never . . . Ezmet, it was there all along. In La Seu."

"When? When did you find them?"

"Six months ago. I sent your office message after message, but for some reason, you never replied. Ten years ago, I had them dig deeper until we found an entrance into the basilica. As I was saying, we were able to break through the layers of earth six months ago. And then, five months ago, we were able to enter. Everything inside is intact—from the pointed archways to the ribbed vaults, everything. Even the gargoyles are intact. It is as though the earth gently turned over and covered the basilica, preserving it. It's in perfect condition." Nikolaj grinned and shifted in his seat, looking as if he wanted to jump up and down in his excitement. "They are as if they had been there, waiting for me to find them."

"Are you sure it is them?"

"Yes." Nikolaj nodded effusively. "They are just as you told me they looked. Dark, mysterious, hooded figures, but they are trapped inside the basilica. They have been made as if they are a part of the building."

"The priests had imprisoned them there, yes." Ezmet fisted his hands, unable to contain his own excitement. "Is there any way we can get them out?"

"I don't know yet. That's why I'm here. I need your permission."

"You have it." Ezmet rang for his assistant. When the man entered, he introduced him to Nikolaj. "Thomas. Make sure that he gets everything he asks for."

Thomas nodded but didn't look up. He had been tapping on his pad, inputting all of Ezmet's instructions. When he finally finished, he looked up. "Is there anything more, your majesty? I can start on these immediately."

"Send in some refreshments and something for Dr. Nikolaj."

Thomas nodded and left the room, quietly closing the door behind him. Ezmet walked around his desk and sat on the chair beside Nikolaj.

"Now, tell me. Why are you really here, Nikolaj? Francis is on Earth. You could have just told him you wanted to speak to me."

The look of confusion returned. Nikolaj looked at him quizzically. "Ezmet, I don't know what you're talking about. Earlier you said that Francis had spoken of me. How is that even possible?"

The realization hit Ezmet. "Are you saying that Francis hasn't called you? We've been vacationing on Earth for five months now."

"I'm sorry, but you are confusing me, Ezmet."

"Francis came here to Thosolla six months ago, and we met. I recognized him as your son. I couldn't miss it, not with the way you two resemble each other. We've been together ever since. There was a family emergency, and I had to leave him in my house on Mount Toubkal. But don't worry, my aunt, Xephine, has sent my guards to get him so he can join me here. I haven't asked him yet, but I intend to marry him. He is my *Mastre*, after all."

All the time he was talking, Nikolaj was shaking his head. "I don't know what you're talking about. My son had been in a coma for over ten years. He and his mother were together when an earthquake struck. His mother, my Ana, she didn't make it. The rescuers were able to dig him out, but he'd been exposed to the elements for too long. He was aware for a while, but the toxins in the air had done their damage. He fell into a coma three days after he was found. I thought you knew that."

Ezmet could only stare at Nikolaj. He didn't know what to think. He closed his eyes and shook his head. "Hold on, I'll show you that I am not fooling you." He stood and walked back to his seat. Opening a drawer, he pulled out his private tablet and showed Nikolaj. He had taken hundreds of pictures of Francis. Alone. In the kitchen cooking. In bed, sleeping peacefully. There were several with him naked, but it was in a separate folder, and he didn't show them to Nikolaj.

"This is my *Mastre*. This is Francis. The identity he showed when we first met said that his full name was Francis Nikolaj. I asked him how he was related to you, and he said that you were his father. He looks exactly like you, Nikolaj. Is he lying?"

Nikolaj flipped through the images, staring at each one, the tips of his fingers tracing Francis' profile. "How can this be?" His voice broke, and tears began to fall. "How can he be alive?" He looked up and met Ezmet's gaze. "They called me . . . the hospital. They told me he'd died. I buried him six months ago."

Ezmet considered Nikolaj, but saw nothing but grief. There was something strange going on, and he needed to figure it out.

"You said that you had been trying to send me messages. Which office did you send those messages to?"

Nikolaj continued to look down at the image of a laughing Francis. Ezmet had taken the picture in their bedroom only the week before. He had been tickling Francis and had captured the perfect moment. "As always, I send all my messages through the security division. Through Lady Xephine."

CHAPTER EIGHT

Eleven o'clock.

Francis didn't have to see a clock to know what time it was. He opened his eyes to the darkness, but unlike the other times, he could see very well. In fact, it was as if he were a part of the darkness. Something tugged at his senses, and he turned in the direction it came from.

The bare walls rippled, and the trio stepped through. There was no stopping the inevitable. Francis' feet hit the floor, but he didn't feel the cold as he stood facing the door.

The doorknob turned easily under his hand, and Francis pushed the door open. He met no one as he walked the length of the dimly lit corridor. He turned one corner, and then another, not needing a map to know where he was going.

Something moved to his left, and he stopped to watch in detached curiosity as the nurse, and the masked man who was her constant companion, walked toward him. Probably on their way to the room he'd just left. Of course they didn't see him—neither did they react when they passed through him. Francis continued on his way until he reached the end of the fifth corridor. The tugging felt stronger here, and he felt rising excitement within him. They were there. The ones who needed to see what had to be shown.

Forty-five minutes until midnight.

Francis didn't hurry, but it was getting more and more difficult to ignore the call. His target was near—he could feel their hearts beating in excitement. There was an exultation to their rhythms, a joy of committing. That joy would not last.

The elation would turn to terror once they realized there was nowhere to run.

He stopped in front of a door and sent out his senses to see inside the room. Once there, he saw a man and a woman talking excitedly. Francis recognized them for what they were. They were vampires. Not mixed, though. They had been humans once.

"He's on his way," the woman said. Her grin was one of deep satisfaction.

"How sure are you that we're not going to be discovered? He always knows, Xephine," the man said.

"He has always counted on us to keep the kingdom safe, even from its own people. He trusts us . . . me, explicitly." Xephine ran her palms down her skirt. "He has to pay for Ezra's death."

"Ezra was a fool! He shouldn't have been caught. All he needed to do was to take Ezmet into his confidence, and then leave us to do the rest."

Xephine sighed and started to pace. "I know, Maxim. Ezra had to marry that human of his, and look where that got him. All our hard work and they had to ruin it all."

"Well, who would've thought *The Knockers* would find out?" the man who had to be Maxim said.

"Which is why it is so important that we keep Ezmet from bonding with his *Mastre*! If they get together, they will be unstoppable."

"I'm not worried," Maxim said, standing up to pour himself a drink. "We got rid of my brother and his *Mastre* . . . we can handle Ezmet. He doesn't know about Francis."

At the mention of his name, Francis turned to take a closer look at Maxim. Forty minutes until midnight. Beside him, the trio were getting agitated, and he sent them soothing thoughts. They had to have the evidence before they could exact justice. They had time.

"He trusts us so much . . . he doesn't even know we have Francis. The drugs we're pumping into him will eventually kill him."

"I wish we could hurry up that part. I hate waiting," Xephine said. She joined Maxim where he stood and took the glass from his hand.

"Well, he's coming." Maxim poured himself another glass and drank from it.

"I still don't understand who or what this Francis is," Xephine said as she took a seat on the sofa in front of a window. She frowned up at Maxim. "He should be dead. Well, he was, and then he was alive. How is that?"

"The mystery of the *Mastre* has always been that, a mystery. Something that no one can explain. Even before Thosolla, our family always had the *Mastre* to contend with. And *The Knockers*."

"Well, we got rid of them once, we can do so again. We cannot allow Ezmet to gain his full inheritance. If he does, we're finished."

"Oh, we'll end him. Don't ever doubt that."

"Can't we just shoot his ship down?"

"Xephine! Have patience, my love." Maxim sent Xephine an indulgent smile.

"I hate waiting," Xephine repeated.

Waiting was something Francis enjoyed. With waiting, he could discover and learn more. Learning was something he'd found he truly enjoyed. The trio settled beside him, and they waited.

Time passed. Thirty minutes until midnight.

Francis reached out into space and time and closed his eyes. He searched until he felt the familiar touch. His lover was angry, his thoughts full of revenge. There was a momentary pause, and then, Ezmet felt his presence.

Francis?

Francis wanted to respond, but their bond was not yet

complete. Instead, he sent Ezmet images that he was safe.

How is this possible?

With a gentle touch, he soothed his lover, sending him calming thoughts filled with love.

I am coming for you.

Francis didn't respond.

Fifteen minutes until midnight. Francis let out a sigh and opened his eyes. Inside the room, Xephine had a deep frown on her forehead as she looked around her.

"Did you feel that?" she asked Maxim.

Maxim was looking about the room, too. He stood up and looked up and out the window.

"There's nothing out there."

"Is there something wrong with the temperature system? Did that man of yours even fix it?"

"Of course he did," Maxim snapped as he turned back to Xephine. "That was not a drop in temperature. It was almost like a draft."

"How can that be?"

"If I knew that, Xephine, I would tell you."

"Do you think . . ."

Maxim hurried over to the desk and immediately began punching controls. He shook his head. "No. Francis is still there. He should have already been given his shots by the nurse."

Xephine put down the glass she'd been holding and rubbed her hands over her arms. "But where is that draft coming from? No. It must be —"

"No. It is not *The Knockers,* and Francis is unconscious."

Xephine took a deep, unsteady breath. "How long until Ezmet arrives?"

"Another five minutes. I'm already tracking his descent."

"In three minutes, Francis will be dead." Xephine grinned.

Ten minutes until midnight.

The excitement had finally caught up to Francis. He felt

Ezmet exiting the ship. Several Thosollan night guards followed him, all tall and pale-skinned. All wore determined looks and held dangerous looking weapons. Francis smiled. The weapons were powerful, but they were not for him.

Five minutes until midnight.

Francis watched the guards turn the corner. Beside him, the trio's hearts swelled with pride and love. Finally, the time had come. Finally, they were all going to be together. Ezmet came into view, and Francis wanted to run to him and hold him close, but the expression on his lover's face made him stop. Gone was the calm demeanor he was used to. Instead, the Thosollan in Ezmet had surfaced. He looked taller and slimmer, his eyes glowing ice-blue behind purple lids, his fangs descended. The ridges on his brows had protruded, and his pale lips were tinted a ruby red. His hands were outstretched, his elongated fingers tipped with long, sharp, purple nails and clawing the air. It was as though he knew he was walking into an ambush and would spare no life defending Francis.

Three minutes until midnight.

The realization that Ezmet had learned of Maxim and Xephine's betrayal made Francis' smile turn sinister. Now that his lover was here, he could finally read what he'd been unable to because of the distance between them. At last, the truth was clear. He had the evidence he needed. He closed his eyes and called to the trio.

It was time.

The guards kicked open the door. Inside, Maxim crouched ready to attack, while Xephine stood slowly. Her lids lowered as she widened her stance. Blades of black onyx fell from her wrists and dropped into her hands.

One of the guards stepped forward. "By order of the King, Lord Maxim, Lady Xephine, you are both under arrest for treason."

"Over my dead body," Maxim growled.

"If you wish it so, Uncle," Ezmet said. His lips curled in disgust. "I know you had Francis kidnapped. Where is he?"

"You're too late, Ezmet," Xephine drawled. "He's dead."

"No, Aunt. I can still feel him. Our bond may not be complete, but he is still alive."

"Not for long," Xephine said. She took a step nearer to Maxim. "Once he's gone, you will be, too. And then the rightful king will sit on the throne."

"Who? Uncle Maxim? You? Was that all that was important to you? To be king?"

"That, and much more, Ezmet. Much more."

One minute until midnight.

Francis listened and learned. With Ezmet near, he could reach into Maxim's and Xephine's minds. He almost recoiled at the memories he found there. The murder of Ezmet's father, the death of the previous *Mastre*, the imprisonment of *The Knockers*, it had all been because of them.

It is time, The Knockers breathed out. Francis smiled at their excitement.

Yes, it is time. Francis bowed his head and allowed the inevitable. The wind picked up around him, whipping his hair behind him. He felt the rush of division and then, finally, it was done.

Together, they reached out and knocked three times on the open door. *The Knockers* opened their eyes and absorbed all thought and knowledge. They saw the widened eyes of the guards. They saw the frightened faces of the vampires called Maxim and Xephine. They turned to see how Ezmet fared and smiled at him, sending him their unconditional love before turning once more to face the traitors.

Xephine screamed. The blades she held dropped in a resounding clang on the floor. Maxim held out a hand, as though he could stop the inevitable.

Ezmet's features relaxed, returning back to normal.

The Knockers stepped forward, their faces hidden under their robes.

Midnight. The sound of silence dropped around them. Not even the wind outside made a sound. Like a tsunami, a whispered word swept through the room.

Justice.

The trio moved as one, turning their backs on the vampires' lifeless bodies.

Payment accepted. Justice enacted.

Francis opened his eyes to the ceiling. He was back in his bed, and as he looked around, he saw that he was alone. A contented sigh left his lips, and he smiled.

EPILOGUE

Ezmet stood looking out his window. He was in a reflective mood. As King of Thosolla, he was the most powerful vampire in the Galaxy. He had been young when his father had taken the mantle of responsibility after his own father had died saving his people after the volcanoes had erupted, killing millions of vampires and humans alike. It had been his father who had been tasked with giving the order to leave Earth. It had been he who had signed the sacred covenant when he'd met his *Mastre*. The Thosollan female had proven to be his father's savior, and Ezmet had been the product of their love. Ezmet, the first Thosollan vampire, a mixture of vampire and Thosollan, was an oddity even to his own family. Ezmet had been young when his parents had been killed on Earth. When both the vampire king and his *Mastre* had died, everyone had thought *The Knockers* had disappeared with their deaths. After the latest development, however, Ezmet was more confused than ever.

Francis was not only the *Mastre*, but apparently, he was also *The Knockers*. No one knew what to think about the revelation. The trio were feared for their uncanny ability to hunt down the guilty. That no one knew of The Knockers' origins or the true extent of their powers only enhanced the uniqueness of Francis and Ezmet's union.

The news spread like space dust, and just like that, the protests halted. Vampires, Thosollans, and humans all stopped their speculations and were now waiting with bated breaths for Francis to be introduced. There was no question that once

242

he'd found his *Mastre*, Ezmet's position would be secured forever.

"Your majesty?"

Ezmet turned to see Katala standing in the doorway.

"Katala, come in," Ezmet said, waving the man in.

Katala bowed his head respectfully and walked in further into the room. "The doctors called. Francis has been found in perfect health. They are confused, like we all are. Xephine and Maxim had overdosed him on poisons I cannot even dream to pronounce, but they're all gone from his system. Not a trace."

"Have you spoken to Nikolaj? To his father?"

"Yes." Katala nodded. "Nikolaj hasn't left his side. He has no idea what's going on with Francis either, but the doctors said they would continue to investigate."

"That's good." Ezmet nodded. "Call the hospital and tell them that I will be visiting my *Mastre* in an hour."

"Sire, can I say something?" Katala looked nervous.

Ezmet frowned at him, wondering whatever else surprise he was going to have to contend with.

"Speak."

"Sire, ever since Francis' arrival on Thosolla, the protests have died down. He's only been here two days, and already the police are saying that not one crime has occurred. I must emphasize, your majesty, that this is a worldwide phenomenon. And there's more." Katala licked his lips, and he scratched his head. "The opposition leaders, vampire, humans, and Thosollans, they have all sent word, separately of course, that they wish to speak with the *Mastre* and agree to ceasing all conflict." Katala took another step forward. "What is Francis, sire? I know he is the *Mastre*. But *what* is he?"

Ezmet saw the uncertainty on Katala's face, but he also saw there was no fear in it. "He's *The Knockers*, Katala. Francis is *The Knockers*."

Katala let out a noisy breath and began to tremble. Watching him, Ezmet knew Katala was on the verge of hysterics. *The Knockers* were feared by everyone, but Ezmet somehow knew that he would forever be safe with his *Mastre.*

"Should we be afraid of him? He did exact justice on Xephine and Maxim."

"Not Francis. *The Knockers.*" Ezmet nodded. "And yes, they did. But then we also know that they would only punish the guilty, those who would threaten our world. *The Knockers* are the arm of justice and retribution, vengeful creatures that neither forgive nor spare anyone who dares break the sacred agreement between Thosollans and humans. They came back when they could, using Francis as their vessel. They returned and began to correct the wrong. First, with Ezra and Christian." Ezmet shook his head. "I still can't believe that Ezra wanted me dead. I loved him like a brother, and he chose to betray me."

"It was Xephine and Maxim who ordered his every move."

"And he never once thought to go against them."

"*The Knockers* came just in time." Katala's trembling had stopped. He bowed his head once more. "Your majesty." Ezmet nodded his permission to leave. In silence, Katala showed himself out of the room, leaving Ezmet to contemplate on the challenges he had to face.

Four weeks later, both Ezmet and Francis stood on the palace balcony in the capital. Before them, hundreds of thousands of Thosollans looked up, their cheers wishing them joy and happiness thundered in the air. There was no doubt that the legitimacy of Francis' position as the embodiment of *The Knockers* and as the king's *Mastre* ensured Ezmet's position as the ruling vampire king.

If in the past few days Ezmet had worried about Francis being accepted by his people and his family, that day, that minute, there was no doubt. Already, the reappearance of *The Knockers* ensured the peace and continuity of the sacred covenant.

No shocked faces looked up at them, and there were no rumors circulating about any injustice done by *The Knockers*. Ezra's name, along with his parents' and his husband's, had been expunged from the roster of the royal family. There was no judgment, either—no shocked mouths gaping at the sight of Francis. There were speculations, however.

People whispered about how peace would now settle on Thosolla for millennia. With the long lines of the vampire blood running through Ezmet's veins and the surety of Francis surviving the years because although *Mastres* could die, *The Knockers* would never allow harm to fall on their vessel.

Only hours before, both of them had stood before the Prelate who invoked the formal benediction to their marriage.

Ezmet looked down at his right hand, at the ring of intertwined white and red gold. He'd asked Francis to marry him while he was still in his hospital bed. Now, Francis wore the matching ring on his hand. It was not only a symbol of their everlasting love for each other, but it was also a symbol that they were one.

That night, Ezmet lay beside Francis. Across his chest, he held Francis' pale hand in his, caressing the back with his thumb. He found that he needed to touch Francis. He had to see for himself that his *Mastre* was safe and healthy. It wasn't a compulsion or a need—it was a necessity.

"You're thinking," Francis said. He rested his head on Ezmet's chest.

Ezmet looked down and met his gaze, a worried frown between his brows.

"I nearly lost you."

His frown cleared and Francis gave him the sweetest smile. "I was never *not* safe, my love."

"They kidnapped you and tried to kill you."

"Yes, they did."

When Francis didn't continue, Ezmet shifted until their faces were only inches apart.

"What happened to you? You've never told me."

Francis reached up and caressed Ezmet's cheek. "When I was a young boy, my mother died. What my father does not realize is that I also died, but *The Knockers* had somehow been released from their prison when the quake struck, and they needed a vessel. They needed me. The doctors didn't know that, of course, and when I fell into a coma, they thought it was because of the toxins I had been exposed to. What the doctors didn't know was that I needed to regain my strength so *The Knockers* could bring me back here, to Thosolla, to exact their vengeance on those who had dared to harm your family. They knew you would need me. When I awoke, they brought me here, and the rest, you know."

"But who did your father bury?"

"My body. At least, I think it was my body. I am confused as well, but the fact is, I am here now. With you."

"You're not human."

"Not anymore, but neither am I vampire."

"What are you then?"

"I am the *Mastre*. I am *The Knockers*. The one who is master. Your husband." His lips quivered, and tears fell down his cheeks. He leaned across the short distance and kissed Ezmet on his cheek. "Bite me."

Ezmet's fangs descended at the request. He nuzzled against Francis' neck and ran the tips of his fangs against the vein that pulsed there. At last, when he could no longer resist the temptation, he bit down. Immediately, rich blood flooded his mouth. The unique taste that was all Francis took over his senses. Francis encouraged him, moaning his name, humming his delight. Ezmet moved closer until Francis raised his leg and crooked it around Ezmet's, pulling until their cocks were in line with each other. The solid heat only served to encourage Ezmet, making him suck harder until at last, he felt satiated.

Reaching down, Ezmet gripped the cock lying next to his and found it taut. He knew Francis was ready. At once, he dragged himself down until he was face to face with that hot cock. It was no different from that of other men, or his for that matter, other than in size and shape, but Ezmet's mouth watered at the thought of tasting it. He opened his mouth and swallowed the temptation, not hesitating, even when the tip of the cock touched the back of his throat. He didn't gag. He relished it. He continued to suck and lick, and suck some more, loving the sounds Francis made at his every pull. And then Francis stiffened beneath him, and Ezmet sucked harder. Willing Francis to let go. When at last Francis did, he couldn't even jerk from the way his body stiffened. Ezmet kept going until finally, at last, there was nothing left to suck. When he had licked Francis clean, he drew himself up until he was face to face once more with Francis.

Their gazes met and held until Francis broke the connection by leaning up. Just before their lips met, Francis let out a sigh.

"I am your slave."

ABOUT JO TANNAH

I grew up listening to folk tales my father and nannies told either to entertain us children or to send home a message. These narratives I kept with me, and finally, I wrote them down in a journal way back when I kept one. Going through junk led to a long-forgotten box, and in it was the journal. Reading the stories of romance, science fiction and horror I had taken the time to put to paper brought to light that these were tales I had never met in my readings.

The tales I write are fictional, but all of them are based on what I grew up with and still dream about. That they have an M/M twist is simply for my pleasure. And I hope, yours as well.

Twitter: @JoTannah
Facebook Author Page: https://www.facebook.com/jotannahauthor
Website: http://jotannah.com
Goodreads Author Page: https://www.goodreads.com/JoTannah
Email: jotannah1@gmail.com

Unchained

By

Jo Tannah and Lynn Michaels

An unchained vampire rises above the human carnage to find unexpected love.

Yas may not be human, but he quickly realizes his love for Hunter goes beyond humanity and its conventions.

With vampires on the brink of extinction, the remaining few are kept as exotic pets, prized for the aphrodisiac qualities contained in their blood. Yas was specifically bred, born in a cage, and knows no other life. As he nears maturity, his physical needs become more difficult to meet.

Hunter8279 is a cyborg, genetically engineered to hunt and control vampires. His entire programming is scrambled when he sets eyes on the vampire he's been engaged to watch over. Now Hunter's priority is to free Yas from captivity. When Yas' master refuses to grant his freedom without a fight, their life is not the happily ever after they'd hoped for.

DEDICATION

Lynn:
To Yas. He captivated my imagination from his very first appearance on the page.

Jo:
To my family, for bearing with me until I found my writing footing once more.

CHAPTER ONE

Yas

Yas hissed.

"Submit!" Hunter8279 bared his teeth. A growl escaped as he clenched his fists.

Yas crouched low, balancing his weight close to the ground. He glared up at Hunter through the tendrils of black hair that had fallen over his face — observing the cyborg's reaction to his testing him. Hunter took a step to the left. Yas moved to the right. His whole body was taut, ready to attack should Hunter make a wrong move. Still, the sun was high up in the sky, and he was weak because of it. If only it were dark, then his strength would come to full force. Yas had to make a decision soon. Neither of them were human and there was a lot to learn about interacting with species different from his.

They had been circling each other for over an hour — the hunter tracking its prey. But Yas was no prey. He may be one of the last of his kind, but he knew how to defend himself. Yas was patient. He liked the thrill of the hunt. Being caged his entire life had taught him that patience was his strength. That same patience had paid off only hours before.

He relaxed into his crouch, ready to move at a thought — fluid, effortless. Before him, Hunter8279 relaxed as well, but his teeth were still clenched. They stared at each other for long minutes, neither one moving. Neither were willing to submit.

"Why can't you just submit?" Hunter roared out, but he

did not attack. "You know you want to."

Yas observed the way Hunter watched him. He narrowed his gaze on the pulsating vein by the side of Hunter's neck. How was he to subdue the cyborg? He tilted his head to the side when Hunter's muscles contracted minutely. Again, Yas lunged left when Hunter shifted right.

"Yas, please," Hunter begged. "Come to me. Please."

Yas tilted his head to the side, again. Something inside him pushed him to do as Hunter asked, but that same something told him that Hunter should be the one to give in.

He held Hunter's gaze in his and offered a close-mouthed smile. Slowly, he pushed himself off the ground, keeping his arms at his sides. He leaned slightly forward and sniffed. He smelled frustration but not fear. Anger, but it was not directed at him. Love. Hunter narrowed his gaze on Yas.

Yas widened his smile and took a step forward. He knew that Hunter was already making calculations, but he wasn't afraid. As long as he kept his posture unthreatening, Hunter would never attack him.

The closer he got to Hunter, the more he heard the ragged breaths. It betrayed Hunter's need for him. Finally, he was standing in front of Hunter, and he smelled the rising arousal and desire from him. Love.

As Yas reached up and touched Hunter's bicep, he made sure he proceeded slowly. Except for his harsh breathing, Hunter didn't react, didn't even flinch. Neither did he let go of Yas' gaze.

Yas bit his lower lip. Hunter closed his lids. He took one step closer, and then Yas found himself wrapped in Hunter's arms. In a blur of movement, Hunter ran across the desert floor, and Yas laughed out loud. Hunter's only response was to tighten his arms around him.

"Now is not the time to be naughty, my love. Be still. We need to get out of here."

Yas didn't say anything. Instead, he simply breathed in his mate's scent. There was nothing more enticing and intriguing than the blood of the cyborg. He closed his eyes and nuzzled into Hunter's neck.

Never before had he tasted true freedom until Hunter had come into his life. His kind had been hunted to the brink of extinction, and Yas had known nothing but the cage. But Yas had been liberated from the metal bars that had kept him a prisoner. He was no longer a pet to be gawked at or have his blood drawn for his Master's enjoyment. All his life, the cage had been his only home where he'd barely been fed enough to keep him alive.

Things had changed when he came to maturity, and his vampiric needs came to the surface. He'd been defanged, but they'd grown immediately back. The faster they grew, the more frequently his captors removed his fangs. Synthetic blood had no longer been enough to sustain him. As he matured further, his strength grew, and his despair deepened with it. Until that one day. The day he had been offered a gift. Although at the time, his master had thought he'd hired someone that would keep Yas in line.

He'd woken from the latest procedure that removed his fangs to the sweetest, most beguiling scent, and it awakened a hunger in him. It was no ordinary hunger. He didn't crave blood. He needed something else. Yas could still remember the pain of surprise when new fangs dropped from his gums. Fangs that were longer, bigger, sharper than he'd ever grown before.

At first, he had been confused, and then Hunter stepped up to look at him from beyond the bars. Yas instantly recognized Hunter as his. There was nothing he wouldn't do for him, and he hoped that Hunter would feel the same.

To his delight, Hunter had forgone protocol and opened his cage. That was the night that Yas tasted what true blood was, and his strength multiplied exponentially. The more he drank, the more his link with Hunter deepened. They'd tried to hide it, but his master, his keeper, discovered their growing closeness and sought to separate them. Yas growled low when the memories of what could have been returned.

"Don't think about it, my love," Hunter whispered in his ear. The kiss on his cheek made Yas snuggle closer, anger quickly disappearing at the simple touch. The action didn't slow Hunter down.

"I can't help it. I'd never *killed* before." He shook his head as he tried to rid his mind of the invading images—of blood splattered everywhere. The moans of pain and terror continued to scream in his ears.

"I have, and I know it's a painful memory, but you saved my life."

"I didn't mean to kill all those people. I didn't mean to drain them of blood."

"Yes, you did." There was no judgment in Hunter's voice.

"Yes, I did." Yas opened his eyes and admired the determination on Hunter's face. "They were keeping me from you. They had chained you up. *Like me.*"

"Rest, my love." Hunter dropped another kiss on his face. "The sun will not set for another hour. Soon, you'll be able to run with me."

"Where are we going?"

"Somewhere safe. Someplace the humans won't find us."

"You're human as well."

"Only a part of me is."

"Do you have a specific place in mind?"

"Yes."

When Hunter did not say anything else, Yas drew a caressing finger down the back of his neck. "You're not going to tell me, are you?"

"It's not that I don't want to, I have to make sure it's still safe. Branagan bought my services, and he may have gotten hold of classified information."

"I wish I had killed him."

"I know. Don't feel bad about it."

"He was a father to me."

"You don't have to explain anything to me, Yas. He cared for you. In his own way."

"He cared for his exotic pet." Renewed anger bloomed inside his chest. Yas thirsted for more than blood. He wanted justice.

Justice for his kind—justice for Hunter.

"That, too."

"When I see him next time, he will die." Yas grinned as an image of exactly how he was going to make Branagan pay came to mind. It was going to be slow and painful.

"I know."

"I love you, Hunter."

"I love you, too, Yas. Now sleep. I will wake you when we get there."

CHAPTER TWO

Hunter

Hunter8279 carried the vampire, Yas, across the desert and through the sand. The sun overhead weakened his beloved, but he knew damn well how temporary it was and how strong Yas would be at sundown. It both scared and thrilled him in measures. Yas could be so animalistic — he was no human with their frail emotions and obscure morals. No, Yas was pure vampire, and Hunter was closer to that feral vampire side than he often wanted to admit.

Regardless, Hunter never imagined it would come to this. It had not been the plan. Not that first day, anyway. He'd taken Branagan's contract — the pay had been irresistible — and didn't waste time reporting for duty. He had watched hours of video of Yas before arriving at his assignment, curiously drawn to the creature. His long, black hair, his pale skin. Yas had moved with the grace of a predator. Clearly, he didn't belong in a cage. Their first face to face meeting confirmed it.

When those ice blue eyes met his, Hunter slammed the cage open out of desperation, needing to see him, to be closer to him, to feel him in person without the bars separating them.

Even now, his skin was cold to the touch like ice, but underneath that was a raging fire. That fucker, Branagan, had no clue what he had been holding on to. Neither had Hunter.

Hunter8279. That was his name. His calling. Not all that different from Yas. He was a cyborg, *engineered*, rather than bred. They'd created him to control vampires, and he had done exactly that. Hunter was a killer who could take down a full-grown vampire with speed, accuracy, and deadly strength. But beneath the gaze of his Yas, he turned to mush.

The desert sand clung to his face and pulled at his boots. Walking became slogging and still, the sun beat down on him. Any mere human would have been dead by now, but he wasn't entirely human. His internal systems switched on and off, making little corrections and adjustments as they traveled. If he continued, he might be in danger of overheating, but they didn't have much farther to go.

The terrain changed, leaving behind the endless dunes for more rugged ground. Mountains rose out of the rocky sand. Cactus and other brush dotted the land around them. Hunter's eyelids flicked, knocking off the lingering dust. He accessed his navigation system and searched for the appropriate landmarks.

"Why'd you stop?" Yas whispered, but Hunter could hear him clearly.

"Why aren't you sleeping?"

"You woke me by stopping."

Hunter tightened his arms around Yas. He would never let anyone hurt him again. "Almost there."

Yas nuzzled into his neck and made that soft purring sound that melted Hunter's iron heart. After their first encounter, he'd thought to trace the records to see if somehow their blood had been shared. Perhaps being from the same family line would explain their unusual attraction to each other, but he hadn't found anything. The blood they'd used to create Hunter8279 was from a completely different, and now extinct, line of vampires. Yas had been bred from precise lineage, and from what Hunter found, it had been well documented. Yas was worth a fortune, and Branagan wouldn't let either of them go so easily. Yas for his value and Hunter for his betrayal.

He hoped his oasis remained undiscovered.

"There." Hunter moved forward again—course-corrected. "We should be there before sundown."

Hunter's boots crunched over the gravel. He kept a steady pace through a valley with more vegetation that gradually became lusher as they progressed, possibly indicating a nearby water source. He made a note in his memory banks but continued to move forward. There was no time to stop.

Ahead, an odd rock formation jutted up into the sky as if it were a finger pointing to heaven. Hunter kept it to the right of them until he saw the next landmark, a chain of mountains that extended to the northeast. He turned west. A few more miles to go, and thankfully, the sun had started its descent. The air would quickly become cooler, easing up the pressure on his systems.

Miles of rocky terrain wound through the mountains. Eventually, he came to the correct chain. The rock formations became more strangely deformed. They passed beneath an arch, then around them, other arches, circles, and towers of rock appeared. He searched for the one that looked like an eye. When he found it, he stopped.

"Yas. We have to wait. We'll need to climb."

"Climb?"

"Yes. But I must be sure it's not a trap. If Branagan discovered this place, we could be walking right into—"

"Don't say it," Yas hissed.

Hunter growled in response, then found a shady outcropping of rock to set him down. "We wait." He looked out into the vast blue sky. It seemed to go on forever, encompassing everything. He flicked his lids to navigation-mode to determine how long they'd have to wait. "Only a little longer."

Soon, the sun went down enough for Yas to come alive. When he stretched his long arms over his head, the t-shirt that he wore lifted, exposing his stomach—pearly white and kissable. Hunter licked his lips, unable to tear his gaze away from the delicious view. Yas tugged it back down and glared at Hunter, suspiciously. "Where to?" he asked with a raised eyebrow.

"Come on." Hunter grinned up at Yas before taking his hand. He tugged him up off the ground, then led him around to the far side of the eye-formation.

"Up there." Hunter pointed up the side of a mountain. It wasn't as high as the surrounding peaks but steep enough. The rocks smoothed out on the far side where an opening into the cave system would be. If it hadn't been found, there would be supplies stashed inside. Every hunter had caches around for emergencies. This was the first emergency Hunter8279 had ever had. He scowled, thinking of the hunter faction and his history. He wanted to erase it. Wanted to be a vampire—to run through the night with his vampire lover, but he couldn't run from the truth, and Yas wasn't his lover. *Yet.*

He shifted his internal systems, preparing for the climb, and scanned the area for other life signs. His sensors picked up nothing but a tiny desert rat far off in the distance. With a relieved exhale, he led Yas up the mountain. The vampire took the climb as easily as any hunter would. With the sleek agility of a cat, he scrambled and leaped to the next plateau with effortless grace.

By the time they were close to the cave entrance, night had fallen in full. It was pitch black, except for the glittering stars above. He had no doubt that Yas could see perfectly well in the dark, but Hunter had to adjust his vision.

"There," Hunter pointed to a shadow along the rock.

Yas stopped. "You sure?"

"Yes. Go."

Yas huffed but moved in the right direction.

It proved to be the entrance, exactly as Hunter had said.

"Told you."

"Indeed." Yas wrinkled his adorable nose.

Once inside, they made their way down into the depths of the cave, and only when they were well away from the entrance did Hunter flick on a torch to see by. It didn't seem to bother Yas either way. Hunter panned the light around until it fell on a large trunk.

"There."

"I see it," Yas said, flashing a grin at Hunter.

Together, they moved toward the trunk and opened it. Inside, there were rations of food, water, blankets, and extra clothing. Nothing would fit Yas. Everything was sized for a hunter's broad shoulders and long, powerful frame. Yas, although tall, was slight and nimble.

"This is all useless to me," he grumbled.

"Well, I'll feed you after I eat something." Hunter broke open a ration pack and a bottle of water. He choked down the thick cracker. It had been created to be the exact nutrition he'd need, but it tasted terrible—like cardboard and dirt. He downed the entire bottle of water to drown the taste as much as hydrate his system.

Yas watched, bobbing back and forth, ready to strike. He licked his lips. The lusty look on his face made Hunter's dick hard. Yas launched himself at Hunter so fast that his optical system didn't even have time to adjust.

In a reflexive move, Hunter dropped the packaging to catch Yas, and with the vampire in his arms, he exposed his neck, prepared for what came next. Yas' fangs slid out—long and sharp—and pierced his neck, painlessly cutting through the tough skin like a laser through, well, almost anything. The first draw made Hunter's hard cock press uncomfortably against his pants.

"Yas . . ." He needed to reconnect with his vampire. He wanted to toss him to the ground and fuck him hard. "Let's get a blanket. Yas . . ."

Yas pulled his teeth back slowly and made a hard, obvious swallow. He wet his lips and with tense arms, pushed away. When he finally put his feet back on the ground, he rolled his neck and began to walk in circles, his arms at his sides.

"Fine, but I'm not done. Not by a long shot." Yas stopped pacing and looked at Hunter. He licked his lips again—the look in his eyes intensified.

"Good." Hunter spread the blanket out and stretched out on it. He flipped the button of his pants open. "Show me."

CHAPTER THREE

Yas

Yas fought the urge to throw himself on top of Hunter. The call of his blood made his gums throb in anticipation. Something below his waist throbbed as well, and then his cock jerked. He looked down at himself.

"What are you doing?" The sound of Hunter's voice snapped Yas out of his musings. He pointed at his growing dick.

"I'm confused."

"What about?"

Yas frowned and poked a finger at his crotch. "Why is it getting so hard? I'm hungry for your blood, but I don't know why this is hungry too." He examined Hunter's face for some kind of answer. Instead, he saw Hunter's eyes widen. At first, he didn't know how to interpret the expression, but then Hunter laughed. The cyborg actually threw his head back and *laughed*.

A fire burned inside Yas, making his blood boil. He stared at Hunter's hysterical form. Tears were falling down his face as he lay there, cradling his stomach with an arm. Yas was no stranger to amusement. He'd borne the brunt of it from as far back as he could remember. Master had delighted in showing off his favorite pet. But while all those times brought back memories of humiliation and pain, Hunter's laughter stirred something deeper inside of him. It was as though Hunter knew Yas was missing humor and fun in his life, and he had

263

the curious desire to laugh with him. The only problem was, he didn't know what was so funny.

Yas had learned patience from a young age — he'd avoided getting killed because of it. He waited until Hunter's mirth died down. When it finally did, their gazes locked. Yas didn't give Hunter the chance to recover. He sprang into the air and landed with his knees on either side of Hunter's torso. He whipped both of Hunter's arms over his head, quickly placing his arm over them to hold them in place. Hunter looked up at him in open-mouthed silence. Yas leaned over until their noses were only a breath away.

"You laugh at me," Yas said through his teeth. He didn't take his eyes away from Hunter. His hunger grew, and his fangs dropped. But he craved more than blood. Hunter's breathing grew erratic. "You want me," Yas whispered, applying more pressure over Hunter's arms when he made as though to push Yas off him.

Yas fought the urge to bite Hunter and get his feeding done because the body beneath him stirred a different kind of hunger. He couldn't rush through this. He wanted to know why his cock was stiffening between their bodies and why Hunter's was getting bigger and harder beneath him. Did Hunter crave him as much as Yas craved Hunter?

Hunter's steel-gray eyes narrowed and swept Yas into their intensity. Yas wanted to look away, but he knew that by doing so, he would be handing Hunter a gift he wasn't willing to give up. *Not yet.*

Hunter stopped struggling, so Yas lifted a hand and ran his fingers over the short, silky black hair that lay flat against his scalp. He studied the chiseled features. He'd memorized every angle of the beloved face that first day they'd met. What had really drawn Yas to his cyborg was how impossibly long his black lashes were. They cast more than shadows over his face — they lent mystery, hiding more than it revealed. But Yas knew what his hunter hid. Hunter was so intriguing, and he wanted to know more. The cock beneath him twitched and pulsed against him, making Yas look down at where their bodies pressed together.

"I thought you wanted to feed from me?" Hunter asked with a shaky breath.

Yas smiled over his fangs. "I do." He pushed himself closer, and he focused back on Hunter's gaze. A shiver shuddered over the length of his body, and his cock hardened some more.

"What are you waiting for?" Hunter's warm breath brushed against Yas' mouth.

Yas didn't respond. Light as a feather, he slid the tips of his fangs over the curve on Hunter's neck, making the cyborg inhale sharply. Yas could sense Hunter's composure collapsing. He continued to stroke with his fangs, watching Hunter arch his back against the rough blanket they lay on. A growl escaped Hunter's lips, but the sound only managed to encourage Yas to tease his tongue against the salty skin. It brought him closer to the pulsing vein there, and he tilted Hunter's head back so he couldn't move. Hunter shifted, but when Yas didn't feel anything more, he looked down. That's when he caught sight of Hunter clutching his long, thick shaft in his hand. Yas had no idea when he had managed to take it out of his tight trousers, but the sight of those fingers stroking the thick shaft made him feel as though he were headed toward a breaking point. He wanted to know where that road led.

Hunter grunted beneath him, sighing out a low-pitched moan that sent vibrations down Yas' body. That's when he realized he'd moved his head and sunk his teeth into Hunter's neck. The blood pooled in his mouth and the sweetest taste hit his palate, like the honey his master had once made him lick off a piece of bread they'd shared. Only better. Hunter threw his head back, arching up more. The move threatened to spill Yas off him, but Yas didn't mind. He allowed his body to slide over on Hunter's side. Hunter followed suit, pressing his body on top of Yas.

Managing the maneuver made Yas laugh into Hunter's neck, having yet to release his fangs. Gently, he withdrew. Hunter hissed at the parting, but Yas licked over the puncture wounds and allowed his saliva to close them.

"Are you done?" Hunter whispered close into his ear.

"Hmm . . . yes. I think so."

"Then, if you wouldn't mind," Hunter said, pressing tiny kisses on Yas' lips. "I would like to show you all about sex."

"Hmm . . ." Yas smiled at the cave ceiling. Stalactites hung over them like stakes ready to be thrust into their bodies. "I was wondering what that's all about."

"Well, you did ask," Hunter said, pressed himself closer. Yas felt something hot and hard throb against his leg.

Yas craned his neck until he saw exactly what it was. He looked back up at Hunter, awed at the challenge there. For an answer, he jutted his hips forward until his own hardness brushed against Hunter's. "Teach me."

Hunter slid his fingers under Yas' chin and pulled him in closer. The scent coming off his cyborg entranced Yas, and he wanted to know everything about sex, right then and there.

"Do you trust me?"

"Do you doubt it?"

"Naughty vampire," Hunter whispered before swooping in to take his lips in a hot, open-mouthed kiss.

Yas sank into the caress. He'd only tasted Hunter's mouth one other time, and that had been before they'd escaped. Hunter slid the clothes off their bodies, not once pausing to separate their lips for more than a second.

The care by which he moved made Yas arch closer. His cock tightened, wanting to burst out. Hunter guided him lower onto the blanket. Yas didn't know what was going to happen next, but he couldn't quite contain the groan of pleasure when Hunter finally ended their kiss only to slide his mouth down Yas' throat. He was open to Hunter's teaching, and he wanted no other man to touch him. Hunter was his, as he was Hunter's. Whatever had bound them made them mates as far as Yas was concerned.

All logical thinking was swept off to the side when Hunter glided his hand up Yas' leg until it rested on his waiting, aching cock. He raked his fingers wide against the flat of Yas' pelvis, making him shiver with need. Yas pushed up, wanting to hurry Hunter, but Hunter caught his wrists and pressed them over his head. Yas grinned.

"Play nice, my hunter," he said.

"I always do, my vampire," Hunter said with a throaty laugh. He bent his head and flicked a tongue over his lips.

Yas surrendered to the delicate touch. Hunter kissed him again, his tongue delving deep into his mouth, teasing his senses, making him gasp for air. His lips dropped down to his neck until they reached his chest. Each nipple was taken in a soft bite before they were sucked and slathered with strokes of the tongue. They'd gone highly sensitive under Hunter's touch. Yas felt like his skin was on fire

He groaned out when Hunter's hand gripped his pulsing cock, making him ache for something . . . more, anything . . . ache for penetration. He didn't understand what it was he really wanted, but the feel of Hunter's body, the way he milked his cock, spawned warm vibrations in him.

Hunter continued to play with his cock, but then his grip grew tighter and stronger, the friction getting hotter and hotter. When Yas could no longer stand it, his body began to stiffen and his back bowed up. Wave upon wave of pleasure swept through his body, and he yelled out. The world exploded, and he could feel the center of his being spill out into Hunter's hand. He begged Hunter not to stop, and Hunter gave it to him.

CHAPTER FOUR

Hunter

"Hmm . . . that was so different, so delicious," Yas said, a small smile curving his red lips. He raised his arms over his head and began to stretch. The tips of his toes pointed as he lengthened his muscles.

In fascination, Hunter watched Yas stretch beside him. He was such an intriguing creature and reminded Hunter of the predator cats of old, now long extinct—all muscle and restrained strength. Constantly on the alert without looking it.

Earlier, Yas had taken his initiation like a champion and to his surprise, had recovered quickly. Hunter wondered if it was too soon after their first time, but, just then, Yas turned, and the look on his face erased whatever doubts Hunter had for initiating another round of sex. Yas' heavy lids, the soft bite on the lower lip, that was all the permission Hunter needed. He reached out and caught Yas in his arms once more, pulling him closer, and leaning over so their lips touched. For a moment, Yas didn't respond, but then he returned the kiss, almost feverishly as though he couldn't get enough of Hunter.

Hunter opened his mouth wider to receive Yas' tongue and shifted his hips closer so his cock would rub against Yas'. His body seemed to lose the very last of his earlier hesitation, all the remaining vigor collecting in his cock. Yas leaned back a little but continued to lap on Hunter's mouth. Hunter could hear his own loud sighs echoing in the cave.

Yas raised his arms and wrapped them around Hunter's neck, drawing himself closer once more, purring low in his throat. That sound was ecstasy for Hunter. His heart swelled with unfamiliar emotions. Mostly they were painful and unbearable, and he couldn't imagine living without them. Their kiss deepened, and Hunter felt himself getting lost in the moment, the deeper it went.

Yas broke the kiss with a lick over Hunter's lips, then leaned back to gaze into his eyes. Hunter couldn't read the message there and opened his mouth to ask what it was that Yas wanted, but Yas urged him gently back onto the pallet. Yas' left hand reached down and lifted Hunter's balls and cock.

A wicked smile hovered over his lips, but he dropped down before Hunter could say anything. When he kissed Hunter's balls, running his tongue over them, mouthing them, and feeling them tenderly with his teeth, Hunter closed his eyes and fell back. Yas' initiative was a sweet surprise. So when Yas continued to suck and lick at his cock until Hunter's legs slid apart and when the pressure became a little too much for Hunter, he reached down and caught Yas' silky, black hair in his hand then gently pulled him off.

Yas lifted his face, and Hunter pointed to the lube he'd taken out earlier. "Are you ready for your next lesson?"

At first, Yas looked mystified. A moment later, his eyes widened, and the confusion turned to excitement. At once, Yas took the jar and opened it. He sniffed at the contents before dipping his fingers inside to scoop out the gel. He sniffed at his fingers again. "What is this?"

"It's gel. A lubricant."

"What's it for?"

"We need to put some on you, and me, so you don't get hurt when I . . . get inside you." Hunter had an idea that Yas didn't have the necessary information about sex and how to go about it.

"How do we do that?"

Hunter opened and closed his mouth several times, at a loss for words. He frowned and scratched his head. "I'm going to put my cock in you."

"How?"

Hunter closed his eyes. How was he going to explain? He could do the whole textbook information by showing Yas the educational films, but that would take too long. Opening his eyes, he sat up and met Yas' curious gaze. "Do you trust me?"

"Yes." The lack of hesitation delighted Hunter's heart. Yas had given him unconditional love, and now an unconditional trust. How could he have lived without Yas in his life?

"Will you allow me to show you instead of explaining? I promise to stop if you tell me to."

"Why should I tell you to stop? I want to have sex with you," Yas said, tilting his head to the side. His brows furrowed in confusion. "I've seen the films. I know what part goes where."

Hunter's own frown was almost painful because of how confused he was. "Then what are you asking me about?"

"I wanted to know *how* you're going to do it because I can't think of how your size is going to get in me. You're kind of bigger than the ones shown on the educational films my Master showed me."

The laughter bubbled in Hunter's throat. He'd never been so relieved. He sat up and took the jar from Yas' hand. "I'll show you, okay?"

"Good. Now we're fucking," Yas said, sounding excited. He turned and flopped on his stomach, folding his arms to support his head. He looked at Hunter who had gone still, too surprised to say anything or move. "What are you waiting for? Do it! Fuck me. Or whatever. What do you call it anyway?"

Hunter couldn't resist, Yas was simply too adorable. He bent to drop a kiss on his bare ass before smoothing the lubricant over his cock. It had softened earlier, but Yas taking the position had revived it, turning it dark red. He shuddered as he fisted his cock, liking the feel of the friction. It was nothing compared to how he imagined it was going to be once he was one with Yas.

"Relax," Hunter said, feeling his heart race. He rubbed fresh gel over Yas' anus, pushing thick globs of it deep. He knew he was probably overdoing things, but he didn't want Yas hurting. It was going to be his first time, after all, and no way was he ever going to hurt his Yas.

Slowly, gently, Hunter pressed his cock against Yas' opening, expecting resistance. Incredibly, Yas let out a breath, and Hunter gently slid in. Yas gasped and stiffened but didn't move away. Hunter stilled, allowing Yas to get accustomed to the invasion. When Yas gave a small nod, Hunter pulled out slowly before pushing in again. Again and again, he lanced into Yas until at last, Yas began to respond, pushing back and moaning.

Hunter reached around to find Yas' cock and fisted it in his hand until it stood straight. The combined stimulation made Yas groan out loud, and hearing it gladdened Hunter's heart.

Soon, his own groans joined Yas' and the cavern echoed with the sounds of their pleasure. Hunter rocked his hips harder, back and forth, feeling as though his cock were on fire. Yas' moans grew louder as if he could feel what Hunter was going through. The heat grew to almost unbearable temperatures until at last, Hunter let go. He shot himself in spurts inside Yas. He felt Yas' ejaculate coating his hand.

For a moment, the world stopped spinning. Hunter was still riding the spasms while beneath him, Yas froze. It was as though he were held immobile by the cock that still speared him. Yas groaned and jerked, the movement pulling Hunter back to the present. His body began to tremble as though it were unable to process the chaos it had gone through, but then the trembling began to subside, and Hunter knew peace.

CHAPTER FIVE

Hunter

"Oh my . . . if I hadn't slept all day, I'd sleep right now. I feel so good . . . sated." Yas curled up beside Hunter, cuddling into his side.

Hunter wished he could stay that way forever. He tugged Yas a little closer, but he squirmed away. "Come back here, Yas."

"Hunter?"

"Yeah?"

"What's next? We can't live here. I want to go out. I want to run."

"I know. Not yet. Branagan will have—"

"Fuck Branagan! I want to kill that bastard."

"Shh . . ." Hunter pulled Yas to him. He wanted to protect what was his, though he knew damn well how powerful Yas really was. He'd seen him break thick, metal chains. Yas could have escaped ages ago. "How long were you there?"

"I . . . always . . ."

Hunter kissed the top of his head, carded his fingers through his long, dark hair. "We need to figure out our next move. We need to be smart. Like it or not, Branagan isn't going to let us walk away. He's going to want you back."

"He's been using my blood, you know."

"Using?"

"It makes him . . . I don't know . . . young? He feels . . . *vigorous*?"

274

"He's a twisted fuck."

"You have no idea."

Hunter rubbed his shoulders, soothing his lover. "You're never going back. Not if I can help it."

"Good. So. What now?"

"I need to think." He had contacts, other hunters, but he didn't know if he could trust them. Branagan would be coming for them, and he'd likely hire another hunter or two to track them. It was only a matter of time.

Yas nuzzled against him. "Think hard."

Hunter laughed. "Now you know something about sex, that's all you want to think about?"

"Huh?"

"Think *hard*."

"Shut up."

"Like your cock . . . *hard*."

Yas smacked his shoulder, playfully. His lips twitched as though he were trying not to laugh. "Stop. That's not what I meant."

With another small kiss to Yas' forehead, Hunter gave in. "I know.

They were quiet after that. Hunter needed to think through all the different possibilities. There had to be a way to save Yas. A way for them to be together.

The only thing that kept replaying was that they couldn't do it alone. They were going to need help.

Hunter had the capability of connecting to multiple networks to search for information and contacts, but he didn't dare use it. As soon as he did, Branagan would be on to them and able to track them.

"Yas . . . this is impossible."

"Why?"

"We need help, but I can't reach out to anyone."

"How would you reach out, anyway? We're in a fucking

cave, Hunter." He sounded incredulous, and every new emotion he expressed delighted Hunter.

"You're amazing. You know that?"

Yas rolled to his stomach then crouched on his legs.

"Don't pounce on me. I'm not joking . . ."

"Fine." Yas swayed back and forth as if weighing his odds before giving in and sitting down. "So, answer my question. How would you contact anyone from here?"

"My cyborg parts. They're equipped for communication and other things, but even my emergency channels are going to be monitored. Branagan will have them checked, and the hunters are going to help him with it. They can't have society knowing you're loose. There would be panic."

"Okay. I get it. Maybe I can help."

"How can you help?"

"Let me try. I'm a fast learner." Hunter stared at the vampire. Yas was so naive and had been kept from so much of the world, what could he do? "I'm not going to hurt anything. Stop looking at me like that."

Hunter huffed. "Fine." He turned away from Yas. "I think I saw something we can use in the supplies." He shuffled through the contents until he found a headset. "This will work." It had a separate wireless sensor plug that he popped into the slot behind his left ear.

"Hm . . ." Yas flicked at Hunter's ear and peered behind it.

"Now, this goes over your head. Like this." He slid the contraption over Yas' eyes so he could see the interface then turned it on.

Yas gasped. "Oh! Is this . . . in your head?" He reached out and fumbled with the display, touching Hunter's neurons in the virtual representation, but that made his head hum as his circuits responded.

"Yas . . . this is not a good idea."

"Wait. This isn't unlike the one the Master used."

Hunter could sense or feel the device working through his systems. He'd handed Yas a lot of power over himself with that thing. He wasn't sure why he'd done that.

"I need your number. Wait. Is that the eight two seven nine?"

"Uh . . . yeah."

"Why numbers?"

"Easier. I guess."

Yas moved around the cave as if dancing with the interface. "Easier for whom? The creators? The masters? The hypocrites?"

"I don't know. Yas, what are you doing?" Hunter's neurons clicked and shuffled while Yas accessed the communication protocols.

"Just a sec."

"Do you have any idea what you're doing?"

Yas chuckled. "Actually, yes. This is very much like the device I stole from the Master—"

"Don't call him that."

"You're right. He's no master of mine. Not now. I didn't know better when I was younger. But . . . okay . . . here we go."

Hunter could feel the communication line. It was secured and scrambled. He turned to face Yas in wonder. "What did you do?"

"Just contact whoever it is you need to reach, Hunter." Yas ran his hand over Hunter's shoulder. "It will be okay."

"I'm impressed." He really was, and Hunter was not easily impressed.

Yas clicked his tongue and gave him a playful wink. "You should be."

Hunter had no idea how smart Yas really was. For him to be able to hack the communication system and secure a line was simply incredible. Hunter couldn't even do that. He could take advantage of it, though. He initiated a connection outside of the hunter network. He needed someone he could trust, and he could only think of one person who might be able to help.

The connection clicked, opening digital pathways that reached out to his friend, his brother—Hunter8280. His wombmate. Hunter's visuals flipped on for a virtual session.

In a few seconds, a holographic image stood before him. "Nine. Missed you. What's wrong?" Eighty's face looked so much like Hunter's own, rugged, inflexible, and worried. Eighty knew he wouldn't call unless there was a good reason.

"I need help. I don't know how to explain it. I . . ."

"Let me guess. Ran off with the vampire you were supposed to be protecting?"

"How—"

"Because the call to hunt *you* has been issued." He held up a device and shook it at Hunter.

For a brief moment, Hunter8279 panicked. His heart rate sped up, and bile rose in his throat, but he swallowed it back. He was a hunter. He always remained calm. "And what will you do?"

Eighty sighed. "Help you. What do you think? You're my brother. Plus, I have some news that you and your vampire may be interested in." He made some hand motions, waving them around, then he pushed on something. A file landed in Hunter's data port.

"Eighty? What is this?"

"Names and locations of vampires being harvested for their blood. They're being treated worse than animals. We're hunters, bred to protect. We cannot allow this to continue. We're hoping you and your vampire will help us. In turn, we will help you." His thick eyebrows lowered over his eyes as he angered.

"They're going to help us, Yas," Hunter said turning to

watch as Yas prowled around the cave, acting like he wasn't paying a bit of attention, but Hunter knew better than that. Then it hit him.

Hunter focused on his brother once more. "Eighty?" He asked. "Who's *we*?"

"A group of hunters. You know most of us. We're joining forces over this. We . . . we all have the same blood. We were created to guard and control them. We never abuse them. We were not made to torture vampires. It's against our encoding." It was the motto they lived by. They'd known their purpose from a young age. Hunter didn't disagree with it, but he wanted more than that — with Yas. Deciding to help the other vampires, though, that was an easy decision.

Yas peered around Hunter's body to face Eighty. "Of course we'll help. What do we need to do?"

Eighty regarded Yas for a second before letting out a soft whistle. "We suspect there may be something more than we were led to believe about vampires."

Yas danced through the interface once more, sending Hunter's internal systems into a tizzy. Hunter blinked when his drive began analyzing and correcting. Whatever Yas had done, other than the obvious alterations he was encoding, made Hunter think that they may have a chance going against the likes of Branagan.

"We're making a plan now, I see. Good. We're in." Yas didn't blink, appearing fully engrossed on what he was doing. A focused Yas looked adorable the way he sucked his lower lip in. Hunter had no doubt that his Yas was going to be valuable in coming up with a good strategy.

Eighty watched and chuckled. "Your little vampire is quite the surprise, Nine."

"Oh, he is indeed." Hunter crossed his arms over his chest and watched Yas' arms caressing the air, and simultaneously, his circuitry.

"Shush, you two," Yas said, not taking his eyes off what he was doing. "Branagan will be coming for us soon. We have to deflect him — time to get busy."

"What are you doing?"

CHAPTER SIX

Hunter

Yas huffed and rolled his eyes, but he didn't stop whatever it was he was doing.

"I've hacked into Branagan's security and patched the others in. That's nothing. I also breached his inner private files. Always knew I could, if I wanted."

Yas walked over to stand behind Hunter. He slid his hands down Hunter's shoulders, but Hunter wasn't sure which one of them he was trying to soothe.

"I guess I never wanted to. I . . . I didn't want to know what his files said. About me." Yas sounded melancholic.

"Yas . . ." Hunter started to turn, to comfort him, but Yas stopped him.

"Wait. I'm not finished."

Hunter stood still, patiently waiting for Yas' next move. When more tingling sensations jazzed through his head and body, he began to feel a little concerned. "Yas? What are you doing?"

"I'm upgrading some of your whatchacallits."

"Whatcha-what? Yas? Do you know what you're doing? This is my head we're talking about." Hunter started to turn once more.

"I do know. Now stop moving." He slapped Hunter's shoulder. "We need you tip-top."

"Why?" Hunter frowned at the cave wall in front of him. He suspected he didn't want to know what Yas and Eighty were up to. Of course, Yas didn't bother to answer.

"Okay, Eighty. Are you good?" Yas said after a while. He sounded smug.

"By the blood of the holy! This is . . . this information confirms what we had and more." Hunter's brother sounded overwhelmed as he ran a hand through his thick hair that looked so much like Hunter's own.

"Information?" It might have been Hunter's head they were connecting through, but he couldn't see a damned thing they were doing. Yas patted his shoulder before placing a kiss on Hunter's cheek.

"Do you have the security information to enter the estate? That's the most important piece right now," Yas asked Eighty.

"Affirmative." Eighty saluted. Hunter thought his face was going to split from how broad he was grinning. "See you there." Before Hunter could say anything, Eighty ended their connection. Hunter sighed. He really should say something, but he didn't. Yas was Yas. And, well, Eighty was Eighty. He let out another sigh. There was no use getting in the way of two determined men — or vampires. *Whatever.*

Yas seemingly ignored Hunter's sighs of resignation. Silently, he continued to flit through Hunter's circuitry for a while longer. The sensations increased, warming his body. Finally, Yas circled around and stared into Hunter's eyes. "How do you feel?"

Hunter grunted. He didn't want to admit it, but he actually felt good. Horny. He thrust his hips forward.

"What? Oh? Look at you." Yas' smile turned sultry. He leaned over Hunter, an evil glint in his eye.

"You're going to take care of me, Yas?"

"Everything you did to me felt . . . amazing. You want that too?" Cheeks flushed, Yas' eyes widened as his gaze met Hunter's.

Mesmerized by Yas' look of wonder, Hunter felt his own

excitement rising. "Oh, yeah. I want that."

Tentatively, Yas reached down and grabbed Hunter's hard cock. His fingers were cold, even with Hunter's blood pumping through his body, but it still felt nice. Hunter thrust his hips upward, tunneling through Yas' grip.

Yas tightened his fist and gazed into his eyes. Hunter couldn't stand it any longer. He humped furiously, trying to hold his dominance back while simultaneously chasing that elusive orgasm. He closed his eyes and concentrated, but it wasn't quite working.

Abruptly, he shifted and pushed Yas down to the blanket and pressed his shoulders to the ground. He loomed over the smaller vampire. He wanted to see Yas' face. Wanted to fuck him—mark him. It was too soon for marking, but Hunter needed more—needed something else.

He pulled away from Yas' tight fingers and sat up, turning around and lifting one leg over him until he sat straddling him. He grabbed his cock at the base and rubbed it over Yas' face, against his lips. "Ready to see what this can do?"

Yas wiggled beneath him. Hunter didn't know if he was going to stay put and accept it or fight for dominance. In this instance, he couldn't have it. Hunter needed to have control.

Hunter stroked his dick and dragged it across Yas' cheek. He groaned at the sensation of the temperature contrast—icy face and hot palm. He fucked into his hand and poked the crown of his cut cock against Yas' lips. "Be still," he growled when Yas wiggled again.

"Can't . . ." Yas sighed and grabbed Hunter's ass. Then in a surprise move, he stuck out his tongue, licking the tip of Hunter's cock. "Mmm . . . tasty. Make more."

Hunter hissed as he squeezed out another drop of his pre-cum, watching hungrily when Yas didn't turn away. Instead, he leaned closer and began to lick it up. The sight and sounds pushed Hunter closer to the edge. He needed release—

needed Yas.

Those ice-blue eyes shifted up and met his with a heat that was impossible to ignore. With his gaze locked on to Hunter's, Yas' wicked tongue flicked out against Hunter's cock.

The tingle built and spread, then Hunter came. Exactly like he had imagined it—squirting out over Yas' face.

Yas laughed and closed his eyes, while Hunter used his softening dick to smear the mess into Yas' skin.

"Damn, Hunter . . . my dick wants to be hard again. But it can't."

Hunter chuckled at Yas' innocence. This time, Yas chuckled with him. "I'll get something to wipe your face, though I'm tempted to leave you like that."

"Ha! I'm tempted to let you." His tongue flicked out again, and he licked some of the mess from around his mouth. "I like it." He said the words so matter-of-factly that Hunter couldn't help but laugh again. "Is sex always this much fun with laughing?"

"No, not with everyone. But it should be."

Hunter carefully disentangled himself from Yas, making sure he didn't kick him in the face as he lifted his leg out of the way. Going to the box, he rummaged around until he found a cloth. He wet it with water from a bottle, then proceeded to cleaned them both up. First Yas and then himself. Afterward, they lay on the blanket, stretched out side by side. The ground was hard and not very comfortable, but it was heaven for Hunter.

Yas quickly maneuvered his body around Hunter. There was no hesitation to his movements, and for some reason, that sank deep into Hunter's heart. He didn't want this feeling to end. This unexpected love. He would kill anyone, destroy anything that would get in between them.

"I'm worried, Yas. What plan do you have? You told

Eighty, but not me."

Yas let out a sigh and gently stroked his chest. "You're not going to like it."

"Then why are you doing it?"

"I have to." The matter-of-fact manner of his speech made Hunter tense. What was Yas hiding from him?

Hunter leaned up so he could see Yas' perfect face. "No, you don't. Hey, we're in this together. Talk to me."

Yas stared at him for a long while. His eyes looked sad as though he were reluctant to tell Hunter. That made Hunter's fear increase.

"I have to go back to him," Yas said. "I have to be on the inside to make the plan work. If he's still hunting me, your team will never get close enough. We have to make him trust me. It's the only way."

Hunter could only stare at Yas, contentment turning into sudden anger.

"No. You are not going back without me. Period."

Yas rolled his eyes and rolled out of Hunter's embrace. The sudden absence only made Hunter's anger rise. "Yas, come back here."

"I am not going to talk to you when you're in a *mood*, Hunter." Yas got to his feet and began to pull on his clothes. "I didn't tell you my plan because I knew you were going to overreact. I was correct."

Hunter growled low in his throat when Yas walked away. "Yas. I said come back here."

"No."

"Yas!"

CHAPTER SEVEN

Yas

"**Y**ou're either insane or have a death wish."
Yas ignored Hunter's yelling and stretched his arms up toward the cave ceiling.

"Yas? Are you listening to me? I won't allow you to go ahead with this plan. You are not, I repeat, *not* going to put yourself out as bait."

Still, Yas didn't respond. He knew his silence only increased Hunter's anger and frustration, but he'd made his decision. Nothing else would work. If they went in there and attacked Branagan's estate, there was a forty-five-point-ten percent chance they'd all end up dead.

"Are you even listening to me?" Hunter flung his arms to his sides as he paced. He grumbled to himself and kicked the floor every other step. The dust swirled around his boots. Yas wanted to assure him his plan was the only one that would work, but one look at Hunter's glare directed his way, made him look away. If only to hide his amusement.

Branagan's estate had been designed to withstand any kind of attack from without or within. There were the numerous hired guns that guarded the gates and perimeters for one. Then there were the dogs which weren't easily subdued, but Yas didn't want the loyal canines to get hurt — they'd slept with him in his cage and kept him company most of his life. No. He couldn't risk getting the dogs hurt.

Yas paused his stretching when another plan bloomed in

his mind. He could definitely use the dogs to his advantage. They knew him, and he should be able to control them. He tilted his head to the side, watching in his mind's eye the different scenarios of how to do it. Finally, he nodded. *Yes. That plan could work out quite well.* But only as a last resort. He really didn't want to lose any of the dogs.

"You're not listening to me. Are you trying to get me angrier with you?" Hunter's growly voice speaking in his ear brought Yas back to the present. He assessed Hunter's stricken expression before bringing up a hand to caress the spiky cheek.

"I'm sorry. I got caught up in my thoughts. I didn't mean to ignore you," Yas said soothingly. "I've been so used to being alone. It won't happen again."

Hunter gazed at him for a long second before sliding closer. "I know you're used to being alone and keeping things to yourself, but I'm here now. We're together in this. Talk to me."

Yas searched Hunter's face. He knew he had to tell him something, but he also didn't want to lie. It was best not to tell Hunter his plan. Otherwise, Hunter wouldn't let him do it and that might end in catastrophe. Also, they needed the element of surprise, and surprising Branagan was the only way to get him alone. That way, he would be easily eliminated from this world. Only then would it be safe. Only then would the others get their chance of getting rescued.

His vision reddened at the thought of the list that Eighty had sent. There were so many like him out there, and they were all being treated like animals. Milked of their blood for the entertainment of humans. No one deserved to be tortured all of their lives. Whatever their ancestors were said to have done over a thousand years ago, Yas and the others didn't deserve to pay through slavery.

"I have a plan, but I can't tell you everything until we talk to your wombmate and his companions. We have to make sure they are one hundred percent into helping out. If not . . ." Yas paused momentarily and then shrugged. "If not, then we don't proceed."

Wordlessly, Hunter kissed Yas. There was a desperation to it that only hardened Yas' resolve. He had to make this work.

"I trust you," Hunter murmured against his lips. "Now come, I want you to familiarize yourself with my weapons. We can't let you go inside that estate without knowing how to shoot a gun."

Yas allowed Hunter to lead him to the back of the cave. Hunter had laid out several mean-looking weapons on a table. Some of them were sleek and elegant-looking, and some were tiny and looked like toys. Yas caressed each with the tips of his fingers.

"Show me how to work each," Yas said. He might as well learn the purpose of each weapon and how to use them.

The next evening, Yas looked up at the moon. Hunter's other brothers in arms had yet to arrive, and Hunter was focused on cleaning his guns and sharpening his knives. Yas took the opportunity to slip into his gaseous form and send out one text message to his Master's—no, not that—Branagan's private cell number. He really must stop calling the man *Master*.

The night was still young, but already he could feel himself getting stronger. He didn't mention the call to Hunter or the changes he was going through. Every time he fed on Hunter's blood, something inside of him altered. The first thing he'd noticed was that his vision had sharpened.

All his life, when he had been trapped in the cage, he had always felt stronger during night time, but at the same time, he'd always felt weak. There were times his vision blurred to the point of blindness. Now, all he needed to do was focus on a spot, and he could see the tiniest speck of dust floating in the air around them. His mind worked faster too, and he could think of plans upon plans, rejecting some, contemplating others.

Gravel crunched beneath booted feet. Yas turned and faced his lover.

"I've got to go, Hunter. This is the only way we can get in there, kill Branagan, and save the others."

"What do you mean leave? Now? What the hell are you talking about?"

Yas sighed. "He will think I killed you and became afraid of the wide-open space — too afraid to stay outside, I've run back to him. He can be that short-sighted and egotistical. I've known him all my life. Mas — Branagan will think this was a momentary rebellion and also that his control over me is all-encompassing. He'll think to punish me, and because the first auction was interrupted, he's going to attempt another one to recoup his losses."

"If I allow this," Hunter began, but then stopped when he saw Yas' disbelief. Yas cleared his expression, put on a sublime one, and waited for Hunter to continue. "If we do this, he's going to hurt you. He's going to bleed you dry. Maybe kill you."

Yas rolled his eyes, but then walked over to Hunter to placate him. "I know exactly what he's going to do, Hunter. It's why I know this is the plan to follow." He patted his hand on Hunter's chest. "Look. I know you don't want me to get hurt, I don't want you to get hurt, either. But if we're going to go after Branagan, my plan is the way to do it. And that means I'm going to be bait."

Hunter's gaze grew intense. "No, Yas. No."

Yas leaned forward and pressed his lips against Hunter. At first, Hunter didn't respond, but Yas put all of the love he felt for Hunter into it. It took a moment, but then, he felt Hunter's body relax. Yas broke off the kiss and took one step backward.

"I sent him a message. Branagan. I told him I was meeting him in an hour. I'm sorry. Don't be angry."

Tapping on his new abilities, he adjusted his molecules to change into tiny water droplets. The look of surprise on Hunter's face morphing into anger cut through his heart.

"Come for me."

CHAPTER EIGHT

Yas

From several hundred feet high, Yas swooped down the desert plain, twisting and winding through canyons and crevices. If he had muscles in this form, he knew that the ones on his face would have strained from the grin that stretched across it. He sang and hummed through the air, a feeling of lightness in his being. Much as he was enjoying this shape — the speed made for faster traveling — it lacked the comfort from when he had been cradled in Hunter's arms. They'd only been separated for less than an hour, and already he keenly missed Hunter.

He let out a sigh and almost laughed when it came out like a howl preceding a storm. In mere minutes, the miles flew beneath him, and he wondered if he could travel with Hunter like this. It would be fascinating to see how he would react.

Yas regretted having to leave Hunter like that, not telling him what he had in mind, but he'd had no choice. After analyzing all the probable scenarios, only one plan had the least deaths involved. Hunter may not believe it, but Yas found killing a really painful affair. Even now, he couldn't unsee the humans he'd killed, the way their necks rolled after he'd snapped them with a twist of his hand.

His form moved in a crazy pattern when he shuddered in horror at the memory. No doubt, he would kill again if the situation called for it, but that didn't necessarily mean he had to like it. Also, the blood had tasted off. There had been a bitter, chemical aftertaste that had clung to his taste buds. Not like Hunter's blood, which tasted rich and fresh, and surprisingly potent.

Branagan was a monster who only kept him alive so he could drink his vampire blood and have sex. Yas' form once more shuddered in disgust, the movement making his form drop about ten feet closer to the ground.

Branagan loved his orgies and invited many of his friends and associates over to the estate so they could partake of Yas' blood diluted in red wine. The mixture allowed the guests to have sex with everyone all night. Thankfully, Branagan had been too selfish to share his secret pet, so his guests never found out where he got his steady supply of the highly valued, and rare, aphrodisiac. Since Yas had matured, he could only wonder how his blood had changed and how drinking it would affect humans. He had a feeling that one of the main reasons why Branagan did everything he could to suppress Yas' maturity was because mature vampire blood had a very different effect on humans.

A movement on the desert floor made him pause. His molecular form hovered lower until he deciphered that it was a vehicle on the road. He narrowed his vision to examine it, flinching back when he recognized the driver. It was Duke, Branagan's trusted bodyguard. Yas would never mistake the man's square-jawed, brutish face set in a perpetual frown, for anyone else. He'd endured the sting of his backhanded strikes and kicks to the stomach more times than he cared to remember. Beside Duke was Raymond, another bodyguard he recognized, but Yas had never interacted with him.

Yas dropped down until he hovered right beside the vehicle and peered into the back seat. Branagan was talking on his phone as usual. The man was never without the device, always giving out orders to whoever was on the other end. Yas was glad he was in this form for now. He didn't have to feel his heart pounding from the fear of seeing his keeper. Another point for the gaseous form. He stared at Branagan for a long time until he knew he had to go on ahead to where he'd agreed to surrender once more into the hands of his torturer.

Yas sped ahead of the SUV and searched for someplace to land. He needed at least a few minutes to take form and take on the behavior of his immature self. It didn't take him long to find the spot and immediately settled over it and began to concentrate on the physical form he was to take. Although Branagan had been there to witness the start of his evolution during his dramatic escape, he was sure that Branagan had been too angry to notice all of the subtle changes that came along with his maturity.

As soon as his body took shape, he shed the newly acquired aura of strength and confidence to take that of a frightened and helpless vampire. For added measure, he contrived to leave gaping wounds on his body. With those in place, he took one more sweep. He made to lower himself to the ground when he noticed that his clothes looked impeccably clean and tailored. Yas imagined a dirty, bedraggled look and willed it into place on the material. He only stopped when he felt satisfied with the results.

No sooner had he crouched low on the ground than he felt the vibrations of the approaching vehicle. It would take it another two or three minutes before Duke would spot him, so he sat and raised his knees so he could hide his face against them. He began to shake.

Yas didn't look up when the sound of a vehicle came to a stop. He didn't move when the doors opened and shut. He didn't flinch when a large hand roughly took hold of the back of his shirt and pulled him up. He opened his eyes and met the black ones in front of him.

"Now, now, Duke, be gentle with my pet."

Yas cowered at the sound of his Master's voice, while his feet dangled in the air for another brief moment before Duke lowered him. When his feet touched the ground, he didn't stand. He let out a whimper and slowly began to crawl toward Branagan. Over the hot, sandy ground, he moved on all fours, never raising his head, until his fingers reached the tip of his Master's leather shoes. With a trembling hand, he extended his fingers, stopping only when they were barely an inch from the shoes. He waited. Patiently.

"Look up, my pet. Look at me," Branagan ordered in a soothing voice. Yas didn't hesitate, immediately doing as ordered.

Branagan was a tall, thin man in his early sixties although he'd had several surgeries and looked to be in his mid-forties. His blue-white hair was superbly styled, and his brown eyes had an amused glint in them, although Yas knew the teasing was all a cover-up for a cruel personality. His tanned skin looked dark under the SUV's headlights. With the light behind him, he appeared to be a poorly drawn caricature of a man.

"You have been very naughty," Branagan said. Yas didn't lower his eyes. He would have to wait until given instruction to do so. Branagan let out a dismissive sigh, waving a hand toward the SUV. "Do get up and get inside the car. We'll wait until we get home before we talk."

Yas stood up but kept his head down. With his shoulders slumped, he walked past Duke and Branagan. Ahead of him, Raymond held open the door to the back seat. Yas didn't look at him when he got into the car. He settled behind the driver's seat and held his wrists together out in front of him. Branagan settled beside him while Raymond opened the trunk. He came around to Yas' side and took hold of his arms. Yas stared straight ahead as Raymond locked the chains around them before doing the same to his ankles. He was used to the process for this had been the norm whenever he needed to travel with Branagan. When Raymond was done securing the chains, he took his seat beside Duke in the front, and then they were on their way.

Yas looked out the window, not wanting to betray his amusement at the pathetic security measures. As a young vampire, the touch of steel on his skin had hurt to the point of incapacitation. Now, he felt nothing. To keep to his character role, he let out another whimper.

Branagan reached out and patted his knee. "I regret that the chains hurt you, my pet, but it's only for a few hours. When we get home, we'll take them off, hmm?"

Yas didn't answer, but he did nod his head and continued staring out the window. It was pitch dark outside, yet he could see quite clearly. No one spoke for the next three hours. Pretending exhaustion, he closed his eyes and leaned against the window and planned. He made sure to let out a pitiful whimper every now and then, though, to keep up with the role.

CHAPTER NINE

Hunter

Yas had been gone for hours before Hunter caught sight of Eighty and his colleagues. He zoomed in his vision to see two other hunters with him in an open-top jeep, driving across the desert, sand flying behind it and appearing as conspicuous as possible. If Branagan had spies looking for them, that would surely give them away.

They stopped close to the mountain, out of Hunter's view. There was nothing to do but wait and trust. And worry. Yas had been gone so long. He dreaded what he was putting himself into with Branagan. They had to hurry and stop this.

Come for me.

Yas' words echoed around in his head as surely as they'd been permanently implanted. It riled him up.

By the time Eighty finally breached the wall of the cave, Hunter was livid. "He left hours ago. He's being tortured. We have to go now!"

"Hey . . . easy, easy . . ." Eighty dropped his gear and reached out to give Hunter a bro-hug, slapping him on the back. "I've missed your ugly mug."

"Not possible. You see it every time you look in the damn mirror." Their familiar exchange helped ease his panic.

Eighty chuckled. "From what I've seen, your vamp can take care of himself. We need to focus on our part of the plan."

"I know. What's with the big show? Exposing yourselves like that. If he has spies—"

"He doesn't. Branagan didn't waste time. Word is that he's got Yas, Nine. He's already preparing for a big to-do at his estate. He's not looking for you. At all."

Some of Hunter's apprehensions disappeared, but he still narrowed his eyes at his wombmate. "Why's that?"

"Thinks you're dead."

Hunter snorted. "As if."

"Doesn't matter, Yas' plan worked perfectly, so far. Let's get the gear split out and get going. We don't have much time."

The two other hunters behind Eighty were in the process of opening up their packs, taking out weapons and other equipment. Everything about it was customary, normal. Hunter had worked in countless hunting parties before, and they appeared to be exactly that. He raised his eyebrow and nodded toward the other two.

"Oh, right. This is Five and Twelve."

Hunter studied the cyborgs. Except for their height and build, neither resembled the other, or Hunter and Eighty. They obviously came from separate lines, and from the look of their enhancements, they were older too — by several generations.

"Can we trust them?" Hunter didn't bother to lower his voice.

Eighty nodded and squeezed Hunter's shoulder. "Five broke out a vampire being tortured about three months ago and has been on the run ever since. The vampire died, anyway. His master had drained him too thoroughly by the time he got to him. Now he wants revenge."

He reached out and shook Five's hand. "Sorry to hear that."

"Not as sorry as I am." Five didn't hide the misery in his eyes. Hunter didn't know what to say, so he shifted his gaze back to the other cyborg.

"And this is Twelve."

The hunter grunted at him in response. There was an air of gloom about Twelve's posture as though he'd gone through a misery he couldn't quite calculate.

"He didn't get his vamp out before it was killed," Eighty said in a low voice.

"Oh."

"He was my mate. I got my revenge on his keeper, but there's more I can do." Twelve looked away and began assembling a laser blaster. Hunter let out a whistle as he stepped nearer to take a better look at the weapon. Where Twelve had gotten it was beyond him as it was supposed to be still in development.

"What we do know is that Branagan's planning to auction Yas off to these same idiots who think vampire blood is for fun and games. They treat vampires as if they were nothing more than a commodity. A bag of blood, created for their pleasure." Hunter could hear the disgust in Eighty's voice.

Hunter turned to Eighty. "And you? Did you have someone?"

Eighty looked away briefly. He looked as if he were weighing his words before revealing too much. "I have someone," he finally volunteered. "My vampire, Vitza. I don't know where he is. That's part of the intel I'm hoping to get from this douche and his party."

"Okay, I'm convinced. Let's do this. Tell me again how we're going to get in."

Eighty rolled his eyes. He pulled a similar weapon as Twelve's out of a backpack and began to check it. "Duh ... Yas is helping. He's sent enough information to make this easy."

The four of them discussed the plan, each contributing his part. Once it was solid, they talked about vampires. Hunter could see the heartbreak in their eyes as they talked about their vampires — their mates. They'd never be whole again, but maybe they could get some satisfaction in helping Eighty find Vitza. And helping Hunter secure Yas' safety as well.

It hadn't always been like this. When vampires were plenty, they were treasured and revered, and feared, of course. That was part of it, maybe too much of it. The humans tended to destroy what they feared — what they couldn't control. But even beyond all that, vampires and cyborgs were evolving into something new. This mating thing . . . they didn't know how it came about, but Hunter had a suspicion that it had something to do with the vampire blood the creators used when they tweaked the newer generation of cyborg. Hunter looked at Five, technically a fifth-generation cyborg and immediately reassessed his theory. Maybe it hadn't been a mistake at all.

"We need to go now, Nine." Eighty's voice shook Hunter from his thoughts. His wombmate stood at the front of the cave. Eighty's stocky build blocked the rising sun, creating dark shadows across the floor and across Hunter's heart. As he picked up his weapons and strode toward the vehicle, Hunter hoped they would be successful in this mission. He couldn't imagine living like Five and Twelve. Broken and alone. Then again, he also suspected that their vampires had not reached maturity, not like his Yas had. With grim determination, he pushed his somber thoughts to the side and focused on the mission. He was going to get Yas out of that estate alive and whole, or he would die trying.

CHAPTER TEN

Yas

Yas shivered. He didn't feel the cold of the laboratory, or the chains on his wrists, but they didn't know that. He looked in the mirror to his left, willing a look of terror on his features. Yas didn't want to raise any suspicion by staring too long at it. He'd seen enough and quite clearly. What he'd seen looking back at him in that mirror was exactly that — a weak vampire — but he also saw what he'd felt ever since Hunter had walked into his cage, into his life. Hunter had triggered his maturity.

Hanging his head down, his chin to his chest, he knew he was the picture of abject misery. He didn't need to allow anyone to see evidence that he was no longer a young or weak vampire. Yas peered under his lashes and stretched out his senses. He watched and listened in on what Branagan was saying. Branagan stood there on the other side with another man, a lab technician who Yas didn't recognize.

"Are you sure we got him back in time?" Branagan opened his hands in front of him in a graceful wave of movement as though giving permission to the technician to speak in his presence. It was a mannerism Yas had always associated with Branagan.

"We're not entirely sure, but yes, we think so," the technician said. "No one's seen a fully evolved vampire in almost three hundred years, so we're carefully monitoring his physical condition."

"I want you to be one hundred percent sure. The auction is in half an hour, and I don't want to have a repeat of last time."

"We've drawn enough blood from him to weaken any vampire, especially one his age, but in case of doubt, we're prepared to knock him out."

"Good, good," Branagan said. He let out a long sigh, and it sounded like a cross between a whimper and a chuckle. "I will let our clients in for a brief taste of the aphrodisiac. Make sure he's ready." There were footsteps, a door opened and then closed. Yes, he had been bled, but only a little. Not nearly enough to weaken him. Yas didn't know if it was because it was Hunter's blood, but the technicians had difficulty maintaining blood flow. Yas' blood had coagulated within the plastic tubing in seconds. It took them ten tries to finally get a quart of blood. His mouth curled into a smug smile. Seeing his blood so syrupy only confirmed his earlier theory that it too, had changed in properties. The only thing he didn't know was if it was still a potent aphrodisiac or if it was some form of toxic poison. He shrugged, rolled back his head, and straightened his spine. They would find out soon enough.

Behind him, another door opened and closed, and he risked a glance back to the mirror. The technician was no longer there. Ahead of him, the door to the room opened, and the same man came in, followed by four others. They were all wearing white lab coats. Yas considered their movements and focused on the tray they had rolled in with them. Yas shifted his gaze to the door and again, willed his sight to see through the walls — two armed guards were standing there. Thanks to Hunter, he now knew the weapons they held were automatics, and their bullets were laced with silver. Yas stifled the chuckle that bubbled up his throat. Foolish humans, to think that diluted silver could hurt him. He shifted his gaze once more to the technicians.

The one who had been talking to Branagan walked up to

him with an air of overconfidence and arrogance. Keeping to his role of a submissive vampire, Yas pretended to flinch when the man twisted his arm to expose the underside. Another technician handed him a syringe, which he took and aimed at the vein in the crook of Yas' elbow. Yas looked down and immediately saw that it was a silvery fluid. He took a tentative sniff, and when the scent of concentrated garlic hit his nose, he growled. He'd underestimated the technician's abilities. It seemed the man knew his vampires. The mixture would render a vampire paralyzed.

A red haze of instinctive fury took over. Yas pulled on the restraining chains and broke them. He wrenched his arm out of the man's hold. He evaded the man's attempt to stab him with the syringe. With the side of his palm, he dealt a sharp blow to the man's chin.

The man staggered back with a yowl of pain. A wave of irritation swept over Yas, so reached out and grabbed him by the back of his neck. In one lethal move, Yas simultaneously twisted and bent the man's neck. The resulting sound of vertebrae breaking and snapping cartilage was like music to his ears.

Satisfied that the man was dead, Yas turned his attention to the remaining four men who appeared to have frozen where they stood. Their inaction was their demise. In a blur of speed, he made quick work of slicing across their throats with his long, black nails.

Yas grimaced at the way the men grasped at their throats in an effort to stem the gush of blood.

Pathetic creatures, these humans.

He clicked his tongue in disgust as he looked around him. There was blood everywhere, the white of the lab coats and the paint on the walls emphasized the gore. The clock on the wall revealed his carnage had lasted a mere two minutes. He still had time to spare to get to his cage and pretend. A realization hit him then, and his smile broadened. He found he liked to act. With that thought in mind, he took off the manacles that were still on his wrists and left them where they dropped. Yas walked around and over the puddles of blood and opened the door, surprising the guards standing outside. He could feel his strength increasing. Instinctively, he knew it was because it was nearing evening.

The guards were slow to react. Once their throats were ripped out, Yas quickly pulled their bodies into the room. He searched the corridor and saw no one, but he did see the three cameras angled in his direction. These were easily dealt with. Yas took on the shape of his molecular form and silently went on his way to where he knew the auction room was going to be. As he passed another clock on the wall, he noticed only thirty seconds had passed.

Yas stopped in front of the door of the auction room, but he didn't enter immediately. He rematerialized and stilled as memories of his incarceration flooded his mind. Yes, it seemed that he had a weakness, and it was his rage of missing out on freedom. Rage would do well for him for it stirred a passion inside him that made him feel stronger. That night had fallen helped as well.

His skin prickled in anticipation. He sniffed, searching for a specific scent and caught it immediately. Branagan was in the room. But then so were a lot of others — most likely clients who were there to view him. Yas took a deep breath and allowed his body to take on the form of tiny water molecules, slid under the door, and went directly to where he knew his cage was.

A black, silky material draped over the metal cage blocked anyone from seeing inside. That worked to Yas' advantage as he rematerialized. Quickly, he wrapped the chains around his wrists and ankles, crouched low on the ground and waited. Outside the cage, he heard a voice advising the audience the auction was about to begin. The swirl of conversation stopped, then Branagan began to speak.

"Ladies and gentlemen, welcome to my home. My friends, I have invited you here tonight because I have something special to offer you. Something so rare, it was believed to be extinct. I must admit, I have had this creature in my possession since its infancy and am saddened over what I have to do. It's not that I no longer enjoy it or no longer want it.

"On the contrary, I wish I could keep it with me forever, but I cannot. The merger with AnalytIQ has been completed, and I fear I would be too busy to care for my pet." Applause followed, and Branagan paused.

When the clapping died, he continued with his speech. "As you may all know, new acquisitions can take up all of our time. Investments need a lot of attention. It needs to be pampered, cuddled, and *whipped* into the shape we want it to become. I came to realize that I no longer have any choice. I deeply regret this, but I must let it go. I must let go of something I truly treasure to someone who will not only enjoy having it in their homes but can make full use of its extraordinary gifts. This is where you, my friends, come in. I wouldn't wish for my favorite pet to get lonely. Ladies and gentlemen, I present to you, *Homo Nosferatu Vampiris!*"

The curtains dropped, and right on cue, Yas looked up and dropped a mask of terror on his face. Momentarily blinded by the bright light focused on him, he didn't have time to consider what to do next, for out of nowhere, popping noises beat a staccato rhythm. Wide-eyed, he looked up only to see the audience scramble about. A guard standing in front of his cage dropped to the floor. Dead. More popping noises followed, and the room erupted in chaos. Hunter's scent reached him.

Yas hissed at the crowd.

A voice barked out, "What the fuck, Hunter? Couldn't you

keep to the script?"

CHAPTER ELEVEN

Hunter

The hunters drove to the far reaches of Branagan's estate and entered through a little-used gate. Yas had given them the security codes and schematics of the main house.

A part of him wished they could have stayed at the cave. When Yas had turned into mist and vanished, it broke Hunter's heart a little, but he swallowed that pain down. It was time to get Yas back. That was all that mattered to him.

Eighty led them through the brush to the main estate. Their entrance would be a loading dock for supplies. It would have been somewhat busy, getting ready for the big auction earlier in the day, but with luck, it would be deserted by the time they arrived.

As they approached the huge, red brick building, Hunter's sensors indicated the time. "Hurry! It's started."

Twelve dashed off. His job was to kill the power and return to the main ballroom where the event would be held. The others would go there and secure the exits. No one would get out. They weren't killers, but they knew what had to be done. And they'd damn well do it. Once they dispatched the crowd — and Branagan — they would get the information on the vampires being held captive. With that information, they'd be able to hack into whatever system they needed to find and rescue the others.

After that . . .

Hunter planned on taking Yas far, far away from this

country that so blatantly disregarded intelligent life. Yas was special and amazing. He was brilliant with abilities that Hunter hadn't ever imagined. He needed to live. To be free. Hunter would make that happen, no matter the cost.

"This way." Eighty bumped shoulders with him. "Nine. Come on."

"When this is over, I'm changing my name." He was intelligent life, too. He deserved a real name and not a number.

"Good, but get your head in the game now."

He wanted to help his brother. Eighty had shown him what love and respect meant as children. They had been raised on a hunter farm, but they had always stuck together, always. Eighty had his back then and now. "I'm ready. Let's go."

Eighty used Yas' codes to lock the doors. "I'm adding some extra codes to keep them sealed."

Hunter could hear Branagan's booming voice inside the room. The bastard was talking about Yas as if he were nothing but a trained animal, some kind of house pet. The notion infuriated Hunter. "Mother fucker," he muttered.

Eighty smacked his shoulder. "Stop. I know. We need to get inside. Five is already entering through the stage door."

He nodded, and they circled around to the service entrance. Two security goons blocked the way. Before they could put up a fuss or signal an alarm, Eighty shot one between the eyes, and Hunter shot the other. They both dropped where they'd stood. Eighty shoved them to the side with his booted foot. "Let's go."

They went inside and secured the door behind them. The room was dark with tables and chairs spread around. Some people stood near the back, but most were sitting, facing the stage. Hunter and his brother had entered from the side. He could see Five sliding behind a curtain on the stage.

Center stage.

Where a spotlight shone down on Yas inside a cage. He put

up his hands to hide his face. Hunter saw them tremble as if in fear, and then he curled up on the floor. Rage boiled inside of him. His Yas should cower to no one. Without thinking about how he was breaking off from the agreed plan, he raised his weapon. The stock of the gun pressed into his shoulder. He aimed . . . not at Branagan, but at the guard who stood beside the gate of the cage.

They had planned for the signal to be the power cutting off. They were supposed to wait until that happened to make a move. Hunter couldn't. Not with Yas there on that stage. Hunter's heart broke with Yas' obvious misery. He didn't hesitate — he took the shot.

The guard dropped to the floor, and Yas' head jerked up. He hissed into the darkened crowd. A look of surprise popped up on Branagan's face. Then he narrowed his eyes. "Do not panic," he called out, but it was too late.

Chaos erupted. The guests all moved at once, some diving to the floor and under tables, some running to the doors. Hunter was shoved to the side. He glanced around the room, determined to find his target.

Eighty and Five shot people down without discernment. The crowd screamed. Hunter's chest tightened. They hated doing this. Killing indiscriminately was not what they did. They only harmed when necessary. This was necessary. These animals had been hurting vampires. That was more important.

Hunter pushed through a small crowd, throwing a man to the floor. He put a bullet through his skull, then pressed on. He needed to get to Yas on the stage.

There was a loud pop followed by the lights going out. The power had been cut three minutes after Hunter had taken the first shot.

Nothing Hunter could do about it now. He shifted his eyes to night vision and shot down several guests who got too close to him.

He leaped over several prone bodies and crawled up on the stage in time to see Twelve enter the side door, then fling himself into the melee. Yas was no longer there, and neither was Branagan. Hunter feared the worst.

The only thing left on the stage was the dead guard and chains lying inside the cage. Hunter turned to search the crowd. He saw blurs of movement, something speeding across the room too fast for his vision to hone in on. It must be Yas. He sighed in relief. Yas was safe . . . more than safe, he was zipping around the room, helping the hunters.

Pride welled up in Hunter's chest. He'd jumped the gun, but Yas—his lovely Yas—had everything under control.

Hunter tried to keep up with Yas' movements, but he couldn't. He finally gave up and did the next important thing on his list—he searched the room for Branagan. The fucking coward must have taken off. He wasn't around the stage or in the dwindling crowd. For Yas, he needed to find the bastard, but where was he?

Chapter Twelve

Yas

Yas had every intention of joining Hunter when he spied Duke on the other side of the room. He stopped in time to see him let a knife fly in the direction of Hunter's back. Yas didn't hesitate. He sped across the room with a speed that surprised even him, intercepted the knife and threw it back across the room. Duke froze, his eyes widened in shock before slowly sinking to the ground. Yas didn't think the man could survive having a knife stuck in his throat. He turned once more to search for Hunter, but his cyborg was already on the stage and looking about him. Once more, Yas sped his way but got distracted when he spotted another of Branagan's men aim at someone who looked like Hunter.

Yas sped in the guard's direction. The man never even realized he was there before his neck went in a one-eighty turn before dropping to the ground. Again and again, fate seemed to stand in the way, keeping Yas from joining Hunter. Finally, sick of all the interruptions and distractions keeping him from his lover, Yas rolled his eyes and decided enough was enough.

Willing his body to change into his gaseous form, he swept over Branagan's clientele and one by one, broke their necks. There weren't many because the two other cyborgs were picking them off one by one with their weapons. They were most likely Hunter's brother and friends.

When the last of the screaming humans was silenced, Yas

floated above the room searching for Branagan. The man was nowhere in sight, but Yas could sense his presence and scent his fear. He stayed up there for a minute, thinking over the possibilities of the man's location when he saw something move under a table that had managed to stay up while the rest were either upended or broken from bodies crashing on them.

Yas lowered his form right beside where Hunter stood looking around him. When he rematerialized, Hunter jumped a foot in the air. Yas stretched out a hand to catch him on his shoulder and guide him back to the ground.

"Yas, for fuck's—" Hunter growled out.

"Shh . . . ." Yas placed a finger over Hunter's lips to silence him, pointing with his other hand in the direction of the table. His gaze never looked away from where he'd spotted Branagan.

Yas did his vampire magic trick—appearing beside Branagan one second, grabbing him by the scruff of his neck and vanishing, only to reappear beside the table in the next. He pulled Branagan out, ignoring his screams of terror. His face was as white as a sheet, and his hair was in disarray. Yas grimaced at the smell of urine and something else coming from him.

"Well, well, well," a cyborg said, who looked so much like Hunter they might as well have been twins. Yas thought this must be Eighty, Hunter's wombmate.

"Hello, I'm Yas. You must be Eighty." Yas pulled Branagan over to where Hunter and Eighty stood.

"Hello, Yas. Meet Five and Twelve." The cyborg even sounded like Hunter. Yas already liked him. He threw a quick glance at the two others. They were both taller than Yas, but neither as tall as Hunter and Eighty. All the hunters were stocky, and Five and Twelve had massive shoulder muscles, making them seem even bigger. They also had sad eyes. It was clear they didn't enjoy killing any more than Yas did, but they did what they must.

"Hello, Five. Hello, Twelve."

The two gave him a silent salute. Yas turned back to Branagan.

"Hunters, meet my *former* master, Branagan." Yas pulled a chair into an upright position and sat a now silent Branagan there. His former master looked as if he'd lost all of his confidence and didn't know what to do about it. Branagan kept stealing glances at Yas and back to the cyborg standing before him and back again.

"I think he's a little confused," Twelve said.

"Let's unconfuse him, then," Five said, as he stepped forward. Branagan flinched back, and if Yas hadn't been holding on to the chair, he would have fallen out of it.

"No, no. I think we owe this one to Yas, don't you think?" Hunter asked.

Yas sent his mate a beatific smile for his suggestion and then blew him a kiss. Without waiting to see how Hunter reacted to his love play, Yas crouched down on his knees and peered into Branagan's face.

"Hello, *Master*," he cooed.

Branagan's eyes widened at the seductive tone. Behind him, he heard four harsh, indrawn breaths from the cyborgs. Yas threw a glance over his shoulder and chuckled. Except for Hunter who didn't bother to hide the stiff erection beneath his pants, the other hunters placed their hands on their groins.

"Tone it down a bit, sweets," Hunter said, casting an amused looked at the other hunters.

Yas dipped his head and turned back to Branagan.

"We're going to have to ask you a few questions, and I want you to answer them truthfully," Yas continued, subtly modulating his voice, to compel obedience from the man he once regarded as his master. Branagan's face relaxed under his control, his eyes going flat as he stared into space. Yas stood up and waved Hunter and his brothers over. "You can ask him anything you want."

Hunter stepped in front of Yas and held his gaze for a moment before turning to Branagan. Yas searched for another chair. He sat there as the cyborgs got all the information that they needed from the compliant Branagan. Until they were finished, Yas would patiently wait for his turn. He had time.

Three hours later, Hunter crouched before Yas, placed his weapon over his thighs and put his hand on Yas' knee. He looked tired and relieved at the same time, but there was an aura of grimness about him.

"Did you get all the information you needed?" Yas asked. He reached up and caressed Hunter's cheek.

Hunter nodded, tilting his face ever so slightly to kiss Yas' palm.

"Yes. We got it all."

"You don't sound happy."

Hunter sighed and ran a hand down his face. "No. It's all good, but I'm tired." He met Yas' gaze. "After we get out of here, I want to take you somewhere safe."

"Another cave?"

"No," Hunter said, amusement leaching into his voice. "Another country. There are places out there where vampires and cyborg live in peace. At least, that's what Eighty told me. I want to give it a go."

Yas leaned down and brushed a light kiss on Hunter's lips. "Yes, we will give it a go."

A smile broke on Hunter's face, and Yas couldn't resist kissing him again. "First, I must make things right."

Hunter threw a glance over his shoulder. "I'll wait for you." He took to his feet and waved his brother cyborgs over. When they reached them, Hunter tilted his head toward the exit.

"Yas needs some time alone with Branagan." The three cyborgs didn't say anything but merely dipped their heads briefly in Yas' direction and left.

Yas approached Branagan and stood looking down at him. "Awaken," he said.

Branagan jerked and blinked about him in confusion. He began to straighten his rumpled shirt and combed his fingers through his hair only to freeze when he realized who it was standing beside him.

"You," he said.

"Yes, it's me. But I'm no longer your pet. Remember Hunter8279, the cyborg you hired to guard me?"

Branagan's gaze flicked over to where Hunter and the others were moving through the exit before looking back at Yas.

"Well, turns out he's my mate." Yas shrugged and walked behind Branagan's chair. He placed his hands on Branagan's shoulders, felt the man tremble under his touch. The nails on his fingers lengthened to sharp points. Branagan's trembling increased as Yas caressed the skin on his neck with the pointed tips.

"I promised myself I would make you pay for what you did to me and my kind." Yas leaned down until his lips were in line with the pulsing vein on Branagan's neck. "Before we get there, I need to know the answer to a question."

"What question is that?"

Yas smiled at the space in front of him. "I was wondering about my blood and how it would affect humans after I matured." He leaned down and pressed his cheek against Branagan's temple. "Are you as curious as I am?"

Ten minutes after Hunter and his brothers had left him in the room with Branagan, Yas came out to find them talking quietly among themselves. Hunter gave him a welcoming smile.

"All done?"

Yas nodded with a sigh of relief. "Yes. All done." He gave the cyborg a happy smile. "He answered my question brilliantly."

"And what question was that?" It was Five who asked.

Yas leaned back into Hunter's chest, perfectly comfortable in the arms of his lover.

"I made him drink my blood one last time," Yas said.

When he didn't continue, Eighty gave him a glare, and Yas' smile broadened even more.

"And?" Eighty asked.

"He didn't take it too well."

"So, he's dead then?" Hunter asked.

Yas leaned up and kissed Hunter's jaw. "Yes. He's dead." He didn't say anything more. Thankfully, Hunter and the others didn't ask any more questions. He could still see the ecstatic look on Branagan's face before he started to choke. Yas didn't think anyone could survive their blood boiling. He was still thinking about what he'd discovered when he heard barking in the distance.

"It's time to go, Yas," Hunter said.

Yas nodded and moved to follow Hunter, but the barking didn't stop. "Wait."

"What is it?"

"Wait for me," was all Yas said before he shifted to his molecular form.

With the stars high above, his preternatural speed gained strength as he flew. When he got to where the barking was coming from, he took shape. In front of him were fifteen cages, each one occupied by huge, hairy, bear-like dogs. The resemblance to the canine family ended there. Each stood over forty inches and weighed no less than two hundred pounds each. Also, their eyes glowed an eerie aquamarine. They were gentle yet protective creatures that could take down an immature vampire. All fifteen quieted and sat on their haunches, heads tilted as though curious about what Yas was about to do next. The genetically altered breed of dogs had been designed to do their master's bidding, to control immature vampires, but they didn't fear Yas, nor he, them. In fact, they treated Yas as part of their pack.

Caged for most of their lives, they were no different than Yas. After drawing blood from Yas, Branagan would gift him with some playtime with the dogs. Through time, they had become a pack. They were family. With grim determination, Yas broke the chains that kept the cages locked. One by one, the dogs ran up to him, tails wagging, whining, and whimpering their welcome.

"Settle," Yas said. As one, they sat by his feet and stared up at him with adoration in their eyes. "Come."

When Yas returned ten minutes later, he couldn't help laughing at the looks on Hunter and his brother's faces.

"I knew your vampire was awesome, Nine, I just didn't know he had vampire dogs with him as well," Eighty said when one of the dogs approached to sniff at his boot.

Hunter took Yas in his arms when he finally reached him.

"You're incredible, you know that?" Hunter kissed the top of Yas' head. "I love you."

"I love you, too. Now, can you get me out of here? I hate this place. Take me somewhere safe, where we can be together without fear."

"Where your dogs can be safe as well?"

Yas nodded. "Yes. They're kind of my brothers, and like me, they were chained and caged."

"And now you're free." Hunter led him to where their vehicle was hidden in a copse of overgrown trees.

"Yes, now we're free." Yas took one last look at Branagan's estate, the looming structure full of shadows and death. It was the only home he'd known, but with Hunter now in his life, he would never go back. He didn't know what the future would bring him and Hunter, but from where he stood, there was only a promise of a future and love. That was more than he could ever ask for.

EPILOGUE

Hunter

It had been a long road to get to Noridge, but Hunter never felt happier. He watched the view speed by outside the window as Yas lay curled beside him under the blanket. Hunter hadn't lowered his guard until the transport he and Yas were on had crossed the border. There had been a moment of fear when the transport stopped at the border checkpoint. He'd thought the authorities would board and arrest them. But none of that had happened. Only when the transport's speed increased had Hunter finally allowed himself to relax, but not by much. Yas had slept on as those in charge on either side conferred and exchanged documents for safe passage.

The long vehicle moved silently but swiftly as it crossed the border. One second they were still in Praem Shar and the next, they were in Noridge. For Hunter, it was as though his whole life had flashed before him in an eternity of the longest minute he'd ever experienced.

According to what Eighty had told him, Noridge was one of the most progressive countries in setting civil rights laws for vampires and cyborgs alike. They had been the first to discover the mating link between the two species and passed laws that granted sanctuary for those seeking its protection. That had been over a decade ago. Hunter wondered how that information had been kept secret for so long, but that was all for later. Right now, he was glad that he and Yas had been granted asylum.

Eighty had prepared the documents for them. It had been difficult at first for they had to create an identity for Yas. Also, there had been the question of the dog hybrids that Yas refused to leave behind. It had taken them eight bizarre months hiding in caves and other abandoned places. The wait had been excruciating, especially as he and Yas had moved about constantly—never staying in one place too long. Food and supplies had not been an issue thanks to Eighty.

They finally got the word that they had been granted asylum three days before. Eighty contacted them and said they needed to be on a cargo train at a specified time. Hunter took him at his word, and he packed them up and moved them out with haste.

Eighty met them at the meet-up point. He handed over their new identification papers before introducing them to the Captain. Once the required exchange was done, Eighty said his goodbyes. He'd found a lead on his vampire, Vitza's, whereabouts. Hunter was glad that his wombmate's vampire was still alive, but Hunter couldn't join him in the search without risking his asylum status. He was gratified to see Five and Twelve in the distance. They would keep Eighty safe. He could only hope that they would all make it out alive and join them in Noridge.

He and Yas had been given quarters on the second deck. Yas' pets were in their cages below deck. Thankfully, they were intelligent creatures and paid heed to Yas' caution they keep quiet. The creatures never let out a single howl during their three days of travel—not even when Yas had to delay feeding them so as not to alarm the passengers and crew.

Hunter let out a sigh as he ran his hands through Yas' dark locks. "Babe . . . I want to tell you something."

"Hmm . . ." Yas leaned to the side, exposing his face from under the covers.

"Now that we're here—"

Yas jerked upright, craning his neck in every direction. "We're here?"

"Yes, we just crossed over."

Yas tossed the covers back and jumped to his feet. "Yay!"

Hunter scowled up at him. Immediately, Yas quieted. "What?"

"I want to tell you something," Hunter said with a sigh.

"Oh, okay." Yas settled down, taking the empty seat beside Hunter. "Tell me."

"I want to change my name. I don't want to be a hunter or a number."

"Okay. What should I call you?"

Hunter smiled. That was his Yas—so sweet and willing unless you crossed him. His strength was even more of a turn on.

"Fida."

Yas raised one perfect eyebrow. "You want me to call you Fida?" Yas screwed up his face. "What does that even mean?"

"It means sacrifice or redemption."

Yas leaned back into his seat, a thoughtful look over his face, but after a moment he smiled at Hunter. "Yes. That's fitting." Then he pounced, pushing Hunter—no, Fida's shoulders to the mattress. He took a slow, upward sniff along Fida's neck, letting out a soft purr that usually preceded his feeding.

Fida felt his cock tighten in his pants. That purr never failed to arouse him. They both sighed when Yas sank his teeth into Fida's neck.

Fida could hear Yas' thoughts inside his head. *"I love you, Fida."*

"I love you, too," Fida said, relaxing under Yas' weight. When Yas finally retracted his fangs, Fida was about ready to burst. Yas leaned back, placing his weight over his knees. His pink tongue licked at the droplet of blood on the side of his mouth. Fida had never seen anything or anyone so sexy.

"Now I have to fuck you." Fida pushed himself up to a sitting position.

A slow grin bloomed over Yas' red lips. "If you can."

Never one to let go of a challenge, Fida reached for Yas who was still straddling him, but in a blur of movement, Yas disappeared and then reappeared. Hunter found himself pinned under Yas. He bucked his hips upward, catching Yas unbalanced. Gaining the upper hand, Fida wrapped his arms around Yas. They wrestled each other, each giving and receiving until Yas finally had Fida pinned once more.

"I have something in mind." Yas grabbed the lube they'd left on the window sill and handed it to Fida. "Work me open."

Using thick, deft fingers, Fida made quick work of the process. Yas was still loose from their earlier frolic, so it didn't take long. While he was prepping him, Yas had taken advantage of his position and unbuttoned Fida's pants. Naked at last, Fida got on his knees, pulling Yas by his hips and positioned him. Before he could even attempt to mount his lover, Yas changed up again. Swinging his long legs over Fida's thighs, he made quick work of straddling him and sinking onto Fida's thick cock. Fida gasped. It all happened so quickly. Yas slowly started undulating, pulling at his cock. The heat was incredible, and he let out another gasp.

"You like?" Yas half moaned, half sang.

"Yes . . ." Fida wrapped his fingers around Yas' hips and watched him glide, up and down. He marveled at the intense expression on Yas' face, but that was how Yas did everything.

Yas measured his pace and slowly brought him to the edge of climax, and Fida could no longer hold back. He bucked up into Yas, his fingers digging deep into the skin over his hips. "Fuck!" He gritted the words out, feeling the muscles on his neck tighten as he bit down over his lip.

"Yes . . . my hunter . . ." Yas moved faster. The heat escalated.

They pounded into each other as if it was the last time they would ever connect, though they both knew that wasn't true. They would be together for a very long time. Once a vampire became fully evolved, they could live forever. No one knew how long. And cyborg? They had vampire blood and DNA built-in. They aged very slowly. And better, living in Noridge would be safe for them both. No one would dare touch them here. Not while they had asylum status.

Yas yanked at his hair. "Fuck me, Hunter . . ."

"Not Hunter — say it — call me Fida."

Yas groaned as he fucked harder, tilting his hips and banging into that special spot. "Fi . . ." He came hard, shooting his essence between them.

Fida followed with stars behind his eyes and a cool vampire in his arms. Exactly as it should be.

ABOUT JO TANNAH

I am a wife, mother and blogger by day, a writer by night. It can be difficult, to say the least, but it is a challenge that keeps me on my toes.

I grew up listening to folk tales my father and nannies told either to entertain us children or to send home a message. These narratives I kept with me, and finally, I wrote them down in a journal way back when I kept one. Going through junk led to a long-forgotten box, and in it was the journal. Reading the stories of romance, science fiction and horror I had taken the time to put to paper brought to light that these were tales I had never met in my readings.

The tales I write are fictional, but all of them are based on what I grew up with and still dream about. That they have an M/M twist is simply for my pleasure. And I hope, yours as well.

Twitter: @JoTannah
Instagram: https://www.instagram.com/jo_tannah/
Facebook: https://www.facebook.com/profile.php?id=100012354600386
Website: http://jotannah.com
Goodreads Author Page: https://www.goodreads.com/JoTannah
Email: jotannah1@gmail.com

Also from Jo Tannah

Compelled, Winter Roses, Grass Stains and Flip Flops, Around The Block, His Christmas Valentine, His Gentle Incubus

Tales from the Archipelago: Kilig, The Secrets He Keeps

Taboo Series: Taboo, A Taboo Christmas, Taboo Pleasures, Christmas Unwrapped, The Summer Knows

Hidden Series: Hidden Evils, Hidden Dimensions, Hidden Fates

Rise of the Symbionts: Royal Guardian, Royal Consort, Royal Symbionts, Tarragon

CyNapse Security, Inc.: Objectified, Kaleidoscope

The Adventures of Marcus Kildud: The Hunt

Chronicles of the Serai: Heart Held Hostage

The Phantom Hunters: Waylaid

With Ann Mickan: Lemonade Stand, A Lemon Flavoured Christmas

Free Stories: Sock It To Me, Tell Him

About Lynn Michaels

Lynn Michaels lives and writes in Tampa, Florida where the sun is hot, and the Sangria is cold. When she's not writing she's kayaking, hanging with her husband, or reading by the pool. Lynn writes Male/Male romance because she believes everyone deserves a happy ending and the dynamics of male characters can be intriguing, vulnerable, and exciting. She has both contemporary and paranormal titles and has been writing since 2014. Her stories don't follow any set guidelines or ideas, but come from her heart and contain love in many forms.

Facebook friend: https://www.facebook.com/lynn.michaels.71465

Lynn's Loonie Bin—Facebook Readers' Group: http://bit.ly/LooneyBinonFacebook

Twitter: https://twitter.com/sljasble

Goodreads: https://www.goodreads.com/author/show/8430620.Lynn_Michaels

eXtasybooks profile: http://www.extasybooks.com/lynn-michaels/

Instagram: https://www.instagram.com/lynnmichaels69/

ALSO FROM LYNN MICHAELS

A Blessing in Disguise

By

Catherine Lievens

Being turned into a vampire is a malediction—or a blessing in disguise.

Dryden lost everything in the late 1800s when he sacrificed himself for the man he loved—his freedom, his lover, his humanity. He's been a prisoner and a slave since then, and he knows there's no way out of it except death. The man who turned him won't let him die, though, and Dryden can't see another way out.

Morgan has been looking for Dryden ever since he volunteered to take Morgan's place for punishment after he robbed a powerful vampire. He knew Dryden was turned into a vampire, so he did the same. He and his maker, Silvester, have been drifting around following leads since then.

And now they've finally found Dryden.

DEDICATION

(Remove this and insert your dedication . . . if no dedication, disregard and I'll remove when formatting)

CHAPTER ONE

Dryden kept his gaze on the floor. It never paid to look Rochester in the eyes.

"There's a party tonight," Rochester drawled.

Dryden gritted his teeth. He didn't answer in any way, didn't show that the news affected him. He was still sporting the scars of the beating he'd gotten during Rochester's last party.

"As always, I expect you to be there for the guests. Give them what they want, when they want it, including the live snacks."

And *that* was what Dryden had been punished over last time. He'd learned his lesson, though. As much as he wanted to help the poor humans, he couldn't do it again. Another torture scene would drive him crazy, and that wasn't what he wanted.

No, he wanted to die.

If he'd been able to drive Rochester to the point that Rochester killed him, he would have pushed, but Rochester knew he wanted to die. He'd known ever since he'd turned Dryden into a vampire, and he'd made sure Dryden never would. Every time Dryden had tried to take his own life or push Rochester to the point of no return, he'd failed.

And he was still there, in Rochester's house, in his power.

"You know, sometimes I still wish I'd ignored your offer," Rochester said. He sounded pensive, but Dryden knew better. Rochester always knew what he was doing or saying, and he made sure it caused the maximum amount of pain.

"Your boyfriend was so much prettier than you. He'd have made for good entertainment, if you know what I mean."

Dryden knew. He supposed he should feel lucky that Rochester had never wanted him that way, which was one of the reasons he'd begged to take Morgan's place back when he was human — when *they* were humans. Dryden wasn't human anymore, and it had been so long that Morgan had to be little more than dust in the earth by now.

Dryden missed him.

He'd missed Morgan since day one, but he'd learned to deal with it. No matter how much he was tortured, he never regretted it. He could too easily imagine what Rochester would have done to Morgan if he'd been allowed to turn him into a vampire and enslave him for the rest of his life, and it was so much worse than what Dryden had gone through.

"I don't like it when you talk about him," Lucia, Rochester's wife, said.

"Sorry, dear. I was just having a chat with Dryden here."

"Talk about something else, like maybe how he shouldn't let the snacks escape this time. I don't think you were hard enough on him to make sure he learned the lesson last time."

Dryden hated both of them. Rochester, with his golden good looks that made him appear more like an angel than the monster he was, and Lucia, dark in contrast, her lips always red, be it with lipstick or blood. Dryden wanted to see both of them dead, and he'd kill them himself if he could.

But Rochester knew that, and that meant Dryden was chained to the wall in his cell every morning, just in case. And when he wasn't in his cell, when he was forced to do Rochester and Lucia's bidding during the night, his ankles were chained together so he couldn't run.

He had no way to escape. He'd tried more times than he could remember, and they all ended the same way — with him in pain and knowing he'd have to go through this again and again until Rochester decided he was bored. Since it had been more than a hundred years, Dryden was starting to doubt he ever would.

"I can't do anything right now, my love. He needs to be able to serve tonight."

"Pity. But tomorrow?"

"Mmm, why not? I suppose it depends on how well he works tonight."

Dryden hated them. He hated being talked down to. He hated having to serve them, having to watch the depravities they got into and clean up after them.

But this was his life, and until he found a way to end it, it was what he'd have to go through.

"Talking about this makes me . . ." Lucia said.

Dryden hoped they were going to tell him to leave before they got naked. They were beautiful to look at and to watch, but it was like watching two venomous snakes ready to strike. And at least snakes were animals. They didn't know better. Rochester and Lucia did, but they chose to behave like monsters.

"Leave," Rochester snapped.

Dryden didn't wait for him to repeat himself. He walked out of the room as fast as he could with the manacles around his ankles. The door slammed closed behind him, but the sound wasn't enough for him not to hear the loud moan.

He shuddered in horror. Those two were terrible in normal situations, but they got worse when they wanted sex. He counted himself lucky that Rochester had never wanted him that way and that Lucia was too jealous to want to share her husband. Of course, what she didn't know didn't make her angry, but Dryden wasn't going to be the one to point out Rochester had at least four other people in his life. Dryden might want to die, but he'd rather it happened in a more peaceful way than having Lucia tear his head off.

She hated him and who he reminded Rochester of. Sometimes, it gave Dryden a certain satisfaction, but he knew when to stop pushing, or when not to push at all.

Dryden hadn't been told what to do, so he went to the spot in the garden where he spent the most time. It was private, hidden between trees and wild bushes. Rochester and his wife didn't care about the garden, even though it was beautiful. The only part they made sure was taken care of was the section right outside the house, and it was only because sometimes the parties expanded out from inside.

Dryden looked up at the tall wall that ran around the house and the garden. He'd tried to climb it several times, even though they'd arrived at the house only a month or so before, but he wasn't able to. His ankles were bound together, and the wall was smooth. If he ever managed to leave, it wouldn't be that way.

He sighed and sat with his back against the wall. He wasn't going anywhere. He'd given up that hope a long time ago, and in the moments in which he couldn't help thinking about it, he reminded himself that he had nothing waiting for him out there. He'd been in Rochester's hands for more than a hundred years. Everyone he'd known, including the man he'd loved, was dead and had been dead for a long time.

The only thing Dryden had to live for was revenge, and sometimes, it didn't feel like it was enough.

Morgan hit the wall with his fist, relishing the pain.

"That's not going to solve your problem," Silvester drawled. He was on the couch watching TV. Morgan had no idea what the movie was, and he didn't care.

"I haven't been able to solve my problem in a hundred and twenty years. I doubt anything will solve it."

Silvester sighed and turned the TV off. "Are you done

taking your anger out on the wall?"

Morgan rubbed his face. He wanted to do much more than hit the wall once, but the converted warehouse they were staying in wasn't theirs, and while he could pay for any damage he caused, he'd rather not. "Yeah."

"Sit down."

Morgan's first instinct was to tell Silvester not to order him around, but he pressed his lips together and flopped onto the couch. He pushed a strand of hair back and looked around for a hair tie, but of course, there wasn't one around.

He huffed.

"Damn it, Morgan. What's wrong with you?"

"I didn't do anything!"

"Yeah, you did. Why are you so freaked out? It's not the first time we've followed a bad trail."

Morgan pulled on his hair. "I know."

"What is it, then?"

"I really thought this was going to be the right one." And it had been so long. Morgan had been looking for Dryden for a hundred and twenty-something years. He'd lost count after a while, but he knew it was much longer than he'd thought it would be in the beginning. He would never have had a chance to find Dryden if he hadn't begged Silvester to turn him into a vampire. As it was, he still hadn't found the love of his life, and he didn't know if he ever would.

Silvester patted Morgan's thigh. "I know it's hard."

"You do? I can't remember, did you lose someone you loved the same way I did? Did the man you love sacrifice his life and his freedom so you didn't have to be enslaved?"

Silvester held his hands up. "Right. Sorry. If you're going to be this bitchy, I'm going to go and let you brood."

Morgan took a deep breath, then another. Silvester was right. Morgan was freaking out, but it had nothing to do with him, and it wasn't going to help. "I'm sorry."

Silvester smiled. "I'd have left you behind a long time ago if I didn't want to hear you rant and bitch, Morgan. I understand how disappointed you are, but we have eternity to find your man."

"I know." But that meant Rochester also had eternity to torture Dryden, and Morgan had no doubt that was exactly what he was doing. The man was a cruel asshole. That was why Morgan needed to find Dryden as soon as possible.

Silvester rubbed Morgan's back. "I know it's hard, and no, it's not because someone offered himself to take my place as a vampire and as a slave. But I've been through a lot, Morgan, and while we might not share the same experiences, it doesn't mean I don't know how much you hurt. I want to find him as much as you do."

"And to kill Rochester."

"And to kill Rochester."

Silvester had never gone into details why he wanted to kill the man, and Morgan didn't care. The only thing that mattered was that they had a common goal — to rid the world of Rochester — and that sooner or later, they'd do just that.

But first they had to find the guy, and they'd been trying to do that for the past hundred-plus years. Rochester was a professional at disappearing, though, and Silvester and Morgan had never managed to be in the same room as him. The same city, yes, and even the same neighborhood sometimes, but Rochester always managed to leave before Morgan could get his hands on him.

"What if we're too late?" he asked, his voice barely more than a murmur. This was something he tried not to think about because it hurt. It hurt, and it made him wonder if everything he was doing was going to be for nothing. What if Dryden was dead? What if Rochester had taken care of that years ago?

But what if he wasn't? What if Dryden was still alive and

in Rochester's hands? No, Morgan couldn't stop until he was a hundred percent sure that Dryden was safe or dead. He'd never forgive himself otherwise.

And he still wanted Dryden. He'd never forgotten his lover, and he doubted he ever would. But time was passing, and it was wearing on him, every day a bit more. How long could he go on like this? How long could Dryden, if he was still alive?

Silvester got up and held his hand out. "Come on. It's time for some training."

Morgan huffed again. "Training? I'm pouring my heart out to you, and you want to train?"

"Yep. No better moment. It's obvious you're thinking too much, and you know this is the best way to get rid of those thoughts. Obsessing over them and what you might have done wrong won't help you, but training will. We have to be ready for Rochester."

Morgan took his hand and let him haul him to his feet. "Are you ever going to tell me what he did to you? Who he took from you?" he asked.

Silvester hesitated. "Maybe once he's gone. What he did doesn't matter to you, though. It's not relevant to your mission."

"It's important to you, though, and I care about you." Sometimes, Morgan wondered if it wouldn't be easier for him to be with Silvester. But there was no way he could forget Dryden, and besides, he wasn't in love with Silvester. They were friends, maybe best friends, but it would never be more than that.

Silvester smiled, but it was forced. "I know. I think you're a bit too down right now for me to tell you my story, though. You need to regroup and try again."

"Are you ever going to tell me to give up?"

"No. I don't think you should. Dryden is out there

somewhere, and you're the only one who knows that and who's doing something to try to help him."

"You are, too."

"I am, but you're the important one, the one he'll be glad to see when we finally find him. Now come on. Enough talking. It's time to put those muscles of yours to good use. You're going to need to know what you're doing when you find Rochester."

Morgan already knew what he was doing. Silvester had made sure of that after he'd turned him. But Silvester was right—the more Morgan trained, the better it would be. He was going to find Rochester and kill him, and he was going to get Dryden back.

No matter how long it took him.

Dryden hated this. He didn't want to have to guide Rochester's *guests* to the back room. He didn't want to stand there while they attacked drugged and terrified humans. He didn't want to have to leave the near dead humans there once the assholes were done eating them.

But he had to.

He'd rebelled against Rochester last time, and it hadn't ended well for him. As much as he hated not being able to help, he had to choose between them and himself, and this time, the choice was easy—almost too easy. It made him uncomfortable with himself, but he'd learned to ignore that kind of feeling a long time ago.

Dryden wished he could go back to the party, even though it meant he'd have to go around offering glasses of blood. At least he wouldn't have to listen to the whimpers and moans of pain.

"That was a good one," the woman he'd brought to the backroom said as she rose.

She'd been straddling the lap of one of the male humans, and while she'd sounded like she'd enjoyed the position and the biting, the human hadn't. His eyes were wide and glassy, and he reached for Dryden, but Dryden looked away.

He hated this. He wanted to help, but he couldn't.

The woman pushed her red hair behind her back and slunk toward Dryden. Dryden tensed, already knowing what was going to happen. Some vampires mixed feeding and sex as easily as if the two belonged in the same situation. Dryden supposed he might have done that, too, if he hadn't been turned in the circumstances he'd been. But for him, life as a vampire had always been about blood and pain, not pleasure, and that would never change.

No matter how many beautiful women tried to get into his pants.

She stopped in front of Dryden and ran a finger down his chest, pulling the collar of his shirt to the side. He reached up and pushed it back, but she wasn't having any of it. She slipped a fingertip under the shirt and fingered the thick scar that was there, just under his collarbone. It made Dryden shiver, and not in a good way, both because of the memory the scar brought up and because he didn't want this woman to touch him.

Dryden stepped back. "I'll make sure you get back to the party safely."

The woman arched a brow. "Safely? Why, do you think someone is going to attack me on the way back?"

"Of course not." But Rochester didn't want any of his guests left alone in his house. He didn't trust them, just like they didn't trust him.

She pouted. "I'm not going to be able to convince you to have fun with me?"

She could have forced Dryden if she'd wanted to. He was surprised she didn't, but he supposed not everyone Rochester knew was an asshole. That didn't make this woman a good person, but she could be worse. Or maybe she *was* worse, but Dryden didn't know it because she was being nice in this situation.

He didn't care, and he didn't want to find out.

He stepped to the side so she could walk ahead. "Please, after you," he murmured, slightly bowing. He hated these signs of submission, but by now, they were ingrained in him and came almost naturally. Rochester had been training him in this ever since he'd turned him into a vampire.

Dryden shuddered when he thought it could have been Morgan in his place. Morgan had always been the strongest one of them both, at least mentally, but things would have been so much worse for him if Dryden hadn't taken his place. Rochester hadn't wanted him only as a slave like he was using Dryden. No, he'd wanted Morgan for his body, because Morgan was small and had long hair and Rochester had wanted him in his bed since the first time that he'd seen him. Rochester hadn't been married to Lucia back then, so no one would have stopped him.

Dryden had. He still didn't know why Rochester had agreed to the exchange. He'd wanted Morgan, and Morgan had been the one who'd snuck into his house and had stolen from him, not knowing that he was opening their lives up for something much more dangerous than cops and the law. Dryden didn't know why, but even after the years — decades — of torture, he was glad Rochester had agreed.

"What's your name?" the woman asked.

"My name doesn't matter."

She arched a brow. "It doesn't matter, huh? I bet Rochester doesn't want you to say it. Am I right?"

She was. Dryden had never found out why, but Rochester had made sure he knew not to tell anyone who he was and the history they shared.

"I'll take your non-answer as a no." She frowned. "Hey, are you—"

"Auriel. Are you monopolizing my slave?" Rochester drawled.

Dryden hadn't even seen him, and he fucking hoped the man wouldn't think he'd been about to speak. Of course, even if he didn't think Dryden had, it didn't mean he wouldn't take the opportunity to torture him a little. The asshole lived to cause pain, and he particularly liked inflicting it on Dryden. Dryden often wondered if it was because he'd taken Morgan's place, allowing Morgan to slip from Rochester's hands. He had no doubt Rochester had been planning on somehow getting Morgan anyway, but Morgan had disappeared right after Dryden had been taken, just like Dryden had ordered him to. Dryden had been surprised since Morgan hadn't been known for doing what Dryden wanted unless he wanted to. He'd never taken orders well, and that was one of the reasons his life would have been hell if he'd been in Dryden's place right now.

Dryden slunk away, leaving Rochester to talk with the red-haired woman. He didn't want any part in their conversation, and the longer Rochester's attention was on someone else, the better it would be for him.

He went back to the back room to clean up the blood spills and to make sure the man Auriel had drunk from was okay. He was still slumped on the couch, but he was breathing, which was more than Dryden could say for some of the other humans in the room. He knew they'd all be dead by the end of the evening, though, so he steeled himself and ignored their cries for help as he made the room presentable again—Rochester's words, not his.

The chain that bound his ankles together didn't make things easy, and he had to shuffle around, but he was glad to have something to focus on. He had to make sure he didn't walk too fast, because he'd end up on his face otherwise.

"What do you think you're doing?" Rochester asked from behind Dryden. There was a barely contained fury in his voice, and Dryden wasn't sure what he'd done to deserve it. Of course, he only had to breathe to make Rochester angry most days, but still.

"I'm cleaning up," he said, making sure not to look at Rochester.

"With Auriel."

"I brought her here, made sure she had what she wanted, and walked her back. That's all."

"She's curious about you."

"She tried to get me to fuck her."

The anger on Rochester's face faded a bit. "That's why she was asking questions?"

Dryden shrugged. "I don't know. She tried to get me to fuck her, and I said no. I don't know how she took it or why she wanted it, although she'd just fed, so it's probably just that I was the only man able to perform in the room." There was no way any of the humans there would have been able to get hard, even if they hadn't been drugged up to their eyeballs. They'd been fed on, and they were terrified. No one would want to have sex in those conditions.

Rochester didn't look a hundred percent convinced, but he nodded. "Good. Continue to do your job, and don't talk to the guests. Actually, why don't you stay here with the snacks and make sure they survive until the end of the party? Some of them don't look as fresh as they ought to."

Dryden tightened his hands into fists. He felt the urge to attack Rochester and tear his head off about five times a day, but he couldn't react to his words. "Of course," he said instead, hoping it would save his hide once the guests left.

He knew how unlikely that was, though.

CHAPTER TWO

Morgan swung his fist toward Silvester's face, but Silvester was faster and ducked, hitting Morgan in the stomach as he did so. The air whooshed out of Morgan's lungs — and contrary to what most people believed, vampires *did* need to breathe if they wanted to stay alive. He pushed through it, though, and managed to hit Silvester on the side with his foot.

Silvester grinned, but before he could retaliate — and Morgan knew he would have — someone knocked on the door.

They both froze and looked at each other. No one knew they were in town. They moved continuously, following rumors about Rochester and his people. That was why they were there, but so far, they hadn't been able to pinpoint the area where Rochester was staying. They didn't even know for sure he was in town, but Morgan was hopeful.

He always was. Even after more than a hundred years, he still hoped and prayed that Dryden was out there somewhere, that Rochester hadn't killed him, even though so far, he didn't know for sure that was the case.

"Are you expecting someone?" he asked Silvester. Silvester was the one who always dealt with other vampires. Morgan didn't particularly like them. He didn't like the fact that he was one of them, but there hadn't been another way to make sure he'd have the time to find Dryden.

Silvester shook his head. "No. But I told a few people where I was. It's probably one of them."

He headed to the door, and Morgan untied and retied his

hair. He ought to cut it, but Dryden had always loved it long.

"What are you doing here?"

Morgan arched a brow at how harsh Silvester's voice was. He was usually soft-spoken, even though he was deadly and strong-willed.

"I thought you'd be happy to see me."

Both of Morgan's eyebrows shot up at the woman's voice. She sounded seductive, and that was at odds with what Morgan knew about Silvester. He'd never actually seen him with anyone, but then, he didn't think Silvester had seen *him* with anyone either. Of course, Silvester knew Morgan was gay, since they'd been looking for Dryden for decades.

"I'm never happy to see you, Auriel. What do you want?"

"I have information." Auriel sounded brisker now, as if she'd realized that trying to get into Silvester's pants was a moot point.

"On what?"

"On the man you're looking for."

Morgan felt like he'd been punched. He never interacted with the people who claimed to have information on Dryden, but right now, he wanted to grab that Auriel woman by the shoulders and shake her until she spilled every single detail. That was probably why Silvester didn't let Morgan talk to their informants, come to think of it.

"Are you bullshitting me, or do you really know something about Dryden?" Silvester asked.

"That's his name? Rochester didn't want me to know it."

She knew something. Morgan was sure of it, and he hoped Silvester could see it, as well. Morgan didn't know what Silvester's thing was with this woman, but he needed to get over it, because this was it. They might finally be able to find Dryden, and Morgan wouldn't allow anyone to mess that up, not even Silvester.

"Keep your hands where I can see them," Silvester warned

before he opened the door wider.

A stunning woman with red hair and even redder lips walked in. She barely glanced at Morgan before turning her attention back to Silvester. Morgan was glad, because her gaze was stone cold.

"Why are you looking for that guy?" she asked. She stepped closer to Silvester and reached for him, but he stepped back and shook his head.

"Just tell me what you know, Auriel."

"What do I get for it?"

Silvester sucked in a breath. Morgan would have promised her anything, but it was obvious she wasn't talking to him, and no matter how much he wanted to, he couldn't make a decision for his mentor.

"What do you want?" Silvester said between gritted teeth. He was tense, his jaw tight.

"You know what I want."

Morgan was pretty sure Silvester would have paled if he could have. "I can't."

Auriel swung her hair behind her back. "Then I guess I have to go. Good luck finding your man, though. He might even still be in one piece after Rochester is done with him."

"Stop," Morgan cried out.

Auriel did. She looked at him and cocked her head. "And you are?"

"Who I am doesn't matter. What do you want? I'll give it to you."

She looked Morgan up and down and wrinkled her nose "No, thank you. I'm not into men who look more feminine than I do."

Morgan wanted to punch her and ask her if he looked feminine after that, but he pressed his lips together. Silvester knew Auriel, so he probably could handle her better than Morgan. That was true for almost anyone. Morgan wasn't a people person, especially not when said people were vampires.

"Is there anything else I can give you?" Silvester asked. He sounded desperate, although Morgan knew he was the only one to realize that. Whoever Auriel was, she didn't know Silvester as well as he did. He'd been living with his mentor for more than a hundred and twenty years, and he'd never seen her.

Auriel made a show of thinking about it, and Morgan already knew her answer would be no. She was playing. She enjoyed Silvester's distress, and Morgan would have told her to fuck off if Dryden hadn't been at risk. He was pretty sure what she wanted, and he didn't know if Silvester could give it to her. He didn't *want* Silvester to have to do that, but he kept his mouth shut. They both knew Morgan would throw him to the wolves when it came to Dryden's safety and his life.

"Nope. You know what I want. You've always known. I guess I'm lucky I happen to finally have something you want," Auriel said.

Silvester's whole body was tense when he nodded. "All right. I'll give you what you want—*after* you tell me what you know about Dryden and I can verify that you're not lying."

Auriel strode to the couch and gracefully sat. "He's with Rochester. There was a party last night. I was there, and I saw him."

"How do you know it was him?" Morgan asked.

"He has a scar, right? I heard Silvester was looking for a man with a scar under his collarbone."

Morgan swallowed. "He does." Silvester had put that bit of info out so people knew who to look for. Morgan didn't want to think about how Auriel had seen the scar. Not yet.

"The address," Silvester snapped.

Auriel licked her lips. "Are you sure I can't have a taste of my prize?"

"No, and you won't get anything unless we get Dryden back here safe."

She huffed. "You're no fun. All right." She leaned toward the coffee table and scribbled something on a piece of paper she found there. "Here's the address. You know where to find me once this is over. And don't think I won't come looking for you if you try to leave, Silvester. I've been waiting for this for a long time, and I won't let you wiggle your way out of it."

She got up and left, leaving behind the smell of her perfume and goosebumps on Morgan's skin. It felt like something was crawling all over him, and he could only imagine what Silvester was going through.

"You don't have to do anything," he murmured. He couldn't look away from the note on the coffee table. He was both afraid to touch it and eager.

Silvester sighed and rubbed his face. "Of course I do. We finally found Dryden. At this point, I'm ready to do just about anything to get him away from Rochester and reunite him with you."

"What does she want from you?"

"Don't worry about it, Morgan. Come on. We have other stuff to focus on. I'm hoping that by the end of the night, Dryden will be with you. I don't know if we'll be able to come back here, but we've already planned for that. Now that we have an address, we need to plan."

Morgan was torn between wanting to make sure Silvester would be safe and finding Dryden, but Dryden won.

He always did.

Dryden supposed he should feel lucky Rochester hadn't come around yet. He was probably sleeping the party off with Lucia—he'd overindulged in blood and drugs, just like he always did. He'd no doubt be in a foul mood when he finally woke up, and *that* was when the problems would start for Dryden. He was Rochester's favorite punching bag, and it didn't matter that for once, he hadn't done anything wrong the night before. Rochester would find a reason to beat Dryden. He didn't need one, of course, but he liked to invent them, as if it made him feel better. It might, for all Dryden knew. But since they didn't make *him* feel better, he couldn't have cared less.

Dryden had cleaned up just like Rochester had ordered him to. All the humans had been dead by morning—some from blood loss, others because a guest or two had become violent, a few of drug overdose, since that was the only way vampires could get high. The more drugs they got into their human snacks, the higher they got, and since they didn't care if humans made it out alive or not, it was a win-win situation for them.

Dryden's heart ached for the lives that had been stolen. He hadn't known any of the humans, not even their names, and he never would. He wished he could, because he knew that most of the families would continue to hope and pray for their loved ones to be okay.

They weren't okay. They were dead, and they'd died horribly. Dryden hadn't been able to do anything about that, but he wished he could go to their families and try to comfort them, give them answers.

That would never happen, of course.

Dryden sighed and pressed the back of his head against the cool wall behind him. There wasn't much in his cell—a mattress he did his best to keep clean, a too-small blanket, a bucket, and an empty mug that had contained cold blood. Dryden wasn't allowed to touch the blood he served at the party, and he was lucky when Rochester remembered he had to eat, too.

He'd never bitten a human. Rochester had tried to force him, because he knew how tortured Dryden was over that issue, but it was the one thing Dryden would rather die than do, and Rochester had eventually given up. He still made sure that Dryden was the one taking care of the humans during his parties, because he knew it hurt him.

Dryden heard the footsteps long before Rochester got to his cell. He didn't open the door, just looked at Dryden through the bars. He looked bad, but Dryden wasn't surprised. He always looked bad after a party—reddened eyes, blotched skin, hair all over the place, and expression like he'd seen something that disgusted him. Of course, that might be due to Dryden's presence.

"The humans are all dead," Rochester drawled. His voice was rough, though, instead of the smooth tone it usually was. Dryden wanted to ask him if his wife knew he'd been on his knees for at least one guy last night, but he liked his balls where they were, and for some reason, Rochester hadn't cut them off—yet.

He liked having Dryden in his power, but he also liked to have Dryden serve him, and that wouldn't be possible if Dryden was mutilated. Rochester's posh asshole friends wouldn't like the sight.

Dryden ignored Rochester, even though he knew it wouldn't help.

"You wish you could have helped them, don't you?" Rochester asked. He knew the answer to that, of course. He wouldn't ask otherwise, because he didn't like surprises, and he *hated* when Dryden got mouthy.

"Answer me, Dryden," Rochester snapped.

Dryden growled and showed Rochester his fangs. The man had the power to push him until he snapped, which he knew and took advantage of any time he could. Dryden hated him a little bit more for that, and for the fact that it worked every.

Single. Time.

"You're lucky I'm not in there with you, but don't worry. I'll let you out as soon as I feel better, and you'll pay for snarling at me," Rochester said. His voice was light, as if he was talking about the weather, but Dryden knew what it meant.

By the end of the night, he'd be bloody and would no doubt have at least a few broken bones.

He sighed. There went his relaxing night, and after last night, he'd needed it.

Rochester was laughing as he left, his footsteps fading away. Dryden settled back against the wall. It would be useless to try to get out of the cell. He'd been there only for a week or so, but all the cells Rochester put him in were the same, and Dryden had given up trying to get out. It would only make Rochester angrier, and he'd take it out on Dryden's body. Besides, even if Dryden did manage to leave the cell, he knew guards were walking around the house, both to make sure no one escaped and that no one came in.

No, if there was even one possibility for Dryden to escape, he'd have found it years ago. That didn't mean he'd given up, but sometimes he wondered why he should even try. There was nothing for him out there. His family was long dead, as was Morgan. He was a vampire in a world he barely knew anymore.

New, softer footsteps made Dryden look toward the door. He frowned, wondering if Lucia had decided to come around to tease him like Rochester had, or maybe to torture him a bit. She hadn't appreciated that Rochester had mentioned Morgan the night before, and Dryden wouldn't be surprised if she decided to take it out on him. It wouldn't be the first time.

Dryden stretched up to try to see who it was when the person stopped in front of the door, but he couldn't see anything, just the top of someone's head. The hair was blond, and

Dryden couldn't remember any of the guards of the slaves being blond.

He pressed harder against the wall when the person jiggled the handle.

"Fuck."

Dryden blinked at the whispered swearing. He didn't recognize the voice, either, or rather, he knew he'd heard it before, but he didn't want to fool himself into thinking he had because it wasn't possible.

"Are you sure it's the right one?" a voice he *knew* he didn't know asked.

"Pretty much."

Dryden could almost hear the eye-roll. "Have you checked?"

"No, but this is where the guard told us to come, right?"

There was a sight, then a brown-haired man with a beard peeked in through the bars. "Dryden?" he asked.

Dryden wasn't sure what to do. "Yes." He supposed it wouldn't change anything to confirm he was Dryden. Was this a new torture Rochester had come up with? Had he asked someone to tell Dryden they were freeing him only to laugh at him when he believed it?

"You're better at this than me," the first voice said.

The man at the door disappeared. The handle jiggled again, and Dryden could hear the scrapes of something moving in the lock.

Then it clicked open.

Dryden swallowed and prayed that whatever this was, it would be quick and painless, although he knew better.

The door creaked a bit, but it didn't stop. The brown-haired man stepped in, but he didn't come near Dryden. No, instead, he stepped to the side and let someone else pass.

The blond-haired man. The man with the voice Dryden thought he'd recognized.

Morgan.

Dryden blinked and wondered if Rochester had somehow managed to drug him. Was he seeing things? That was the only explanation.

Morgan crouched next to Dryden and reached for him, but he stopped before touching him. "Dryden?" he asked, and it hurt Dryden's heart because it sounded so much like him.

"I think I'm going crazy?" he murmured.

Morgan smiled. His eyes shone with tears, and he shook his head and reached for Dryden's chains. "You're not, although I understand the feeling. I've been looking for you for so long, love."

There was no way this was real. Dryden continued to think that even when Morgan managed to get the cuffs off his ankles. He helped Dryden to rise, and Dryden stumbled and found himself in his arms.

Jesus. His imagined Morgan even smelled like Morgan had. It was slightly different, with a hint of copper, but it was the smell Dryden had yearned for.

"Come on, love. I'll tell you everything you want to know once we're out of here," Morgan murmured.

Dryden let Morgan guide him to the door. Even if he *was* going crazy, he didn't care.

He was with Morgan.

Morgan was pretty sure Dryden was in shock and that he believed he was either dreaming or that he'd gone crazy.

Morgan would probably have thought the same thing if he'd been in his place. They hadn't seen each other in a hundred and twenty years, and as far as Morgan knew, Dryden hadn't even known he was alive. He'd made sure that Rochester never found out, and from the looks of it, Dryden wasn't allowed any visitors.

He looked good, though. He hadn't changed since the last time Morgan had seen him. He was a bit thinner, and his eyes had a haunted look, but Morgan hadn't expected anything different, not with what he knew of Rochester.

He just hoped he wasn't too late to save Dryden.

Morgan didn't expect their relationship to be like before or to still be a reality, but that didn't mean he wouldn't help Dryden get out of Rochester's claws. That was the reason he'd asked Silvester to turn him into a vampire, after all.

"Can he walk?" Silvester asked as Morgan guided Dryden out of the cell.

"I think so."

"Good. Let's go. Someone is bound to notice the dead guard sooner or later."

Morgan stepped forward, but Dryden didn't move. He was staring at Silvester. Morgan understood he was in shock and everything, but they needed to move, even though he wanted to give Dryden all the time he needed to get better. "He's a friend. You can trust him," he told Dryden.

Dryden hesitated, then nodded. He finally followed Morgan, and Morgan breathed easier. He kept Dryden's hand in his as they walked back the way they'd come from—toward the garden. They'd have to jump the wall, but Rochester didn't have many guards, so they should be able to get home without too many problems.

Or so Morgan had hoped. He was surprised when a voice behind them asked, "What's going on here?" just as they reached the door to the garden.

Dryden went ramrod straight, and Morgan knew why. He'd have recognized that hated voice anywhere.

Rochester had found them.

He looked at Silvester. They had to do something, and Morgan knew what he wanted. "You want to do it?" he asked.

Silvester shook his head. He reached for Dryden, and

Morgan passed him on. Dryden clung to him, so Morgan kissed his forehead, then turned to face Rochester.

Rochester's eyes went wide. "You."

Morgan forced himself to smile, even though the only thing he wanted to do was stick his foot up Rochester's ass until it poked out of his mouth. "Me."

"I thought you were dead."

"Surprise, I'm not."

"I can see that." Rochester looked past Morgan, at Dryden. "And you've come for the man you love. How precious. I'm not going to allow you to take my slave away, though. Our contract was clear. He took your place as my slave until *I* decide I've had enough." He hummed. "But if you want, we can do an exchange. You stay here, and he goes."

"Or we could both go, and I won't kill you, no matter how much I want to." God, Morgan couldn't wait.

Rochester laughed delightedly. "Kill me? Sweetheart, you look like you couldn't kill a fly even if you tried."

And *that* was where Rochester had it wrong. Morgan had always been short and thin. He'd always been feminine, and he didn't care. He *liked* the way he looked.

But he wasn't just his looks. He'd worked hard since Silvester had turned him, and he *knew* he could kick Rochester's ass. The fact that Rochester underestimated him because of his size and his aspect was a bonus. It would be that much satisfying to kill him.

"Morgan—" Dryden said behind Morgan.

Morgan knew what he wanted to say. He wanted to tell him he'd stay, that he'd go back to his cell and continue to go through hell just because Rochester was an asshole. Morgan still didn't know why he'd fixated on him the way he had, and it had been a hundred and twenty years.

"Yes, Morgan," Rochester mocked. "Listen to Dryden. He's been a nice little slave, you know. He doesn't even fight when

I ask him to take care of the snacks during the parties, not anymore. He used to, but he's so mellow now. He's not you, of course, so I haven't touched him, but maybe I will now. Or do you want to take his place? Because that would be so much better for me." He licked his lips, and Morgan had enough.

He acted before Rochester could say anything else. He didn't want to have to listen to him anymore.

His fist hit Rochester's sternum. He put as much force as he could behind the hit, and he thought he'd heard something crack. His fist had definitely caved something, and he grinned, satisfied both at that knowledge and at Rochester's shocked face.

It wasn't even that hard to kill Rochester. Morgan had made him up to be a formidable adversary over the years, but he wasn't. He clearly hadn't been training, and he only managed to avoid Morgan's fists and kicks a few times before Morgan moved around him, grabbed his chin, and slid the knife he'd been keeping in a holster tied around his thigh over the thin skin of his throat.

Blood spurted, getting Rochester's nice white shirt and the floor in front of him dirty. It wasn't over, though. Morgan didn't want to risk Rochester coming back to haunt him and Dryden. He wouldn't be dead unless Morgan took his head or his heart out, and Morgan wondered which one would be easier — and more satisfying.

"I'll do it. Go," Silvester said.

Morgan hesitated. He wanted the pleasure, but he knew Silvester had been waiting for this moment for a long time, and he trusted him to finish the job. Who killed Rochester didn't matter. What did was that he'd soon only be a memory.

Morgan nodded and let go. Rochester's body slumped on the floor. He made a gurgled sound while emptying himself of blood. He'd need to kill a human if he wanted to get enough of it back to survive, but Silvester would make sure he didn't live that long.

Morgan handed his knife to Silvester and took Dryden into his arms again. "You're free," he murmured, kissing Dryden's forehead.

"What's going on, Morgan? Are you—are you really here?"

Morgan smiled. "Yeah. Yeah, I am. Come on. We have to get out of here before someone finds us."

Dryden straightened. "The guards."

"We killed a few of them on our way in. Do you know how many there are in the house?"

"No. Rochester never lets me leave the cell unless there's a party or he needs me to do something."

Morgan gritted his teeth. He wanted to turn back and beat Rochester to death. He wanted to ask Dryden what had been done to him over the years. But they didn't have time for that now. He needed to get Dryden to safety. *Then* they could talk. They'd waited for more than a hundred years. They could wait another hour.

A scream made both of them jump. Morgan turned around, shielding Dryden with his body.

Silvester was getting up, the knife in his hand bloody. He wasn't looking at Morgan, though. No, he was looking at a dark-haired woman standing in the hallway and staring at them with shock and hatred in her eyes. She stopped screaming, but only for a moment. "What have you done?"

"We need to get out of here," Silvester snapped. He turned around, grabbed one of Dryden's arms, and dragged him away. Morgan didn't hesitate—he followed.

He didn't care who this woman was. He'd done what he'd come here to do, what he'd been working on for more than a hundred years.

"I'll find you, and you'll pay for this!" the woman yelled. "Guards! Guards!"

They *really* needed to get out.

Morgan didn't know how they managed not to encounter more guards. Maybe all the ones available had run to the woman, neglecting their post and leaving the garden wide open for Morgan, Dryden, and Silvester to run through it. They didn't bother to hide. They couldn't afford to waste time.

Silvester and Morgan ran with Dryden stumbling between them. Morgan knew he wouldn't have been able to do this without Silvester, not this part. He'd have gladly killed Rochester, but being a vampire didn't change the fact that he was shorter than Dryden and that he wouldn't have been able to drag him to safety on his own.

They had to help him climb the wall, and by then, they could all hear the guards running after them. Morgan climbed the wall first, reaching down to haul Dryden up while Silvester pushed him. Once Dryden was sitting on the wall, Morgan slid down, but before he could reach for Dryden, Silvester, who'd climbed the wall, too, waved him away. "Go start the car. We'll be right behind you."

Morgan trusted Silvester with his life — and with Dryden's. He ran to the car they'd left hidden between some trees and slid into the driver seat. By the time he was backing off toward the dirt road, Dryden and Silvester were on the ground, rushing toward it. They scrambled into the back seat, and they were off.

CHAPTER THREE

Dryden's head hurt. He'd been given too much information in the past few hours, and he didn't know how to work through it and wrap his mind around it.

Morgan was still alive. He was a vampire. He and his vampire friend had killed Rochester and taken Dryden away. Dryden was free.

He was free for the first time in more than a hundred years, and he didn't know what to do with that knowledge.

"This isn't our place. We're borrowing it," Morgan said as he led Dryden toward a dark warehouse. The sun wasn't up yet, but the sky was starting to get lighter, and the need to be inside was like an itch between Dryden's shoulder blades.

"I actually bought the place," Morgan's friend — Silvester — said.

Morgan stopped and looked at him. "What? Why?"

"I like it."

Dryden stared at both of them. Where had Morgan met Silvester? How? How had he become a vampire? Who had turned him? Was it Silvester? Why had he wanted to become a vampire in the first place? Dryden had a hard time believing he'd done so just to find him, but he had a hard time believing pretty much anything right now. His world had tilted on its axis for the second time, upending his life and thrusting him into a situation he didn't know how to deal with.

"She's going to know where to find you now," Morgan said. He pulled Dryden along again, and Dryden followed him.

He'd follow Morgan anywhere, and he hoped he wasn't imagining him. That would destroy him. Although maybe it wasn't a bad thing. Either he had Morgan back and he was free, or he'd gone crazy, and he'd eventually kill himself. At least now, he could. No one would try to stop him just so they could torture him some more.

"I doubt she's going to stick around much longer, not without Rochester. Who was she anyway?"

"His wife," Dryden croaked.

Both men looked at him. He looked at the door in front of them.

"Rochester was married?" Silvester asked.

"Her name is Lucia. She's a horrible person."

Morgan's hands tightened on Morgan. "Did she hurt you?" he asked.

Dryden nodded.

Morgan's eyes narrowed. "I can go back and kill her, too."

Dryden shook his head. "No." He couldn't be away from Morgan. How could he be sure he'd see him again if he left?

"Let's get you inside, then. Sil, do you need to leave?"

"Why would I need to leave? It's my place," Silvester.

"That woman who came to tell us where Dryden was. She wants something from you, and even though you won't tell me what, I know you're not eager to give it to her."

Woman? "Someone told you where I was?"

Morgan smiled. "Come on. We can talk about all of this after you've eaten and showered."

Dryden wanted to get all the answers he needed now, but he couldn't deny he was bone-deep tired. He felt like he'd been tired for the past hundred years, and he was starving—and he probably stank, which was the last thing he wanted when he was back with Morgan.

God, Morgan. Dryden couldn't believe he'd gotten himself turned into a vampire for him. He wasn't sure that was what had happened, but what other explanation could there be?

He let Morgan steer him into the building. The furniture was nice, modern and clean, but Morgan didn't give him time to look at the couch or watch TV. He gently dragged him toward a door in the back. "This is the guest bedroom. I've been staying there, and you can, too. You can have the bed if you'd rather not share it with me. I can sleep on the couch."

Morgan was talking a mile a minute, and it made Dryden smile. He'd always been that way. He talked too much when he didn't know how to deal with his feelings. Dryden used to help him calm down and think, but he wasn't sure he was up for the task right now.

"I'm going to go talk to Auriel," Silvester said.

Morgan froze. He dropped Dryden's arm and turned around. "You can't go."

"I told her I would, and she held up her side of the deal."

"But—"

"Look, Morgan, I know you're worried about me, but you don't need to be. I know what Auriel wants, and I know I won't be able to give it to her. I'll let her try, though. I told her I would if the info she gave us was good, and it was. I won't go back on my word. And I'm old enough to take care of myself, so don't worry. I wouldn't do this if I wasn't sure." He smiled. "You've got Dryden back. Focus on him, not on me."

Had there ever been anything between Morgan and Silvester? Dryden wouldn't blame Morgan. It had been so long, and Morgan couldn't have known for sure he'd ever find Dryden. The fact that he had was a miracle, and Dryden was glad Morgan hadn't faced the past hundred and twenty years on his own.

"You're sure?" Morgan asked.

"Yes. Take care of your man. I'll be back soon."

Morgan and Dryden watched him leave. Dryden licked his lips. "What is he going to have to do?" Dryden hated the fact that anyone, let alone one of the men who'd rescued him, would be forced to do something they didn't want to do.

Morgan sighed. "I don't know, not for sure. He and Auriel, the woman who came to us yesterday to tell us she knew where you were, they know each other from before. Silvester hasn't told me how or why. He's secretive when it comes to certain aspects of his life."

"You've been friends a long time."

Morgan looked at Dryden and smiled. "We have. He's the one who turned me, you know? And he stayed with me while I looked for you. We've been all over the world together, hunting Rochester and trying to get to you. I hate that he has to do this, whatever it is." He took Dryden's hand. "Come on. I'm sure you can't wait to get a hot shower. And I have clothes for you once you're done."

Dryden laughed. "I won't fit into anything of yours. You know that."

Morgan rolled his eyes. "I know. I've been buying clothes for you ever since you disappeared. I swap them when they become out of fashion, but I always choose comfortable stuff. Are pajamas okay? A soft pair of pants and a t-shirt?"

"I'd wear a garbage bag, as long as it didn't come from Rochester." He gave Dryden decent clothes when Dryden had to be there at his parties, but the rest of the time, Dryden had to make do with ragged clothes.

Morgan cupped Dryden's cheek. "I'm so sorry you had to go through all this because of me."

Dryden shook his head. "It wasn't because of you."

"Yeah, it was. If I hadn't snuck into Rochester's house, if I hadn't robbed him—"

"He didn't have to turn me into a vampire and torture me for a hundred and twenty years, Morgan. Even though you stole from him, he didn't have to be a cruel bastard. He was because that's what he is. If you hadn't stolen from him, he'd have found another way to get to you. Once he saw you, he was obsessed with you. We both know that."

Morgan nodded. "All right. Let's talk about this later. You need a bath and blood."

Dryden had been told what to do for more than a hundred years. He'd been forced to listen, to obey. But he didn't have to anymore. He knew Morgan was nothing like Rochester and that he'd never force him to do anything, not even to take a bath, and that was what gave him the strength to straighten his back and shake his head. "I want to talk, Morgan. Now."

Morgan rubbed his face. "I know you do. And I want that, too. But I hate to see you like this. I want to scrub Rochester off your body and your mind, and since I know the second one isn't possible, I'll settle for the first one. Even if you only take a shower, Dryden. Please. I want us to be able to forget Rochester."

Dryden licked his lips. "Why don't you come scrub him off my skin yourself, then?"

Morgan blinked. "What?"

"Take a bath with me." They'd never done that, and now they could. They had the time and the means. What could be better to draw them back together?

Morgan wanted to say yes. He'd never wanted to say yes more in his life. Could he, though?

He had no idea what Dryden had gone through. He knew Rochester had wanted to turn him into a vampire because he was attracted to him and that he and Dryden had different body types, but that didn't mean Rochester hadn't touched Dryden. The thought made Morgan want to go back and kick his body, but he had to think about it. What if Dryden was pushing himself because he'd missed Morgan? What if he was traumatized? Who wouldn't be after spending a hundred and twenty years in Rochester's hands?

And fuck, what if Dryden didn't want Morgan anymore?

Morgan would never regret looking for him and saving him, but what he'd done didn't mean they would fit together as well as they had before. They hadn't seen each other in a long time, and they'd both been through a lot, Dryden more so than Morgan. But a hundred-plus years were enough for both of them to change, and that might mean they wouldn't be together anymore.

The thought paralyzed Morgan. All those years, he'd thought about Dryden and what they'd do once they were re-united. He'd known Dryden would be traumatized, but he hadn't thought about the possibility that what they'd had was gone.

"Morgan? You can say no. I'll understand if you do. I know I don't look good."

"It's not that." Morgan didn't want Dryden to think he didn't want him anymore. He was as beautiful as he'd been when they'd last seen each other, even though he was too thin and bore the scars of Rochester's tortures.

"What is it, then? Are you and Silvester . . ."

"No. No, he's my best friend, but we were never together. I'm just afraid of hurting you."

To his surprise, Dryden smiled. "You won't hurt me. And trust me, I've been through a lot of pain. Nothing you can do to me will hurt me."

"It's just that I don't know what Rochester did to you, and I don't want you to be uncomfortable, since both of us will be naked."

There was a glint in Dryden's eyes when he answered. "Trust me, I won't be uncomfortable. I've been dreaming of having you naked and in my arms again for decades. I'm still not sure it's really happening, to be honest, but I decided to go with the flow. If it's a dream, I don't ever want to wake up, and if I've finally gone crazy, well, I hope I'll never be sane again."

Making the decision was easy. Morgan grinned at Dryden and took off his long-sleeved t-shirt. He dropped it on the floor, then reached for Dryden. Dryden raised his arms, but Morgan shook his head. "Let's go to the bathroom first. I'll draw the bath. *Then* I'll get you naked."

Dryden pouted, but he allowed Morgan to pull him to the bathroom. Morgan dropped his hand when they walked in and turned the water on in the tub. He checked the temperature and plugged it, then contemplated the bath salts and liquid soaps Silvester owned. Why did he have so many? "Do you have a preference? There's lavender, rose, bubble gum, banana. Who wants to smell like bananas?" Morgan took the shea butter one, opened the bottle, and gave a careful sniff. "Oh, this is nice. What do you think?" he asked, turning to look at Dryden.

Dryden was smiling, and Morgan couldn't help but smile back. It was almost like a dream, and he was afraid to wake up and find that he hadn't found Dryden.

"Whatever you like, Morgan. You know I've always let you pick pretty much anything."

That was true. Morgan dumped half the bottle of soap into the water. He wanted there to be a lot of bubbles and foam. He knew Dryden was scarred, had seen some of the signs on his arms, and he suspected there were more under his clothes. If Dryden didn't want him to see them, he could hide under the foam.

Anything to make sure he was relaxed.

Morgan didn't look at Dryden as they undressed. He wanted to, but he didn't know how Dryden would take it. Besides, what kind of man did that make him? Could he ogle a man who'd been a slave and a prisoner for more than a hundred years? Well, he could, but he wouldn't, not until things between them were clearer. He wasn't sure when that would be, but if Dryden trusted him enough to be naked with him and to share a bath, he hoped it wouldn't be long.

Once naked, he shielded his cock with his hands. "How do we do this? One side each?" The tub was big, big enough for two. Maybe buying the warehouse hadn't been such a bad idea, although Morgan would be glad to leave this town and never come back.

But that was something to talk about another day.

"That's okay."

"You go first."

Morgan listened to the soft sounds of Dryden's footsteps, then to the water sloshing around in the tub. "You can turn around, Morgan. And you didn't have to look away in the first place." Dryden sounded amused.

Morgan looked at him. "I wasn't sure. I don't know what happened to you, what was done to you, or if you still want me. Because you have to know that me rescuing you doesn't mean you have to be with me again. I'll understand if you don't want to."

Dryden sighed. "Why don't you get in the tub? We can talk while we're soaking."

Morgan didn't hesitate this time. When Dryden said something, he meant it, or at least, that was how things had been back when they were together.

He settled down in front of Dryden, their legs bumping against each other. They'd never shared a bath, but Morgan could get used to this. He *wanted* to get used to it, to be able to do this every day if he wanted to.

Dryden was mostly hidden under the foam and the bubbles, but he didn't look like he was actively trying to shield his body from Morgan's sight. He leaned back against the tub and sighed deeply. "God, I can't believe I'm here right now. It's like a dream."

Morgan found Dryden's ankle in the water and gently squeezed it. "I have a hard time believing you're in front of me. But it's real, Dryden. You won't ever have to see Rochester again. You're free."

Dryden didn't move. He was frozen, with his eyes wide and his mouth slightly open. Morgan was starting to worry when Dryden's lower lip trembled, and he scrambled toward Morgan, slipping and splashing water everywhere. Morgan caught him as he threw himself into his arms. He wasn't sure what was happening, so he went with the flow. When Dryden plastered himself against him, straddling his thighs and holding on tightly with his arms, he didn't push him away. He wrapped his arms around Dryden's back and held him close, running his fingers into Dryden's too-long hair and gently pulling onto it until Dryden's breathing slowed.

"Okay?" Morgan asked.

Dryden turned his face against Morgan's neck. "I don't know if I'll ever be okay again."

It had finally hit him, hadn't it? Morgan had wondered how Dryden could be so calm and mellow after everything, and now he realized he wasn't.

He rubbed Dryden's back and waited, unsure of what to do. Then Dryden said, "Tell me, please."

"Tell you what?"

"What happened. How you can be here when I thought you'd died decades ago."

Morgan relaxed against the tub and held Dryden. "There's not much to say. When Rochester left with you, I wanted to follow and save you. I knew I wouldn't stand a chance, and since he'd turned you in front of me, I knew I had time. I hated the thought of leaving you with him, though, so I went back to his house, but it was empty. I don't know how he did it, but only a few hours after he took you, you were both gone as if you'd never been there. I knew you were a vampire, though, and that the only way to rescue you was to become one, too. I started quietly asking around, visiting the worse parts of town." Morgan snorted. "Would you believe I met Silvester in a pub? I thought I'd have to go to the docks or whatever, but no."

"And he turned you."

"I had to insist. It took me a while to befriend him and to convince him, but I finally managed after I explained why I wanted it. I found out later that he hates Rochester, but he'd never told me why."

"And he's helped you all these years?"

"He has. We've been living together since then, training and following the rumors and gossip about Rochester. Following *you*." Morgan swallowed. "And now that I found you, I don't ever want to let you go, Dryden. Please tell me you want the same thing. Please." Because Morgan couldn't imagine a life without Dryden, and he didn't want to find out what that was like.

Dryden couldn't have ignored the longing in Morgan's voice even if he'd wanted to. He was stunned at the thought that Morgan had been looking for him all along. Even if he considered Morgan might be alive, it was hard to believe he'd be so focused on coming after him, especially for so long. It had felt like an eternity. It had *been* an eternity.

"You went through all this for me?" Dryden asked, glad that Morgan couldn't see his face. He hadn't meant to jump on Morgan, but he'd been swamped with feelings he wasn't ready to deal with, and he'd needed him. Morgan was the one person who'd always been there for him, to comfort him, and that didn't seem to have changed, thank God.

Morgan huffed. "Of course I did. And you didn't answer my question."

"That's because I don't know how to answer it."

"Just tell me what you want right now. I can deal with anything, I promise. I just need to know I have a chance to be part of your life again."

Dryden sighed and snuggled closer to Morgan. He wanted to say yes. He wasn't sure they could have what they'd had before, though. Actually, he knew they wouldn't. They'd both changed. That was the one thing Dryden was sure of. How had they changed, though? Could their new selves fit together the way they had before?

"I want to be with you," he told Morgan. He didn't want Morgan to wait for an answer and suffer. He sounded so eager to do whatever he could for Dryden.

Morgan's shoulders relaxed. The water surrounding them was warm, and it made talking about this easier.

"But I'm not sure what to do right now," Dryden continued.

"Well, you're going to soak for another while, then you'll eat, and we'll go to bed."

"We can't stay here. Lucia is going to come for us."

"Lucia? That's Rochester's wife?"

"Yes. They've been married for a few decades. I didn't think they actually loved each other, but maybe she cared for him more than I thought. I don't know. I mean, they're each as horrible as the other, and cruel, so it's weird to think they have the ability to love. But she really sounded in pain earlier, when she found him dead." Not that Dryden cared. He wanted to, because he was afraid of not feeling anymore, of becoming like Rochester and Lucia, but he couldn't bring himself to be sorry for a woman who'd made his life hell.

And if that made him a bad person, he'd learn to live with it.

Morgan rubbed his hand down Dryden's back. "I know it's been a long time. I know we're not the same as we were back when we were human, and that you're going to have to learn how to be free again. I know it's going to be hard for you, and I'm ready to tackle any problem head-on and help you through whatever life will throw at us. I've been looking for you for more than a hundred years because I never stopped loving you, Dryden. I realize we might not work anymore, not as lovers, but I'd like to try, and if we find out we don't, I'd like to be your friend, like we were before I realized you were in love with me."

Dryden laughed. "*I* was in love with you? Because I distinctively remember you looking at me like I hung the moon ever since you were what — twelve?"

Morgan pinched Dryden's side. "Shut up. It's not my fault you were my only wet dream. I knew I loved before I realized what it meant."

Dryden sighed happily. This, the way they behaved with each other, gave him hope that they could have what they'd lost back. He wanted to. He wanted Morgan. He wanted to get some normality back in his life, and honestly, he couldn't imagine himself without Morgan. He knew learning to live again wasn't going to be easy, and being with Morgan would help. But that wasn't the only reason Dryden wanted to be with him, or even the main one.

He'd never stopped loving Morgan. He'd never stopped wishing for him, hoping that one day they'd be reunited. Of course, he'd thought that would only happen when he died, but that didn't change anything. He had the opportunity of living the rest of his life — and it would be a long, long one — with the man he loved. After all that had happened to him, he deserved it.

He leaned back and cupped Morgan's face with his hands. Morgan's eyes widened. "I love you, Morgan. I never stopped loving you, and I hope I never will."

Morgan blinked. "Does that mean you want to be with

me?"

"It does. I've never wanted anything more. I've dreamed of this moment ever since I last saw you. I never thought it would be possible, and I'm not about to say no to this."

Morgan's smile was one Dryden had dreamed of every time he'd closed his eyes over the past hundred years. It bloomed on his lips, illuminating his entire face and making him look even more beautiful—as if he needed to. Morgan had always been gorgeous, and even now, Dryden had a hard time believing he'd chosen him.

Morgan's eyes shone, and Dryden didn't want him to cry. He kissed him, sighing against Morgan's lips.

It was just like before. They fit together just as well, and it didn't take them long to slide back into familiar gestures and movements. Dryden rocked his hips against Morgan, suddenly eager for more, for as much as he could get.

Morgan moved back. "Are you sure about this? Rochester—"

"Never touched me, not the way you think. I promise. Nothing you can do will remind me of him." And Dryden so craved this moment. He was taking his life back, and being this close to Morgan was part of it.

The water splashed around them as they moved. Morgan kissed Dryden again, his tongue pushing into his mouth, dragging along his. Dryden kept his arms tight around Morgan, not willing to let him go. He couldn't remember the last time he'd wanted release, the last time he'd yearned for something this much—except for death.

But he wasn't going to die. He was a vampire. If he was lucky, he'd never die, and he'd stay with Morgan forever.

They rutted against each other, their movements achingly familiar to Dryden, yet different—more intense, more hesitant after their long separation. Dryden didn't even care that he'd come embarrassingly soon. He doubted Morgan cared, either. He just wanted to be close to Morgan, to be one with him again.

Morgan grabbed Dryden's ass cheeks with both hands and hauled him close, his lips never leaving Dryden's. They were frantic now, both of them trying to get there, to fall off the ledge.

Dryden was the first to do so. Morgan slid a finger between his ass cheeks. He didn't push into him, but he massaged Dryden's hole, and the memories that brought back along with the stimulation made Dryden shudder. He bit Morgan's lower lip and cried out, his cock pulsing without even needing to be touched.

He scrambled to get a hand between them. It wasn't easy, not when everything was slippery, including their skin, and when Morgan didn't seem to want to let him go Dryden ended up tickling Morgan, and when Morgan laughed and tried to push him away, he grabbed his cock and stroked.

He remembered this well. He remembered everything about Morgan, all their moments together, and he couldn't wait to make more memories with him.

"I love you," Morgan murmured again and again as his back bowed under the pleasure.

Dryden felt awkward, but he didn't stop, and he relished the moment when he felt Morgan's cock pulse in his hand. Morgan shot between them, painting both their chests with his seed, making Dryden his once again.

Dryden had thought he'd die in Rochester's hands, and he'd never been happier to be wrong about something.

EPILOGUE

Dryden leaned back in his chair and laughed at Morgan and Silvester. Morgan snatched an olive from Silvester's drink, then threw it back in his face, nailing him in the middle of the forehead. Silvester growled. But they all knew he was teasing, joking around. Dryden would have been wary of him even only a few months ago, but he was learning.

He'd come a long way since Morgan and Silvester had rescued him from Rochester's claws. He couldn't believe he was in Rome, Italy because they were running from Lucia. Dryden wasn't sure how smart it was for them to be in Italy since that was where she was from, but it had been two against one. Besides, he doubted Lucia would find them easily. He wasn't even sure she was still looking.

He knew she'd gone around lamenting what had happened, but from what Dryden knew of her, he doubted she'd play the grieving widow for long. She'd probably inherited everything Rochester had owned, and that was enough for her to live for a long, long time without having to worry. She'd no doubt be ready to find herself a new husband in a few years. She might have threatened them when she'd found them in her house, but Dryden suspected it had been mostly to show the guards that she hadn't had anything to do with the murder and to get their pity.

"You okay?" Morgan asked, leaning closer.

Dryden nodded. "Sorry."

"'S okay. I know you're going to spend a lot of time in your head for a while. I was just checking." He kissed Dryden's

371

cheek and smiled.

Dryden looked around. He still wasn't used to being able to kiss Morgan in public. They hadn't been allowed to do that back when they'd been human, and Dryden had spent the time since then chained in a cell. He'd had no idea how much the world had evolved outside the cell until Morgan had freed him, not beyond seeing the changes in the houses Rochester owned. He had no problems dealing with a fridge or a shower, but holding hands in public still made him panic. He was working on it, though. He wanted to be the man Morgan deserved, the man he'd been looking for for so long.

He *could* be that man. He knew it. He just had to try.

He smiled at Morgan and forced himself to stop thinking about what people might do if they realized they were together, and about Lucia. He didn't want to think about her ever again.

"We can go home if you're not feeling well," Silvester suggested.

Dryden shook his head. He wasn't comfortable, but he never was when he was in a public place, and there wasn't much more public that the terrace of a coffee shop on Piazza Navona. Silvester and Morgan had insisted they go there, even though they couldn't eat anything. They'd gotten drinks, though, and the piazza was gorgeous — and nothing Dryden could have ever imagined seeing, neither when he was human nor after he'd been turned.

"Why don't we go take a walk. We should take advantage of the nice weather while it lasts," Morgan suggested.

"Or maybe we can just go somewhere else," Silvester suggested. "Maybe South America? We haven't been there yet, not with you, Dryden."

Dryden smiled. "It's almost as if you want to drag me around the world."

"I do. You deserve to see the world. You've been locked up

for too long."

Dryden still wasn't sure why Silvester didn't seem to mind him, but he wasn't about to ask. He knew Morgan and Silvester were only friends, and Silvester didn't seem to care. If anything, he always did his best to make sure Dryden was included in everything. He never decided to move them, or even to go somewhere for a drink, without asking Morgan and Dryden first. It still puzzled Dryden, but he liked it. He hadn't had control over his life for too long.

They left the piazza and headed back to the apartment Silvester had rented for them — or maybe bought. He seemed to be inclined to do that when he particularly liked a city or a place. Dryden had been worried about the money in the beginning. He didn't have anything to his name. Morgan had reassured him that he had plenty of money, though. He'd even showed Dryden his bank accounts, and Dryden had been stunned by the amounts he'd squirreled away. Morgan had just laughed and told him he'd had plenty of time to invest, but Dryden had no intention on asking more questions. He didn't even know where to start when it came to Morgan's computer or his phone.

But he was grateful for everything Morgan and Silvester had done for him, and for everything they were still doing. "Thank you."

Silvester rolled his eyes. "Stop thanking me. You're Morgan's man. I'd do pretty much anything for him, and that means for you, too. Now come on. We should walk to the Colosseum. It's pretty at night."

They weren't in a hurry. Dryden liked the city this way, with the people around them slowly going home, leaving the streets to him and his friends. Dryden felt safer when there weren't many people around.

Silvester squeaked. "Shit."

Dryden blinked. He didn't think he'd ever heard Silvester

swear, but he understood why when he followed his gaze and saw the woman from the party, the one with the red hair.

She was standing on the sidewalk and glaring at Silvester. She pointed her index finger at him. "You."

Silvester raised his hands. "Auriel, I tried to give you what you wanted. You know I did."

"You're an asshole. I should tell Lucia where to find you." She smiled. "Actually, I think I'm going to do just that. She stopped looking for you, but I'm sure she'll love to get her hands on you after what you did to her husband."

Silvester looked at Morgan and Dryden. "Run."

They did. Dryden wasn't sure why, because it wasn't like Lucia could get there any time soon, but he was holding Morgan's hand, and Morgan never let go. They ran toward their apartment, and Dryden knew they were going to have to pack and leave. He hoped they'd have enough time to get to the airport.

"What the fuck happened with her?" Morgan asked once they were in the apartment.

"Nothing," Silvester answered.

"Bullshit. What did she want from you for telling us where Dryden was?"

Silvester raked a hand through his hair. "She wanted to sleep with me."

Dryden gaped. "And you agreed to it?"

Silvester rolled his eyes. "Of course I did, and we got you back, right? So it was worth it."

"Why is she pissed at you?" Morgan asked, going straight to the point like he always did.

Silvester sighed. "Because she's a woman. I told her I only liked men. I've told her every time she tried to get me in bed. She never accepted it, but she had to last time, since no matter what she did, I couldn't get hard."

Dryden blushed. This was something else he wasn't used

to. He'd never have talked about sex with anyone but Morgan before, but Silvester didn't seem to care. He didn't ask details about Morgan and Dryden's sex life, but he also didn't have a problem telling them they'd been loud.

"Do we have to leave?" Morgan asked.

"Do you think Lucia is going to come here?" Silvester asked instead of answering.

Dryden closed his eyes and smiled. This might be a disaster at first sight, but they'd been planning on leaving Rome soon anyway. Accelerating that by a few days wouldn't change anything, and truth to be told, he was eager to see more of the world.

He'd hated being a vampire since the moment he'd been turned, but he didn't anymore. Being turned would give him the opportunity to be with Morgan and to see the world, to be happy like he hadn't been in too long, maybe ever.

It had been a blessing under the form of a malediction—a blessing in disguise.

ABOUT CATHERINE LIEVENS

Catherine lives in Italy, country of good food and hot men. She used to write fantasy as a child, but it was reading her first gay erotic romance novel that made her realize that that was what she really wanted to write.

After graduating from college in English language and translation, she divides her day between writing, reading, taking care of her son and reading some more.

You can find her on Facebook and Twitter or on her website: authorcatherinelievens.wordpress.com

Email: lievens.catherine@gmail.com

Newsletter: http://eepurl.com/c-uvKn